C0-DKM-901

STRAND PRICE
$5.00

Also by Anthony Fowles
DUPE NEGATIVE

Double
Feature

A Simon and Schuster Novel of Suspense

by

Anthony Fowles

SIMON AND SCHUSTER · NEW YORK

Copyright © 1972 by Anthony Fowles
All rights reserved
including the right of reproduction
in whole or in part in any form

Published by Simon and Schuster
Rockefeller Center, 630 Fifth Avenue
New York, New York 10020

SBN 671-21461-6
Library of Congress Catalog Card Number: 72-88052
Manufactured in the United States of America

Double
Feature

CHAPTER ONE

When you kill someone you think it's the end of everything. But slowly you come to realise that life goes on. Do it pat like the cat in the adage and it turns out that the awesome, plummeting descent to the freezing unimaginableness of hell is of no more lasting importance than losing your virginity, or a married man's first adultery. It's trivial enough to live with if you do it to the right people. And for the right people, of course. That's why there are still so many soldiers knocking about.

That's how it was with me, anyhow. Pretty much. With the more or less connivance of the British police, I killed a couple of men I thought needed killing. And myself thereby too, I'd thought, to make up the set. Self-destruction by indirections. Everything happens in threes. I thought that afterwards, after this formal artificating of my spiritual death, nothing would ever matter. But I was lyingly fooling myself—or, at any rate, I'd overlooked one thing, Lestrade. I'd forgotten that nothing much had mattered beforehand anyway. I emerged from the black walling of my tunnel of death to be confronted, not by retribution, not by insanity, not even by the latest permutation handed down by the equivocal majesty of law and justice. It wasn't at all like the film. It was not The End or any head-on confrontation, but merely a reunion with that most easy-going, most terrible of sidekicks, Time.

What do you do? If you're a middle-aged cameraman you go back to your flat at the epicentre of freelance film-makers and wait. In the gloomy chill of the fag-end of an Ealing winter, I waited. Sooner or later there would be a knock at the door. Sooner or later the police, or somebody, would come. Either that or the white-hot roar of a pain beyond comprehension

7

would tell me in a compressed eternity that I'd been, in turn, gunned down. I waited to see which. I waited and I turned down jobs. I turned down a job for Ikon Films that once I'd have given my right eye for. Now that there seemed every chance I might lose that eye all the way through to the back of my bored-out skull I had to tell them No. You can get away with it if you're the Rear Admiral of the White but producers don't cotton to one-eyed cameramen round the set. They look unsightly.

The clock tick-tocked on and I sat reading Nabokov and waited. I called up Ronnie Schell and, via a long cock and bull story he was still naïve enough to believe, arranged to make him an indefinite loan of my Eclair and other gear. I went through the motions of stipulating that he maintain it and return it in the same etcetera, etcetera, etcetera. As I'd discovered, I always leave an escape clause. He was overjoyed. He was just getting a foothold in the dunghill of the film world and, properly put to use, the camera was worth a small fortune to him. As for me, I had no need for small fortunes. In the black briefcase on the shelf above the leather wing armchair was a medium fortune of my own, cheek by jowl with the Dryden Juvenal. All in dollar bills of small denominations. Oh, my Hamilton and Lincoln long ago! Kill the right people at the right time and you can live on, not with John Wilkes Booth in the Seventh Circle, but in Fat City. A nice fat city, like Dallas.

Twenty-three days after I acquired that money I was vouchsafed an answer to my no-man's-land vigil. It came of an evening, not with a distant, unheard cough from a telescopic-sighted Remington, but after all and just as I was opening a fresh can of beans, anticlimactically, with that off-hand harbinger to all the massive realignments of our lives—a phone's sudden routine ringing. Outwardly routine myself, I wiped orange-brown juice off my finger, threw the Kleenex in a basket as I crossed the living room and lifted the receiver.

'Powell?'

Always let them come to you. Counterpunching has more style.

8

'Speaking.'

And listening. I could already place the voice.

'This is Porter. Remember?'

Indeed I did. A straight cop who bends the law in pursuit of justice is not lightly to be dismissed from memory.

'Sure,' I said. 'What's up? They throw you off the force?'

I didn't hear laughing.

'No way,' he said. 'It's you the knives are out for.'

'Oh? Just because I tried defusing the population explosion?' I had to assume we were wired for Special Branch sound.

'No, not that. They know, of course. But I tidied it away. A murder and suicide. Open and shut case.'

'Thanks.'

'It's what you know. You still have that film?'

'My famous roll of incriminating film? Sure, still got that.'

'Where?'

'Bank. Safety deposit box.'

'Hmmm. If I were you I'd put it somewhere safe.'

'Yeah, funny ... It's the Americans, then.'

'Probably. Not that I know directly. But probably. They can't be happy about you knowing about one of their top men defecting. They can't be happy about knowing they don't know how much else you know.'

'Nothing. The film and von Eckhart is all I know ... what about your end?'

'The people here are unhappy along the same lines. Two murders with the file only officially closed. They see you as a walking mills bomb in the midst of our fair country.'

'So let them arrest me. I'm past caring.'

'They know how much dirt you can dish. Our late M.P. had damn near a State funeral.'

'Requiescat. The bastard.'

'Yes. But that's our secret.'

'Until my trial.'

'Exactly.'

I felt that quiver of fear. Perhaps it came ghosting down the open line. Perhaps it was the baleful presence, lurking close, of my premonitory familiar.

'... Am I just going to be ... disappeared?' I said.

Come on Powell, no mealymouthing.

'Killed?' I said.

'Not by us,' Porter said. 'Not our style, now, is it?'

'What is?'

'That's why I rang. You'll be contacted, I'm pretty sure, any day now. You'll be—invited—to leave the country.'

I laughed. Loud and clear I laughed out loud.

'They can't do that! They can't deport me! I'm as British as they are!'

'Come on, they don't work on that level. They have their own system underneath the system. Try getting a job. Try using your bank account. See how often the Inland Revenue can write in a week. Try jay-walking—one foot off the kerb—and see how big a book they've got to hit you with.'

I felt my back going up with the alacrity of an adolescent's prick. A new game was all but afoot and I'd be off the side lines.

'Let them try,' I said. 'Just let them try. I'll take it all. And I can always sing.'

'Singers need audiences,' he said. 'They'll never let you find one ... My advice is—frustrate them. Leave now. Your way. Under your own steam. You don't have ties.'

Oh true. How true. How very conveniently true.

'How do I know this isn't them talking now?' I said. 'A soft-sell job through you?'

'Come on,' he said.

'Or on your own account. You're deeply implicated. Accessory to murder. Conspiring to pervert the course of justice. If I talk you're the first of the living to bite the dust. You've the biggest interest in getting shut of me.'

There was silence. The silence was aggrieved and hurt.

'That's not worthy,' Porter said. 'I don't play that way.'

I thought.

'No,' I said, 'you don't. I take it back.'

That's another one you have to give me. There was more quiet.

'What'll you do?' he said.

'I shan't budge.'

Far away, somewhere way across a cold and darkened London, he sighed faintly.

'OK. It's your decision. You can't say—'

'I haven't been warned. Yes. Thanks. That much I appreciate.'

'It's OK,' he said. 'Nothing.'

'Not by us you said,' I said.

'... Hmm ... ?'

'You said I wouldn't be killed "by us". Who might I—'

'I can't vouch for the Yanks,' he said, suddenly insular and nineteen-forty. 'They work on bigger budgets. They don't play cricket. They tend to be anally compulsive about wrapping up loose ends, not leaving things to chance. But your guess ...'

His voice trailed away as if he'd suddenly lost interest. Tired. I remembered he was only two years off retirement.

'Don't worry about me,' I said.

'I might,' he said. 'We got one back for the Ebro, eh ... ? Take care.'

'Thanks again,' I said.

A dry clicking and a whirring. He'd hung up.

With the receiver still at my ear I knew as a racing certainty that I didn't want to shift and wild horses wouldn't drag me. As I cradled the receiver I had the impulse shooting through me that I should: my lines and life were free; free as the road, loose as the wind. That was it! A road. The path to somewhere. Somewhere new. An end to this sitting endlessly waiting on my arse at the dead centre of nothing and, instead, a broad, white, on-driving clean slate of a highway, down which, all options open, I'd travel to fresh fields ... Like where? That's the ever-present fallacy. Here and now is zilch. Let's go someplace else. Back to the past where we were oh so happy. On to next week, next year when we'll be oh so happy again. Off to far away where, in a brave new world, the dust of this town off our shoes, we'll start all over bright and shining. Sure. You bet. Sure thing. When the going gets rough we all babble of fresh fields.

So, played out, in two minds, spoiling for a fight, for a flight, I did what everybody nearly always does. I lay low and said nothing, waiting still some more. I didn't do a thing. Wait and see. See what happens. It may never come to that.

It did, of course. It always does. Another nine days, in this case, was what it took. Nine days of dreary drizzle from sky and television. I was able to keep careful count. After Porter, my phone hadn't rung the once. And why should I break down and ring the life-time friends I'd met last month who'd said, who'd always said (and always say) they'd be just sure to ring. Not once. Things like that set you to noticing the tick of time. And looked for, un-looked for, knocks, abrupt and peremptory upon your evening door.

No Kleenex needed this time, just some Haydn to turn off. Warily, set, in spite of myself, to throw a punch, I crossed the arbitrary, unresolved silence crashing through the room and opened up the door. A man stood there. A stranger. Not a flatfoot whose corns I'd trod on in my last tender waltz with the boys in blue.

'Richard Powell?' he said. It was just a question.

'Come in,' I said.

He was about my own age, tall and, in a boozing bookmaker way, seedy. Too fat, too red veined, lank hair too thin and scrawny. And not a boy in blue. He wore a Lewisham High Street raincoat open over a grey flannel suit two shades too light. The mustard sportif suede boots formed the perfect accessory—along with the black briefcase. He had one too.

I wasn't going to invite him to sit down.

'You can guess why I'm here,' he said.

I dummied up. I played it tight, close to my vest.

'Yes,' I said.

'Good,' he said. 'We'll get on.' The voice was adroitly commonplace.

I didn't say anything.

'They've been talking about you,' he said. 'You'd be surprised how much they've been talking about you.'

'Talk is cheap,' I said. 'Particularly talk like that. And if they have, it's nothing that you know anything about.'

The red-veined cheeks did not flush redder. They didn't pale with sudden anger. I knew then that they'd picked a good man for the job.

'Just give me the verdict,' I said.

'Smart, aren't you?' he said. 'Just because you know something. They want you out of the country. There's a plane leaving Heathrow at eleven tonight. Pack your bag. You're going to be on it.'

'It used to be the stage,' I said. 'Where's it going?'

He hesitated.

'Come on,' I said, 'I've got to find out sooner or later.'

'Alaska,' he said.

I snorted.

'What if I don't want to go?' I said. I'm not proud. I can trade clichés with the best of you. He sank to the occasion.

'You don't have any choice.'

As he said it, I knew I had. Life goes on, yes, but after you've travelled through the strange landscapes of risking and taking life where only nerve stretched to the utmost is there to sustain you, the return is to a world of everyday diminished scale. It's all small beer. Nothing matters. Or only very personal things. Like giving dubious authority a bad time. I could still enjoy doing that. That was true. I had enough embarrassing Anglo-American information up my sleeve to ... And yet I couldn't. Porter was right. There'd never be a public trial, a straightforward charge. It would be Star Chamber, Dutschke stuff. We live in Maudling times.

I think it was my mind's mention of that name, the face it conjured, that tipped the final balance. They promised endlessly a national extension of the dank, wet-blanket weather outside. The Great Navigator might see it otherwise but, way on down the track, midway through this our mortal life, I wasn't going to live on, die, under a morning cloud. I'd go. I'd move on out. It wouldn't be better. It would be rough and tumble, hand to mouth—an end, however elegant the total scene, to all home

comforts. But there would be maybe a sense of action, movement, goals and aims. And maybe not. But at least in blindly
offering myself, laying myself on the outward extending line,
I'd be earning the right to a promise of those things. By any
rights of justice I should earn the positively-charging increment
that initiative bestows on those who switch off life's automatic
pilot. And yet ... and yet ... There is no justice. I stared hard
at my windows. It all came down to them. Blackly reflected in
their as yet uncurtained panes was my living room and all its
things, the fire I'd tried to bank against the surrounding, outer,
darkness. Perpetually, patiently, the hostile darkness pressed its
forehead gently, irresistibly against the brittle films of glass,
bound, it knew, eventually—a decade or a century from now
—to shatter them and win inexorable entry. Braver then, to
venture out and meet trouble halfway. You can't counterpunch
the latent. Why are you going out into the dark, Powell? Because it's there.

I turned and looked around the room and felt the sour bolus
of resistance hardening. The room lacked chrome and moulded
plexiglass laminates and the latest inflatable Italian Sunday-
supplementia. No copy for a fish-eye lens. But it was a room
where Sir Joshua Reynolds, dropping in to try a glass of port
and compare professional notes, might have found himself at
his ease and at home. My home. Abruptly robbed of Haydn.
Sharply I realised that I didn't want this churl mindlessly ending
the long parade of books collected—not my works, my betters
—on my shelves. I didn't want the few survivors from my old
divorce, the canterbury, the small vitrine on the brass-railed
sea-captain's desk, trundled indifferently away. I thought of my
Citroën wagon. I didn't want authority's brief, petty hammer
knocking them all down to some professionally dropsical and
tipped-off dealer.

'I'll be ready three weeks from now,' I said.

Richard Powell, the world's greatest living eighteenth-century
film-maker.

'The paperwork's all done,' he said. A tiny concession. 'You'll
have—'

14

'Do it over.'

'I can see I'm—'

'Come back then.'

'The plane is all—'

'Look,' I said, 'go back to the car outside and tell your boss waiting carefully while you do the heavy gang stuff that in three weeks' time he can have me meek and mild. Force me now and I'll fight all the way. And I'll sing too. Now you tell him that! He knows what I can do and he knows what I can say. Now, get out of my house.'

He stood for a moment, not disturbed, appreciating my performance. He held his eyes squarely on mine for the obligatory don't-tell-me-what-to-do-or-when-to-go couple of beats.

'Well, I can go and see,' he said.

He turned and went out, shutting the door. I moved across and caught for the first time the stale nicotine odour his coat had leaked into the room. It was all the scene had lacked. I closed the door. I didn't know if he was coming back. While I was waiting to see I reached for the gin. It would make no difference now. I'd made up my mind I wasn't going to go for three arbitrary, just-for-the-hell-of-it-I'll-show-you-who's-boss weeks, and I wouldn't. He hadn't returned after thirty minutes so I returned to the lepidopteral prose. I went back to the gin, too. It was too late, in this country, to begin phoning anybody. I read on until I'd forgotten sufficiently enough about the man's cheapening intrusion to be able to go to bed. As I was staggering through the ivory gates of sleep it struck me that if Reynolds was to come round for port or chocolate I'd have to get some tapers and some tobacco in.

Sir Joshua never showed up. The man in the grey flannel suit came back, though, three weeks later, and by that time the yellow pages had done their work. The car was sold, the furniture in storage. The rooms were empty now and like all empty rooms smaller and ineffably sadder. More diminishment. A room made empty of all personality had been left to the slow death of old age. When there is nothing left remarkable, brightness falls from the air and the remembered echoes fall fainter, fainter into nothing.

I hadn't called Molly. The temptation to do so was too irresistible. You have to have standards in dealing with ex-wives, especially the ones who've requested never to hear from you again. I'd let her be another dying fall. I was glad when, a little later than before, the man's knock sounded again and I could pick up my luggage—the briefcase and one leather duffle bag—and go. Why not? It would make a break. It was probably high time. The new broom could sweep it clean of all those literary allusions.

I went out through the hall for the last time, maybe the last time, and, perhaps for the last time, the sudden sector of white glare from the light above the front door steps made me feel vulnerably naked to the eyes outside in the encircling dark. There were some there tonight for sure. He followed me out. I gave him credit for having changed his shirt. Otherwise he was dressed the same. He overtook me and suddenly there in the Ealing side street was an oversized Daimler limousine. He opened the rear door and I got in.

A greyhound of a man sat languidly in the far-flung corner of the back seat. While my guide pulled down a taxi-style occasional seat I took the other corner and waited for my eyes to dilate. The last man, the chauffeur, set the car in motion. It made a noise like a well-bred sigh. My guide sat watching me, big and intent, from opposite. But I ignored him now. He'd served his turn. I kept my eyes upon the other, silent man and, as the street lamps made their own spasmodic scrutiny, tried to take his measure.

He was Leslie Howard grown old and grey. Grey hair, grey tweed overcoat and, greyest in a way of all, his face. A backstairs Robespierre from God knew what Ministry. A discreet club or college tie beneath the stiff white collar. Unconcerned, he didn't quite look at me. A gentleman.

It was impossible to like him. I couldn't let him get away with it in total silence.

'Where am I going this time?' I said.

16

'Alaska, like you've already been told,' the guide said.

'I wasn't talking to you,' I said.

The lean head turned aristocratically to outface me.

'Alaska,' he repeated. He didn't have Howard's voice. The Wellington sneer had long since pinched all music from it.

'Persistent,' I acknowledged. 'What if I come back round trip? My lease still has four months to run and I just might feel like exercising the option.'

'I really shouldn't do that if I were you, Mr Powell. It's really all in your own interest. I'm sure you appreciate that.'

He was the man from the Home Office squashing the documentary on National Health Service euthanasia. He'd put more drawl into his voice.

'After all,' he went on, 'that's but a trifle now.'

'Here,' I said. If the quotation thing was determined to dog me we might as well get it right.

He didn't like being corrected. He turned and looked away. I didn't pursue. It was impossible to like his voice and I'd had my little victory.

'Here are your papers,' his heavy man said. 'Use this passport now.'

'No visa?' I said.

'There's a vaccination certificate and an Alien Registration Receipt Card. Your new passport says you entered America at Fort Lauderdale two years ago and left six weeks ago from New York. For a resident alien the green card does instead of a visa. Just show it to their immigration and there'll be no trouble. Now let me have your old passport.'

I hesitated a moment and then gave it to him.

'My genuine passport, you mean.'

I looked at the photographs on the alien card and the fake, but not shiny new passport. Lifted from the copy on my last application renewal. An unused face, taken when I was young, stared hopefully at me from a portrait nine and a half centuries ago.

Meanwhile, back in the present, Robespierre reached into an inner subfusc pocket. His grey hand withdrew, holding with

17

studied, worked-at distaste, a white foolscap envelope. The envelope was as fat as the hand was lean.

'In view of the inconvenience of your—disruption,' he said, 'we thought fit—'

'Keep your fairy money,' I said.

It is hard for a grey man to blanch, but, as he repocketed the envelope and averted his stare, he managed it. Well, public school—maybe he was. It gave me a point of sour cheer. I'd been on the point—from sheer bloodymindedness—of accepting the money. It was only taxes I should take as I ran to make H.M.'s accountants' noses bleed. But I'd done better in turning it down. My refusal had, just perceptibly, jolted his stereotyped, class-bred world picture. His untranquil silence gave assurance that from time to subsequent time he would recollect the incident and feel disquieted.

The car purred down the sodium-yellow way towards Heathrow. There was nothing else to say and nobody said anything and with a sharper stab of awareness than I would have guessed possible I realised I was grateful for it. The hard reality of my situation—that I was taking a last farewell of London—came home to me. Not to my intelligencer brain but to somewhere on the edge of thought where nerves spread strained and intuitive. I was bidding a long goodbye to Greenwich with its austere greys and whites against the blackness of the Thames and winter sky; to the quickening roar of approval from the crowd as Palace took the field; to the old and empty pubs on City evenings. Goodbye to all that. The people and the things I'd gladly pay to go without—Frost, the *Guardian*, my namesake Enoch—I'd find them all waiting for me at the other end, wherever I fetched up. People. As the limousine swept into the main gates of London Airport it came to me that not one human face had swum its way upstream to swell the conscious montage of what I'd miss. Not even my ex-wife's. *Tu oublieras aussi Henriette.*

I wrenched my mind back to the present and made myself watch points. It might be functional as well as therapeutic. From a score or so of location trips I knew the layout of the concourse. I pretty well knew instantly when, with a soft slur-ring of tyres, the car had deviated from the main sweep round the ugly terminals. A smaller road, less well lit. A sign: No Entry. A slowing down but never quite a stop as, the driver flashing something to a man, we rolled on through a checkpoint. A phallic barrier rising. Acceleration on to tarmac while high beams cut into the momentary blackness. A plane at rest, loom-ing up as in a film and then picked out by our own headlights. A coming to a halt.

'Here, take your things.'

Cold night winds knifing and not a further word. Escorted up the ladder-stairway thing. Ducking slightly as I moved inside the cabin, blinking in the light.

'Good evening, sir.' Bowing. An oriental face. Taking the ticket from him and not from me. Momentary hesitation.

'Goodbye, old chap. Have a good time.' For her, but not for me.

Some half-caught words and then the heavy scrape of metal down below and a quick whoosh of air as someone locked the door.

'Seat 72C, sir. Towards the rear.'

A long walk down a tunnel-length of faces, each one hostilely inquisitive behind the strained indifference to know what man-ner of important man had delayed their flight. No, I wasn't famous. Resentment stayed as recognition failed to come. Bags bumping. How long these airline interiors stretch on for. HMG had done me well. Tourist. At last, one of the several empty seats, 72C. As the engines revved to taxi, I thankfully sank down.

It was a Boeing flight of JAL, straight commercial, nothing laid on for me, flying over the pole to Tokyo via Anchorage for refuelling. I took this in mechanically and I struggled with culture- and with dislocation-shock, and with the sick dis-ease induced by ersatz cabin pressure. It made my skin feel clammy on both sides. There's little, finally, more sordid than an aero-plane ride. Pan Am makes the going grate. I felt an edge of hysteria. I needed focus for stability. I homed in on the stewardess. Orientals: they had the jump on occidental girls under Western eyes, but underneath the pretty face you saw, as with all airborne waitresses, a rather ordinary girl, harassed, fatigued, uneven powdering betraying washroom grooming. But managing somehow. Tokyo Rose smiled for me and brought me gin, not sake. I paid her with a new dollar bill. I blessed St Juniper and sipped and, with hours ahead of me in which to think, made my brain go limp.

Time and vast distances droned away. I drank and thought of nothing. Interruptions came: the predictable teriyaki dinner, more edible in its unfamiliarity than its infra-red mini-grilled BOAC counterpart, and then, with a drawing down of blinds, the movie. Foolishly I hoped for a Kurosawa or an Osu. I might just as well have hoped for a Timmerman. What I got was the already credibly dated confection about lonesome cowboys, easily riding to rendezvous at a New York midnite, with a purblind lighting cameraman, an operator under the patronage of St Vitus and a latent adult director. Strictly one concept per set-up. The accolades the thing had garnered were sad reminders of the headlong descent in ad-mass taste. One day I must produce 'The Faggots of Flushing' and make my fortune. I tried. I gave it twelve minutes. Then, alert again, once more oriented to the realities of my present situation, I took the earphones out. So much for the fabled Japanese hospitality. But never mind. I was ready now to think.

It really wasn't the first stage out of town. Alaska wasn't happenstance. My putting off of the day showed that. The repetition of the destination was as organised as the deliberate smoothness of my actual embarkation. They knew I knew America, had lived there. But not the frozen north. And charity was not their line. Alaska's claim to fame was still not its oil but its remoteness. I thought of my old unfriendly acquaintance with the CIA. Both dead. Increasingly I saw that this was one stage in particular—the one that ran from out of Sioux Falls and all the way down to the Little Big Horn. Or my name wasn't Custer.

I put back the earphones and, an old man biting back his

tears, pretended to watch the movie. When release came, I counted off five minutes and wandered to the front of the cabin and the magazine rack. What would look most likely? I picked up *Life* and wandered back. Now, from my own indifferent mask, it was time for me to vet my fellow travellers. Some oriental businessmen. They all look alike to me. Two Negro US Army sergeants. So do soldiers. Empty seats. A pretty Caucasian girl. She looked up, caught my eye and looked away at once to keep me at arm's length. Or so it seemed. I wandered on. An old lady asleep. Ditto a young couple. Four business types, burly, unrefined, obviously American. A lone American asleep. More Japanese and then my seat. I sat down. Nothing. In the film there's always at least a pair of nuns.

I read for ten minutes or rather, such is *Life*, flipped advertisements vacantly over and then got up again. This time I moved to the toilets in the tail-end section. More faces appearing from behind fat headrests as on I unevenly pressed. More distancing looks from people intent their personal airspace should not be violated. And there—bullseye! A white man, middle-aged and by himself, grew motionlessly rigid for the space of just one heartbeat as I looked straight at him. I moved on and away and went into the john. I peed and in that claustrophobic intimation of the coffin, my breath coming unreasonably fast, tried to order my thoughts.

Of course he would sit behind me. For observation with the most extensive view. But, hell, I was jumpy, abruptly torn from out my element, bound to be fanciful. Was it possible that on the strength of just...? For the nineteenth thousand time in my tired life, I forced myself to trust my brain. The first impression always, not the subjective, embroidered re-run. It had only been an instant but I'd caught it as sharp and as explicit as a freeze frame. But not through any viewfinder. Out there. For real.

I dried my hands and came out through the door fast. Celerity was rewarded. I had a glimpsing impression of the tail-end of a head being turned sharply away. Strike two. On impulse, hardly progressing forward, I sat down on the rearmost empty seat. I watched and waited staring at the neat black hair only several rows ahead—just as he must previously have stared at me.

Nothing happened. The head did not react. Twenty minutes passed. Hostesses came and went. I asked for coffee as a sort of cover and sipped its instant mediocrity. A man came down the cabin from far off, the lone American I'd seen asleep. His eyes stared absently at my vacated seat and then flicked swiftly on to my *bête noire*. I scrunched right down. A sign had passed. Without a pause the eyes flicked on to take in the toilet. Still no hesitation. As he came near a devil made me stand and block his passage. I looked him in the eye.

'Oh, pardon me,' I said.

A hard man, as tall as me, younger and fitter. A cipher face. We *pas de deuxed* out of each other's way. I went back to my briefcase and its money. There was a toilet at the front, much closer to his seat. Two heavies. There's Western scripting for you. For no good physical reason I found myself breathing in short, gulpy bursts. The Adrenalin Kid. In fast, thick pants. I'd need them in Alaska. Buy them from Marks and Spencer.

I broke the panic off. I tried to think objectively of what might unkindly happen when I came to leave the stage.

My ears ached and a lousy numbness pained my sense. We were coming in to land.

'Fasten seat belts, please.'

Ah so. Click. The Boeing settled into its approach run, distributing faint nausea with its sharp descent. Everybody radiated a smiling and alert composure, exposing thus the common fear, the unspoken group certainty of the holocaust only seconds away. Everybody except me. I had my own particular doom-dealers to preoccupy me : Mr Marks behind and Spencer up in front. I glanced out of the window. Man-made lights, small but rising fast, moonlight on snow, on river or on ice, outer darkness joining land and sky. Incredibly beautiful and colder to behold than the smile producers give unknown writers. Prophetically my scrotum shrivelled further. Fear—and now the cold.

22

A hop a skip and a glide. A good landing.

'You may unfasten your seat belts now.'

Click.

'For your own safety we ask—'

A well modulated, Japanese, American-accented English voice. Better than live would have been, and deader—a tape, then, in this age of Sony. I tuned it out. The Boeing wheeled and taxied. A softer voice, hesitant and charming.

'Local time in Anchorage, Alaska, is ten fifty-five p.m. For those of our passengers disembarking here we would like—' Ten fifty-five p.m. The plane had kept even pace with the antipodean sun. Once again I'd travelled fast and furiously, merely to mark time. Jarring for an instant, the plane halted.

My scrotum had its head screwed on OK. The cold would knife right through your bladder. God knew, knowing American bureaucracy, how long I'd have to wait in international and johnless limbo. Taking my briefcase this time, I pushed past rack-reaching passengers and went into the toilet to pee and stall for time.

I didn't hurry. When I came out Marks was gone, but Spencer, sole occupant of the long, narrow cabin, was fumbling with some luggage. OK, already. Nothing I could do. I grabbed my other bag and, lurching down the aisle, kicked him sharply on his nearest ankle. Pure malice. I didn't say a word. That he said nothing too beyond his grunt had to be an error. Obviously it hurt him more that I wasn't a dour pro conniving at espionagic insultation.

'Thank you for flying with us, sir. Have a good trip.'

I nodded to the bowing offspring of Tojo's buck-toothed bandits and, clambering down the stairway, set out to make acquaintance with the land of her second cousins much removed. At once an icy gust, withering in its contemptuous intensity, came whipping across the tarmac from the lost graves of countless Eskimaux: that, it said, was before the gold and oil. I hunched my shoulders and ducked my head acknowledgingly; its point made, the wind dropped, but it had been a blast to conjure with. As I hurried after stragglers across the

23

well-swept fifty yards of apron, a risen spirit half a pace behind matched its doppelganger stride to mine. Ghostly it breathed just past the edge of vision, the cold conductor of my self-destructive soul. But welcome now. I'd need cold steel to deal with Marks and Spencer. The wind had blown favourably for me.

I gained the double doors and barged on through. Warm air. Signs. 'US Citizens—Straight Ahead.' No deviationist need apply. A second arrow sinisterly set me on the path to Immigration and Customs. With no alternative I joined the dwindling line as Spencer came in through the doors and civically marched straight ahead. Still further to my left the group of passengers continuing on stretched legs and yawns in transitory no-man's land. Beyond all barriers, in promised land, two huge Alaskan State Patrolmen, faggot Mounties, sky-blue Smokey the Bears, stood heavily ill at ease. I saw their guns and thought: 'America.' No sign of Marks. The line performed its subtle peristalsis and I shuffled on.

It was true I had no choice. I'd thought it out. You can't fuck Immigration and survive. Living in the States before had told me that. My Ealing guide had told the superficial truth—the green card ought to see me through. The question was: now that I knew I'd been set up, was the fix in to nail me on a technicality? I didn't think it was.

I saw Spencer go through his equivalent checkpoint.

They wouldn't, surely, use the law on me. The penalty for travelling on falsified and forged papers—even if HM Government supplied—had to be the last thing everybody wanted, deportation. Arrest would be too open and too vocal. Proper procedures—

'You want to let me have your passport and visa, sir.'

I'd reached the counter and a sharpfaced, crew-cut fox of a man. I handed him my papers.

'Uh-huh ... Where did you leave the US from, sir?'

'New York. Six weeks ago.'

'Uh-huh. And what was the nature of your trip abroad, sir? Business or pleasure?'

'A little of both. Mainly business.'

'What is that, sir?'

24

'I'm a film producer.'

'Uh-huh. What is your US address?'

'Los Angeles. 1459 N. Seward Street.'

I'd checked. The green card doesn't carry an address.

'Kind of a long way round.'

'I've never been up here before. I aim to take in a few days sightseeing. The air-fare's hardly any more.'

'Uh-huh.' Then, 'If you'll just wait here, sir. I'll be right back, I'm sure.'

He turned and disappeared into a windowless back office. I stared at its green wall while panic, mind-dissolving fear, ran through me like a tide to unnerve the temper of my resolution. In a dream I stood while heat and cold sent hidden shivers pulsing up and down. Imbecilic fool! I'd borne a half-baked image in my mind of kindly policemen going by the book. Me! I hadn't seen the cynically deft going-through of motions. The charge, the warrant never quite produced, the file mislaid, the hamfists buried in the stretched-out stomach, the night-time ride and rendezvous with squat, bland-featured men. While in that room infra-red light spelled out the secrets of my treated passport, I stood as fixed as possible, trying to stem the swirling flood of images. My ghost laid spiritual ice fingers on my shoulders and whispered of the comfort found in flight, in heedless, endless, use all your breath and more, flight. I forced myself to stay, tried not to move. If I didn't move at all perhaps it would pass away. Someone behind me muttered with impatience. The man came through the door and without blinking once returned to stand and face across from me. There were flecks of grey in his eyebrows and large, grey pores disfiguring the wings of his nose.

'Fine, Mr Powell. Thank you. Have a good stay in Anchorage now.'

He gave me back my stuff.

'Thank you,' I said, quite mechanically. I didn't check the papers I got back. Somehow I moved along. My knees had the rigidity of rippling waters. Welcome to Earthquake City. But first the Charybdis of Customs.

My eyes took in the waiting uniformed official, short and balding, watching me approach and suddenly my lost resolve returned. I felt a sense of shame—my ghost had witnessed all—that I should have known so juvenile, it seemed, a crisis of nerves. On edge was fine, it tuned the reflexes: but over edge was fast downhill to death.

'You board your flight at London, sir?'

'Yes.'

'How long are you planning to be with us in the States?'

'Indefinitely. I'm a returning resident alien. My home is in Los Angeles.'

I remembered to half harden the 'g' in the local affectation.

'Oh yeah. What's in that bag?'

'Personal effects. Clothes mainly.'

'Uh-huh. How about the case?'

'It's full of money?'

'Huh?'

'Money.'

'Let me take a look.'

I opened up the briefcase. Ageing, losing his hair and growing fat, he stared into it wistfully while the assembled portraiture of close to fifty thousand dollars stared stonily back.

'That's a lot of money,' he said at last. 'You're taking quite a chance.'

'I like to have it by me. It's the sentimental value.'

He grinned. An honest man.

'You ever heard of traveller's cheques? American Express?'

'This is the latest thing. It cuts out all that paper-work and book-keeping. Besides, the interest rates are lower.'

'That's for sure. OK. Go right ahead. A guy with dough like that's no need to cut corners.'

I smiled and moving right along entered the land of the free. Across the hallway plainly watching me stood Marks and Spencer. I looked around for inspiration.

It was a well built complex, neither large nor small. Vinyl covered seats, Hertz and Avis desks, the counters of the airlines that flew in. Glasgow, Belfast, San José—somewhere near that scale. And quiet now, subdued, two thirds of the desks closed down, the lighting somehow dim. It all conspired to tell me I was tired. But as the people wandered to and fro in search of bags and all that airport people seek, I figured that I'd stick around a while. Dim as the lights might be, they were a whole hell brighter and more public than the icy dark outside.

The tannoy shrilled and, as I walked across to see the Avis girl, announced the arrival of Alaskan Airways flight 021 from Fairbanks.

'Elastic Scareways,' the girl giggled.

'I bet you've used that before.'

She gave me silver what my dollar bought and told me of the best hotel downtown. Like the hostesses she didn't come up to the ads. Marks and Spencer sort of watched. I went up to a Coke machine. The tannoy yelled the boarding of Alaskan Airways flight 021 for Seattle. I hoped it was a Boeing. Otherwise they'd shoot it down on arrival. I raised the minute twenty-five-cent Coke up to my lips and froze with disbelief. Heading for the gateway marked Alaskan Airways 021 walked Mr Spencer along with Mr Marks.

It was too much. I ought to laugh out loud. Here I'd been, ace paranoid par none, screwing my nerves up to the sticking point and, all along, my doom-dealing adversaries were nought but watchful couriers. I should feel flattered. Better, I had no true knowledge that they were even that. Paranoid indeed. Probably no more than hurrying businessmen Seattle bound. Relief washed through me with the drink. The world was one big sparkling Coke commercial. Things go better with ... Idly now I watched them leave—the acquired operator's habit of watching action even after 'Cut!' so long as film still rolled. Thus it was, how I'm not quite sure, that I caught their signal to the man of about my height and age who entered just as they went out.

CHAPTER TWO

I slept fast and I woke up fast—a sure indication my anxiety level was high. There was no twilight period of dislocation. The moment my eyes opened I knew exactly where I was. That seemed to suggest I must still be in the land of the living. To coin a phrase. If you could call this living. To coin another.

I sniffed the air, literally. No gas. I looked slowly round the cell—early Hilton writ small—of the Wayfarer, Anchorage's high-priced, scaled-down tower of Babel. The vinyl sterility had not been violated. The lock was still locked, the chair still angled against the door. Nobody had pitoned their icy way up thirteen exterior storeys to force my window and propel from a blowpipe, fashioned from a bamboo found only in the inner-most jungles of New Guinea, a death-dealing dart steeped in the unantidotal venom of a Papuan vegetable alkaloid. It was my lucky day. Not that I could have quarrelled if I'd woken up a cold, mottled, bloated. pin-cushion and dead. In registering I'd betrayed instantly the desk clerk's faith in me. I wasn't really Bernard Schwarz, realtor from Des Moines—nobody ever *makes* himself Jewish, right, Tony *bubele?*—and some hotels might have felt justified in puncturing that false persona. Still, it was interesting. Interesting that I still found interest in finding myself alive. With a rising curiosity that I'd thought all but gone for good, I discovered the topic not without its savour.

I pressed my luck further and got up. By concentrating hard upon the small mechanics of washing and shaving in an alien bathroom, I succeeded, momentarily, in smothering anticipation of the thousand ruder shocks I could suspect my flesh would be imminently heir to. Only then did I look at my watch. It told me it was 1.35 p.m. Alaska Standard Time, Zone 2. I knew

28

then I could feel refreshed and reconditioned as well as alive. I'd nearly slept the clock round since the giggling Avis girl had rented me a big cream-puff Plymouth in which to oscillate away from the air terminal and Marks' and Spencer's relief-man. For all of ten miles, twenty minutes. It was all Fifth Avenue to a Maoist orange that he now resided, already privy to my cover, a fellow traveller at the Wayfarer, and that my room number was as surely lodged in his memory bank. I set out to cross his path and rode the elevator down to the ground, I mean first (remember that, Powell/Schwarz) floor.

The third man was sitting strategically in the lobby. I looked at him and he looked at me. I walked through the lobby to the coffee shop and he got up and walked after me. I sat down at an empty table. He sat down at an empty table and looked at me. I looked at him. I found him lean, middle-aged, nondescript —an assistant bank-manager. But an assistant bank-manager whose colourless unwavering eyes compelled me, in spite of myself, to drop my own and grope for a menu.

I tried to breathe more slowly. A second, icy breath seemed to infiltrate the air around me. The ghost had come West, too. Steady. I made myself assess the prices. That didn't help my pulse rate, either. Even allowing for the long, destroying, inflationary years that had passed since my last times in the States, they were astronomical. When people in Alaska talk about the 'lower forty-eight' it's not geography that's on their minds, it's the cost of living. I could damn near buy their whole polyurethane hotel, give or take ten million, but these prices, with their lost economic horizons, stuck in my craw. I had, in any case, forgotten the massive, syrupy overkill employed on American breakfast menus.

'And how are you today?'

The chirpy, chippy waitress with the face like the great tundra.

'Fine. Just fine.'

I said it in American to cut off any reception speeches.

'Well, good.'

Four vowel sounds.

29

'And what'll it be?'

'Just coffee.'

The sun went away. The tundra refroze.

'All rightee.'

She whisked the menu from my hand and in removing her middle-aged bulk from my line of vision exposed again to my refocused eyes the changeless stare from my private basilisk. Another waitress approached him. Curtly, he ordered coffee without once looking at her. He looked at me.

'There you go.'

I drank coffee. Bitter, reheated more than enough to matter, American. I looked at him and thought. It was rational to suppose he didn't know I had caught that look of the previous night at the air terminal. Nominally, we were total strangers with nothing in common, no connection. OK. Now he was advertising his presence, psyching me, blowing cold air by spectral proxy on the back of my neck. He must know I'd be on guard—that I wouldn't take him for a persistent faggot, say, whose bark was as tough as his final bite. Okay. So why did it pay him to advertise?

Maybe a change of location would round out the plot. I left money on the table, went out to the lobby and rode the elevator all the way up to the top floor, site of the originally-named Penthouse Bar. I shouldn't knock it. There was booze inside and, where Anchorage had the civilised edge on Acton, unlimited time in which to absorb it. I went in to finish my breakfast.

Daylight, diffuse, already darkening but harsh, assailed my eyes. Plate-glass windows did for walls in here, affording quadrilateral views of the city and its setting as they trebled the heating bill and raised the tariff. It was reasonably eye-catching stuff, but more attractive still was the centrally located bar serviced by a deft looking Asiatic—Filipino, probably. Business was slow and he looked pleased to be rescued as well as surprised when I ordered a bottle of champagne. Not to eat below had actually been a smart move. It allowed my globe-trotting metabolism maximum time to re-set its clock.

30

Deftly indeed the barman returned with the bottle and did business with it. The four or five other inhabitants scattered at random tables looked up as the cork sounded but were safely encapsulated as individuals again by the time I took my first sip. It was Californian, but none the worse—or cheaper—for that. No sign of the third man. I wandered over to the win-dows to play at taking in the view. Perhaps I was mistaken.

I fought off the habitual acrophobia by lifting mine eyes up from the tiny, magnetically attractive street below unto the hills out beyond Cook Inlet. Snow-covered, fading mistily into the white grey sky, they sat implacably elemental, waiting to re-encroach upon the twenty square blocks that presumptuously made up the quilted heating pad of a city. They knew with utter certainty that some millennium or another they would— just as the ice, thick to God knew how many feet in the inlet, would reassume the iron grey ribbon of water that some breaker had kept artificially open. At a quayside a freighter, it must have been quite large, was off-loading some heavy looking cargo —a bustling, cheerful sight even at this distance and one that unfairly sent an unlooked for stab of anger paining through me. What was I doing here when I could be in a grimy, cosy, Wapping Thameside pub? Well, it didn't matter. I sought for dis-traction and it came as Fate made it up to me, at once, in the form of what might have been a fighter-bomber coming in to land at an obviously military airbase on the edge of town. Sub-dued blue and silver against the greys and whites, it homed speedily, noiselessly over the water, seeming to glide. Perhaps it was darting in from the new breed of hermits at Point Barrow where, credulous eyes on their daily more obsolescent scanners, they sat immured, the first, most northerly bastion of those pledged to keep the world safe for Wall Street. The plane was very low now, and I moved to follow its skimming descent down to the compulsive instant of landing. I never saw it. The shift of viewpoint revealed, hard across from me, staring with the same implacable blatancy, my man in Alaska.

I went back over to the bar and my bucketed champagne and poured another glass. I waited for five minutes. He watched me. He didn't come over. Okay, so he didn't want to talk. Okay, he only had one reason, then, for advertising himself like this. He wanted to throw a scare into me. Okay, so he was doing a pretty good job. There was only one reason, to continue, why he wanted to scare me. He wanted to flush me out from cover, set me running, get me to move out where I'd be alone. There was no driving out of this town at this time of year. Ten to one he had something worked out for me between the hotel and the airport. Smart thinking, Powell. That really narrowed it down.

I slapped bills on to the counter, got up quickly and told the again surprised barman to present the remainder of the champagne with my compliments to the gentleman over there. I went down in the elevator, wondering if I was overdoing the cock-snooking at the opposition but deciding that all I had going for me at the moment was the possibility of unbalancing them and maybe shaking something loose. We'd see. I went out and by walking fast, almost running, managed to survive three freezing blocks in only my hard-worn grey production-meeting suit. I dived (dove, Powell, dove) into the ritzier of two sports outfitters shouldering on in neighbourly competition.

Inside I bought sets of thermal underwear and socks and woollen Bean shirts. I bought a down-lined parka that cost its weight in money but would have warmed the Siberian cockles of a Solzhenitsyn hero, cross the bay. I got it in taupe. Not, as the salesman thought, because I was after geese, but because I figured that in the not-to-be-thought-of last resort it would be better camouflage than deer-hunter's red. I didn't mention I'm against blood sports. I bought two pairs of boots, heavy, fleece-lined, and a long PVC duffle bag to put it all in. Then, as an afterthought, I asked for and was given a cubicle to change in. I used it and came out a new man. Frenchy Lafitte the lumberjack. By the store entrance, ostentatiously not buying a bowie knife, was Champagne Charlie.

I walked straight by him and out on to the sidewalk where, protected from the elements by my new clothes and from him by the sprinkling of passers-by, I could afford now to take my time. More of a store dummy as yet, Lafitte moved awkwardly, self-consciously. But now down at street level coming home to me for the first time on the chill, electric air was that added dimension of excitement, that quickening of expectancy and pulses all Europeans feel as they turn on to the American pike. I felt an anticipation of pleasure at renewing acquaintance with the American Way that drove back into misty oblivion all fond memories of Wapping. Here, a long twilight held the sky and neon signs, old friends, winked their glittering approval of my return—Sears, well of course, Rexall Drugs, and that's the spirit 76 Station. The cars, pastel-coloured sharks, glided by, alluring, glamorous and shoddy. Anchorage, I realised, with sharpening recognition, was like any small-to-medium city in the cold Northern Mid-West. Identical, in fact, but for the faces. Here, the faces of the whites were unrelieved in a stolid, square projection of power, red-necked right between the eyes. Their Caucasian steps rang on the swept sidewalks with an arrogance unalloyed by the note of insecurity a Chicagoan's tread betrays. And where in Chicago omnipresent Negroes would carefully have transmitted a casually goading uppityness, here the occasional Eskimo face was barren, inert, dispossessed of even commonplace expression. Gloomy. I rounded a corner and bang in my viewfinder was a Triple-A tow truck lugging a crumpled Chevvy. It was exactly right. The final detail in the reinitiation ceremonies. I felt an instant cheering. Despite the Shadow knowingly dogging my steps for the last ten blocks I felt almost happy. There might be life in it yet. Passively I'd let them prise me from a past I'd streaked with blood and a future I'd turned to infinite emptiness. But here I was in the Promised Land where, it was said, anything, even the great myth of a fresh start, might be conjured out of the wild blue new frontier.

Like buying a gun. I hadn't had it in my mind but the moment I saw the hockshop I jaywalked across the street already ninetenths sold. It was your typical run-of-the-mill American pawnshop. There were plenty of guns going. There was really no reason to pause. But I did. Some vestige of the fastidious, an English sense that guns are always dramatically superfluous, made me hesitate outside. I walked slowly up and down as if intent on the pattern of radios and cameras within the window. A gun. Apart from shooting a couple of people dead, I knew next to nothing about the things. They weren't my style. They —a reflection in the window caught my eye. I turned. Squarely across the street still watching and following was the ubiquitous Alaskan Creeper. That did it. I'm malleable, I can be bent. I went inside. When in Rome . . .

The proprietor, a sort of lightly-shaved grizzly, ended by selling me a .38 Police Special, a Colt automatic. He told me it was a good reliable model. I said yeah, that was the one where they got the torsion bar bug licked and he said 'Huh?' He said and I agreed that it should do the job. Neither of us said what we thought the job might be. I got it and nine rounds of ammunition, all he had in its calibre, for sixty-five bucks. Maybe you could beat that if you had a hammer but all I had was cash. He put it in a brown paper bag for me, such a discreet, grunting death-dealer, and, with fidus Achates still in tow, I carried it back to the hotel.

I checked out my briefcase from the hotel safe and went up to my room. No time bombs, tic polongas, US marine corps or machete-wielding nymphomaniacs. Just the constant four barish walls squaring the stale air of loneliness. Methodically I transferred the thick wads of dollars—a different sort of ammunition, a different sort of game—to the limitless pockets of my new parka. I tried to think, to plan, but no plans came. With the world before me, I needed direction, specifics. I was toying in Freudian abstraction with my Police Special when, like a sword through the cerebellum, the phone rang.

I wheeled to look at it. White, slightly old-fashioned, it was a sculptured piece of bone with skull-like affinities. It shrilled insistently, instinct, it seemed, with waves, with voices, of menace, age-old vocal runes prophesying woe. Lift the cold receiver and the reservoir should be tapped, flooding through me in an enervating, will-destroying race. It rang and rang. I didn't answer. It was one of two things—a wrong number, or the men set to watch me, and worse. In which case it was another move to unnerve, unbalance me. Threats down the line, perhaps the baleful intimidation of a live, open silence. I didn't need that. I needed direction, a campaign plan, but the initiative had to come from me. My one sad asset was the interior lines of my unattached one-ness—it was for me to unbalance him before I made the break. In mid-ring, the phone stopped abruptly, now that I'd grown used to it. An after-echo lingered, sighing its regret. It had to have been him. Nobody else knew I was in town.

I wasn't going to get stampeded, either. I waited thirty-seven infinite, interminable minutes and only then, when a sudden whirr of voices in the corridor outside gave a partial guarantee of security, went quickly out through the door and down again in the elevator. As its doors slid open like a film wipe he was centrally there, the first thing visible in the reception area. I walked a fast four blocks and, more attuned now, dived through the swing doors of the Malemute Saloon.

Nobody was whooping it up. The long mahogany Western-style bar to the right was taken up by as long a line of solitary, self-communing Eskimos waiting for their next relief handout and the next bright young University spark to come over and insistently feather his fledgling documentary reputation with a liberal study of their plight. They would suffer the impertinence of his BBC invasion as they now suffered the throb and boom, all bass, from the mighty-Wurlitzer-styled jukebox—impassively. High on their stools, heads forward and down, they paid no heed, keno players waiting for numbers in a dying language, to the girl mechanically gyrating to the cliché rhythms of some bush-league Motown disc. She did it on a stage the size of a suitcase against the far left wall, lit by a cheap black-light rig. Three men sat apathetically at three separate tables, silent, looking at the girl with eyes too tired to conjure lust. The record resolved, there was that dry click those machines give and, as my corporeal doppelganger walked in at the door, I went over and selected an Aretha Franklin number. If you're going to do it, do it right. He sat on a stool at the end corner of the bar right by the door. I pulled out a chair and sat at a table where I could watch him. The music started.

35

At once I was sorry that I'd fed the machine, for by doing so I'd sentenced the girl to another three minutes on the treadmill. As the beat came on again, she was obliged to dash down behind her the towel she was using—sweat glistened on her in the artificial light—and bump and grind away again. I looked at her, surprised because she was an Eskimo. Her body was beautiful but all wrong for a job like this. The tasselled pasties designed to mask her nipples half covered her small, high breasts. The crude violet slash of upcutting g-string revealed narrow, lithe hips, lean thighs and flanks. Where there needed to be pendulous red-hot-momma flesh, she was modelled in exquisite colouring to a fine, sinewy, gracefully slight scale. Her sleek of dark, straight hair, the angular refined bone-structure behind the desperate grin pasted on across her face, suggested Japanese cherry blossom rather than US beer hall. There was a hurt, frantic look lurking in her eyes. And with good reason. She knew she was a rotten dancer.

'What'll it be?'

The barman had come across, first cousin to the man who'd sold the gun inside my parka. As honest as the local day was long.

'Coors.'

No draught beer in Alaska.

He brought over a bottle and a glass, intent on reducing manual fatigue in his labour-intensive work, allowed me to do my own pouring.

'A buck,' he said. He'd already served my friend at the bar. A whisky.

I gave him his dollar and raised the glass to my lips. First of the day; first, this time around, of the Continent. Maybe the last. I drank. Light, a hint soapy—and brewed with a thousand memories from a decade away, of warm, shallow Hollywood, soft evenings spent behind old frame houses and the susurrations from a lilac sky. The music stopped. From behind the counter, close to where my guardian angel sat, the barman shouted:

'OK, Elsie.'

She reached down swiftly, thankfully and from behind the

36

stage fetched up a kimono-style wrap. Still draping it around herself—it was exactly right for her—she stepped down from the stage and made towards the back of the bar. That was when a half idea, a hint of direction, came to me.

'Hey, Elsie,' I said, 'want a drink?'

She stopped and looked at me. I had the feeling you always do of feeling mean and dirty and taking advantage while she looked at me with a shy sort of naïve shrewdness, wondering.

'OK,' she said.

And that was how Elsie the Eskimo Go-Go Dancer came to be sitting at my table in Anchorage, Alaska.

The barman was back. I looked at Elsie.

'Beer,' she said.

The barman looked at Elsie like she should have said something else.

'You get thirsty up there,' she said.

'Two beers,' I said.

The barman went away.

'You shouldn't have said that,' I said, 'he doesn't have you here just to drink beer with the customers.'

'It's what I like. Besides, it doesn't matter.'

'Nothing matters ... What do you mean?'

'Mr Latham's giving me a tryout here for a month. This time of day, when business is slack. The month's nearly up, I guess, and I guess that's going to be it. I guess I blew my big chance.'

She grinned, wryly, resigned, hurt a great, great deal. Her voice had a trace of lisp and moved in sing-song, childlike cadences. I kept getting a sense that she was a Geisha lost in a cold land far from home. The barman came back with two beers. I gave him five and told him to keep the change. It had the effect of wind on granite.

She drank without fuss. She really was dry.

'So,' I said, 'you haven't done this before?'

'No. I just got into town looking for...'

'Where from?'

37

'Juneau. It was dead down there so I came up here to look for work, I guess, and he had a sign in his window. I guess I figured I could cut it and it'd be better than—better, I guess, and he said he'd try me one month.'

She was very nice, very sweet. I played with the idea.

'But I guess it's not me,' she said. She grinned. 'Hell,' she said, 'I had to spend my first break altering the costume down to fit me. I should have known better right then.'

'Maybe it's better this way,' I said.

'Oh sure,' she said flatly, 'sure. I make a great little waitress. Hey, you talk a little funny. You German or something?'

'I used to be British.'

'Oh. You live here in Anchorage now?'

'Just passing through.'

'Oh. Where's home?'

'Hollywood,' I said before I could think and felt sorry in the instant. There's a force in old clichés. Her eyes really did seem to light up.

'Gee,' she said, 'I'd like to go there some day. But, hell, I've never been out of Alaska, even. I guess...'

Her voice trailed away. She didn't want to embarrass me by hinting, even, at the obvious proposition. She didn't want, I could see, to consider it. People that believe in fairy tales get hurt, she'd learned, and Prince Charming doesn't hang out in saloons, she'd learned. But I could tell from the echo of hope in those eyes, she didn't believe. And why should she, when I was sitting there considering which of my two magic wands I should pull out first? I had no right to involve her. None at all. But it would be a gas, such an absolute gas, to see my watcher with the rye trying to split himself, be in two places at once. He was watching us now with an absolute in concentration. I couldn't begin to guess the sinister, depthless convolutions he'd impute to this casual pick-up. That was what made it right. The thing with which I could improvise an initiative, assume a direction, a plan. I took an enormous risk—the risk that at thirty paces he couldn't lip read.

'I could buy you an air ticket to Hollywood right now,' I said.

She gave me a fast look and then a slow one. It was the same one as before. Guarded, trying to be shrewd but wryly admitting that she hadn't been around long enough to know the score and would have to finish the job using trust.

'What would it mean?' she said at last. 'Sleeping with you?'

'Yes,' I said, 'probably. Sooner or later. You're very pretty.'

She ducked her head.

'I finally met the guy who thought so,' she said.

'Yes. I think so.'

'You'd live with me in Hollywood?'

'Probably not. We'd work something out. You'd want to go your own way. Sooner or later.'

'Maybe not,' she said, '... don't even know what you are, what you do.'

'I'm an insurance salesman.'

'Oh.'

Hope died cleanly with the lie where the truth would have raised a quisling army of fantasies.

'What the hell,' she said, trying to be tough, 'fat-gut Latham's only going to gyp me anyhow. OK, mister, you got a date.'

I tried to make my smile not look like a leer. He'd never ceased watching us.

'Fine,' I said, 'swell. Listen, can you drive?'

'Sure,' she said pridefully, 'I'm an American.'

'That's fine too. Where do you change?'

She tossed her head.

'In back.'

'OK, here's what you do. Go and change into your things. Slip out—'

'I'm supposed to do another session.'

'Forget that and all the other sessions. Here, take this.'

I gave her a hundred-dollar bill. Then, in a way that he must have been able to see but masking exactly what they were, I gave her the keys to the rented Plymouth.

'Car keys?'

39

'Don't flash them around. I'm staying at the Wayfarer. Those belong to a hired car I've got. A Plymouth. It's in the underground car park. The number's on the tag. I have to make a call. Get changed, slip out the back way, pick it up and meet me on the corner—that way—in fifteen minutes. Trust me.'

With no pockets she was still clutching the note. She got up looking at it.

'You trust me?' she said.

'Sure.'

She smiled happily.

'OK,' she said.

'See you, Elsie.'

Watched by a suspicious barman she disappeared through a rear door. I drank some beer. Everyone was watching everyone. A perfect image of life. Now I could enjoy watching Argus.

He was plainly agitated. For the first time his eyes flicked off me. They were on the door she had gone out by. They were back on me. Back on the door. His hand fiddled with the shot glass he didn't drink from. Fiddling while Bernie sat doing nothing. Obviously he was waiting to see if she'd return. It was poetry to watch. He was worried. For all he knew, Elsie the Eskimo Go-Go Girl might have been queen of the Richard Powell International Conspiracy against Voyeurism. He said something to the barman, who nodded, looked at his watch and frowned. Abruptly, conspicuously not looking at me now, he had slipped from his stool and was gone.

Beautiful. I had him on the run. Trying to cover two bases at once. We could drive to the airport now, hide out there, grab the first plane to just anywhere and fly on finally at leisure. I drained my glass. There should just be time—Drive to the Airport! It was with the glass in mid-air that the thought came to me, arresting me a second in mid-emotion, frozen by its horror. For that instant icy, skeletal fingers brushed up on end the hair at the back of my neck. My dark deathly angel was hollowly declaring his approbation of my lethal complacency. As I thrust the chair askewly back a great interior shriek clamoured accusingly inside my skull. Fool! Criminal fool!

As I charged through the door, thought had already hardened into hideous certainty. Deadweighted, like a jockey putting up way too light, by the gun and the wads of money in my coat, I sprinted the four blocks flat out, frenziedly, as terror drove me past the astonished looks of people, who or what I couldn't have begun to say, shuffling into my swerving path along the sidewalk. My foot skidded away from under me where snow had been poorly swept aside. Somehow, the taste of blood burning at the back of my throat, my heart being squeezed tighter and tighter in sharper and sharper spasms, I kept my precarious balance. As I ignored the hotel entrance and made straight for the car-park ramp, a thin film of sweat seemed to bathe my skin, conducting the bitter evening cold to me all the faster. I reached the ramp and plunged, heedless of what might be coming up, down its steep descent to underground. With the angle I gained an insane, uncontrollable momentum, my feet instinctively careering on and forward just enough to keep me upright. Too late. Not quite simultaneously there were three things: a blinding white flash of light; a vicious whoosh of air blasting past, and a noise, louder and more physically painful in that containing, artificial cavern than I could have believed possible. Dresden, Hiroshima, Coventry, Hanoi. And explosive shock which, whether directly or magnified by my overstretched senses, sent me smashing down, unnerved, jarringly hard, full length upon the coarse, oily concrete. Skin was torn from my hands, a fingernail went and, as I rolled, a kick from a steam hammer that took the last breath from my body brought me to a brutal halt against a huge concrete pillar. With the impact my head snapped up to a sickening crunch and for moments I sprawled there fighting off nausea while a distanced world span swimmingly by. Then, somehow, with no consciousness of intervening time, just a terrible sense that there was something I must do, I was standing swayingly on my feet, staring at the unimaginable.

What had been a car was now a holocaust. The hood, corrugated, charred, had been blasted three-quarters askew and thick livid smoke shot through with dark, orange flames was belching violently upward from a twisted mass of engine entrails. Intense, maniacal hissing shrieked that the radiator had gone. The entire front end was twisted. At forty-five paces I could feel the heat. Ridiculously, impelled by a guilt aghast and numbing me towards the outwardly heroic, I moved forward. The stench of burning rubber grew thickly stronger. As my angle of vision changed I could see that the windshield had completely disintegrated, its frame savagely contorted, and that the driver's side door was buckled as from a high-speed collision. The smoke and flame subsided an instant before roaring up again with redoubled fury. In that split second I caught a glimpse of something hanging, impaled obscenely yellow-white for all its crimson lacing, in what was left of a splintered steering column. Mercifully the smoke billowed back and as my eyes began to water at its sting I caught a smell in my nostrils more foetidly sweet than rubber. Of its own, it seemed, my stomach began to retch. Pointlessly, I was still, half-doubled, gagging, moving forward when a sudden spurting flare from deep inside the car's interior drove me headlong, on instinct, sorely to the floor again. With a breathtaking *varoom* the Plymouth's fuel tank exploded like a second bomb. My ears rang. Something hot and sharp brushed burningly across my cheek. I staggered up to my feet. All I could see was fire. Three or four clusters of flame were licking upward from the vinyl roof of the adjacent Charger. A thin fiery tongue was snaking its way underneath. In that moment I heard above the flame-thrown roar the sharp clatter of voices and feet descending the staircase. I turned and, driven by a rage already tempering to a hardened cold, ran painfully back up the ramp. There was nothing I could do. For her, that is.

As I came up out of the ramp into the night the chilling air hit me. Involuntarily, as it again seemed, one arm supporting me against the wall, I was abruptly sick, vomiting liquidly, splatteringly, down on to the sidewalk. Then it was over.

I felt shiveringly, internally cold but I felt clear-headed. Nobody had seen me. I walked towards the corner of the hotel in

42

the direction of the main entrance and, just as I turned it, heard the muffled, subterranean boom of a third explosion. The Charger had been detonated. I caught sight of myself in the window of the inevitable lobby boutique. Superimposed on the vacuous smile of the dummy—pasted on like Elsie's in her last dance— was my own grimed reflection, hair up and on end, soot or something on my cheek, stains on my sleeves. Shivering still, I took the time to take stock. I could now feel singeing on my eyebrows but none of my new clothes had actually been torn. As always, buying expensively had been wise. I took out a comb and a handkerchief. Using them both and a good deal of spit I managed an elementary wash and brush up which promised to conceal that I'd just ascended from an inferno. Then, the possessor once again of a purpose in life, I pushed open the plate-glass doors of the hotel.

Small knots of people, staff and clients were standing in broadcast clusters about the large lobby. A few talked mutteringly, while most were listening with that abstracted, fear-in-the-eyes look of people straining to catch noises outside and far away. It reminded me of London shelters in the early blitz. As I headed for the elevator I shook my head with a subdued grimness as if I had been out reconnoitring, only to find my worst fears confirmed. A mink-coated matron whose henna-hair was a come-on one generation behind her face grabbed me by the arm. Unbelievably she had a plastic button—'We've seen the Eskimos of Wainwright'—snuggling luridly within the exorbitant luxuriousness of the fur. Her fat lower lip trembled a full two seconds before the threadbare voice found utterance.

'... Is it a ... the earthquake?' she said.

Soberly I nodded.

'Keep the panic down,' I said.

Her face, draining instantly of a lifetime's sugar-coated complacency, was still in my mind's eye, giving me one small block of satisfaction on which anticipatorily to whet my revenge when the elevator doors cleared open before me and I found myself confronting across a three foot abyss the man who, having placed a bomb inside my car, had followed me obviously and insistently to make me run headlong in panic to my own incineration.

Intent to murder gives you verve. His hand was still clutching his suitcase, his fish mouth still working convulsively sucking in air, as, oblivious to local standards of etiquette, I whipped out the automatic with a speed that only hypertension, nerves stretched to battle stations, could have generated. I had the safety off as quickly. I lunged forward, pushed him hard into the innermost corner of the grey steel box, risked taking my eyes off him for a second, and pushed the Close Doors button. Two decades later, while we stood and patiently waited, the doors juddered together. The elevator was big, its capacity set at twelve people. I backed against a side wall, trying to evolve a game plan.

'Go up and press button fourteen,' I said, 'and see that's all you press.'

Tough guy talk. He did as I told him.

'Now back off into the corner again.'

He did so, sullenly, but no longer astonished or afraid. He was in some kind of control of himself again and making plans of his own. I stood too far away for him to rush me. We rode up in earsplitting silence. No thirteenth floor, of course. The lift drew to a smooth halt. The doors opened. I gestured with the gun.

'Get out, turn left and keep walking.'

On thick carpeting I followed him down the long, awe-somely empty catacomb of a corridor.

'Stop outside fourteen-fifteen.'

Turning his head to look at numbers he did so. I stayed some feet away. Awkwardly, using my left hand to get at a right-hand pocket, I dredged out the room key on its heavy metallic tab and tossed it sharply to him. He caught it, on re-flex, one-handedly.

'Open the door fully wide. Leave the key in the door. Switch the light on. Walk slowly into the middle of the room, put down your case and stand there turned round facing me. Keep your hands away from your coat.'

44

His grey eyes had been growing harder, more confident. Now a flash of unease, of naked worry flickered back across them and across his grey, neutral face. Once upon a time they would have got Wendell Corey to do the part.

'I reckon we can reach some satisfactory—mutually satisfactory—arrangement,' he said.

It was the first time I'd heard the voice. It too was neutral or, if my heightened imagination hadn't read too much into it, perhaps a Southern accent had rigidly been ironed into almost-conformity.

'I reckon,' I said. 'Do what I said.'

Very circumspectly he did all of it and stood there looking at me, impassive again, now that he saw I wasn't going to shoot him in the back. I retrieved the key from the lock, kicked the door shut after me and went on into the room. The light was bright after the muted corridor. The drapes were drawn open. But the highest building in Anchorage isn't easily overlooked. I was getting an idea of sorts now. If I was very lucky it might have enough self-sealed circuitry about it to give me a head start.

'You have a gun?' I said.

He motioned to the suitcase.

'In there,' he said.

I walked cautiously forward, holding my gun low, pointed at his belly. At arm's length, using one hand just like they do in the movies, I frisked him. He made no move. He had a gun in a shoulder holster under his left armpit. I fished it out, stepped back and threw it on the bed way out of reach. Tensions irradiated the room. It was altogether different a place from the cold emptiness that the shrilling of the phone had invaded.

'Now you've upset me,' I said.

'Can't blame a guy for trying. I had a telex on you. Seems like you've been using bullets like they're going out of style.'

'Maybe. I don't intend using any now.'

He grew, somehow, taller. Confidence restored the tone to sinews fear had previously slackened. Still neutral. He might have passed for an insurance salesman too.

'We can do a little deal,' he said. 'I never met a man on Raker's payroll who wouldn't wheel and deal.'

His hands gestured, began to move.

'Don't move,' I said quickly. 'I can change my mind about the bullets.'

The idea took on more definition.

'Raker's—'

'No deal. Take off your clothes.'

'Sure,' he said, 'I tried to get you. It's my job. You know that. You understand. Orders. But listen! It doesn't stop here. Your buddy Raker's next on their hit-list! They're going right to the top. Give me a—'

'Shut up!' I yelled. I had it now, complete and irresistible. Cold and implacable and just. And lo! the ice shall appease what fire hath wrought. I grew icy. Yelling was out of place.

'I don't need a deal,' I said. 'All I want is an out from this whole affair. I've got an escape plan. All I need's a head start. This is a way to get it. Get your clothes off.'

He stared at me blankly.

'All of them?'

'All of them.'

Still basically incredulous, he slowly took off his topcoat. He took a step as if to throw it on the bed.

'Uh-uh,' I said. 'Just on the floor.'

I could see clearer and clearer what I wanted to do.

'Now the jacket,' I said.

He removed the jacket and let it fall. Then, standing ungainly on one leg and then the other, an ugly duckling of a flamingo, he took off both his over-heavy American shoes. He took off his tie. As he reached for his belt I began to feel the baleful cobra of my sadism leering up inside me. He'd seen a lot of me of late but I was going to see a hell of a lot more of him. I felt a distinct voyeuristic pang of glee and if I'd ever felt invited to the woodchopper's ball I might even have detected the kindling of a faggot's burning interest. But I like my vices straight. I motioned to him to go on and, hopping from one leg to another—how unwieldy a man is getting in or out of clothes,

46

what fun this was suddenly becoming—he pulled off his trousers. His socks seemed too long in their self-support up his surprisingly thin legs. Hopping again he peeled them off. They left indented rings in the bulge of his calf flesh just below the knee.

'The wristwatch,' I said.

He took that off. He wore it with the dial inside the wrist. He laid it carefully on his jacket. Now he was reduced to the mandatory American tee-shirt and boxer-shorts. I waved the gun again. Very slowly he peeled the shirt off. It stuck for a long instant over his face and I was tempted to blast him then and there while his awareness was choked in the opaque panic limbo of the yielding cotton. But that would never have done. He dropped the undershirt. He hesitated. I waved the gun again. Betraying with even slower movement his disbelieving agony, he took the shorts down and off. He straightened up and stood there, hands unnaturally at his sides, like a bad actor asked to do nothing. He didn't quite want to cover himself and so acknowledge the humiliation he felt. He'd never been a locker-room man. I looked at him for a long while in silence, stretching out his embarrassment. Naked, he looked older. His arms were surprisingly without muscular form, just long and very straight. His shoulders seemed rather rounded. His belly had the sad protuberant look of all stomachs whose muscles have finally gone for ever, a little pot destined only to bubble up bigger and bigger. Man to man he didn't really have too much to worry about but I could feel the cobra coiling, readying to strike.

'Ever hear about the plastic surgeon who hung himself?' I said.

He mumbled something inaudible, reduced to God knows what pre-adult stage of incoherency. I cut him off in midmutter.

'OK,' I said crisply, 'put the shorts back on.'

He bent gratefully to retrieve them. As he did, I stepped sharply forward, reversing the gun in my hand, and with all the force and deliberation I could muster I smashed the butt down on the back of his skull.

Things in life don't always go like they do in the movies.

With a guttural, neanderthal grunt he sprawled forward on to all fours. Then, in a manner I hadn't at all bargained on and would never have imagined possible he slowly turned and lifted his head and looked up at me. He might have been a sick dog. His eyes were glazed and filmy and I thought of how I had felt on cracking my head in the basement parking lot. But he still knew what was happening. His features had sagged themselves into a curious pleading blur.

'Olivares,' he said thickly. 'Rafael Oliv—'

Thought of the basement helped me. I applied his own mercenary's rules and gave him no quarter. Without pity—without enough—I hit him again with the gun. It takes one to know one. This time he went sighing, full-length face down upon the floor. Suddenly I remembered I hadn't put the safety back on. I applied it and then hit him twice more. At that angle it was like chopping firewood. Violence is all. With the fourth blow, I drew a trace of blood. I stopped then and stood up. I was sweating more than my efforts seemed to warrant.

Swiftly I took the duffle-bag I had bought earlier in the day and tipped its unwrapped contents piecemeal on the bed. I took his revolver, snub-nosed and fat-bellied like him (do people always look like their guns?) and, after breaking it open and removing the bullets, put it in the left hand pocket of my parka where it could offset the right-side drag of my Police Special. Up the Arsenal. I picked up his topcoat and searched its pockets. For a moment I went giddy with shock. The key to his room wasn't there. He'd been on his way to check out, and I'd assumed it would be there. Perhaps he hadn't intended to stop at the desk at all. Perhaps he'd done it already. I should have got it from him first. I was still an amateur.

I snatched at his jacket. The key was there. Twelve-o-five. I sighed, and rammed jacket and topcoat into the duffle-bag. I bent and scooped the rest of his things in after them, including the watch he'd handled with such superfluous meticulousness, so ingrained can habits become. To get at them I had to drag him a little to one side. His skin felt clammy. It was an unpleasant and sobering reminder of what I had yet to get through.

Ignoring my few personal effects in bathroom and closet, I zipped the duffle-bag shut. I put it on the bed. From my pockets I took bills, about sixty dollars' worth and small change. I scattered them on the bedside table, adding from my pockets my Swiss Army knife—sorry about that, old faithful, but needs must when the devil drives—a Sheaffer and a lucky Irish penny —things I hoped were international enough not to seem from England. I pulled dog-eared tags off the grip I was losing now, retrieved my spent air ticket from on top of the chest of drawers. Then I went to the window. As I'd checked, it pivoted horizontally. I opened it wide, looked out and, after a necessary second to steel myself, looked down.

In the tiny street far, far below, darkly glistening with occasional pools of light, all was quiet. My room was on the side of the hotel, one hundred and eighty degrees from the car-park ramp entrance. That was where the crowd would be tonight. But on cue a siren distant in the city wailed the probable approach of another fire truck. I hoped it was another. Merry hell must be breaking out down there by now. That must be scanned. I was going to have to get out of this place sooner or later and the Plymouth—and what was in it—would point like an accusing arrow straight at me. If they put a cordon ... But first things first. Making myself do it, I craned out of the window nearly as far as I dared. In the darkness, at that height, I ran no risk. I looked left and right, twisted my head up. I might have been an astronaut going through a careful checking procedure during countdown. Two rooms away on my left a light shone, but diffusely, its curtains drawn. Everywhere else I was surrounded by a blank wall of darkness. Fine. I drew my head back inside and, in the process, unthinkingly looked down. My stomach contracted, turned over. The street lay glinting malignantly at that far-off, straight-down distance, exercising its atavistic allure. A nerve thrilled in the dark side of my mind. Drawn, fascinated, I projected on to my imagination the precipitate ecstasy of that shrieking, committed, voluptuous fall down the sheerness of the man-made cliff face. A blast of icy air swirled round me. My familiar was at my side, willing me

49

to push my luck out there. The wailing siren neared, reached a keening pitch, a will-destroying song. Shuddering, I turned, impulsively it seemed, and faced into the room.

It had gone flat. The release of action, the crisis at the window, had bled it of excitement. The edge of pleasure, however vicious, was dulled. It was like the aftermath of sex. It was the same old room. Only a man, stark naked, lay stretched out prone within it. The aftermath of sex, perhaps—only I still had a partner to satisfy. Fatigue, rich and royal, swept down upon me, but, feeling that this was the last time I could summon the effort, I braced myself to stave it off and faced the obscene, no longer postponable moment.

It was obscene. It had been smart, easier to make him undress himself. But as I turned him over, lugged him to a sitting position and pulled him across my shoulders in a bastard fireman's carry the icy clamminess of his flesh was like the kiss of serpents. I staggered an instant, my knee buckling. He was heavier than I'd expected. But not, technically, a dead weight. I could feel his heart beating faintly close to my right ear. I edged sideways with him. It seemed very important not to get a smearing touch from his dangling genitals directly upon my own skin. He made no groan or twitching movement. He was out cold. I was rather glad of that, but all the same when I got to the window I hesitated a moment. Then I remembered the sweet sickly smell spreading from the burning Plymouth. With that I tipped him out. I, Richard Powell, man without a country or a calling, man without a woman, man once again without a purpose, tipped him out. In such dejected fashion he fell a four-second finite eternity. When he hit, the noise came unbelievably loud up the satanic well. A bursting, splattering pop. The sound of my splattering vomit greatly magnified. He'd be strictly a Christiaan Barnard special now. There were no screams, no cries, no squeal of brakes hastily applied. I turned, seized hold of the duffle-bag, my brief- and his suitcase and stopped at the door. The bad penny had turned up. And dropped. Hearing no corridor noise, I let myself out into what was now, more than ever, a catacomb.

That was how, also in Anchorage, Alaska, I avenged the

premature death of Elsie the Eskimo Go-Go Girl.

It had been better not to worry about fingerprints. Everything wiped clean would have looked instantly suspicious. Suicides don't do that. I couldn't control, of course, how recognisable his fragmented burst pod of a corpse would be. With luck, not a hell of a whole lot. So, when as seemed more likely, they found the teeth, the charred and blackened female bones inside the gutted Plymouth, they might detect the workings of an open-and-shut case. They'd trace me from the car. He was the same height and build and colouring—I didn't like to think so, but he was—as I. It might just pass: remorseful suicide after murder. The nudity had just the touch of crazed, irrational appropriate-ness. Suicides, of course, leave notes to say they are not loved. I hadn't been able to get that fancy with forgeries or extortion but there has to be one exception that proves the rule. That he'd pressured me—and I'd almost not bothered—into registering pseudonymously was royal luck for which I couldn't take the credit. It allowed me now to keep my passport. Otherwise, registered as myself, I should have had to leave it as conclusive proof of either my dead identity or, more likely, of my living guilt. It would have been conspicuous by its absence. All right. I didn't have, hadn't left, credit cards, ID's, a social security num-ber in the name of the late Mr Schwarz. So maybe they went up in the car. Checking in Iowa was going to show the man didn't exist in any case. That was another switch that ought to buy me time.

Using the fire escape stairs, I went down one floor. En route to twelve-o-five I passed one lady, elderly and rich. She seemed oblivious of fire and murder taking place around her and on the morrow would, I knew, be oblivious of all French-Canadian bell-hops. Twelve-o-five. The same side of the hotel. I let myself in and, shutting the door after me, went over to the window. Noth-ing stirred below on the cold side-street. I went back and switched on the light. No naked blondes on the bed. No gunman breath-ing softly through his mouth. The identical room to mine but a mirror image. A mirror image therefore of the same sterility. As brittle as a mirror, too. It was so empty, so apparently untouched by human hand that an aura of unchanged reality pervaded its unpalatial ordinariness. At any moment a melancholy horn would sound in a far-off forest and, on the instant, all would vanish away and I would stand forlorn on a barren, windswept heath. That's how it seemed. Or maybe, after my good deed for the day, I was entering into delayed shock.

I shook that off. I had to make time. I went through the room looking for any personal effects his precipitous departure might have induced him to leave. Nary a one. The cupboards were bare; as clean, befittingly, as a hound's tooth. Fine. I sat down on the bed and unzipped the duffle-bag. Methodically now I went through his pockets. Small change, a comb—clever of me not to leave mine upstairs—about a hundred bucks in small notes in a billfold, a nail clipper, a book of matches with the name and address of an LA bar, The Silver Peso, but not a cigarette. I repacked the bag and transferred my attention to his case. It was the glamorous sort that create instant covetousness when you see them in shop windows—a folding, two-suiter flight bag with zippy, pouchy pockets set into the outside. Buy one and the jet-set world's your oyster. Or, at least, your lemon. It wasn't locked. I unzipped it and laid it open. Laundered shirts on cards, nondescript ties, a tropical lightweight suit, rather soiled, and—bingo!—on the other side, beneath pyjamas, one of those simulated-leather folders for passports, tickets, travellers' cheques and such. Crammed.

I opened the thin green passport first. It's nice to know the name of anyone you've introduced to vast eternity. The done thing, really, even after a *fait accompli*.

He had one claim to fame. The only man I'd ever seen who exactly resembled the likeness of his passport photo. David Lester. Commonplace, really, for syllables I'd no doubt blabber on my own deathbed. If I died in bed. I turned the pages rapidly on, needing not to think. A lot of stamping, lots of visas. He'd come into the States only eight days ago himself, arriving at LAX from ... interesting, Saigon, apparently. Suddenly, *à propos* of nothing, it came into my head that I should have stayed my hand, been less singlemindedly bent on levelling the score. On the threshold of the unconscious he'd thrown up a name. He'd been trying to buy time, a reprieve, with it. It might have paid me to listen. Killing emotionally can lead you into fatal errors. I should have had more patience. Irritated, I laid the passport aside. A discreet leather billfold caught my eye. A credit card holder probably. One-handedly I flipped it open. Not plastic money, but even more interesting. A not quite identical photograph, a fuzzier more blurred likeness, stared heavily back at me from his recent past. Gold embossing and photostatted document joined official forces to proclaim sergeant's rank in the LAPD. Only this time the name was Carter. What I'd splattered over the pavement had already been a split personality. Like a good Boy Scout I pocketed the police ID and, displaying equal initiative, reached for what promised to be an air ticket. Then some variation in the light's refraction, the subtlest suggestion of an altered value, made me look up.

He didn't carry a big stick but he could sure tread softly. What he did carry was an adequate-sized handgun. It was pointed straight at my belly and its mouth looked like the Lincoln Tunnel.

'You're not Lester,' he said.

CHAPTER THREE

'He just stepped out,' I said. I didn't have the presence of mind to say it in American.

The gun in his hand described a lazily threatening arc.

'So who are you?' he said.

'Just what I was going to say.'

I couldn't understand why my mouth was so dry when everything was aqueously taking place five fathoms deep. Unreality as glassily thick as water engulfed me. I clenched my fists, commanded my brain not to drown. Slowly fantasy ebbed. Now there was nothing to it.

'That's scarcely so strange a coincidence,' he was saying. 'I don't believe we've ever met before.'

Cool. I tried to shrug, tried to smile, tried to seem as nonchalant as he seemed. I had to keep him guessing, had perhaps in the next five minutes literally to live off my wits. A matching nonchalance. It wasn't easy. At first, second and third glance I had never seen a man with such style and polish, never, indeed, seen a man so downright beautiful. About thirty, he had a face of perfect symmetry that avoided all the vacuity of a pretty male model by being, just, Asian. Perhaps over a very long life you might finally come to gauge the precise proportions of the lineage. I tried to make the most of what I still had coming. Gauguinesque skin the colour of wet sand was stretched taut across bone structure modelled with an edge. Someone had coordinated the long straight nose to the fluid slash of a mouth. The eyes were deadly patent, as full round as my own. Eurasian. I couldn't get past that.

'Then why don't we wait for our mutual friend to return and introduce us correctly?' I said. It lacked something of George

Sanders but for a first take in these circumstances it was heroically close. For a split second I seemed to detect his assurance waver. Perhaps my own stretched nerves had lied. Please, brain, an inner voice went on, please brain come up, come up with something. Moving across the room with a suddenness that defied simile he whipped the air ticket out of my hand. He backed off out of harm's way and examined it.

'OK,' he said sharply, looking up. 'Enough. I'm the house detective. You want to talk first before we go downstairs.'

It wasn't a question but a command. But as I smiled again, there was, for this first time, a touch of spontaneity in it. As he said it, I sensed, I knew unequivocally that he was lying. The patina of his composure was way above any corridor gumshoe's reach. And I knew, equally as certainly, that if he was lying he was outside the law. Outside of any conventional law, at any rate. All things considered, that was marginally the better.

'Your accent,' I said. 'It's most interesting. You're totally fluent, of course—most impressive—but your accent's English, isn't it? I mean rather than American. If you take my point. And yet there's a hint of the continent. French, I suppose, although the obvious isn't—'

'I want information,' he said, 'not insolence. Put your patronising English hands up in the air. Higher.'

Slowly this time, he came forward again. Methodically he emptied my pockets. Cagney would have knocked aside his gun arm and jabbed him to the floor, but I didn't have a box to stand on and I can't dance. The unnerved slackness around my knees seemed to promise that any moment I might not even have legs. I stared helplessly at his field cannon, trying not to shudder while he removed my papers, the Lester/Carter police ID, the two guns I'd acquired in such short order, the small fortune in bundled dollar bills. Perversely, it was losing the last that hit home to crumple my morale one further cramp and make me feel the more defenceless. The Christian in me should have rejoiced, but I was brought up with shares in the Salvation Army Assurance Society Ltd. He flipped through my passport.

'All right,' I tried, 'I'm just a plain old-fashioned thief. Only a pretty good one. I thought I'd just taken Lester for every last—'

'Mr Powell,' he said, 'Lester never carried this much money on him in his life.'

I waited. Think, think!

'I've grown impatient,' he said. Ice was at the heart of his poise. The gun lowered slightly as he took deliberate aim.

'Talk,' he said, 'or I shall hurt you very grievously. The left knee first.'

Less than defenceless now. Naked. I knew exactly, down to the last intimate congealing in the bowels, how Lester had felt frontally exposed to my sadism. I suddenly felt that there was a God, that He was not mocked and that His retribution was not only swift and terrible but finely ironic. From His viewpoint my universe had diminished to the gold-brown finger around that trigger.

'It wasn't so much a case of stepping,' I said. 'Actually, Lester leaped out.'

I jerked my head towards the window. The unwavering menace of the muzzle fractionally relaxed. A dart of interest glinted in his eyes. Watching me carefully he moved sideways to the window and looked down. He stiffened slightly. This was a room with a view.

'You see,' I said.

Moving as carefully, my hands out at arms' length, I crossed to the other end of the window. I did it casually, with the same lack of concern I show tiptoeing through a bed of ranch-bred tarantulas. Down below at the bottom of the black abyss was an unmissable focal point. About eight ants were standing on the edge of a glowing jewel of light, the common pool from the headlights of two toy cars. One of the toys had a further red light on its roof. The light glowed on and off, on and off. In the centre of the circle of ants, the centre of the pool of light, there was something else, far away, too fuzzy in outline to identify. I looked back at the gun and on up to its owner. Both were once more bestowing their undivided attention on me.

'Lester?' he said.

I nodded.

He shook his elegant head.

'Not underneath this window,' he said.

'Under mine.'

'Did you kill him?'

'Maybe.'

Since my tactical gaffe about being a thief I knew more than ever that my one hope was to zap him with the unknown, to stay anonymous, be subtly outside of pigeonholing and being hence a candidate for routine handling. Routine disposal. File this in the basement, Miss Jones. As I prayed to myself for some exotic catalyst, he returned implacably to basics.

'Who are you?' he said. There wasn't going to be a third time of asking.

The gun came up to level at my chest. I forced myself to speak.

'There's a corpse splattered all over the snow down there and ringed with half the police in Anchorage. There's a king-size fire roaring away in the basement garage. The other half are down there. The whole joint must be jumping with cops. They'll have a cordon thrown round the place by now. You don't dare pull that trigger.'

At my own words my blood ran cold. Soon it would run hot. I'd made a second error, this time the fatal one. Conversationally, I'd issued a challenge. His sense of aesthetics would demand that, a mandarin among assassins, he shoot me.

'Precisely because of that,' he said, 'the noise will constitute a very small risk.'

'You'll still have to get out.'

He smiled, such an angelic, satanic, doom-laden smile. My jaw ached as I braced myself for the gouging tearing hammer-blow. With that tensing a door locked deep in the labyrinth of my mind sprang unbiddenly open and a word, a name, flew out.

'Besides,' I said, 'how would you explain it to Raker?'

That got to him, how I could tell I'm not sure. The call had got through to the Governor. The gun dropped a reprieving fraction from the horizontal.

'What's Raker to you?' he said.

'What indeed?'

We stood, two men, not talking. Time raced by, crawled by, sped by, stood silently still. Steadfastly, Gibraltar set on blancmange. I looked at him. Nothing in his face altered but in that endless instant the European in his features vanished away. The Middle Kingdom was ascendant. Was this Olivares?

'Supposing I was to tell you I'm looking for Raker,' he said.

As unobtrusively as possible I took the deepest breath of my life and gathered all the omniscience of total ignorance.

'I've never known him not consider a pitch,' I said, 'a deal. Not at the right price. Supposing I said that I could take you to him.'

'...Then I would be obliged to make you divulge his whereabouts.'

'I'd probably divulge a lie. On the other hand...'

'Yes?'

'If you made it worth my while...'

'You would take me to your leader,' he said. 'How mercenary.'

He was considering.

'Don't fish,' I said. 'Everyone's a mercenary.'

'Not quite,' he said. 'Where, generally?'

'You've got the answer in your hand,' I said. 'No, not the gun, the airline ticket.'

'Los Angeles,' he read.

So that's where. Well, naturally. Everyone gets to go there. It was no worse than any other place. Better, maybe, as at least I'd once known my way around there.

'How much?' he said.

'We can talk about it as we go.'

He gestured with the gun.

'You appreciate that you'll have this in the small of your back every inch of the way.'

'We can work something out.' I'd said that to someone else up here. 'You might just get away with paying me my own money.'

He smiled. The European came back into his face.

'Let's regard that as a surety against sharp practice,' he said.

58

'But of course. You can have my word too.'

'An Englishman's bond.'

'We could shake hands.'

'Let's take that as read, shall we? Mine are rather full just at present.'

Melvyn Douglas and Franchot Tone. I nodded at the window.

'They'll be a damn sight fuller,' I said, 'trying to get by the law.'

He looked at me. He was calculating again. I could tell.

'Oh,' he said wonderingly, 'I thought perhaps you had some—'

'Not a chance.'

Not without charm, timing it well, he smiled.

'We'll rush them,' he said.

CHAPTER FOUR

Warm, and therefore tireder than hell inside the cabined drowsiness of the DC8, I stared through the porthole by my left ear at the tiny man out there in the sub-zero night below. Encumbered by untold layers of insulation, zippered, kapoked and anoraked, he moved across the apron as in some ponderous homage to the Michelin tyre man. He waved his arm finally, as languidly awkward as a man submerged in oil. The plane began to taxi out to the runway—a black, light-flanked ribbon between the parted white sea of the snow. As the perspectives pivoted I looked back at the receding terminal. No screaming, light-flashing police cars came sirening across the white sheen, the darkness, to turn the intercepted plane from her course. As far as the hissing cabin pressure would allow me I breathed a touch easier. My pulse was down below two hundred for the first time since, on a marginally warmer occasion, Washington crossed the Delaware.

The end of the runway. The opening throttles sent a tremor through the riveted cabin and we gathered speed. The ghost's icy presence waned. Incorporeal, he constituted a less lasting threat to my equilibrium than the pressing problem of the gun in my right rib section. First things first. I glanced that way.

'Smooth take-off,' he said happily. Normal businessman-to-man small talk.

I lapsed into continuing silence. He smiled sweetly. Johnny Coolie. A man could come to love him, I suppose. I suppose. The stewardess, all American short-stemmed beauty, came lurching heavily down the aisle dispensing synthetica. I looked straight through her as fatigue, rich, luxurious, seductive, swept over me in the too-cramped blessed seat. Two continents and minimal sleep can take it out of you. And two killings, of course. All I needed now was a flight-deck shoot-out between Cubans and Jordanians. Then I'd have the set. I yawned, closed my eyes, disengaged the thought clutch. Images came. Instant replay of the not-to-be-believed.

A bulletless gun in mid-air. The world's longest elevator ride. Walking out of the Wayfarer. Right past, waved on by the grey-eyed cops. H'm. The smooth, beautiful Eurasian face. He was Johnny Cool, all right. No one could have engineered it more adroitly ... The late Lester's police ID had been the key. Still up there in the hotel room he'd gone straight to it. He looked at it, looked at me.

'Can you handle an American voice?' he said.

'Kind of,' I said. I saw his plan. 'It's pretty hard, though, if you're English.'

'Harder if you're Bantu.'

'What about the photograph?'

'With these things even when you're the sitter you have to have luck to get a likeness.'

'Maybe.' I was getting more shakes. There was no let-up. Another six furlongs in the adrenalin stakes. Still, there was a chance. In this anti-visual age nobody looks at anything any more.

He was breaking the shells out of the fat-bellied Lester gun. He snapped it shut and threw it, empty, over to me. He flipped the ID after it.

'You say there's a fire in the basement?' he said.

'Yes.'

'You're Sergeant Carter, Los Angeles Police Force. You're taking me in on suspicion of arson.'

I nodded. It was the better choice.

'Now. Put this money in the attaché case.'

I did so. When it came to money, this was an open and—

'Let me carry it. You'll want to whip that card in and out as fast as you can get away with. Understand?'

I said that I did.

'We'll use the back way. The brighter ones will be out front. The card was a fake, his cover. Let's go one better.'

He grinned conspiratorially. His eyes glinted again. The odds had to be high against us but, no question, he was enjoying himself. He moved to the door.

'Let's go,' he said. 'Oh—I'll tell you this much. It's in both our interests to get clear. But bear in mind, I beg you, if anything goes wrong, you'll be the—'

'Sure,' I said, 'sure. I saw that picture too.'

Nobody was in the corridor. Each with a hand in his pocket, his on a gun that was loaded, we walked parallel, the width of the corridor apart.

'Round here,' he said.

We made it to the service elevator. This must have been how he'd come up. I pushed the button and something whirred into humming life. It was still working. It arrived empty. We got in.

Once again two men locked in the intimacy of a stainless steel box. Both with racing brains. I tried to order priorities. If I dived headlong as the doors opened I could probably miss his bullet, get off with a wounding. He was probably bluffing. Whoever he was, shooting me would only help his vindictiveness. Nothing else. Maybe I could pin the Lester killing on him. His word against mine. No. No chance. My own presence on US soil was far too tenuous. Fifth floor, fourth floor.... Why not give in altogether? What was left to me, anyway? Third floor. My own bloodymindedness. I bitch therefore I am. A poor thing but mine own. Nobody else's. The longer it was postponed, the lesser the inevitable defeat of extinction. The elevator stopped, but my stomach kept on fluttering.

The short distance to the service exit seemed amuck with men in blue, and some in plain clothes. No Press it seemed. One laundry skip. No Alaska State Police—all Anchorage cops.

Seven pairs of eyes swivelled in scrutiny as we stood there. It was opening night on Broadway.

'Move on out,' I said, like in the movie.

He'd taken up a position in front of me. They could all see the bulge in my jacket pocket. He'd had to put both his hands at his sides as he moved forward. He was a gambler. If I wanted to I could pull the rug right out from under him. Correction: a good gambler. I'd hit the deck with him. Besides, I couldn't see a rug.

I prodded him past two or three scattered flanking men. Two uniformed, Police-Specialed cops mounted guard on the exit, footmen style. We walked to meet them. We never made it. A plain clothes officer jutted himself into our path. He was short, chunky, granite-hard Caucasian.

'What goes on?' he said. He wore a hat. He'd seen the movie too.

There was a wall-mounted light to my left. I swivelled to get my head between it and him, showed him the card and nodded at my prisoner in one prayerful movement.

'Extradition to California,' I said. 'Guess you guys'll be holding him up here now.'

A cop confronted by another from another State, a rival Force, he took the card.

'More fucking paperwork,' I said.

'Captain Cantor know about this?' he said.

'I'm on my way there now.'

'This the man?'

'Huh?'

'There's a guy outside on the sidewalk. What's left of him. Fell or pushed. All the way from the top, you'd have to say.'

I let out air between my teeth. I didn't have a whistle in me.

'Hell,' I said. 'I thought it was just the fire.'

'Identification won't be easy,' he said.

He still held the card. Puzzlement, uncertainty, were written on his face. I'd known better reads myself. I played my joker.

'Can you spare me a man?' I said. 'Just to the car, I got a driver.'

He gave me back the card. He shrugged.

'Sure,' he said. 'Don't know what the hell I'm supposed to be looking for here anyhow.

'Jackson, see Sergeant Carter gets to his automobile.'

A big ball-carrier of a cop came forward and drew a gun. Just the business end protruded from the wrap-around ham fist that turned it to a toy.

'Thanks,' I said. 'Christ, what a change from Santa Monica. Boy is it going to cost him.'

They were still chuckling softly as we went out.

It was a change. It was colder than the dead of yesterday. Audibly, Jackson shivered.

'This way,' I said. There was no point in looking up Lester. Not in his downcast condition.

We turned left down thirty yards of quiet, dark sidestreet and I lightheadedly wondered what would happen to the cop. Rubbery, far beneath me, my legs kept on keeping on. I was above it all, high on nervous reaction. I'd abdicated. Let dog eat dog. But nothing happened. Johnny Cool didn't make a move. Jackson did. He shivered. Our exhaled breath made white ghosts in the night. We drew nigh unto the corner.

We reached it. It was like turning from night to day. Light blazed across the façade of the hotel from the headlights, searchlights of two dozen cars. Fire hoses stretched flatly from a brace of hydrants and a tanker fire-truck. That must mean the fire had been put out. I wondered how long we had before Captain Cantor was too. There was no smoke drifting in the Anchorage night. Perhaps the eager and the nipping air had frightened it all away. Or, more simply, where there's no fire, there's no smoke. Only men in heavy clothing, everywhere in lumbering view. There were more police cars than you could shake a can of Mace at. This wouldn't do, Powell. I pulled myself together.

'OK, Jackson,' I said. 'I can cut it from here. See you get some good hot coffee, now.'

'Yes, sir.'

Just like that. We were alone.

'Come back.'

I'd made three steps before he said it. His hand was in the pocket again. It wasn't on account of the weather. I came back.

'Down here.'

Three icy blocks away we picked up a cab.

'What goes on?' he said.

'Fire at the hotel,' the driver said. 'Where to?'

'Shamrock Bar.'

'Where you guys from?'

'Quebec, Canada.'

That was why he'd made his voice so French. He kept it that way when he had me pay the guy off. Alaskan cab fares. Other places they'd get you the car.

'Gee can I use a drink,' he said before the driver gunned off with his newly won wealth.

'Me too,' I said.

I never got it. All I got was the pay-phone by the cloakroom. Ice-cubes tinkled in the next compartment. Gin was in the very air I breathed. I looked at him pleadingly.

'Call another cab,' he said.

'Salaud,' I said.

I used the Yellow Pages. I used the phone.

'They say five–ten minutes.'

'Good,' he said.

'Time for a drink.'

'Stay where you are. You did well. You've got balls.'

'I thought I'd lost them a couple of times back there.'

He smiled. We looked at each other. Whoever had dreamed up the warm, low-key orange lighting to the tiny lobby had known his stuff. It was made to buy drinks in—or to exchange confidences. It came to me that I was getting away with murder. Thanks to Lester's fake ID. It was what you might call a double fake. If it was fake. Maybe Lester was Carter.

'Who are you, Mr Powell?' Johnny Cool said.

It was warm in there, cosy. Euphoria whispered to my nerves to unscrew from the sticking point. I looked at him, slim, smiling, elegant. A light made for confidences. I didn't know the first thing about him, didn't know him from Adam—assuming, as is most tenable, old Adam was Eurasian. He had a gun on me and really there was no need. One thing we had in common— the bearing off of a famous victory. Even if they caught up with us now. It had been famous. A famous bluff. Now, perhaps, as the pace, the tension slackened, now perhaps in the soft light made for confidences was the time to speak, the time to build on the sharing of our great escape an intimacy free of guns.

Slackening! Like a dog leaving water I shook the drowsiness off me. I jabbed contempt into my system to keep it at full stretch. It had been Rafael, not Adam, Olivares. This smiler had a knife. I could trust him, sure. Like Othello trusted Iago. I put an edge into my voice to cut the strands of cameraderie.

'Only one way out of this town,' I said. 'The airport. They'll go straight to it. You lost us time with your fake trail.'

He looked at me evenly.

'Perhaps,' he said. 'There's a plane in forty minutes. Only one tonight. We have no choice but to wait for it. Better here than there, whatever.'

'They'll be looking for two. We'd do better by ourselves.'

He looked at me.

'You've got my money,' I said, 'I'd have to get back to you.'

That was true. I'd get back all right.

His grin this time had lost all friendship.

'Not a chance,' he said.

Outside, with nice punctuation, the new cab had honked.

Nice—a devalued word. Like all of them. Jane Austen. She'd used it nicely. What an insight. She didn't go round confusing life with reality. Nice. Nice clouds out there through the plane's window streaming whitely by the nice sharp wing. Grey really. Pregnant with snow. You could sing that if you had a tune. It was light spill from the cabin that made them white. *Où sont les neiges d'antan*. There's no business like ... nice cabin, nice warm, nice bye-byes.

'You wanna pull down your shelf, sir?'

Miss Lurch, the stewardess, jerked me out of it. I waved the plastic food away. That wasn't nice, it was shitty. Owed her a favour, though: I still had some thinking to do before I could let myself sleep.

Once again—I'd been doing it for ever, it seemed—I hauled myself off the canvas. Only just. The fatigue count was getting

66

harder to beat all the time and I'd no idea, one would say, how many rounds I was supposed to go. Another round. Good thinking. Mine's a gin and tonic. But, nice as it would be to have him pay for one, I'd go without. In the first place it would take the girl hours to break off from her surly dispensation of whatever dead-of-night meal this might be. Secondly, in the informally long duel of wits I was engaged in with Johnny at my side, it would behove me to seem the thing I was not. I must still keep those wits at red alert. I feigned sleep while I tried to take stock.

I was on a plane flying south to LA. That, in view of what I'd left behind, was to the good. They're very hot on litter-bugging in downtown Anchorage. Sooner or later, though, the chase would be on. Probably sooner. Even though embarking had been such a doddle, there'd probably be a compensatorily tough reception party at LAX, armed to their flawless Californian teeth. At Anchorage there hadn't been a thing. No ringing school of shark-like police cars. No plain-clothes stakeout snapping on last-minute cuffs. Only the usual nominal airport security patrol. There'd been seats. We'd bought four tickets, given—it was an internal, domestic flight—false names all round. Twenty sweating minutes drinking coffee oh so casually in the shadowed corner of an all night grill and we had walked the marrow-chilling fifty yards to board, as unquestioned as a pair of sky-jackers. That was how, under some duress, I came to fly out of Anchorage and bade a glad farewell to old Seward's Folly, the once-land of the Eskimo. As a final mix 'em up, I'd suggested we use Lester's ticket. He complied. The perfect gentleman. His treat. It made up for using my money at the counter.

My money. Premising we stayed out of the slam, that was probably the first reality. With amusement I found his taking it had made me avid for it—even beyond my stained, inverted honour. Suspended as I was in total stateless limbo I needed the bread of life to give me leverage. Money isn't everything but it's great when you can't get credit. Once I'd been Richard Powell, lighting cameraman. Now not only occupation but country, station were gone. Without a station you miss all kinds of boats. Without money ... I hadn't lied in saying I'd stick close to him. Getting it back was something to look forward to. It gave me a kind of future. Now there was a switch for you.

And yet, whether or not I died a-Wednesday, there *was* a smack of honour about it. Whatever rapport of shared experience there might be, whoever, intriguingly, he might be, I resented the hell out of Johnny Cool. Nobody had ever pushed me around for so long. Well, not in years. I'd forgotten how to be used to it. One other little thing: he'd been on the point of killing me in that room, I'd not the slightest doubt. He wouldn't kill me up here at a public, pressurised thirty-thousand feet. I could temporarily count on that. And right now it paid me to ride along. LA, *pace* the Police Department, was where the game would start again. Who the hell was he? I'd been worrying at it so long I almost believed I'd seen him before. That was bred of too much fancy. The truth was, I had no idea. One thing, he'd have even less idea about me. Sitting there so composed, the Inscrutable Kid, he must be racking his own brains fiercely. I wasn't even any kind of professional. No affiliations, a complete loner. Not that I should exclusively worry over him. Both our identities were secondary. The big primary issue was: who the hell was Raker? My big buddy. Everybody knew that. Except me. Who the hell was he? There was no one I could ask. I was supposed to be the hired guide. Sod it. Nothing to do until LA. I wasn't going to lose any more beauty sleep over it ...

The ball was well short of a length, going on with the bowler's left arm to miss the leg stump. I pivoted, timed the hook well, knew from the feel that I'd middled it. The ball sped towards the flock of sparrows worrying the outfield in line with the gasometer. Casually scattering, they were unharmed as, landing amid their grazing rights, it skipped first bounce over the boundary, beating long leg running round. That brought up my fifty, made in just under even time. From the other end Mickey Stewart nodded laconic approbation and the sparse strung-out crowd started to applaud. I raised my bat in acknowledgement and, as I did, the wicket-keeper did something very unfair. He began jabbing me in the ribs with one of the bails. Once, twice, three times. I woke up to find myself staring at lank grey hair plastered thinningly back across a dubiously white skull. The seat in front was tilted all the way towards me. The wicket-keeper played for the Third World XI.

'Coming in to land,' he said. Just one friend to another.

I blinked, trying to wake up fast. My mouth felt as dry as boots left out in the Mojave down below. Except I couldn't, surely, have slept that long. And besides, we were still in the greyest of unCalifornian cloud. I stretched, looked out of the window. At that moment the port wing dipped obligingly as the plane banked and we came down out of the grey cloud into a clear, grey universe. There wasn't a trace of smog in sight. It wasn't Los Angeles. The queasiness in my stomach went slightly beyond the inducing of the sharp, crabbing descent. Grey steel water, black-green pines on ridging hills, early morning dawn. Over there a city. Boeing city. Seattle.

'Seattle?' I said.

He nodded, smiled. I belted up. It wasn't a non-stop flight. That must be scanned. I wasn't at home in Seattle. The plane's descent increased in momentum. I settled back to await the agony to my ears. Miss Lurch was nasally prompt to add to it.

'Good morning, ladies and gentlemen, we are now making our final approach to Seattle-Tacoma, where we shall be on the ground for approximately forty minutes for refuelling and for taking on new passengers. During this time, through-flight passengers may leave the aircraft for refreshment in the main concourse. Local time in Seattle is six twenty-five Pacific Standard Time. To those passengers leaving us at this point, the Captain and crew wish to say thank you for flying Western and we sincerely . . .'

I tuned her out as the Apaches stepped up their war dance on my drums.

Twelve centuries later our supercharged mass-grave leeched/ nuzzled home on Mother Earth. Clang, clang, clang went the doorway and an atmosphere of normality returned. If any atmosphere is normal at eight thirty in the morning.

69

'Let's grab some coffee and stretch our legs a little,' said my matter-of-fact Company colleague. The small-hours flight hadn't cramped his style, ruffled his sleek feathers by one millimetre.

'Better take our things,' he said.

As we walked, hand-luggaged, through glass arcades that seemed to intensify rather than filter out the grey glare of the morning. I had a pretty shrewd idea of what he was about. When he studiously avoided the oasis of a compact coffee-shop I knew for sure. It wasn't just that he disliked compact coffee. Maybe—if there was a place for me in it—he had the right idea. We turned a corner. Another endless corridor of brushed chrome, plate glass, vinyl flooring and multi-lingual signs extended away to infinity. A lost echo of Marienbad fluttered whimperingly up and down the long length. We walked on. No Swiss Guards leapt forward to apprehend us. At long last we gained entry to a vestibule thinly peopled, not with courtiers but with grey-faced travellers, yawning desk-clerks and eventually a cab-driver.

'Where'll it be?'

'A good car lot,' the senior partner said.

The driver looked a little early-morning blank.

'You can rent from—'

'No. We want to buy—'

'Just make it Car Row,' I said.

That made sense. The driver nodded.

'Got you,' he said. 'Climb aboard.'

We climbed aboard. I was looked at.

'You brought the money?' he said.

Very droll. All the same, a cheering note had been struck in me. Those are games I like to play—buying cars, swapping mules.

The salesman's name was Ralph. That didn't surprise me. All car salesmen are called Ralph. He was tall and sincere and bald. I could tell he was bald on account of his bad hairpiece. He was friendly and neighbouring. And, as I've said, sincere. And up-standing. It was a long time since I'd seen so upright a bent man. He'd shaved off the moustache.

We found him midway in Car Row where the cabbie finally

put us down. Previously I'd had him make two slow passes the long length of this particular Tin Pan Alley while I cased the seemingly endless lots. There they all were—the gleaming schools of metal fish collectively inspiring as much confidence as a portfolio of Australian copper shares. Here and there, Willie Shoemaker alongside Alex Karras, grinning Nipponese and sportif European franchises had infiltrated the Detroit ranks—Datsun and Triumph recapturing an infinitesimal fraction of what in far-flung wars good old American pragmatism had cost them. With one eye I watched Johnny Cool. You can learn a lot about people by the way they react to cars. Would his face light up as we passed the hot-shot Sports Car Imports lot? He didn't react at all. He'd told me I was going to be in the driver's seat, told me to pick the model. He watched impassive as I went about it.

'Don't get nothing fancy. Get a Chevvy,' the driver said. 'Get it fixed any time, anywhere. Get a Chevvy or a Ford.'

I couldn't see a single Citroën anywhere and, besides, it would have been all wrong. We needed a car that would blend as much as possible with the freeway landscape. A used car. An apple-pie and ice-cream car. I flirted with the idea of a VW—one of identical millions and air-cooled for California. But who wants to ride around in Kesselring's staff car?

'Sounds like good advice,' I said. 'Drop us here.'

That brought us to Ralph the GM dealer.

'Hi there,' he said, 'help you folks at all?'

'Oh . . .' I said. 'Maybe. Aiming maybe to buy a car.'

'Well, we got 'em. What kind of car did you have in mind?'

'Oh . . . I don't know. Hadn't thought too much about it, I guess. Transportation car I guess. Only reliable.'

'They're all reliable here. We give 'em our Six-Ways Gold Seal Guarantee.'

'What's that?'

'Anything goes wrong in the first two thousand miles why you just bring it right back here and we'll fix it for you absolutely free of labour charge.'

'Oh . . . fine.'

'My name's Ralph, by the way.... And yours—'

'Glad to know you Ralph.'

'Glad to know you too, Mr—ahm. How much you have in mind spending?'

'Oh, I don't know. Hadn't really thought. Not too much. Wanted to take a look around, I guess.'

'Well, we got 'em. Take your time. Look around. Any help you might need, why, I'll be right over there in the office.'

I took my time. There were about fifty cars on the lot and for my purposes about forty-five of them would all have done. Maybe it was pointless to play games, a waste of energy and time. But car salesmen are made to be played against. Hard as it is, you've got to try to win against the house. I looked around. Johnny followed me amiably. The quiet friend who comes along with you because he knows about cars and you needed a ride anyway. Next time you sell a car take a close look at the second guy—the one with his hand perpetually in his pocket.

It was in the second row. A late sixties Rambler Cross-Country Estate. Its lines were an appealing touch less garish, more functional than most of its cousins. You have to try harder still when you're number four. Its colour, a mid brown/beige, would camouflage up with pleasing inconspicuousness on the dusty road south. It was an automatic with American Motors push-button-type transmission. That planted an infectious little germ in my brain. I made a big fuss of the Impala saloon next to it.

'Fine car. Fine car.'

Ralph had soft-shoed his way back before being sent for.

'Yes, I guess. Colour's kind of—kind of—you know.'

He didn't, so he grimaced a pantechnicon expression. It could convey anything.

'Sixty-nine model,' he said.

'What's the mileage?'

I'd already taken a look at the clock through the window but I wanted to hear him say it.

'Forty-nine thousand.'

I whistled sharply.

'For nineteen-ninety-five?' I said.

'It's maybe the best buy on the lot. Used to be the manager's personal vehicle.'

He aspirated the noun into three syllables. I just looked at him with my disbelieving Jew expression. There's no prejudice about me.

'Want to take a spin?' he said.

'Well ... may as well, I guess.'

A light came on behind his friendly, neighbouring eyes. He'd got me to put my committed foot in its door. He thought.

He went off to get the keys and, just for a moment, a light flickered in my head too. I switched it off. Hope might spring eternal so long as I lived, but there was no point in fooling myself. I wasn't going to jam my foot down on a gas pedal and, burning screeching rubber, bullet away from my Saigon sidekick. I wasn't Steve McQueen.

'Here we go, then.'

It started on the third time of asking. We all got in. My quiet friend was in back just behind me. I took it round the block, concentrating as much on holding the right side of the street as on its performance. All the same, it had plenty of power.

'It's a real strong car,' Ralph said.

That's something else you'll have noticed. They all say that. All the Ralphs.

'I'm not planning on hitting anything,' I said.

He laughed at that. Genially.

It handled like a supercharged sperm-whale.

'Forget it,' I said.

I drove it back. Quite deliberately I eased it back into the very self-same slot. End of phase one. I started to walk away.

'Maybe there's something else we could—'

'Well—while we're here. How about this one right next door, I mean.'

'The wagon? Oh she's a real fine car. Sixty-eight Rambler. This one's got air. She'll—'

Phase two.

I gave this one a much more extended workout. I took over half an hour. All the time Ralph pitched his sale. He remem-

73

bered not to use the 'manager's personal' approach again, but he wasn't that proof against the insidious power of habit. It seemed that the Rambler was a strong car. It turned out to be a real tight car too. Maybe it was. You can never really tell, of course, unless it's two hundred per cent obvious if there's something wrong. What they may have put in the crank case, packed in with the power-chain, you really can't tell. This one seemed not too bad. The suspension wasn't too spongey, was agreeably hard to my European taste. The steering was similarly positive, not too mushy. It could cruise at seventy for ever. The clock said thirty-seven thousand. Just possibly that was the truth. Perhaps it would do. After all, as Ralph originally pointed out, the brakes were up and it had good rubber. I drove it back.

'Well, gents, what do you say?' Big, bald Ralph.

I shrugged, looked at my Italo-Latvian mechanic.

'I don't know,' I said. 'What do you think?'

He shrugged, looked at me. Pat on cue. Right in the groove. Johnny Cool.

'I don't know,' he said. 'It's your money.'

That was all too bloody true. I looked at Ralph.

'How much again?' I said.

'Sixteen-ninety-five.'

'Yeah, all right,' I said. 'Now what can you do for us?'

'Well—I shouldn't, but you guys've kind of hit a spot, I guess. What the hell. For you, sixteen-sixty. What do you say?'

I didn't say anything. I snorted.

'Well, thanks a lot,' I finally got out. 'And thanks for your time. I guess we've been kidding—'

'Listen. How about making an offer? Try me.'

'Thirteen and a half,' I said. I don't know why. I could have bought half the cars in the place. It was all arbitrary, academic.

'Not a chance.' He shook his head.

I shrugged.

'Why don't you—'

'It wasn't a haggling price,' I said. 'Take it or leave it. I'm not a horse-trader.'

'No way. I mean what kind of trade-in—'

'Thirteen and a half, spot cash.'

He looked at me.

'Why don't you go talk to your boss,' I said. 'See what he's prepared to do for us. Spot cash.'

'There's no point,' he said. 'Not at thirteen and a half.'

I shrugged. He shrugged. I smiled. He smiled. It went on for a long time like that. He said it was bad I had no trade-in. I said it was good. There was a moment when I caught myself thinking that he probably had a second wife and three kids who constantly jeered at him and alimony for his ex to provide and that he probably hadn't made a sale in ten days and probably banked on his commission to get by. I hardened my consumer's heart, true though it all obviously was. Let him think the same about me.

'Thanks but no thanks,' I told him.

Finally he went off to call his boss. I glanced across at JC and grinned. Funny. I still had a gun on me and yet I hadn't enjoyed myself so much since Muller put the third past Bonetti. He looked at me quizzically. Maybe I'd made a mountain out of a molehill. Maybe I should have caved in fast and lulled suspicion. But I hadn't caved in before. And big Ralph would remember two guys who bought like a lamb far more readily than two who haggled. And what the hell. Here he came now.

Solomon had adjudicated at fifteen-fifty—a verdict of unimpeachable impartiality. I didn't push it further. I reckoned we had a draw. Always give the other guy an out. I closed out the deal and we all moved—whither thou goest, thither goest J— into the permanently anchored trailer to take care of the paperwork.

It took twenty minutes and I had to be careful. I gave a fictitious Seattle address—4428½ Second—in case there was complicated stuff about taking cars across state lines. Dimly, I seemed to recall that there was. I wondered whether I dare use my own true name. That might make it possible to register the mighty monster legally in California. But I daren't—I simply daren't. And—I brought my rambling mind up sharply to confront

75

actuality—what the hell was I doing, contemplating bourgeois automotive legalities in LA? We weren't heading south to set up house together. That had been with someone else. The further I could put between me and that car, and the sooner, the better.

Ralph counted the money twice. Then he shook hands. Once. I got behind the wheel. JC sat in the diagonal back seat to me.

'You like driving bargains,' he said. 'Now drive this.'

'Where to?'

'Los Angeles, my friend.'

'I'm not your friend.'

'Ah, well. Perhaps that will change. Who knows? It's a long way.'

'Yeah. I've got to get gas.'

I gassed up the car and got some maps and some local directions. I swung out into traffic pointing the car south. It was behaving well. As soon as you've paid down cash, you always feel they won't. Usually you're right. For a long time we cruised past the endless panoply of hoardings, signs and store fronts. Life, I reflected, framed better than Antonioni. More subtly. That was because life knew what it was doing. We climbed a rise and there was water to our left. And freeway. I turned at an intersection, turned again and accelerated. Only one way to get on to a freeway—fast. In a jam you can brake in less time than you can accelerate to seventy from forty. No trouble. I was on, one of the leviathans hugest that ply the freeway. I got into the middle lane and relaxed. All I had to do now was watch points. The length of the West Coast.

That was how, exercising all my new options, I left Seattle heading South.

CHAPTER FIVE

Drive, he had said. So we did. Two travelling men, salesmen, wayfaring strangers. One up front and one in the back. The chauffeur and the killer. I saw that picture. Lana Turner played the wife. Two salesmen driving, as far as any of the other passing and repassing cars might think. Three guesses which one was going to get the title role. Driving South. Two strangers through this world of woe.

Only it wasn't. It was gorgeous and romantic. Even when tawdry and prosaic. I was an ex-Englishman let loose on the royal American road, and, so does familiarity breed contempt, the gun within the car, the question of who was Raker, both faded into postponement as the rushing highway landscape preoccupied my windshield. The tyres thrummed evenly on the grey, glaring pavement. The sky was big and wide. The grey wind came at us buffeting, breathing a dimension of history, of Cabrillo perhaps, of Lewis and Clark, of denimed thirties hoboes riding on a freight, conquistadores, usurpers of all they surveyed. We were immortals, film-star heroes riding down out of the hills to right all wrongs, settle accounts. We had all the omnipotence that being behind the wheel on a long sustained drive imparts. We were Lombardi's grim heroes piling up the inexorable yardage. He wasn't my jailer, my executioner, he was my comrade in arms. It was a noble ... the highway sped regularly, druggingly, hypnotically into me until after a while it seemed as if the drive was happening exclusively within the hollow confines of my skull, and all the streaming world reduced itself to that.

Or so, for a while, I let it seem. As did he, my silent partner. He scarcely spoke. There were none of those long soul-searching conversations I've known on drives to far-flung locations when, lulled by the motion of the movement, your shabbily suspicious daily guard will drop and show to your surprise you have a soul to search. Speechless, he was a presence, twin brother to the ghostly doppelganger, scenter of ghoulish ironies, that rode at my right elbow, in the corner of my eye or, other times, sat right behind and purred his icy glee upon my neck. Two presences, not finally discomfortable, whose influence familiarly waned the while the road exerted all its wide supremacy.

It's a wonder, I suppose, I didn't drive into oncoming lanes. I pressed the button and drove automatically. And gradually the diners, the wayside, off-ramp commercial frontage coffee-shops ushered in my decompression, brought me to a splash-down in reality. Those red vinyl bucketty counter-stools, those beige-nylon uniformed waitresses wiping clear the just vacated place, that pabulum without one grain of personality—however high, ecstatic, wrapt by metaphysics you may be, I defy you, my putty medal on it, to eat of their apple-pie and not discover your paradise is lost. The Bar-B-Q, The Shangri-Lunch, The Pollywog, Checker's T-Bone Diner, Ronnie's Ranchero Retreat. When the trumpets blare on that awful last day whereon each man shall be judged according to his works, the real Howard Johnson will not stand up.

I selected the wayside stops, telling him in advance. He never demurred. We went to the can together. Three big pistols. He chose the route, telling me in advance. I didn't demur either. I'd probably have gone the same mix-'em-up double-take, never quite rational route myself. From Seattle we followed the inland shoreline straight round to Olympia. I wanted to stop and pick up a couple of six-packs there but the truckers were on strike and the source might just as well have run dry. Whenever we did stop I bought papers, local, national. There was nary a word, not a whisper, of the flying flatfoot. The radio was heavy and ersatz, newsy and acid, evangelical and rabid, but, wherever I dialled, spoke not of Anchorage's aerial ballet. I finally got my beer in Aberdeen, when, leaving the obvious inland route, we turned due west and came out on the coast. I topped a rise and there it was, looking at me with a mild surmise in its one vast unblinking eye, the ebony-blue Pacific.

'I can see the sea!' I said.

He didn't say anything.

'I saw it first.'

He still didn't reply, and I let it go. I knew one important fact about him now, at least. He'd never been on a before-the-war chara trip to Brighton. How old was he, anyway? A deal younger than me. Perhaps he came from a kingdom by this sea and had seen it all before.

I turned in the general direction of Cape Horn, and after a while the feeling began to come over me that I wasn't going to make it in one grand slam go. The feeling crystallised into something more precise—unutterable, blinding fatigue, as if I were sweating on the inside. I mentioned it in passing, but he remained tiresomely inscrutable. A cold, sea-misty night had long since fallen when, at last, he muttered his change of heart and— Hi there, Oregon—eyes aching from the oncoming dazzle of lights, I pulled in, via Kelso, to the Rest-E-Ze Motel on the scanty outskirts of, well naturally, Seaside.

It was a minor-key hotel run by an agency couple who'd collected their faces from a Dust Bowl hand-out. Perhaps it was my tiredness, but I couldn't detect any anti-Semitic tendencies, so I signed in as Julius Garfinkle and, yawning prodigiously and genuinely, let crew-cut Gramps and Ho Chi escort me in their differing fashions to the one room available as our night-time tower. It was the only type they had—a smallish, twin-bedded box with a toilet-shower box tacked on to house the glasses wrapped in sanitised paper. The only window was small but just get-throughable.

'Go ahead,' he said.

Johnny Cool and I were room-mates.

Well ... that was funny. And embarrassing. Embarrassing for me because of the usual, vague but always present sense of shame attached in pulling down your pants in front of a total stranger. Or enemy. Or friend. But, it was going to be a whole sight more embarrassing for him. On top of a tiring day's drive and a trip generally, one might say, not without its sources of nervous tension, he had to get through an entire night without me jumping him, mugging him, escaping. I wandered slowly, tee-shirted into the bathroom, pondering that. I ran the water, took my time. Well, I thought, I think I'm going to give him tonight. I'd no doubt he'd kept me going deliberately to make sure I'd be dog-tired. And he'd succeeded. I was bushed. I couldn't move fast enough, think fast enough, react fast enough to make a play that would hold up all the way to Cape Horn. There was a long way to go. I'd make my break when I could make it clean.

I heard him dragging the room's one easy chair to the door. Perhaps he was figuring on sleeping out the watches of the night in that.

'Which bed would you prefer?' he said.

I had the uncanny feeling he could read my thoughts.

'Oh ... the one on the left will do,' I said. It was the one under the window. Maybe, in the small hours, I would change my mind.

'Very well,' he said. 'You have that one.'

He was so pleasant and considerate, my room-mate. Why, I'd bet that by now he had a Peking U pennant stretched out on the wall.

I was still smiling slightly as I walked back through the bathroom door and the Rock of Ages pile-drove down on my head. I crash-dived into a black and nauseous oblivion, shot through with red-hot red.

I woke up suddenly into almost as solid blackness. I sat sharply up in bed and a depth-charge exploded whitely in my brain. Twisting sideways I was neatly, on reflex, sick down the side of the bed. The fodder from the wayside greasy spoons had earned delivery of a quick come-uppance. I lay back, shivering. I was always shivering and being sick these days. Getting old, Powell. The reverberations from the depth-charge slowly lowered in intensity and stabilised at a steady, distant, ache. If I kept my head still. Somebody must have grafted it into my medulla oblongata while I was under the anaesthetic. I let the vomit lie. Movement was more noisome than stench. I let the sleeping son of a bitch in the next bed lie too. I didn't have an ounce of retaliation on me. I was getting warmer now. He lay there motionlessly. I couldn't hear his breathing. I could make out his bulk now that my eyes had grown accustomed to the dark and stopped watering, but I could not get accustomed to it enough to see his face. I'd no idea whether he was lying there watching my every invalid move, or off high and away on the seventh level of poppyland. But after what he'd done to me I knew where the smart money lay. If he was an opium smoker he was the sort that would rather fight than switch. I was in my underclothes. He'd put me to bed. He'd done that for me too. So considerate. It was warm here. Warm. If I kept still I could float all the way down the river like a log and the Indians on either bank would never know and I could get right past them. If I kept still ... After a while a non-violent, restless, image-filled sleep came o'er me creeping.

Slap. Slap. Slap. He was working at my face with perceptibly less force than he'd applied to the back of my head.

'Wake up,' he said.

I opened my eyes. Life breathed its cold, bright, new every morning glare into them and I shut them. My tongue felt thick and thirsty.

'Drink this,' he said.

He was sitting paternally on the edge of my bed, and somewhere he had found some orange juice.

'It's poisoned,' I said.

'Drink it,' he said.

I drank some. If it was poison, it was delicious. I had to struggle half upright to get it down and I did so gingerly. There was a nagging ache, but no blacksmith's choruses in the cortex, no Fourth of July set-pieces in my skull. All the same, I winced. If I could lull him into a sense of false security, he wouldn't hit me so hard next time. He sighed. He actually sighed. Somebody had cleared the vomit away.

'How do you feel?' he said.

'Great. Just great,' I chortled.

I made a sketchy but slow and deliberate toilet. Take great pains with life's minutiae and you're all set to spring when the big one comes along. As I shaved there was a knock at the outer door and muffled voices. I heard the chink and rattle of china. When, ducking in spite of myself, I sidestepped back through the bathroom door, breakfast awaited me on a tray. Masses of it. Politely, he hadn't made a start. Politely he now helped me to coffee.

'No sugar,' I said.

He watched me sip. Politely.

'How is it?' he said.

'Fine.'

It was. Hot, bitter, good. It cleared an awakening channel through the gunk that coated my mouth, oesophagus and tripes. Now that's what I call good coffee. Especially when served so politely. Only the gun, loaded near his right hand, struck a faint false note. I drank more coffee. It excavated taste buds and an appetite. I found I was ravenous and reached for food.

'There's Canadian bacon too,' he said. 'I thought you might prefer it.'

I did. Infinitely better than the over-fried American bombay duck variety. But where had he learned the difference? I looked at him. Politely, he looked at me.

'Anything you'd like to tell me?' he said.

I smiled.

'Food's great.'

He smiled.

There we were—two sprint cyclists standing on our pedals, each waiting for the other ace to make the first move. I drank my coffee. He ate his eggs. Western style. More specifically, European style, keeping his fork permanently in his left hand. So elegantly. Once again I had the feeling that long ago in another age, another country, I had known him. Had liked him.

'I truly regret having hit you,' he said. 'If you'd only confide in me, it wouldn't have—'

82

'Take a hike,' I said.

'I'd hoped for more suitable accommodation where—'

'Take another hike.'

He smiled. Politely.

'That's not our style,' he said.

So I was back in the driver's seat again. I let out token, strategic groans as I slipped behind the wheel, but for a man short on sleep who'd been hit hard over the head I didn't feel too bad. I made all of five miles before it caught up with me. Then I didn't feel too good.

It was a grey, glaring, low-clouded world that bounced harsh light off the endless road into my bruised and addled pate. We zigged back inland to touch an impassive Portland and then zagged south on the inland highway. It's a big country. While he sat equably behind me, working at his enigma variations, all glamour leaked out of the royal progress south. It became a static, on-rushing chore, a seventy-five-miles-an-hour bore down an endless concrete belt of vast eternity. I needed a divertissement to offset the long, vegetable tedium.

It wasn't far to seek. It's not that big a country. On another time scale I was rushing to LA at an alarming rate and I'd better, I'd just better have a punch to throw when I arrived there. Otherwise the lump on my head would grow into a hole. I'd only gone over it six thousand times already. I tried to see it anew in this cruel fresh light.

Lester had blurted out two names. Raker, the pivotal Unknown Quantity and, as I'd beaten him into his final unconsciousness, gutturally, Rafael Olivares: there could only be about ten pages of Olivareses in each LA phone directory. Beyond that he'd had no cigarettes and the remains of a book of matches from a bar called The Silver Peso. A Mexican name and, presumably, a Mexican bar. That was as much as I might begin to put together when I started to sweat out my bluff in LA. I tried working backwards. West Coast Orientals, Mexicans though there are in thousands, I would premise that Johnny Enigma and Rafael Olivares were not, *mon cher inspecteur*, one and the same. A premise. A step in the dark. Johnny had been looking for Lester. When he'd found me he'd been—I was reasonably sure, as sure as I could be sure—set at a loss. He couldn't place me, fit me into his scheme, crooked or straight, of things. Therefore, in so far as it chimed with his obvious priority—finding Raker—he was playing me along, on and for the ride.

People don't hide their whereabouts from friends and equally, not know their friends' whereabouts. Ergo, Johnny Cool meant Raker no good. Ergo, one of them—or both of them—was completely outside the law. JC had, it was a fair deduction, expected Lester could get him to Raker. Lester had been, manifestly, sent to eliminate me by much the same sort of people concerned to suppress the original Valachi Papers, soft-pedal the Baker case, discriminatorily gun down Black Panthers, defraternise the Soledad Brothers. That made Lester inside what gets to pass for the law these days. I, God help me, had absolutely no connection with Raker. Johnny thought I had. If he didn't like Raker, he wouldn't love me. It seemed that, although in the end they'd pretty much turned out to be his own, Lester had been juggling two balls. Or, to put it another way, I didn't know what I was on about.

I jammed the gas pedal down another five miles an hour worth. I was getting bored with the car, too. I punched on the radio. Some juvenile was singing *Wichita Lineman* in a voice that couldn't take the strain. I elbowed that.

'Slow down. We don't want to get a ticket.'

The wife from the kitchen. So he'd seen it too. A car, black and white, vehicle for satanic nuns, had nosed on to the highway a couple of miles back and was slowly overhauling us. I eased my right foot up a fraction. Two minutes later, armed to the teeth, it flashed uninterestedly on by. It was one of intermittent police cars that we'd seen the length of our trip. At first sighting the integrated colour scheme had set me on a tingling qui vive. Gee, guys, let's signal our distress in Morse code. But I hadn't got around to it. I couldn't remember which was short and which was long. Much as I like Japanese movies, I'd have felt such a fool going down the road flashing OSO.

'You going to hit me over the head again tonight?' I said.

'I was rather hoping to avoid having to do so,' he said. 'But it tends to depend on you, doesn't it?'

'Oh, sure.'

'Win my confidence—by taking me into yours—and there should be no necessity for such crude expediencies.'

I stared straight out through the windshield. The car thrummed on down the highway. The highway zapped back at the car. Evenly, hypnotically, narcotically. I couldn't think past the one roadblock conclusion. I didn't begin to have enough data to snow, stall or con. All I had, and mustn't on any account surrender (my life on it), was my lack of classifiable identity.

'Win your confidence,' I said at last. 'Talk.'

'Precisely. It can be done. I'm not unreasonable.'

'So are they all, reasonable men.'

'I beg your pardon?'

'Forget it.'

A Valiant puffed itself up to foreground size. I pulled out to overtake.

'Listen,' I said. 'It seems to me that I'm performing a great service for you. Obviously you haven't an idea of where Raker is and—'

'You only have to tell me.'

'Tell whom! That's my point. What kind of goods would I be freighting down to him? And what's in it for me? Just tell me that. What do I get out of it? We haven't even begun to talk about that.'

I'd done a nice job of getting worked up. He sat in silence as the endless cyclorama outside whooshed by.

'What's Raker to you?' he said.

'Seems to me I've ... well, let me put it this way: what he is to me could depend a great deal on what sort of an arrangement you and I can come to right now. What he is to me can change. With sufficient guarantees.'

He was quiet for another two miles.

'Whose is the money?' he asked.

'His,' I said, 'technically. What's left from all you've worked through.'

'You're delivering it?'

'Partly,' I said. 'Incidentally.'

I didn't want to come in too low. Sitting in my rear-view mirror, myself a domed and tired old Martian before him, he mused.

'The money can be made up,' he said. 'And a lot more added on top. That's not a problem.'

'Maybe that makes me feel a little better. How much is a lot?'

He sat still saying sweet nothings as more headlong miles unreeled back into the past.

'We'll find a place with two bedrooms,' he said.

Silently I connived at helping him keep his word. As we ran south, geography and memory began to pay me out a tiny thread of initiative. That afternoon, approaching the Oregon-California border through grey, overcast, inland Lincolnshire countryside, we began to encounter the four-wheel-drive pick-ups, the Kaiser jeeps, the camper buses—all with their gun racks nailed to the mast. The déjà-vued terrain clicked into abrupt focus for me. I had been here before. This—full of lakes, swamps, rice planta-tions, reeds—was duck, goose hunting country and it was that time of year. Once in the dim, dear days I'd flown up from Hollywood to shoot the shooters—hearty, bourbon-filled men wading out to the icy pre-dawn blinds with their Remingtons and Winchesters and phallic insecurity. And, from these covert vantage points, the buckshot dice loaded heavily in favour of the sportsmen, the geese, with the ineffable double curve of their wing span, the ducks with the glossy subtleties of their plumage, had been cut to pieces amid whoops and hollers and a reaching for hip flasks from the men with the stunted pricks. And I had filmed this National Sport in all its sacredness and gone on back to the motel each afternoon pleased with my hundred and a half's day's pay. I remembered now as I headed for the same motel, just south of Klamath Falls, and, though a lot of blood had flowed under the bridge since then, considered I marginally preferred killing people. It was an appropriate thought to carry across into Ronnie's Golden Egg of a State.

It was called The Hunters' Lodge Motel. A thing of plate glass, steel frame, vinyl and mock Tudor façading, it was built to a novel and ingenious plan. A jockey parked your car in an area way around the back and after you'd signed in (Fred C. Dobbs —so you changed your name as well) at reception, you were taken to rooms set out on one of three storeys. It was a new concept in wayside halts and as the bellhop ushered us in to our third-floor 'family room' a brilliant coinage came to me.

'Hey,' I said to him, 'I've got a great idea about how you should call this place. Go tell the manager he should call it a 'hotel.'

He stared at me.

'You see,' I said, 'a mixture of house and motel.'

He still stared at me. He was some kind of a dumb gook— much more oriental looking than Johnny C—and he didn't get it. He went out. Of course he got it. It was just that he had taste.

I contemplated my room-mate.

'You want to talk?' I said with malice aforethought.

He considered.

'Possibly, tomorrow,' he said.

I shrugged.

'OK. Possibly tomorrow,' I said.

'You take—'

'—the inner room,' I said.

Concertina doors—more vinyl—separated what could thereby become two distinct bedrooms. I went through to the second, taking deliberate care to leave the partition far from closed. I made more noise than usual pulling off my jacket and pants and none at all pulling them back on. I'd let the road show continue long enough. I was far enough from Anchorage and getting too close to LA for comfort. It was time to flee the fiendish bondage of Fu Man Chu. Given that, it was the best of times, it was the worst of times. Knowing the luck was running out on me, knowing my patience must be wearing thin against my nerves, knowing he hadn't administered another sleeping draught, he'd be expecting me to make my move. And because he was expecting it, he might expect me not to try because I'd be expecting him to be ... I let it ride. I figured that the convolutions of bluff and counter-bluff pretty much cancelled each other out. I lay wide awake in the dark, breathing with the rhythmic stertorousness of a man sleeping the sleep of the just. On the off-beat, I listened. From beyond the great divide there came not a sound. He was as silent as the grave. Hours went by. They never went by so slowly before but they were obliged all the same to keep inexorably moving. It's in their contract. Grunting, I tossed and turned so as to be free of bedclothes and be able to spy directly into his room. It was as black as buggery. I acted my part as the sleeping partner for a long, sustained encore. It was Oscar-winning stuff but all the response it evoked was total, equivocal silence.

The money. He wouldn't expect me to leave without the money. It must be under his pillow, alongside him in bed, tied to his wrist by a cord. He'd calculate I'd have to have it. And he was dead right. I did. But first things first. I would fake him out by passing it up now and circling back.... With a sound like the Fall of the Nibelung I sidled out of bed and crouched down. Silence—heart-pounding ear-splitting silence. Like an Edgar Allan Poe hero I waited, full of a dark primeval cunning. Still no noise. Groping, literally unable to see my hand in front of my face, I found my shoes. I stuffed them into pockets. There had been a window in my room but that was out. It was high, it had a grille I could never remove sans noise and there was no telling what kind of a drop lay behind it. I had to remember I was the Acrophobia Kid. The escape route had to run straight through his room and on out through the door. Crawling, feeling my way through the blanket dark with the clumsy antenna of my hand, I inched forward.

The gap I'd left in the partition was a lighter shade of black. With a child's chilled sense of vampires hovering above me, of fangs waiting to tear me, I made it that far. I'd moved like a snail to find my pulse driving through me with ceaseless pressure, my heart a traction engine. I had a breathless, barely controllable urge to gasp in air. I'd advanced eight feet. I waited.

Two decades later I pushed my head into his room. It was lighter here, blackness that was palpable had given way to grey. A faint illumination, moonlight or artificial, filtered in through the window and now I could make out the long shape of his bed and, as on the previous night, the shadowed bulk of his stretched out form. Was he asleep? Awake? As before, there was no knowing. Nor as the room's furniture fell away to dense obscurity, was there any sign of the briefcase. Well, forget it. Let that, temporarily, go: press on regardless, Macduff and devil take ... a century later I paused in mid-room before my tell-tale heart should awake him. Strain whistled through the atmosphere like sixty-cycle hum. I could hear him watching me. Or thought I could. As before I had every sense he was lying there, his eyes wide open, sardonically watching my grotesque progress. A whole dimension of feeling distastefully ridiculous became added to my stretched to the edge of fear nerves. I had crawled so that, should a sixth sense half awake him, my normal, standing silhouette would not be looming slap, bang straight there in his eyeline. But how pathetic my mouth open, silent breathing, infant's crawl must seem to his amused observance. At any second now his smooth tones, even more English in their derision, would bring me up short, heart hammering, with an elegantly thrown away put-down. It suddenly seemed totally important to avoid such ignominy. Anticipation of such shaming urbanity was worse than dread of a sudden blasting flash, bone slivering into shards as the slug impacted mercilessly home ... And yet ... And yet ... I had reached the door. I paused again. Once more I recovered my silent breath.

It took me four minutes to open the door. Two hundred and forty seconds. Count them. Slowly, oh so slowly, I reached up and found the handle. Cunningly, oh so cunningly, I turned it. Gently I tugged—and a bright bar of light fell wideningly across bed and room. There was nothing I could do. Softly, softly, escape.... I had to have a silent, sufficient head start to get the car in motion. With my face tensed permanently, it seemed,

89

in the grimace of bad expectation, I eased back the door wider still and wider. Enough. Breath still bated, I wriggled through to the deserted corridor. More quickly but as carefully I re-shut the door.

I stood up and on thundering tip-toe made off down the long characterless corridor, unchaperoned, free. It felt strange. But not mine to reason why—not now. Sheer distance between him and me was top priority—or the appearance thereof. Not the elevator. I took the stairs. Two flights and I emerged into a reception lobby of subdued light, faint far-off whispering radio music and no obvious sign of the night porter. I crossed carpet to doors of as thick plate glass, pushed through and went out to be sandbagged by the cold, raw, northern Californian air.

Cold it was. After the central heating I was shivering uncontrollably like a dog as I moved off across asphalt in search of the parking area. No clouds, no doubt, to hold in the daytime heat ... I looked up and, for a different reason, found myself breathless. Across the backwoods American sky, far from the neon and smog of the madding cities, the stars were broadcast with a glittering prodigality. Lambent, icy, in constellations proudly alone, they blazed with gem-like glitter against the black jeweller's velvet. Brought up in cities you forget how dark the true night is. For a moment I stood looking at them, tempted to try reading my fate in their remote, arcane patterning. But then, very properly, my old ghostly familiar came riding on a particular freezing blast to remind me that I didn't know how and that if I didn't haul my star-gazing arse right over to the Rambler I wouldn't have a future worth considering. He was right, bless his little polished skull. It was a silent but not a holy night. We are all of us walking in the gutter, but some of us are looking at the gutter. I got on with it.

He had the keys, of course—had made sure the parking jockey returned them to passenger, not chauffeur. But once I'd found the right lead from the coil, that was only going to delay me thirty seconds. Then I could light out—not for the wide open spaces but just half a mile down the track. I'd stack the car quietly off the road and walk back. I could watch the reception area from the opposite clump of trees. Sooner or later, agitated, he would appear to try pick up the pieces and my trail. If he didn't have the case I'd flash straight up to the room the back way. If he still toted it, things would take longer. But, sooner or later there would be a chance for a snatch. I owed him a knock-out drop. And, at least, in shadowing him, I would at least have purpose again and initiative.

There it was, ice on the windshield. I prayed it was unlocked. If it wasn't, I'd have sore need of my forsaken Swiss Army knife. The door handle was so cold it burned but, yes, it yielded! Unlocked! The door came open and the courtesy light came on. With the relief my breath exhaled a larger vapour cloud. I slid inside headfirst across the long bench seat. The light threw a pale, sickly cast of yellow across the tinny dashboard. More breath-clouds were already fogging the inside of the windows. Now, then ... I ducked down to inspect the electrical entrails beneath the steering column. Red, blue, brown ... it wasn't too obvious. No bombs in this one, though. I'd have to get the hood up. I swung myself up and was confronted by a moment of pure, silent horror.

Rising up like a belated shadow in the misty rear-view mirror, rising up swathed ghoulishly in blankets, rising up like a bad penny, a bad angel, a nightmare of a second ghost with a real-life gun aimed at my head, was Johnny Cool. My heart froze for ever in mid-beat.

'Check,' he said.

It happened one night.

On the morrow low grey clouds had universally blown in from nowhere, colour coordinates to my mood. We made a late start. The grand anticlimax to the events of the night had taken the steam out of everything. After the cold, silent, chagrined march back to Castle Rackrent I went out like a light. I needed no assistance from his hidden persuader. The let-down had left me drained, exhausted. I dreamed on, one block off nightmare alley, until well into the morning. He let me. What a sweetheart. When, in spite of my unconscious knowing better, I woke to go another fifteen rounds with reality, I discovered a trolleyed breakfast alongside the bed. How did he do it? I nibbled toast, drank indifferent coffee and wondered where the hell he got his stamina. Was I that old? I sat there considering, and to help me with the comparison he came silently in through the open partition. Now I had a new problem: where did he find time to groom himself so immaculately?

'Everything all right?' he said.

'Just great,' I said.

He smiled.

'You sleep in the car the night before, too?' I said.

He nodded.

'It seemed—wiser,' he said.

He looked at his watch. He wore it on the inside of his right wrist. Also.

'OK,' I said.

He went out. That was one problem solved. With looks like his he'd have made the best ten list dressed in prison denims. I got dressed myself and we went out into the rain.

Rain was hissing evenly down as we crouchingly rolled out of the motel's gravelled driveway and sheeting down with six times the intensity by the time we were two miles down the road. I could sense now a potential built into the car to wander from any line you might put it into in a hurry. A thick film of water, a constant streaming curtain adhered to the windshield. The wipers, cranked all the way up, gave only an alternating vision of the lashed surface ahead. To the side, on the tailgate window, matching curtains hung burbling, lacily plastered home by the wind. I had the heat on. For a while the dry warmth within induced a sleepy cosiness. I should have been shacked up in some warm pad making love all the more luxurious for the torrent cascading down outside. But Elsie had been brutally murdered and the others had been when that I was ... We rolled through some saturated township, brown, desolate, bereft. It was raining there like in my memory.

Womblike cosiness within the rain modulated into a submarine claustrophobia. There was more to it than the weather.

When we'd hastily ducked into the car Golden Boy had, uniquely, occupied the front passenger seat. We sat no longer as master and chauffeur-slave and I knew that my abortive attempt to escape had caused some kind of catalytic reaction. But what? The rain and I both drove on and he sat there mile after mile without uttering a word. The silence built up until you could slice it. I made myself not turn the radio on. He sat half against the door, studying me rather than the route. I had to work at not allowing my eyes to slide away from the road and subserviently on over to meet his. A gust hammered rain on us with altered rhythm. The compulsion to turn my head was growing unbearable.

'Well now,' he said, 'we can't continue like this indefinitely.'

He had shattered the wicked spell.

'It's gone on long enough,' I originally said.

'Quite. Suppose I tell you why I wish to find Raker.'

'OK.'

I tried to transmit all my tension to my hands on the wheel and leave the rest of me relaxed.

'Actually, I'm hoping to kill him,' he said.

A shiver of hysteria ran through me. We flashed past a lone building. My eye caught a sign: FUJI REALTY. My shocked nerves added another syllable and I knew I'd stumbled on a diagnosis of my condition. I was suffering from a bad dose of it. Any moment now the steering wheel would melt in my hands and this hallucinatory dimension paralleling life would dissolve back to normality. But normality for him was that I might be Raker's buddy.

'That's cool,' I made myself say without giggling. 'But aren't we all?'

'Oh?' he said.

'What's your reason?' I said.

He laughed softly.

'Oh, no,' he said. 'I know nothing about you and I've just made you a very big present. I've laid my biggest card on the table. Before I deal out any more I'm going to have to insist you follow suit.'

93

'I don't know,' I said. 'I don't usually play poker before lunch.'

I still wouldn't look at him. I sat staring ahead at the swimming, Fuji reality of the universe. Now there was more silence and it seemed as though my thoughts were broadcasting themselves out into it. I clenched my teeth to keep them in. Either he was lying or he wasn't. He wanted to see where I stood and maybe declaring murderous enmity to Raker was his best way of drawing my fire, flushing me from cover. Maybe he was Raker's greatest friend.... I had to flip a coin and get a premise. OK, I would premise he was telling the truth. I'd pick up sides in this game. He was against Raker. Therefore, for a while, anyway, I had to be too. Suppose I simply admitted—that wouldn't do. I couldn't get out of my mind the look on his face when he'd first cornered me in that hotel room ... I needed a story. If only I had some data to go on! If he'd talked first, I could have tried bouncing some improvisation off what he'd given away. If he told me the truth. A story. I needed something to give me a guarded neutrality, minimally involved, the immunity of non-alignment. A lie, then—the most dangerous kind—the provocatively transparent one he'd see through at once but with a few seductive hints of underlying truth to keep him intrigued. And me alive.

'OK,' I said, 'let me lay a pretty big card on you. I know next to nothing about Raker and I don't know where he's at.'

For the first time in miles I allowed myself to look at him. With chilling imperceptibility the engaging handsomeness had petrified into the basilisk gaze of the hotel room. If looks could kill Death ran a bad second.

'But you can relax. You don't have to worry,' I lied.

I found I was speaking too fast, dangerously close to blurting words out—any words—for their own silence-filling sake. I didn't get the Victoria Cross for it, but I made myself slow down.

'I have a lead to Raker,' I said, 'a sure contact. It's the way things have been set up.'

'Go on,' he said.

94

I could just hear him. It was the way that venom would talk. The jet eyes had turned opaque.

'I have to backtrack,' I said. 'By profession I'm a cinema-photographer—film cameraman. Up to last year I was working out of Los Angeles, doing—'

'But you're British.'

'Originally. I emigrated out here in fifty-four. I'd decided England was played out, gone soft. I was heading where the work was. Trouble was, I headed straight to where it wasn't. Straight into a slump. Television had hit Hollywood. I was new in town, nobody knew me ... truth is, I never really got over that bum start—'

'Where did you live? What was your address?'

'A lot of places.... Laurel Canyon, Price Street.... The last one was on Seward Street. A rented house. But I left there ... well, I'll come to that.'

He was reacting with the animation of old granite. I had no idea if he knew LA, but his silence yelled disbelief.

'Over the years,' I said, 'I got by. Sort of. I guess I broke even. Just. California's the worst place on this earth to be poor in. I got work of a kind, documentary mainly, and ... well, last year got to be real bad. Worst year since I first came out.'

'You didn't go back to England?'

'To what? Same scene, lower wages. I'd told everyone I'd come back a big man. Loaded. Somehow I couldn't face going back ... Things got so bad I needed a job. Any kind of job. I had an ex-wife gouging alimony out of me every month. Worse than any kind of period pains I can ...'

I let my voice trail off. I was overdoing it.

'A guy told me,' I said, 'I could get a job ferrying cars to Las Vegas. Occasional work I could fit in with filming. So I got to be doing this for this Toyota importer out in Long Beach. That took me to Vegas. One day I hitched a ride back to LA and the guy worked as a dealer in a casino.'

'Which one?'

'The Golden Nugget. He told me how I could get a job there dealing blackjack. And, well, it was permanent, but I did. I

95

turned my back finally on the stinking film industry, pulled out of LA and got an apartment in Vegas. And for the first time in a long time I started to make money. But not as much as some guys. After a few weeks I'd worked that out. There was one guy in particular.'

A car whined past us through the downpour spattering us with spray. I took my eyes off the road and, bracing myself, looked him full in the face.

'A Mexican,' I said.

It got to him. The obsidian of his eyes was highlighted with a fleck of interest.

'The word was out about him,' I said. 'He was running girls. A lot of characters used to come see him. Time was running out on me. I had a right ... I wanted to make up for all those bad years. One day I went right up to him and told him that if he was into anything and could use somebody he could trust me.'

'And?'

'Nothing. Not for a long time. Then last week he came to me and said he had a package he wanted delivered personally to a contact in Alaska. He said it was a deal. I'd have to bring some money back. I asked what was in it for me. He said if I did it well, he'd take me to the guy he worked for and I'd be in. I'd make a jar of money. He said if anything went wrong, like I didn't show up again—there wasn't anywhere I need bother hiding. Well, faced right there with it, I didn't like the sound of it. But from what he said I reckoned I didn't have a choice so I said I'd do it.'

'No doubt that was wise. What was the package?'

'A cigar box.'

'And what was in it?'

'I didn't ask and I didn't look. But three guesses.'

'And you made the delivery?'

'Yes. That's when ... I was told a man would come to me. It was Lester. Or Carter. We made our trade and while I was counting the money like I'd been told, he laughed and pulled a gun. He said this was fifty grand that wouldn't find its way to Raker.'

'And then he relented and jumped out of the window. . . .'

'No! I was shit scared. He was going to kill me! I threw the money at him and dived and the gun went off. He went down bleeding like a pig.'

Nobody could tolerate this farrago. There was a steep embankment down alongside the coming corner. Perhaps I could broadside the car on the rain-slicked road and, forewarned, take my chance of getting out alive and ahead of him. The corner came and I didn't have the nerve.

'He was dead?' he said.

'No. Not then. I—I panicked. I was up to my neck in something much too deep for me. Something I couldn't control. I didn't know why he'd acted that way ... He was going to die anyway. I thought that if I pushed him out of the window at that height they might think it was suicide ... they mightn't even bother looking for a bullet. I cleaned up the blood and then ... I pushed him out. There was a room key in his pocket. I made myself go down there. I wanted to run but I didn't know if he was acting for ... for this Mexican. Or Raker. Or anybody. Figure my position. When I found the police ID I nearly died. Then you walked in and I nearly died again. I ... that's where you came in.'

'So you're taking me to Las Vegas.'

'Los Angeles.'

'Why?'

Frost had formed at the edge of his voice.

'That was the arrangement. I was to take the money back to ... to my contact and meet him in LA. In a bar. But now ... I don't know ...'

'How do you mean?'

Ice.

'I keep thinking that maybe it was all set up. Maybe they thought I'd got interested in their operation and they sent me up there to get rid of me. But ... if Lester was doublecrossing them and they don't know that and I don't show up, they're going to think...'

'Fifty thousand isn't much money.'

'No. Not to them, anyhow. I thought that was because they were trying me—'

'So there's no guarantee anyone will be waiting in LA.'

'Not if Lester was in with them. They could be expecting him. Anywhere. That's why I didn't want to tell you all this. But look, if nobody's there—if we have to go to Las Vegas—I'll still lead you to them, I swear. I swear.'

Slowly, growing more and more rigid with expectancy, I had been pushing up the speed of the car. The faster we went the less likely he'd be to shoot me outright.

'Thus your connection with Raker—if it exists at all—is tenuous in the extreme.'

'I can get you to him, I tell you. I can—'

'What's this Mexican's name? What's the name of the bar?'

This was it. This was what the whole rigmarole had been in aid of. The wipers whined side to side, side to side as we hurtled on into a greyness that could have been oblivion. I looked at him, not needing to act scared.

'Look,' I said. 'I can't tell you that. It's all the life insurance I've got left. I've told you everything else. If I tell you that ... I just don't know who or what you—'

'I ought to shoot it out of you,' he said quite evenly. 'Name by name.'

'Oh, Jesus,' I said, 'I just want to forget this whole ... terrible thing. Maybe you work for Raker. How do I know any more. I don't even know your name. I'll do anything you want.'

'Then tell me the names,' he purred.

'Please!' I yelled. 'Please. I'm running scareder than I've ever been scared in my life. All I want is to be out and away from this. I'll take you there! I'll take you there! For God's sake!'

We were down in the Sacramento Valley now. For some time we had been streaming past farmsteads and green, sodden country, with glimpses, in and out, of the river, brown, foam-flecked, swollen with anger at the mills its dignity had been run through. Now the highway ran parallel to its sweeping course. There was the oncoming lane, a fall away of some thirty grassy yards, a long line of alder trees along the bank itself. His stony, incredulous silence was persuasion enough to wreck the car. As I half watched him from the corner of my eye, I let my left hand fall from the wheel. I moved it the seven leagues distance to the door handle. Even as I did so, even in the midst of my fear and fevered calculations, there was still room for a sour shame. I braced myself for the manoeuvre.

'That won't be necessary,' he said.

He nodded past me at the door. The gun was out of his pocket. The road bent away from the river bank.

'It disappoints me, Powell,' he said, 'that you should prove to be so deserving of contempt. It grieves me to have to associate with such littleness. But life, as we learn, imposes bedfellows on us that can be necessary, however unpalatable. I need you to keep your appointment. I think I can reassure you that your contact will keep that rendezvous—that plans have not been laid to eliminate you. I was not unacquainted with Lester. I have no doubt his attempt to hijack the money was prompted by nothing beyond the prospect of personal and immediate gain.'

He was speaking in the measured phrases of a man employing a second language. It was impossible he'd believed me.

'Because I still need you, and to further reassure you,' he said, 'I am going to do as you suggested and offer you my confidence. You will see then why I have little concern with you one way or another. You will see then why, in exchange for your cooperation, I am prepared to pass this money back to you in circumstances that will make it your own. I gather that, after the safety of your own skin, that is what is nearest your heart.

'Very well. It will not surprise you to learn I am of mixed parentage. I have, in effect, two names.' A name for each of his faces. 'The one is Tran Chau Chieu. The other is Jean-Marie Robin. Kipling, you see, was wrong. You have heard of Admiral Decoux?'

'...No...'

'He was the French administrator who, during World War Two, succeeded in peacefully coexisting in Vietnam with the Japanese. I was born at that time. My father was a French army officer on Decoux's staff. My mother was Vietnamese. She was, very formally, my father's mistress. It was she who first raised me.

'Soon after the fall of the Nipponese Empire, my father and his wife returned to France. It had been discovered that he was suffering from incurable cancer. My mother was broken-hearted but ... It became my father's whim that I should be brought up in France. I exchanged my true mother for a dying father, an alien stepmother of traditional hostility and an impeccable French education. I detested it as much as I detested my step-mother but, in one respect, I shall be eternally grateful for those hate-filled years in that fat Paris suburb. By the time they were over I was a Marxist. A year in your own London did nothing to alter my views. I used to look at those smug faces, unvisited by the marks of any worthwhile thought, and understand every word that Marx and Lenin wrote.

'I decided to return to my native land. The war in what the French imperialists had presumptuously called Indo-China was long since over. There was scope to apply my ideas. The new war, the drive against the puppet regime of Ngo Dinh Diem was gathering momentum. I will not bore you with details. My background, my languages, made me most welcome to certain leaders of the Democratic Republic. I became engaged at a high level in matters of—Intelligence.

'We began to receive uncoordinated and conflicting reports from the National Liberation Front about a certain Jefferson Raker. This seemed curious at first in that he was no more than a Master Sergeant in the United States Army. More reports and allegations reached us: Raker was a Quartermaster immediately responsible for an infinite variety of supplies in virtually limitless amounts. There was some evidence that he had been guilty of misappropriations. It even seemed that we might be able to obtain supplies for our own cause from him. We investigated. It took a long time. He was a lifelong soldier who had been in the service for eighteen years. We had to work backwards through European sympathisers to a time early in his career when he'd been stationed in West Germany.

'What we discovered staggered us at first, then horrified us. Raker was a black-marketeer on the grandest possible scale. Beginning in Germany with petrol, medicines, automobile parts, food, tobacco, he had built himself an unbelievable empire. He had expanded into prostitution and extortion rackets. He had progressed from medicines into hard drugs. Much of his profit, we very much believe, he invested on a world-wide scale in thoroughly legitimate capitalist concerns. All from a base position within the official network of the US military. He grew to have a considerable army of his own, soldier and civilian, working under him within the military framework. Some of these, inevitably, must have been ranking officers above him. When he was transferred—back to the US, to Okinawa—it made no substantial difference. Subordinates continued his activities while he extended them into his new surroundings.

'He probably pulled strings to be posted to Saigon. It was a potential goldmine to him. In the States he had probably branched into trafficking in arms, weapons. It was certainly so in Vietnam. We know that he supplied carbines, mortars even, and ammunition to the NLF in exchange for cinnamon. He had virtually cornered the market in cinnamon. He was directly able to influence the marketplace cost of rice. Most spectacularly, he had organised large scale traffic in marijuana into a personal asset.

'For a while we were very happy with this state of affairs. He was a valuable source of arms, he was a running sore in the US commissariat, a fittingly ironic added burden to the capitalist taxpayer. I saw him myself at this time to negotiate transactions. He was a pig of a man whom I found personally revolting. But it became more than a question of personality. Things began to go wrong. Three times he reneged on the delivery of arms and supplies. And then we learned of more serious facts.

'Using fertilisers and chemicals supplied by the US and intended for the plantations, he was actually compelling a number of outlying villages to cultivate marijuana for him. It was his second most valuable source of income. The continual abduction of thirteen- and fourteen-year-old girls from the same villages will tell you the first. The villagers were, in truth, sympathetic to us and not to Saigon, but geographically they had no option but to comply. American patrols made more than regular visits to them. Raker had them under his thumb. And the villagers were starving. The pittance Raker allowed them for their work was not enough to supply proper food. The head man of one village complained. The next time a patrol came it took him and his sons out into the fields. They did not return. They were found with bullet holes in the backs of their heads and no faces.

'The villagers were brave but foolish. They set light to the marijuana and fled into the jungle. Raker could not afford such an example to be set. Infantry and helicopters came from nowhere to pursue them. As far as we can estimate, nearly two hundred old men, women and children were wantonly slaughtered by this criminal. To encourage the others, you understand. For the military record they became Viet Cong guerrillas.'

I said nothing. The rain had slackened at last. I turned off the wipers. We barrelled on down our own Ho Chi Minh trail as I suspended judgement.

'For a time, to be perfectly honest, there was little reaction in Hanoi over this incident. Raker was useful to us. It was not without precedent in such a dirty and ill-defined war. It was an American problem. But the peace talks had begun in Paris. It was brought home to us that, were Raker to be captured and brought to trial in the North for his crimes against humanity— this before the world's press agencies—it would be a massive and even laughable embarrassment to the US. I was delegated to lead four others in kidnapping him.

'We knew it would not be easy. He never moved without a considerable bodyguard. But everything went well. We infiltrated the South and then Saigon. We had plans to surprise him inside a brothel in the heart of the city. We would drive up in two cars. As the second arrived, we were met with concerted, well-positioned machine gun fire. It was like hell. The three men in our first car went down before they knew what was happening. The car exploded. I was half out of the second. I was hit by what seemed like a steel whip. Somehow the driver pulled me back inside and got going again. We escaped. I lost consciousness knowing that Raker's intelligence network was as efficient as ours.'

'Was it Lester who—'

'No. He was in no position to know. He was at the other end. I will come to him. For the moment you must imagine that I was nearly dying. My driver took me to sympathisers. They hid me, got me a doctor. But it was weeks before I could be smuggled back to the North and five months before I was in any sense on my feet again. In the meantime a curious thing had happened. Raker's time in the military was up. He did not attempt to re-enlist. Abruptly he disappeared—initially to America but subsequently to somewhere we did not know. We have not since been able to discover.

'I am nearly finished. All this happened a year and a half ago. Life—and death—went on. Then we heard word that a US government agent—a man named Lester—was suddenly being recalled to America. This was most interesting. Lester was known to be—corrupt. In particular, he was known to have been on Raker's payroll—turning a blind eye and, presumably, giving him tips on what we might call the military black market. Two constructions could be placed on his recall. Firstly: that his superiors had got wind of his illicit activities and were initiating an investigation. Or, secondly: strings had again been pulled and Lester was en route to reassociate himself with Raker's organisation.

'There was still support in the North for bringing Raker to public justice. I received permission to shadow Lester in the hope that he was indeed making for Raker. To penetrate the American mainland would not be easy—only one man on his own might have any chance—so, alone, by way of Tahiti, I followed Lester to Los Angeles. Within days of our arrival there he—inexplicably, I confess it—flew north to Alaska. Again I followed. As you know, for my purposes, I arrived too late.

'You know now why he was carrying police identification. It was part of his potential cover and potentially useful. More importantly, you will comprehend now why, all things considered, I wish no harm to you so long as you convince me of your cooperation or, at least, non-enmity. My orders still are to abduct Raker but, realistically, that is hardly within the bounds of one man. Most probably I shall be obliged to fall back on the more immediate secondary plan of—execution. That will not be without its symbolic power. Either way, the ultimate decision rests within my discretion. I will not trouble to deny that for reasons of an obviously personal nature, I find little divorce between my public duty and my private inclination. Equally, you will appreciate that as far as I am concerned, the sordid little question of fifty thousand American dollars is neither here nor there. It is a bone I gladly throw you for your temporary mercenary allegiance.'

At last he had finished. The silence flared in my ears. I had a sense that he had never spoken at all, that he had been sitting there throughout in unbroken silence. I had imagined those words, putting them in his mouth to satisfy through the illusion my own buried need. But gradually, as the enervating vacuum of sound was invaded by the pulse of the engine, the even slick of the tyres coming off the road, reality returned. I set myself to thinking.

I had listened with mounting disbelief. But then, towards the end, I had detected in myself a great impulse, a great wish to believe him. It was all true and there could be life in it yet! I could tell him everything and, partners, allies, an incomparably engaging double act blessed with a crusade, we would wise-crack our laconic way to the triumph of right over wrong. Paul Newman and Robert Redford. I suddenly had in him the same sweeping belief that had come to Fitzgerald's chronicler of Gatsby. The same ... the thought helped save me. Gatsby had been, well, other than he'd wished to appear. That belief had contained the reaction of scepticism. Now, much as I might

psychologically need to elevate the fastidious, thoughtfully man-
nered gunman to some moral peerage, I must never lose sight of
the look on his face when he'd been seconds from killing me. My
first feeling of disbelief had to be right. It was hard to reconcile
that stoniness with any political dedication, however quasi-
religious. It had had too much of the personal in it. He had
lied more plausibly, less artfully than I. We needed a referee
to award the decision.

We had driven some miles.

'I don't know,' I said. 'I don't know. You've told me so much
now—'

'I shall still need you, remember, to keep that appointment.
That will hold good even after you've told me the names. With
Lester gone my only possible way to Raker is through you,
through this Mexican. Now—what's he called?'

'All right,' I improvised. 'His name is Manuel Escobar. The
place is The Universal on South Vermont.'

'Good,' he said. 'Very good.'

He didn't ask me to pull over. We kept on going. I suddenly
appreciated why Gatsby had come to mind and why I'd kept
feeling that I'd seen His Handsomeness before. His looks had the
stamp of an oriental Scott Fitzgerald.

We came to Colusa, a half town at the bottom end of the
valley. I tooled down a Main Street where every other car was
a pick-up and every third store sold tractors.

'Pull over there,' he said.

The temperature of my blood dropped ten degrees. Now that
I'd, as he thought, spilt the beans, surely he wouldn't spill my
guts. Not in broad daylight. Not with people around.

'Let me see the map,' he said.

At his behest I worked us back across country to the coast
road. We fetched up in Sonoma. It was still quite early but I was
starving. I had every good reason not to hit the wine but,
strangely, once more there was an incident of reassurance.

Abruptly, that night, he came into my inner sanctum. I all
but leapt for cover in the ten-by-fourteen shoebox. But, wearing

a tee-shirt, he was gunless. Perhaps he had come for me in the other sense. Apparently. With an easy motion he pulled the tee-shirt up and over his head. Then I got his message. Etched around the bottom of his right-hand rib cage, disappearing down below the waistband of his slacks, was a cruelly new cable stitch of a scar. Its shiny glazed pinkness stood out shockingly against the lithe gold body.

'You see,' he said.

He smiled and went out.

I didn't experience a complete renewal of faith in all he had said. The smile did not reach his eyes. Underneath the cloak there was still the knife.

This time it was my turn to make a bolstered dummy for the bed. Even if my registered name was Archibald Leach.

On the qui vive, as we say down the Quai d'Orsay, I sat up all night.

CHAPTER SIX

I woke up with a start, a sense of panic. Somebody had been trying to do for me in a dream that had crash-dived into my unconscious the moment I opened my eyes. Curious. In spite of my fear, at some time in the not-so-small hours, sitting in the too-easy chair, watching the door, I had nodded off. It could have been the last time. Did you see that one—The Big Nod? I was as stiff as a board. Fit punishment. I got up and brewed the courtesy coffee. It was ineffably bad, I would have done better to munch the tinfoil sachet. He came in, catching me off my guard, but only to show me that he was already dressed to the faultless teeth. We made an early start.

The weather had turned. From out of a clear blue sky we now had bright, cold sunlight.

'Il fait beau, aujourd'hui,' il dit.

I didn't react. In the books the hero never lets on he speaks the other man's language and that's how he gets to win. Now I had the upper hand. I could zap him with my vocabulaire of eighty words. I pondered the significance of his choosing to ride in the back seat again.

For a brief, awesome while we touched the edge of the red-wood country. The tall, undeviating trees stretched cathedrally above us, cutting us down to size as they wheeled, the long shadows flashing, about the fixed point of the sun.

'It's a nice day,' I said.

He didn't say anything. He was playing it tight too.

We came out of the trees and didn't cross a river but did emerge again on the shores of the sparkling white-wine sea. Then, way across the sweep of an enormous bite into the coast, I had a hazy impression of a long toy bridge. Distant over there, sitting on the flaw-line, was the fairy, pastel baroque of the Port of St Francis. Well, there are fairies at the bottom of most big cities.

'Keep to the main route around the city,' he said.

Something died in me. I knew then that all along I had been entertaining faint, wishful hopes of San Francisco. In the steep complexities of the one American city I might have paid out good money of my own to return to, there would be, somehow, opportunity and scope to shake loose from Jean-Marie. Now I wasn't even going to get the chance. Once again he'd anticipated my thinking. I wouldn't slip him there. The chase would never be on. I wouldn't get to sip another Irish at the Buena Vista or, wandering through the variegated crowd down along Broadway, duck my head in appreciation of the sound through an open door of my bookish friend the piano sport, striding along after Tatum and my better namesake Bud.

'I'm beginning to feel hungry,' I said.

It was hardly inspired.

'We'll eat later, further south in Highway One,' he said.

We bypassed the town. It didn't shake to its foundations as Gable and Macdonald waved goodbye.

I didn't have too much time to sit chiding their spirits. The road had become a literal cliff-hanger. It took some driving to handle its roller-coaster swoops down to sea level and the tortuous, balancing climbs up out of the trough to round the headland profiles. It was made to take your breath: rock face to the left, plunging sweeps of field from peak to peak, a lush, Northern, rain-fed green. The sea below, now far, now zooming close to hand, was a glissading, iridescent flux of pre-Disney colour. Turquoise and agate interflowed among the stronger blues and shimmering greens as muscles seemed to dipple under a liquid skin. Bars of russet and shark-like, smiling black sinisterly hinted at the temper of more hidden depths. The sun bounced a stabbing dazzle, myriadly fragmented, from off the swollen weight of a surface that recomposed, brilliantly, blindingly, with every fresh roll shorewards of the waves. And all, green, blue, turquoise, black, was offset, highlighted, brought alive by the creamy backwash of the waves upon the rocks. To paint it as it seemed I would have given my right ear.

'Watch the road,' he said.

I corrected our line. From around the corner of the oncoming headland a Citroën saloon appeared. I watched it flee, French blue, into my rear-view mirror, and grew sick of an old passion.

'It's Thursday, let's eat in Monterey,' I said.

'Very well.'

There were hippies on its streets as I searched for a fresh fish restaurant and after, as I travelled on with Charley, the hamburger like lead inside my stomach, much evidence of them bearded, beaded, uniformed upon the highway. We had long since left behind to the North the Winchester- and Remington-toting vehicles of the NRA. The only mobile arsenals now occasionally to be seen were the carbine-extra-optioned Police Specials of the Macemen. Appropriately. The one followed on the other. The present bigoted black-and-whiteness certainly bore no communion, proffered no chance of dialogue in its rigidity with the open child-of-god-like rainbow hues of the beat-up VW buses, made-over hearses, mid-Detroit baroque that now buzzed cheerfully up and down in exterior pursuit of whatever Woodstock or Nirvana they might think Highway One would lead them to. They seemed not to know, and I hadn't the heart to say, that it was at either end the road to Astrapovo.

At the top of Carmel—that cancerous clutch of boutique cells —hitch-hikers, paired and bedrolled, projected deadpan faces and stoic thumbs. Not on the other side, but powerless, I passed by. But the train of thought was given motion. What if ... Thus it was that, losing speed as I climbed a steep left-hander, I momentarily, involuntarily it almost seemed, slowed down yet further on catching sight on the brow ahead of a lone and back-lit silhouette. Handsapockets on the edge of the Big Sur, it had to be a girl. Right. She started to thumb us down.

It wasn't on. However chicken I had made myself out to be, I had no right. I started to jab my foot back down on the gas pedal. In that same instant I felt the muzzle of his gun press hard, against my occipital bulge.

'It's a kind thought,' he said gently. 'Let's give her a ride.'

Life is like the movies—made up finally of significant action, or significant non-action. I should have put my foot down. All the way to the floor. He wouldn't have shot me. But the whole deadly, inane game of cat and mouse, the ceaseless extended war of bluffing attrition had worn my nerves to wafer thinness. When that cold steel channel to eternity came out of nowhere to reflex-jerk my head back, something inside of me snapped too. Something that for too long had been stretched too taut suffered a lesion. The few inches of my foot rising up was the measure of a massive defeat. The car came to a halt some twenty yards past the girl.

'Good,' he said.

I watched in the rear-view mirror. Seizing up a long tube of a grip in her right hand she came loping up to us. Over her other shoulder was a fringed, squarish tote bag, apparently put together from a couple of Indian blankets. It jounced jauntily against her side. There was no guitar. JC was losing the gun. She reached the passenger-side front door and, as I sat without moving, yanked it open herself. Half stooping to bend into the car, light and shadow dividing her face each side of a sharp diagonal, she looked straight at me, smiling very slightly.

'Hi,' she said. 'LA?'

'No—' I managed.

'Your lucky day,' he said. 'Going right through. Jump in.'

Quickly, like all hitch-hikers offered the chance they still half expect to lose, she hefted the grip into the middle of the front bench seat. It brushed my right elbow. She scrambled in eagerly after it. With a heavy, final clonk she slammed the door after her. I waited for an overtaking car, then pulled away.

It happened in Monterey.

We were back up to seventy again. Watching the onspeeding road, I was in that position you always get to with hitch-hikers —assembling a vibratory impression of somebody you can only glimpse in the corner of your eye. Only this time it was different. My foreknowledge of what lay in interior store for her had given that questioning pause on the threshold of the car the permanent, caught in past time, force of an old snapshot. She didn't know it yet, but that moment had been a watershed lifetime away. I did know. And I knew what she looked like.

On my time scale she was young. But not that young. About twenty-three, twenty-four. And not that pretty. About half pretty, like most girls. She had straight, not quite shoulder length hair that was indifferently mousy and yet somehow, as it hung softly, the more feminine for that. Her eyes were ordinary—brown you'd have to say—less of a feature than the soft, natural brows above them. The nose lacked definition without quite being snub, the lips had a similar indeterminateness. They were, if anything, too long, if anything too thin. What saved the face was the slight hollowness about the cheeks. The consequent emphasis this drew to the good bone structure, the firmly delicate chin, gave her an understated, second-class claim to being beautiful. It was all tied in with the faint impression of fragility, of vulnerability, of hope stomped all over but still trustingly allowed to live and hope some more. I knew that in another time, another place, I would have fallen for that tincture of little-girlness and physically molested her with all the treacherous charm of my disciple-needing, equal-shunning protectiveness. My ego-starvation would have felt gratified at having her slight figure kneel before it.

She was breathing a little heavily now—faint embarrassment, strangeness, aggravating her recovery from that quick dash up to the car. I sat there next to her, impassive, my spirit sicklied o'er by the bitter, unredeemable alkali flavour of self-contempt. Betrayal leaves a nasty taste in the mouth. Something else within me that had once had amplitude had shrivelled and turned to stone. That first glimpse of her up ahead had prompted me to slow at the prospect of cramping Fitzgerald's style. Get her aboard, involve her, slip a joker in and get his diverted attention torn between two poles. In that instant the face of Elsie—Christ! they even sort of looked alike—had cut into my mind with an accusatory pallor. I tasted again the fleshly stink from off that holocaust of a first car. And put my foot down. You have to give me that. And then—the gun at the back of my head, a failure of nerve. But it went deeper than that personal defeat. The first black flash of that girlish silhouette had struck another kind of nerve—the one that runs through every dirty-minded businessman. It had been a classic situation and reaction. Sex at first sight. I was every tired and not-so-senior executive or company rep driving back to Surbiton or Queens with one eye firmly fixed upon the roadside for a bit of hitch-hiking spare. Finally, she was in the car because I was your regular, common-or-garden cocksman.

'That was a strange place to be waiting,' said Too Ting Tram.

'I guess,' she said. 'I thought I might stand more of a chance if I walked on some and got out of the pack back there. Guess it paid off.'

Her voice was soft, gentle and low, an excellent thing in women.

'Indeed,' he said. 'Is Los Angeles your home?'

'Oh I guess home's wherever I hang my hat these days,' she said. 'If I ever wore one. LA's just a stop off to take care of a little business and pick up a few things of mine.'

She didn't wear a hat. Blue jeans and a faded, fur-lined flying-jacket.

'I think I get the picture. Cigarette?'

'Thanks.'

Leaning forward he lit it for her. It was the first intimation I'd had that he carried them.

'What's your name?' he said.

'Sam,' she said.

'I'm John and that's Dick,' he said.

'Richard,' I said automatically.

'Hello John ... Richard,' she said.

'Richard's a little the worse for wear today,' he said. 'He didn't get too much sleep last night.'

I was looking straight ahead, not consciously seeing the road any more as I tried to think.

'Where is home then?' he said.

'Born and raised just outside Baltimore,' she said. 'Then my folks moved down to Louisville and I mainly grew up there.'

'I hear that Louisville is very pleasant.'

He was such a nice, unforced and natural conversationalist. So polite.

'If you don't mind spiders. I haven't been back there since ... I liked Baltimore. People forget it's a port. Some days you'd get the smell of all the spices from all the spicelands in the world.'

'But you're obviously not on your way there now.'

I had to think of a way of getting her out of the car and away.

'No,' she said. 'I've been out here a while now. I guess I'm your West coast hippy. Sort of. I'm heading for Taos now.'

'Oh?'

So polite.

'Just north thereof. Some friends of mine have put a whole commune thing together. I had a hand in it and I'm going back to join them. Fastest way there is through LA and out on sixty-six, I guess.'

'Jesus Christ!' I said. 'I knew it! I just knew it! I told you we should keep on going. She's just another damn fucking pot-head hippy out to tell everyone she's ever freeloaded off how to reform their lives.'

I looked full at her.

'What are you going to do up there in shanty-town?' I said. 'Sit getting high among the orient and immortal grass? Take on the mystery of things like you're God's spies? God's elect preaching love? Jesus, the only quality you've any claim to is two hundred per cent arrogance. I know that kind of commune. All those damsels with dulcimers. One great fucking commune of the phallus.'

The road was clear. I turned my head to look at Rin Tin Tin.

'Lay five bucks on her right now,' I said, 'and she'll take us down there in those bushes and do a trick for us both at once, top and bottom. She'll sleep—'

'OK, mister. Stop the car right here,' she said.

With an arbitrary gesture that had style she savagely stubbed out the scarcely smoked cigarette on the bare fascia.

'I'm getting out right here,' she said. 'Alone. That clear? Pull over. I wouldn't want to contaminate your air-conditioned lebensraum—'

Her voice broke off as if guillotined. I glanced across at her and her eyes were wide in frozen horror. I didn't need to look to know why, but I did. He was leaning forward between us from out the back seat, the gun very evident and big in his hand and favouring her.

'Keep driving,' he said. 'You tried, Powell, you tried. But it was no less obvious, I'm afraid, than all your other subterfuges.'

I didn't answer. I kept on watching her. Her eyes were still dilated, her skin stretched tight, drained white beneath its surface tan. She was in shock—that moment of rapidly diminishing disbelief that the worst is actually happening. It was an instant, American reaction. There was no second of thinking it was a gag. The country with a Benedict Canyon, a San Antonio campus, a Dealey Plaza, a Marin County Courthouse has an edge, contains a potential for a violence that is everyday and neighbourhood and not unthinkably exotic or remote.

I tried to flash the girl a look of sympathy, of fellow feeling. She was a million miles away in a dark place, dying a thousand deaths. And only, as she numbly knew, too present. God knew what foreboding images of death, of mutilation were jostling uncontrollably in her mind. I had to try to show her the way the battle lines were drawn. I threw words over my shoulder.

'What the hell are you trying to pull, you bastard?' I said. I knew what he was at.

'I have, as you may have observed, a streak of the gambler in me,' he said, 'and I've just indulged that tendency. I'm happy to tell you that, as your laudably chivalrous attempt to alienate this young lady and force her to leave us convinces me, I consider that I did so successfully.'

The girl was still staring motionlessly ahead. But the deranged glaze had faded from her eyes. She was taking it in. I stayed quiet.

'You see,' he went on, 'I never for a moment chose to give countenance to that tedious rigmarole you went through as to how you came to be associated with our defenestrated friend.

You were wildly unconvincing. On details, for instance. You began by inventing a cliché cigar box that was nowhere in evidence when I happened across you. You gave it such prominence when you began your account, but by its conclusion it had dropped from your mind. And simply because it never existed to begin with.

'But more importantly, I choose to disregard that farrago of unhappy improvisation on general grounds. I've naturally been watching you very closely. Your entire demeanour, your natural attitude does not accord with the picture you tried to draw of a mean and mercenary, small and contemptible, novice opportunist. You didn't do yourself justice, Mr Powell. You're made of sterner stuff. Or, since you're a victim of your own sensibilities, should I say of softer stuff?'

'OK, so I was lying. So what. What's it got to do—'

'Everything. My reading of your character persuades me that you might be indifferent to your own fate but that it would pain you to be the source of harm befalling—'

'You'd be the source, not me. I figured you were mainly lying too. This proves it. You're no avenging saint. Hostages are for fanatics or animals.'

He laughed his well-bred, well-modulated laugh.

'Revolutionaries are fanatics,' he said. 'And saints.'

'At their own expense.'

'Don't let's philosophise right at this moment. Not when we're essentially back to where we started ... There is no Manuel Escobar, no Universal Bar, is there?'

'Yes,' I said, 'the joint exists. And the guy. Only the names were changed to protect—'

I never finished the tired irony. At that instant the girl exploded out from her catatonic state. On top of the speed limit though we were, she lunged to her right like a goal-minder stretching for the puck. Quick as she was, he was quicker. With an efficiency that drew a shrinking gut reaction from me, his non-gun hand came flashing down on her right shoulder with a short, sharp vicious chop. The pain was of the order that evokes a whimper and total loss of breath. Doubling up, left hand reaching up to hold the hurt, she swayed back towards the centre of the seat as I swerved the Rambler back on line. Tears of pure physical pain brimmed in her eyes.

'Wait until we stop, sweetie,' he said. 'You'll get hurt if you don't.'

He sounded like a film director instructing an extra whom he'd never see again. For both our sakes I had to go for a hard-nose line.

'Get rid of the girl. Guarantee me the money. We've still got a deal,' I said.

'I wonder,' he murmured. 'I wonder. You see I can hardly pretend that I altogether trust you now.'

'You still know for sure that—'

'Why don't we just go on a little further while you sit and consider that henceforth more than one life can be influenced by your decisions.'

'You're the one—'

'Really, I think I'd rather not discuss it further for the time being.'

I let it rest. Now that it was two against one I had a feeling that time, for once, was on my side. I looked across at the girl. She looked at me from eyes whose tears were now somewhere inside. If she had deciphered that I was an ally she gave no sign.

More interminable miles unwound. For better than two hours I kept on due south. The three of us sat like co-defendants at a conspiracy trial, maintaining a stiff, unequal silence. The lines of force triangulating round shrilled piercingly through the silence. Why the girl? Why? True, if the LA police were looking for two men, two men and a girl was slightly different. But very, very slightly. It was a minimal shift. What real percentage was there for him in handicapping himself with this extra weight? However hotshot a parlour psychiatrist he might reckon himself, he couldn't surely believe that forced with the either/or choice, I'd sacrifice anything, come what may, for the sake of saving her skin. His suave declaration that I'd behave with such noblesse oblige made me honour bound to sling her out the sledge the first time the wolves got within noshing range. Except ... I had few doubts now that he'd progressed a lesson or two beyond the native-bamboo-under-nails bit of the Torture Tales from the Hills ... Two of us must mean that he really was banking on my hypothetical better nature ... which might mean he anticipated a separation. Perhaps he foresaw me making contact alone and was at his wits' end to know how to keep a hook on me ... If he did want me to blaze a trail, then he was known to Raker's outfit and there was bad blood ... Watching him very closely in the mirror, way behind on points, I answered another bell with the left still jabbing away.

'Listen,' I said, rupturing the electric silence, 'proof of good faith. The guy's real name is Rafael Olivares.' Once again it drew a small reaction. A fractional shift of eyeline—I don't know what. The girl looked at me for a fleeting turned-head second. In that impassive state her profile had the edge on her full face.

'That narrows it down for you,' I said. 'You've only got to shake down seven thousand bars.'

He didn't answer. I got a surer feeling. He knew Olivares and didn't want to know much more.

The sea was still within spitting distance as I swept around the northern horn of the biggest bay so far. Déjà vu immediately engulfed the eye. On high rising ground a couple of miles inland, dominating the centre of the ocean's bow, a building took the eye, discernible at this long range and therefore massive. A ribbon of brown road snaked up to it.

It seemed to me I'd seen this pile before and then I knew that indeed I had. This was the spiritual capital of rather more than half America—San Simeon, the Great Bad Place. We scudded round the shore's arc, vulnerable somehow, a frantic predestined ant under the indifferently baleful eye of a Great Khan. It was strange how so fundamentally hollow a shell could yet project such presence. I marvelled yet again how such a master, such an apogee of mindless acquisitiveness could inspire one of the meagre half dozen or so masterpieces my erstwhile profession had pitifully managed to achieve, and wondered for the first time how long it would be before it was requisitioned as the

Governor's Mansion. That was a pregnant thought. It reminded me that fact, while not truer, is indeed stranger than fiction: that in this Golden Five and Dime State fantasy and reality were only finely distinguishable. It might be a salutory remembrance as the final run-in between me and Chieu grew closer.

We were only about five miles beyond San Simeon, running through a satellite ribbon development of grovelling motels, when he spoke.

'Pull in up there. We'll make ourselves comfortable for the night. I'm sure our good senses will allow.'

I hadn't even turned the headlights on. Alarm pricked at the back of my neck. I got nervous in the twilight zone.

'There's a lot of driving left in the day,' I said.

'I prefer to start early tomorrow and time our arrival in Los Angeles.'

'You're the boss.'

'You've got to let me go! You've got to let me go! You've got to let me go!' It was the girl returning to the present.

He looked at her, a fine-drawn compassion on the sensually ascetic face.

'I promise you,' he said, 'that if everyone is sensible not the slightest harm will come to you.'

Her eyes dilated. Her pallor increased. The charm did not provoke belief. I suspected then that whatever might ensue, he had made up his mind to kill her. It was logical. He had to be a villain. Villains don't dig witnesses. QED.

We checked in. Willard Parks Thatcher. It was even easier for him than before. All he did was keep her covered. She stood in the lobby, accompanied us to our out-of-season family room like a last-act Lady Macbeth. When I opened the door for her she sleep-walked by, the glitter of a strange anticipation in her eyes.

It was the room we'd been in endless times before. A sketch of a closet to the left and opposite the bathroom: then a twin-bedded room and beyond, through the looking glass of an opened sliding door, its mirror image.

'I have to go in there.'

She was looking at the bathroom.

'Of course,' he said.

He followed her in. I heard the sound of a cabinet being opened. He came out slowly holding her grip, her tote bag and his gun. I hadn't run for cover. I didn't sap him down. She locked the door. He pocketed his gun. We listened to the small and private sounds. He beguiled the time with a patient search of her tote bag. There were papers, cards in a small purse. Nothing he read therein disturbed him. She flushed the toilet. There was a silent pause. She unlocked the door and came out.

'If you wouldn't mind going through into the inner room,' he said, 'Mr Powell and I have to talk. Here are your things.'

Stiffly, she went through. He closed the door rumblingly after her. He turned and looked at me.

'Well?' he said.

'I've already given you the man's name,' I said. 'His real name. I think you realised that. Recognised it.'

'If you think that,' he said, 'you'll realise that I'm more interested in the place. What is it?'

I shook my head.

'I don't trust you,' I said. 'But you're right. I'm worried about her. If I give you the name now ... Again, I could be lying to you once more. What does a name mean now? Well, there is a place. Tomorrow I'll take you there. Olivares may not be there—all the timing's off—but you can put word around. But on two conditions. One, I get my money back; two, you let the girl go. It'll be a public situation—there'll be people on the sidewalk, cars going by and such. Let her fade away into the crowd.'

'Agreed,' he said.

He reached into his jacket pocket. Without warning he tossed something at me. The car keys.

'Why don't you go down the road and fetch us all back some food?' he said.

I just stood there. Rigid. An Easter Island transplant.

'We have a deal now,' he said. 'Don't we?'

He nodded towards the second bedroom.

'If anything—'

'I give you my untrustworthy word,' he said, 'no harm will come to her. Not if you're back within the hour. Get lots of coffee.'

Yes. I was back in twenty minutes. I got cheeseburgers and french fries and cole slaw salad and cokes and coffee twice all round. And a knife. I never seriously entertained the idea of scarpering. It was a novel feeling, no question, to be piloting the car alone, free of back-seat drivers. It felt unnatural. The temptation to zoom off towards the vanishing point of the infinite American horizon was there in the landscape. Ramblin' Richard Powell. But, I reflected, as the short-order cook peeled separating paper from the pre-frozen burgers, when you've infinity to choose from, you've got no place to go. When the world's your oyster, pearls are a nuisance. It wasn't places, but people. There was nobody, not a single solitary soul I could run to. He bat better than he knew. The burgers sizzled on the oil-slicked griddle. And it was personal now. I was bypassing the police less to avoid awkward questions about Lester Leapfrog than to ensure finishing the vendetta my way. That's what it had become, a grudge match. Sooner or later I'd get the drop on him and in every way find out what made him run. Even if it killed me. However it turned out it would be an aim, a direction, a pastime. And then there was the girl. He wasn't a gambler at all. Only a guilt-edged investor. There was a quality about that antiseptic, bland depersonalised room that silently cried out for outrage, for unspeakable atrocities to be perpetrated within its blank, unseeing walls. It was America boxed in miniature. I couldn't leave her there, a casual victim to a motiveless malignity turned sadist.

The cook came to the counter carrying the boxed-up food.

'Eight dollars even,' he said.

'That's a nice knife you were using back there,' I said. 'Happens I need one like that right now.'

'It's not for sale.'

'Not for ten bucks?'

'For ten bucks it's for sale.'

He wiped it clean and handed it to me. Outside in the car I slid it down the inside calf of my left sock. I had some kind of an edge now. I drove back, knocked and he let me in. Nothing seemed altered. He wasn't the least surprised to see me.

'Put it on the table,' he said.

I did.

'Now put your hands up.'

Feelingly, he dispossessed me of the knife.

'Tut, tut,' his tongue clicked. 'And you said that I was untrustworthy.'

He divided the food equally. Politely.

'Perhaps you'd be kind enough to take our young friend's share through to her.'

'I'll take my own through too.'

'Just as you wish.'

I left him lord of some fries and slid the partition open.

She hadn't been fluently dismembered as I'd quarter expected, one hundredth wanted to see. She wasn't a trussed naked carcass raw from innumerable razor-thin cuts. She was untouched, sitting slumped, motionless in the darkening room on the nearer bed, her back to me. I'd had the impression she was tall. Now she seemed shrunken, tiny. And frail, of course. She didn't turn round as I came in and at first I thought this was a continuation of her withdrawal from the inconceivable. Then I realised she was watching me in the full-length mirror on the far closet door.

'Have something to eat,' I said as gently as I could.

She made no answer.

'It's good,' I said.

'I'm not hungry,' she said. I just made out the monotone.

'Well have some coffee.'

Mechanically she reached for the poly-whatever-thene cup. She winced carefully.

'Careful,' I said, 'it's hot if you hang on to it.'

She didn't put it down.

'So you're with him,' she said.

'Why?' I said.

'You came back. I thought I—I'd die when you went off. And

121

then it dawned on me that if you came back...'

Her voice trailed away. There was no point in lowering my voice.

'You don't know about all the telephoning I did while I was out,' I said.

That would really have him worried. She looked at me as quick hope flared in her eyes. It faded to puzzlement. She sipped at the coffee, not noticing it. I chomped on my burger. It was rotten. That's another myth.

'You won't believe it, but I'm with you,' I said. 'You don't have to believe it. You'll see. It's just that it'll be easier on you if you do.'

She shivered, looked at me blankly. She wouldn't hitch again for a long, long time. If ever. She bit into her burger. She pulled a face.

'The fries are better,' I said. 'You can swallow them quicker.'

We munched for a while.

'Why me?' she said.

'His idea. He thinks it'll keep me in line.'

'Huh?'

'He thinks I'm a nice enough guy to want to avoid you getting ... slapped around.'

'Are you a nice guy?'

'Not particularly.'

'You came back.'

'He's got something I want.'

She looked at me.

'I'm always getting slapped,' she said.

I think I blinked. Anyway, I let it go. Things were ambiguous enough without having to make allowances for another moaning bleeder or paid-up practising masochist. One was enough. We finished the banquet in a munching silence.

It was still early. If it was his tactic to leave us stewing for a tedious, nerve-wracked time, he was piling up points. I went over to the plywood cabinet and took out the Muscoda Bedside Companion as left by a passing Gideon. I sat on the other bed and started to read. It's not half a bad book. Quite edifying in places. The first section has more muscle than the second. At first glance, anyway.

From time to time I looked over at her. She was a total victim of his plan, and, in its totality, anxiety ill became her. The scent of fear came off her as she continued to sit stock still. The skin strained tight across those face-saving bones ashenly testified to the hollow, visceral, unknowing terror felt within. Once as I looked up a spasm, an all-embracing tic, momentarily convulsed the whole face. Belatedly it occurred to me that for me to be sitting, nonchalantly, as it must seem, perusing the good book, must be an added bizarre twist towards unhinging her. Self-consciously, aware of him, I was trying to devise some small talk that would not be impossibly banal and functionless when, suddenly, noiselessly, she was at my side.

'Hold me,' she said. 'Hold me.'

She was at that stage of reaction which trembles continually, involuntarily. I slipped my arm inside the flying jacket. It could have been made of single layered cheese-cloth. She was as cold as ice. I put my other arm across her and pulled her close.

For a long timeless time, the crown of her head against my cheek, her cheek upon my shoulder, we sat without moving. Her shivering stopped. A sort of warmth generated. We are slaves to our physiology. In the middle of everything, her forlorn-ness the aphrodisiac, I began to think of her sexually.

Coltish was sort of the word. She was older than that and yet, in the rather small high breasts, the narrow neck of waist, the slender flanks, there was a lot of strung out, fragile, thorough-bred adolescence. Without needing to question it for a moment, I knew that the scuffed, indifferent jeans sheathed long, stretched, magnificently lean legs made for entwining, clasping, pulling. Her hair against my skin was soft, finely redolent of all the women—not so many really—I had ever held long times ago in quietly darkening rooms. I could imagine how neatly the tall height of her body would accommodate the length of mine, alongside, fronting, topping. I imagined ... Her head moved away. I let my arms fall. Hair cascaded gently as she turned and looked directly at me. For cheek to cheek telepathy I had employed an unnecessarily strong signal.

Her lips came close to my ear.

'There's two of us,' she whispered. 'Can't we ... can't we jump him?'

Serves me right. I shook my head.

'I made that mistake once,' I said softly. 'He's no pushover.'

'But two of us ... he's got to sleep.'

'Not tonight he won't.'

'No?'

'No.'

Her head drew away slowly, came back fast on a second thought. She was beautiful, after all. Like most girls.

'Did you really telephone anyone?' she said.

Again, I shook my head.

'No,' I said, 'nobody to call.'

Her eyes widened.

'The police!'

'That wouldn't be cool for me,' I said.

'Oh ... But I have friends! Friends who would help! In LA. If we just—'

I jerked my head at the dividing door.

'Phone's in with him,' I said. 'If it's still connected.'

The hope that had animated, relaxed, her face died away.

'Couldn't you try—'

'It isn't necessary,' I said. 'There's a better way. My way. Please believe me ... Sam. Trust me for your own sake.'

Now nothing played across the face.

'Look, it's this way,' I said. 'There's a long poker session going on between him and me and you're just a wild card, poor thing, he pulled in to throw me. It hasn't worked. Tomorrow he and I'll trade information for money and you'll be out of it.'

I was becoming acutely conscious, now that it took on importance, of talking for an audience of two. Why is a silence so inhibiting? I pulled out my pen and picked up the Bible once again. While I made quiet, even 'Relax, now' small talk, I wrote a quick message on its flyleaf.

'Tomorrow. LA. In traffic. Lots of people around. Will crash car. You run. Will squeeze your pretty leg as signal. OK?'

She read, considered, nodded. A steadier, less intense hope revived on that expressive, guileless face. I looked at her questioningly.

'So don't worry,' I said. 'OK?'

She held my eyes and, for a brief and very nice instant, smiled.

'Well,' I said. I got up making a lot of noise and ripped out the flyleaf as I did so.

'You've had an unusual, no doubt tiring day. It'll do you a lot of good to sack out. You take that bed. I'll give you five minutes to get set.'

I slid the partition door open and went through. His back up against its headboard, he was stretched out in shirtsleeves on top of a bed. He was smoking. The gun lay to hand. He regarded me.

'Sorry to break in on your meditation,' I said. 'I have to use the can.'

He gestured me through as to the manner born, the politest gentleman of the bedchamber a mandarin could desire. I closed but ostentatiously did not lock the door. I used the john anyway and in medias res tore up the fly-leaf and jettisoned it in the sounding water. I had the inevitable anxious moment as the tiny pieces danced and swirled in the new influx (American plumbing is so poor) but the Gideons' choice of paper was not of an impervious quality. It sank without trace.

She was in bed. The flying jacket, suede moccasin-style boots and—interestingly, starting trains of thought, ah well—her jeans were sprawled regardless on the floor. She was lying on her back, eyes open, face blank yet not unused, staring at the ceiling. I took off my jacket, shirt, shoes and trousers and slid what remained into the other bed. It was still early.

'Mind if I read?' I said.

'Who sleeps?' she said, not moving.

125

I adjusted the throw from my bedside light so that none of it spilled on to her and turned back to Genesis Chapter IV. That set me thinking too. Everything since has been a replay of that one ... After a while I felt sleepy and turned to switch out the light. She hadn't moved. Her open eyes gleamed faintly as they continued staring up at nothing.

As usual, I had a dream. This one had a hard core of realism. I was on a studio film set. Only this time I wasn't behind the cameras or lighting. I was one of the actors. The other was Tran Chau Chieu. My unconscious had his name perfectly. We were about to do a duelling scene. Pistols, of course. The trick was that the director, a shadowy presence somewhere on the swimming periphery beyond the centre of sharp lines, wanted a vérité effect. He wanted to do it for real. We were all trying to decide who should take the permanent dive and I didn't want to but I seemed under a limelight-stealing compulsion to volunteer. Then, in one of those automatic gear changes that dreams shift through, I was the director as well. I had to decide who would emerge alive—my lean, greying alter ego or surely, that other archetypical superstar, the classic featured Chinois. Without warning I was wide awake knowing something was very wrong.

I flipped the light on. He wasn't in the room. The door was still closed. It was her. She was asleep now. If you could call it that. She was thrashing spasmodically, her head turning sharply from side to side on the pillow as if trying to shake free of the untidy net of her own hair.

'Jamie!' she whimpered. 'Jamie. Oh, no!'

I heard it quite clearly. That's what had woken me before. The noise went down to a low uneven moaning, a patient coming round from sedation. A film of perspiration sheened on her forehead as it turned unceasingly through its arc. I slipped out of my bed and sat with intentional heaviness on hers. It didn't wake her. I reached up gently and started to unskein the tangle of damp hair.

'Sam,' I said, 'Sam.'

Her eyes started open wide in sudden shock. Remembrance

126

burst into them. Her jaw went slack to let out a fierce gasp as with abrupt tense motion she levered herself half upward. I held my hand firm on her shoulder.

'Easy,' I said, 'easy.'

The strain went out of her body and from her face. She lowered herself down, exhausted rather than at rest.

'Hello, Richard not to be called Dick,' she said. 'Is that true?'

I nodded.

'Preferably.'

'Funny. My full name's Samanatha and I can't bear it. It makes me feel four years old.'

She was silent looking at me.

'Do you really think I'm two hundred per cent arrogant?' she said.

'No,' I said. 'That was just envy.'

'You were trying to get me to leave.'

'Yes. Want to tell me about him?'

She looked the question at me.

'About Jamie,' I said.

Dismay, an old private, inner dismay, crumpled the set of her face. She shook her head violently several times. Her lower lip was between her teeth, her cheeks strained up and out, puffing the eyes.

'You want to tell somebody about him,' I said. 'You woke me up shouting his name.'

She began to tremble exactly as she had before. With a visible effort she got it under control.

'You know what you said—'

'...What?'

'About doing it with anyone for five bucks. About putting out.'

'I wasn't meaning to do anything but—'

'I don't need the five bucks.'

Without warning she sat up. With a cross-armed, unfolding sweep that was faintly balletic she peeled off the man's tee-shirt she was wearing. She kicked aside the sheet and blanket and lay naked before me. I could see now the bruise, livid on her right shoulder. As if independent of her will her left leg slid jerkily sideways across the sheet opening, revealing. She began trembling more violently than before.

'Please!' she said. 'Please!'

So, I had it all for as long as would be necessary. A fantasy situation superimposed on reality with momentarily exact registration, no displacement. A rim of softly lit down edged on one side the classic outline of the long stretch of a body, beggaring my previous imagining. The spaced-apart breasts were still well-defined and firm, the slenderly fleshed legs made to take a man, the belly lean with just enough sweet, final, cushioning rise. She was a pre-Raphaelite's palely-loitering lay. The sense of febrility the trembling gave was the ultimate erotic touch. I could feel sex rising in me thick and warm. She was so flatteringly vulnerable ... Remembering to suck in my not all that they once were stomach muscles, I duplicated her peeling. I stepped out of my shorts. I switched out the light. Half alongside her, half across, I joined her on the bed.

It had been a long time between drinks. I had all but forgotten that most seductive element of all within the fleshly delight. The sweet soothing sense of oblivion, of narcotic abstraction from all the thousand shocks, natural and unnatural, that in the guerrilla warfare of the workaday world the same flesh is heir to. For all the trembling, her body was warm and smoothly soft. Another excellent thing in women. Lower than her on the bed, I lay with my head pillowed on her belly, one hand reaching up and across to hold her breast. I kissed teasingly the isthmus of her waist. With my other hand I began to stroke her as she most wanted to be stroked. She moaned, moved under me, trembling now for other reasons. Her own hand, so soft again, moved caressingly in sweeps across my back. I felt immortal longings pricking at me. I levered myself up ready for that moist, velvet, clutching, easing injection, the descent into death and transfiguration. In that instant our eyes locked.

All trembling ceased. She lay there frozen, rigid with an inert tenseness. Strain had bared her teeth. In that denying split second an obscenely sweet taste in my mouth and nostrils triggered nausea and total recall. The smoke fuming from the twisted wreck of car poured on. The flames were not yet extinguished. I was embracing death. There was no feeling now except cold. That was all that the white, vivid, intervening wraith of that tiny, superimposed body could impart. Ice congealed the potential desire at my spine's base. The ghost who always walked with me ran a cold hand where hers had just been warm. His chill applause signalled his delight. And now it was as if, from the recollected room next door, a Valentinoesque voyeur looked on with leering gratification. I subsided as fast as a Nixon bridge to credibility. Shifting the weight of my body, I slewed from off my mounting position and down beside her. I lay there as limp as an over-boiled leek.

Now we were both tense. It was the non-event of the decade. A Marx Brothers Night of Nights. The cocksman had had his figurative comeuppance.

It would have been funny if it hadn't been so sour. The image of Elsie's face, accusing in its inanimateness, kept floating on to my mind. Well perhaps that had been the trouble, the worst mark of all, trying to make out all those expiatory years ago East of Eden. Now this one stirred. Her hand crept down and, cajoling, working at the faint, sticky residue of my late, fore-shortened erection, tried to revive it. The message was imperson-ally mechanical. I reached my own hand down and grasping her wrist made her stop.

'I'm sorry,' she said. 'It's all my fault.'

'Not yours, not mine,' I said. 'It isn't the time or the place.

Violently her head turned and pressed into the crook of my neck. She began to cry, trying not to at first, then, glad to, letting herself sob without control. Hot tears ran down the swell of my shoulder. I listened beyond her sobs. I could hear no sound from the next room but I knew we had a witness. She was shaking again, but this time in a way that had a promise of relaxation in it. I held her. After a while she was spent. She grew quiet and still.

'Jamie is my little boy,' she said. 'He's going on four. But I haven't seen him in two years. I started going with his father when I was a sophomore. I didn't know much. I didn't know a thing. I got pregnant and I had to leave school and get married. Before he'd been the only man I'd ever gone with. All the way. But after I just had to go for every new guy I got near. I didn't like him much, I guess. But it would always work out like this. I'd be all turned on and wanting with a sort of hollowed out, hypnotised, pulled in feeling and then I'd think of how perfect and beautiful Jamie was and how much I loved him and how this man I simply didn't know at all was going to stick that ... thing of his ... right up inside me. And I'd freeze.... Soon as we got to Louisville he went after a divorce. They didn't have to go far for evidence. The court gave him custody because I would exert an undesirable influence on the child. Exert.... They were right, I guess. They sure were.... You're the first who didn't bang straight in and do it to me anyway.'

I could have told her it was because I was a telepathic saint but I didn't. You don't say anything when people come out with wounds like that. You just stick around and stay quiet.

I did exactly that. Her eyes, unblinkingly open, gathered the faint residue of light in the dark room and remotely returned it. Time went by.

'I'm sorry,' she said at last.

'It's OK.'

'I'm just so ... fucked up,' she said.

'Everyone is. It doesn't matter.'

I put my lips very close to her ear.

'Quiet now,' I said. 'You've got that about tomorrow? I crash the car—when we're going real slow—and touch you just before and you jump and run. OK?'

'Yes,' she breathed.

All he could have possibly heard were the sweet nothings of a pair of star-crossed lovers.

'Listen,' she said. 'Afterwards. After I run. I shan't see you again, will I?'

'Who knows? We sail in Time.'

When it comes to the big moments, the need to boom out the ace, I can plagiarise with the best of them.

'I'd have liked to,' she said.

'Try to sleep.'

For a long time she lay in my arms, still awake. Finally she slept. I didn't want to disturb her and the warm succour of another evenly breathing body brought such an old, old balm of content, I didn't want to disturb myself. It didn't matter that he'd find us this way in the morning, suavely thinking his cynic's worst. Still holding her I fell dreamlessly asleep myself.

I found that it did matter. When at an unprecedentedly early hour he woke us, I found the sardonic superiority one layer beneath his bland mask insufferable. I had wrath on which to sharpen my wits as we went south through a grey dawn.

CHAPTER SEVEN

How many miles to the other Sam's town? Around two hundred
and fifty if you start from San Simeon and take the coast road.
Can you get there by noon? Easily, if your rear seat driver has
a pistol not so secreted on his person and he has you out of
your concupiscent bed with a misty Pacific dawn. Southward
again. The mist turned off as the sun rose and there was the
tawny, mottled landscape, faded green and brown, of Southern
California. They have it that way to match the smog.

I could do it all from a reviving memory now, and with little
traffic did it fast. Carpinteria came and Santa Barbara. The oil
sheening across the once blue bay towards the once incom-
parable beaches required an updating entry in my mental guide
book. So did the offshore rigs, its source. A few miles out they
stood on spidery pylon legs like so many gun-towers on the
national boundary of a concentration camp. We left them for
the Chicken Delights of Ventura and Oxnard, the place where
two roads meet. We still kept to the coast, passing a scattering
of desultory surfers pursuing the mirage of endless summer and
older eternal youths breakfasting *en famille* beside their covered
pick-up wagons.

Hearst gave way to Hughes, Miss Davies to Miss Peters. The
Aircraft Corporation's centre for research stood shoe-box senti-
nel to Malibu. Then we were flashing by the pockmarked rear
ends of that sea-facing weekend lure of lemmings. Sky cloudless
blue, the sea breeze blowing stiffly inland, we turned left at that
ocean T-junction where myth ends up short against reality to
follow the smog's wake the length of Sunset Boulevard.

Wilder got it wrong. He should have finished up on Keaton.
That's what I was thinking as I swept round the curves that

Sunset first makes through the nondescript terrain buffering Bel Air from the rude Pacific gales. We passed above a freeway that was new to me—I didn't even catch its name—and then, via half a dozen fast, banked bends, moved downwards into real estate that made me think that after all Wilder had hit it on the nose, as hard and right as any diamond. Colonial mansions, hidalgo haciendas, Florentine palaces, were parked detachedly behind Cadillacs and Rolls and Lincolns. There were more Rolls on show than you'd see in a lifetime up in dole-conscious Derby. The air here seemed scented and quiet to order: the half acres of ersatz grass lawns fresh-picked and frozen to perfection. Prominent on one was a little painted Negro in white riding breeches, green jacket and red cap. He held a whip in one hand and an iron hitching ring for the Bentley in the other. Somebody had painted his face in the latest colour, Placatory White, since Marlowe, many heyday summers back, had drifted by in his thirty-nine Olds. In my need I looked for him now, but his presence remained always just beyond vision. I felt my pulses quicken. I couldn't tell whether it was at the personal reacquaintance with old, forgotten, far-off nights or merely the proximity to all that unreal money. Wilder's document on fantasy stood up. People really did live and have being in those sets of solid papier mâché—chairmen of loan associations, captains of investment, inheritors of real estate, psychiatrists. There were probably even a few movie types left here and there, behind certain brave, archaic fronts.

We might as well get on with it.

'You want me to take you straight there?' I said.

'Why not?'

'All right if I drop my friend off first?'

'We'll do that later, shall we? Where exactly is it from here?'

'Straight ahead. All the way down at the other end of Sunset.'

'Do make sure you don't miss it.'

More recognition—Louis B's palace of philistine stone built on a foundation of God knows what. It loured alongside the fast stretch that brought us, suddenly, to stop lights, a build-up of buildings and, round a corner, the Strip. It had all sprung up since my last time in town. But you couldn't mistake it. There was the same overall feel you get down Tooting Broadway, only with less sense of native style. The boutiques, the fronts for PR hustlers were modishly at one with our age of disposables, grafted on with guaranteed rejection one decade away. When you came to *The Body Shop* there was no shock, no pun involved. You expected it to be a strip joint. Along here, apart from topless waitresses, you could buy clothes and deodorants and records and ice cream and suede and psychedelic décor and public relations and people. And all on plastic money at eighteen per cent p.a. You couldn't buy books or tools or a loaf of bread. Not that it mattered immediately. More to the present point was that here was traffic slowed to any big city's stop-go crawl. Here on the sidewalks high stepping through the lunchtime sunshine and fumes were people, witnesses.

There's always a lot of people out on the streets in Hollywood. It's full of the large-scale unemployed and swing-shift actress-waitresses and red-necked, pop-eyed tourists in awe of the obvious, and oblivious to the implications of the other, more direct hustlers that tread on the labelled, dirtied-over stars gilt-set in the Hollywood sidewalks. These are the people who don't live in the big houses of the dream. The cost of living is a killer but they still love California because it isn't cold and it isn't damp. You don't need much in the way of clothes or a pad. You can put up a brave front on the strength of a tie-dyed tee-shirt. There were a lot of those passing by now. And Billy-Boy buckskin and Existential Black. Kid girls went by with the genuine dead-pan decadent allure of their brittle confidence. The bras they wore under their see-throughs spelt out the duality. I stopped on a red light further up. To the left was a hamburger hash-house with tables on a would-be Continental-style outside terrace. People sat there watching the passing parade two notches too animatedly. They had a self-regarding, self-displaying air you'd never have mistaken for European. Still, they'd make good witnesses. I glanced in the rear-view mirror. Forget it. Just behind, three hippies, hands extended against the patrol car that had swum out from nowhere, were being shaken down and busted.

For possession, no doubt. Possession of alienable rights.

This wasn't the time or place. I couldn't risk involvement with the law. I drove on with the traffic's peristaltic shudder. I got a shock. Somewhere around La Cienega they were demolishing this week's building and you could see murkily across to a long line of high-rise blocks marching along what had to be Wilshire to their rendezvous with San Andreas. The city's towers were not as topless as its waitresses but on all sides a big new high was reaching up to meet, somewhere just out of sight, an even bigger low. So I mused. We were in the sixty-five hundreds now, just east of La Brea. The Strip had petered out and a Ralph's, a Mediterranean Church, filling stations had marked a return to a kind of normality. I paused at a light on Wilcox, needlessly punching up neutral. Then, seeing what was immediately behind—an ugly, angular sprawl of cadmium-yellow Corvette—I knew this was the time.

The light on Wilcox changed from green. My left hand masked the Rambler's pushbutton gear-selector. Our light flashed green. I flipped my right hand on Sam's thigh as with my left I hit the reverse button. I waited a split second to let the 'vette move forward in impatient motion. I trod on the pedal. Abruptly we surged back. There was a sharp shunt forward as, the crunch coming, we hit and then as I tweaked it, another increment the other way. Our arse end rode up over the nose of the 527-cubic-inched, five-speed-manual-boxed, mag.-wheeled, quad-downdraught-carbed heap of glossy junk. I didn't have time to savour the finer delights of my stalling manoeuvre. Swinging round fast as if to see what I'd done, I flung an arm across him coming forward. He smashed down on it with the already drawn gun but didn't have room to swing. It only caused an agonising shaft of pain to run from forearm through to stomach via skull. That was OK. In the same instant as the hurt engulfed me I heard the door click open, caught a glimpse of her heading, tumbling into daylight. He made a move for the rear door but somehow I hoiked him back. She was gone.

'Sit tight,' I said. 'I'm still here. I'll play it out with you.'

He turned to me a face of thwarted stone. The gun came

round. He all but shot me there. There was hooting down the line of backed up cars.

'Put it away,' I said. 'People are looking. The guy's coming up.'

He was. He was storming up to yell at me. He was a kid. A rich kid, therefore. He was medium height and junior Fatty Arbuckle with blond pubic hair across his skull and a moon face the colour of ripe brick. It clashed with the cardinal-bodied, gold-sleeved leather wind-breaker he Californianly wore. Whether from rage or education he was incoherent.

'Whadya ... whadya ... whadya think you ...'

'Got a little ahead of yourself there, sonny, didn't you?' I said.

He had an instant coronary. I usefully occupied the time that took by sliding, Tran Chau Chieu in tandem, out into the street. We were in the middle lane of three. Glaring, grinning motorists were filtering by on either side. I looked about, beyond the gathered, rubber-necking crowd. She was a long gone lady. I wished there had been a Lord to thank. Except that I felt sad. And mean.

'Let's take a look,' I said to Mr Rose Bowl.

'It was your fault! All your fault!' he yelled. 'You came on back when you should've gone on! I've got witnesses! I've got witnesses!'

'Sure,' I said, 'sure. Insurance companies always blame the guy behind. D'you know that?'

'You were liable!' he screamed. 'I saw you! And there was a girl in there too. You were—'

I brushed ignoringly past him and walked to the Rambler's rear end. It was also the Corvette's front. A marriage had been arranged. The cadmium-yellow snout seemed to be doing rather indecent things down there beneath our notice. Behind the tinted windshield one of the world's five great redheads stared haughtily through an unpleasantness that she willed did not exist. Do they always have to go for money?

'Yup!' I said in my Gary Cooper voice, 'looks like we locked horns.'

136

Moonface hissed. The other kind—the horns of Southland—were blowing anything but faintly. The gun went into my ribs.

'Get us out of this,' he whispered, 'before the police come. I'm not joking.'

I didn't think he was. I sidestepped Cardinal and Gold and got back behind the Rambler's wheel. The gun was now about as far away from my left ear through the wound-down window.

'Don't move! Don't move!' bellowed Beau Corvette. 'I want the police to see just how—'

Hitting the right button now I ground the Rambler forward with a scrape and clang and lurch. Apoplexy reigned. A bright bystanding spirit clapped ironic hands. I got out again, surveyed the visible damage. The marriage had borne fruit. To the high-clearing Rambler—not a scratch. To the Corvette—superficial but disfiguring dents and paint scars in an eighteen inch swathe right across the hood. The fold-away headlights were eyes closed in mourning. I grinned cheerily at the ice maiden—the ice woman—within under the red hair and found out what it's like being the Invisible Man.

'What do you reckon?' I asked Tiny Tim.

'Whaa...t?'

'How much? How much to put right?'

'I ... I dunno ... See here, I want to wait until an authorised assessor—'

'Three hundred?'

'Three. ..? I dunno ... I guess...'

He looked back at me with piggy, calculating eyes to gauge if I might pack that money.

'Well, three, I guess,' he said. 'Don't want her husband to know, huh?'

'Give the prick five,' I told my yellow Tonto.

He peeled the bills off like he'd been my long green valet all his life.

'Get it done fast,' I said to Boule de Suif, 'and Daddy need never find out.'

I tipped an imaginary hat to the Red Lady of his wallets.

'See here,' he remembered to get in, 'what about personal injury and shock to my passenger and—'

'See here, ass face,' I said, 'another bleep out of you and I'll smash your face in and make it match that joke on wheels.'

He took a little shuffle forward and then remembered that discretion is the better part of the old college try. He backed off. I brushed by him a second time and got a forearm smash to the gut in any case. But not from him. From her. It had all been for nothing. She was standing the other side of the Rambler by the front passenger door. She looked at me mutely, crest-fallenly, knowing she had betrayed me by coming back. A small death took place somewhere behind my suddenly old, tired eyes. And a small warmth was kindled. On every level the smoggy town was made for jerking tears. She got in the car. I got in the car. He got in the car. I started it up. The light turned green. Behind, the Corvette varoomed into overpowered life and wasting rubber and gas, screeched around us into the Sunset traffic.

'Well,' he said, 'I must confess I find such a sacrificial gesture infinitely touching.'

He was smiling slightly like a card-sharp finding confirmation that the deck was stacked in his favour.

'Yeah,' I said. 'Ain't love grand.'

We drove on in silence.

Not that there was anything to remark on. We drove past Norm's, through Sunset and Vine, that greatest of anticlimaxes, past Mark C. Bloom's, on past all the happenstance short-term architecture of the land of free enterprise. A classic building here was as rare as a shot of Streisand's right profile. Down there a block was the Cedars where, when it's too late, those whose names were once in lights go to have their livers cobaltly bombarded and contract thus disseminated cancer of the bank account. We came to the messy, tawdry junction where Holly-wood and Sunset Boulevards collide and, via the city's presiding genius, The Akron, began the descent to the downtown second nucleus of Sammy's amoebic city. And just before, where Sunset skirts by Echo Park Lake, *The Silver Peso*.

138

I'd pretty much known about where it would be. What I hadn't expected was that this rundown and, in LA terms, ancient section would be another brave front, recipient of a Latin, hippy face-lift. In the bright sunshine there was a sense of gay colours over dirt—of the long since unfashionable made suddenly modish with a few coats of pastel and even primary emulsion. A Spanish supermarket to the left had twenties stucco in inflammatory orange. Pasted on its window, alongside crude hand-lettered Spanish news of 'specials' on meat and frozen enchiladas, were right-wing Cuban, anti-Castro slogans. Three doors away an art-nouveau-ish purple junk shop proclaimed itself a *Den of Antiquities*. From a shadowed doorway that could have led to anything, an archetypal black-dressed señora stared with baleful timidity upon the hostile, impoverishing Anglo-Saxon world. The parked cars were older here, more battered. They helped to give the block the edge of genuinely homogeneous local style that its neighbours lacked. Further analysis wasn't too important. On the right I saw *The Silver Peso*.

It wasn't a complete dive. It was neatly enigmatic, its façade an even series of pale, vertical wooden slats set close together. They were broken by a single-width door recessed in two or three feet at the centre. A long run of black plexiglass above carried the name in unfussy silver lettering. Kicking the hand-brake savagely on, I parked a few lengths down on the same side of the street.

'Over there,' I said.

He couldn't actually shoot us on the spot.

'*The Silver Peso?*'

'Yes.'

'Very good.'

'Listen,' I said. 'I'm in this country illegally. I did kill Lester. I give you that. I don't have any options. Nothing else to do but to do what you say. You've got the name now. You've got the place. Now, when you and I walk in there, let's do it by ourselves and leave the girl to go.'

He smiled.

'You've got it all wrong again,' he said. 'We're not going in there. You are. By yourself.'

'But—'

'Your—friend—here will be in good hands. You know that. Just consider that a pistol shot, discreetly muffled, would go unremarked inside this car.'

'What ... what?'

'You know what I want. A route to Raker. Now go over there and start negotiating one.'

'Olivares may not be there.'

'Take your time. Have a drink. Ask questions. Leave word. We can come back.'

There was nothing else to do but get out of the car and walk along to the bar and go in and try to recognise a man I'd never seen. I looked across at Sam. All the trembling must have been internal. She wasn't motionless, she was rigid. In a way that had no strength. Following the loss of all vitality. Fear, defeat, despair leaked out of her quiescence. And, most of all, a shamed sort of apology. If ever there was a lady in distress this was she, unless you qualified it by—was it there? I'd like to have thought not—an undersense that she was happy in her dolour. I got out of the car and then bent back in.

'OK,' I said. 'See what I can do. Be back soon.'

I didn't waste anybody's time by trying to crack a smile.

Those were the two shots, two superimposed compositions, I carried with me the thirty or so heatwaved paces I took to the door of the bar. It was too hot to think. They filled the gap in my brain. Her sitting there in ashen, frozen full shot. And in the wider two shot, her in identical posture, obtruding on the larger, primary image, the gaoler as well as the hostage. In my mind he stared pleasantly at her from clear candid eyes.

I squared my shoulders, braced myself and, the derivative of a thousand subliminally held Westerns, pushed the door open to walk into the bar. It was instant blackout. There was no pain. Nobody had sapped me. I'd forgotten to anticipate the exposure change of going from acrid sunlight to desiccated, air-conditioned dark. As a voice burbled nasally on I stood halted by this sudden night with a strong sense of the light behind me. Silhouetted I felt set up for every lowdown whisky-drinking bushwacker, every bearer of a Cosa Nostra contract. Eastwood would never have done it like this. I moved forward again quickly, making for the subdued orange glow from a bar that made a letter D with the left-hand wall. Purblind, walking by radar, I made it to the far end, turned its corner and sat down on the high stool. Now I was Eastwood again. I could watch the door. Well, the front one. When the eyes in the back of my head had also become accustomed to the gloom I could watch the rear one over my left shoulder too.

'Yes, sir?'

The barman materialised out of the shadow. He was your archetypal, heavy set, moustached Mexican barman, his skin burnished to a remotely exotic copper by the orange-shaded bar lights.

'Gin and tonic. No lemon.'

'Yes sir.'

He fixed the drink in the tall thin cylinder of a glass. The tonic came not from a bottle but from a set of rubber hoses tied in, somehow, to a compressor unit. But none the better for that.

'There you go.'

He had no accent. I gave him a five dollar bill. Prompted by the need to check my change my eyes made their final adjustment. I let the odd bills of my change lie on the counter and looked around.

It was a pleasantly ordinary bar. A black dress sombrero with silver adornment set amid the liqueur bottles was, mercifully, the only concession in décor to the name. Except that it was almost empty it was a nice, serious place to get drunk in. The three other inhabitants all seemed very serious.

Over at a booth opposite the counter sat the two guys you find in every bar around Hollywood. They're never as young as their clothes and Stanley—it's always Stanley—has always got a million and a half committed, I swear, once they iron out this one little procedural bug. It's a scene, a perpetual off-screen gem, you can always enjoy for the price of an LA drink. It accounted now for the whining voice I'd heard as I came in. If I'd been Sam Spade I'd have suspected them at once, but, almost inevitably, I found my attention on another third man sitting halfway down the long length of the bar.

He had one of the world's great faces—as anyone with Mayan and Spanish and Yaqui and Quezalcoatl knows what else in his blood is likely to have. He was a Segura-size Gonzales who'd been beaten up continually by Federales. He had high Mongol cheekbones that looked broken and made his cheeks two flat converging planes and turned his face into a hatchet. The long thin slit of mouth extended like a cut into the flatness of the cheeks. The nose, broken, mended, broken again, was a thin, jutting, further weapon. It was a face that conjured thoughts of violence, of men suffering from the moment of their coming hither.

I sipped the gin. There was white scar tissue interrupting one black, slanted eyebrow and highlighting the brown-yellow skin. The eyes stared dully, black in deep sockets, at five, six empty bottles of Carta Blanca set before them. The hands resting also on the counter made no move towards the brimming glass that held the seventh. It was a hopeless face. A mask of peasant tragedy. The pride in it had long ago been eroded to the passive, a bleak resignation to what must of necessity be endured. It was made to photograph. If Stanley over there had half a brain he'd have signed a life-time contract with the guy ... Whatever the tonic, the gin was good. That's the better way round. I started to think.

I had to assume that there was a Raker and that the Yellow Fitzgerald out there in the Rambler wanted to get to him. Then why the hell use me as his advance man at so crucial a stage in the tracking? That bore thinking ... The only time my cock and bull Las Vegas story had made a dent had been when I'd woven the scent of a Mexican into its see-through fabric. Ergo, he knew that at least one Mexican hung around Raker. Or maybe ... actually, directly knew him. And knew that he was *persona non grata* himself. So he had to use a front-of-house man. And had no friends. So had to use a hostage ... Maybe he was a North Vietnamese agent of some sort. Maybe he was a fanatic. ... I finished the gin.

'Same again, sir?'

'Yes. Easier on the ice this time.'

'Yes, sir.'

He fixed the drink, took my money. I took a slow sip. There was nothing else to do. None of them, the barman included, had taken a blind bit of notice of me beyond the first, covert, who-are-you-keep-your-distance glance. The two across the way had got to the syndication of the spin-off series stage. The lonesome loner still stared with ancient brooding at his untouched beer. Through the narrow vertical strip of tinted glass door I saw an incessant, irregular flash of coloured metals as the cars swam by outside. Well, it was all OK. This was a nice place to wait, cool and, like all good bars, once you've settled in, reassuringly familiar. Outside in the car it would be hot and sweaty, the sun blindingly brilliant. That would be a place to tense up in. It was tough on Sam but I'd stay here a while, leaving our friend's imagination to work, his fingers to drum. Time went by. The man with the face finally, in a very formal way took a drink of beer. I found that, eventually, my glass was empty.

'Barman.'

'Yes, sir.'

'Same again, please.'

'Like it that way, sir?'

'Try putting in a little less tonic.'

'Yes, sir.'

I paid him. To the low hum of the air-conditioner more time drifted by to the wrong side of eternity. It seemed a lot like the last time I'd been in LA.

'Hey, Richard. Where'll we all be in ten years time?'

'Oh—some bar, I guess.'

Well, I didn't want to think maudlin memories about old conversations with the friends I hadn't stuck by. Maybe I should do something.

'Hey, barman.'

'Yes, sir. Same—'

'Not just yet. I wondered if you might be able to help me out on something.'

He looked at me, his eyes suddenly opaque.

'What kind of help?'

'I just got into town. I'm looking for a friend. Had an idea he hangs out here.'

'What's his name?'

'This guy.'

I pushed the police I.D. of the man I'd killed across the polished formica. He picked it up and looked at it expressionlessly.

'Uh-uh,' he said shaking his head. 'Never saw him, that I remember.'

He started to hand back the mug shot.

'Wait a minute,' he said.

He retreated down the bar and stopped opposite the man with the face. The man with the face looked slowly up. I saw that he'd drunk some more beer.

'Ever see this guy before, Paco?' the barman said.

Paco made the effort of refocussing. He made the further effort of thinking.

'No,' he said thickly. He was the one with the accent.

The barman came back. He returned the card.

'Sorry,' he said.

'That's all right. Thanks anyway. Same again.'

'Yes, sir.'

He got me another. The flurry of activity receded into the past. Past noon. The car must be like an oven by now. Something flickered. There was a change to the rhythm of movement outside the door. Somebody was coming in. I tensed, then relaxed. It wasn't him, but a hooker.

She stood uncertainly just in from the doors having the same trouble with the sudden dark, the barman's running gag, that I had. While, uncertainly, she teetered on four-inch wedge heels I looked her over. It doesn't much matter, I guess, by the time you get to working bars, but she was pretty old and pretty fat.

And not very pretty. Not that that gets to matter either. She was Mexican too. Only that was a joke. As she started to advance into the bar I could see she was wearing a champagne-coloured linen topcoat and a short wig in the same shade. As she opened her pancaked face to speak I sort of thought that her first word might be 'Next!'

'Hiya, Eddie,' she said. 'How's it going?'

'Pretty good, pretty good,' the barman muttered. I'd seen warmer receptions.

'That's good, that's good,' she said.

She'd come three-quarters of the way down the bar between me and the drunk so she could take a look at me. I gave her a stare that was long enough and hard enough to let her know I had her number and I wasn't interested.

'Hey, Eddie,' she said. 'Got a drink for your old friend?'

Silently he poured her a Hamms. It was the least he could do.

'Thanks, Eddie. First of the day.'

She drank a big enough chunk out of it to make me think it was. She pirouetted to look at the moguls. They were about through demonstrating that in Hollywood the bullshit is even thicker than the smog but, as for her, they didn't want to know either. She turned back to the bar looking even uglier. And bored. She took another mansize gulp. Another. Zanuck and Schenk got up to leave.

'Good-day, gentlemen,' the barman said.

He had a talent for exaggeration.

'Quiet,' the hooker said.

'Quiet,' the barman agreed.

She finished the beer.

'Hey, Eddie, sweetheart—'

'C'mon Vera. You know if—'

'Sure. Sure. If you was the owner of this crummy joint you'd look after your little Vera ... You know, Eddie, one day I'm going to have to be angry with you.'

The small setback had sent a line-etching force of resentment into her face. The failure to get a second beer had evoked the flavour of all the myriad other sournesses. The pasted-on brio

145

slumped away and she was suddenly a poor old beaten-up bag, the drunk at the bar's elder sister. The affinity seemed to touch on a kind of feminine logic in her. For the first time acknowledging his presence she turned to him.

'I don't know why I should get sore at Eddie,' she said. 'It's you I should get sore at.'

I didn't catch the faintest reaction.

'After what I did for you.'

This time the sombre mask tensed into an even more angular harshness. She reached into her cheap cream vinyl purse and fetched out a pack of Kools. She got one into her fat round mouth, and somehow, from nowhere, got a smile there too. His stillness made it clear that if she waited for him to produce the light she'd wait for ever. The smile hung on like grim death from the frailest of threads. It fell. Not without bravery she fished out a lighter and did the job herself.

'I guess any gentleman would buy a girl a drink,' she said. He didn't look at her.

'Get out of here, woman,' he said. Beer still kept his voice thick.

She wouldn't face defeat. Perhaps this was a final stand, a test-case battle that her ego said she mustn't add to all the other retreats. He deigned to look at her. His eyes were no longer glazed. In that confrontation of two losers, from the sense of fury pent up behind that hatchet mask, I gained a flash alert of coming violence.

'Beat it,' he said.

'Rafael, amigo—'

With a controlled precision not at all inebriated he smashed her three times across the face rapid-fire with his open hand. She lurched back with the impact, gurgling. I winced, forced myself to stay as aloof and indifferent as the barman had suddenly opted to become. She was beginning to weep now, and, the pain starting to hit home, about to scream in earnest. He was off the stool now and would have struck her again but at that instant came a sudden swell of traffic noise through the newly opened front door. Pushing Sam ahead of him, the briefcase in his left hand, Tran Chau Chieu was coming to look for me. I read this in a split millisecond. As they both stood wavering, temporarily blinded, I had a fractional premonition that the warm-ups were over and the main event was on. I premonish good. The Mexican ex-drunk whirled, faced the door, and, with a blurring of hands, had a knife from somewhere balanced in the right. I yelled 'Sam'. His arm scythed down. We jump-cut. The case was on the floor. The knife was embedded in Chau Chieu's right shoulder. In total silence, we went to a freeze frame. For perhaps a second everything was still. I didn't move a muscle. It was all an unreal million miles away. Then suddenly the whore was screaming high and loud and shrill. Then muffled, grunting, panting as the Mexican, one hand across her mouth was wrestling her to him as a living shield. Chau Chieu clawed at a right-hand pocket. The barman hit the deck. I saw it all and still I did not move. I watched as Chau Chieu sent Sam sprawling hard and fast right at the couple swaying on the floor. There was a gun in his left hand by now. As he dived to his left it went off with a noise like a cannon, unbelievably loud. But not as loud as the single long shriek the hooker gave. She and the Mexican were slewed half around towards me. An instantaneous blotch, black in that light, had saturated the front of the champagne coat, a little above the left breast. Her head went back. The puffed eyes in the round fat face opened to an astonishing wideness as she contemplated the last rotten trick that life had turned for her.

'Jesus,' she said in husky Spanish. Something bubbled gurglingly in her throat. Liquid ran down her chin. Her head snapped down and, dead weight, abruptly limber, she was dragging her man down with her. He gave up trying to support her. He let her collapse and simultaneously jacknifed down behind her. He had a gun in his hand too. She was a dead shield now.

Only then did I think to move. I kicked the stool from under me and crashed down hard and painfully into the angle the bar made with the wall. As the stool flew into open view a second shot crashed out. The stool jerked and splintered, lay still. A residue of sound hung in the air behind a sudden silence that was startlingly and ominously quiet. In the air-conditioned chill, temporarily safe below the counter's height, I started to sweat. I might be all right for the moment but somewhere out there, exposed and vulnerable, was Sam. I didn't want to move. The door to the rear had expanded remarkably. I never knew a door look so wide. When your back's to the wall any out looks like the primrose path to paradise. Without my brain quite sanctioning it I gathered myself and launched my ancient bones out into no-man's-land. I landed with a crunch that sickened right through me, not beyond the open door I'd insanely chosen to ignore but in a bruising welter of crashing table and chairs. A third shot with the same resounding timbre went by me like an intercontinental missile and smashed into the wall. This time it drew the lighter bark of the Mexican's automatic firing in return. I felt as if my balls were two feet wide and hanging in the open air to dry. Expectation of that final whip flailing across my chest had liquefied my guts, converted my legs to un-sinewed, quaking appendages beyond the least control. But some-how I had skidded the upturned table round and was down behind its top. Somehow I was still alive. And somehow I had to get to Sam out there, face down trembling on the floor.

The stalemate was restored. And that sort of silence. I took an endless breath, nerved myself, couldn't do it and then rolled left dragging the table with me. Now I was half inside a booth, half behind the table lid. And straight within the Mexican's line of fire. He was down behind the hooker's body and another stool. Looking at me. That face of triangles was now the mask of death. My balls that had felt so big shrivelled into tiny hollow hunks. My navel was a target's central disc. The empty hands I held up shook like leaves.

'With you,' I said. 'I'm with you.'

The voice came out of my emery-papered mouth in fitting key to match those tiny balls. An epileptic ten-year-old's. You didn't have a thing to fear from me. He turned away to cover Tran Chau Chieu.

He had his little local difficulties too. He'd dived behind the counter's other end. He had to show his face to fire a shot. He had a knife stuck in his gun arm and no chance in the world of getting to the door. He couldn't know for sure the Mexican and I weren't double teaming, couldn't even know for sure I didn't have a gun. It all explained his lying low. None of it helped me get to Sam without risking my life. I didn't move.

Minutes ticked by in my head. Two perhaps. Two hundred. My thudding pulse had lost the tick of time. The whoosh I could hear outside was traffic driving in eternity. My dryness, wetness, my sweating, clammy self was barred for ever from that bright, clean, shiny normal world. I had waited too long. The trembling fit was on me head to toe, uncontrollable, an old man's ague. My teeth were chattering. Odd for a man alone to worry about death. I had a sudden, gathering sense that I would shit myself. That would be too much.

'Cover me!' My mouth had screamed from far away.

I burst from cover full tilt to meet my Maker. I thought I'd take the briefcase on the way. As I lunged gasping at it I was clear within that murderous fucker's sights. Our eyes locked and I consigned my soul to whoever had tried to fashion it. At that instant the Mexican opened fire. Wood was gouged from counter and from wall. On startled reflex Chau Chieu fired lefthanded as I was on the turn. A fiery hammer smashed into my leg. Something tore. A dam was burst and sudden, scalding nausea went flooding to my guts. I was suffused inside and out in thick hot soup. I kicked and stumbled into Sam. The Mexican fired twice more as I pummelled, dragged, pushed her to her feet, on to the rear door. My back felt broader than the Pantage's wide screen. You could miss a barn door and still get Powell between the shoulder blades. A shiver convulsed the spine I thought to lose. Through! A staircase and a wooden door. I wrenched it open, pushed Sam out. I was scalded all anew. Right across the eyes. The sun had drawn the straightest bead of all.

I blinked some kind of watery vision back and looked to right and left. Your everyday back alley, USA. Trash cans, shabby wooden double doors, telephone wires, dust in a dirtied sun. I moved us out of any line of fire. I shouldn't have. My leg, given time to think, screamed back in protest. I made myself not look

149

at it. I looked at her. She looked like I felt, mad-eyed, panting, gasping for breath.

'He lock the car?' I got out.

She shook her head.

'Don't think so. Too busy watching—'

Her tiny voice caught and broke off.

'Look at your leg!' she gasped.

I looked anyway. Another mistake. There was too much bright red blood gathering on my shoe. The trouser leg was too much sodden high and to the back. I felt a stickiness all over. I saw the earthquake start as the sad, uncared-for buildings slowly swayed. Christ! I shut my eyes, lowered my head. I made myself hang on. Behind, on the Western front, all was quiet.

'You drive?' I said.

'Yes.'

'Put your arm round me.'

Two lovers, the trainer and the crippled half-back hobbling off, we started down the short length to the cross street. It hurt. It hurt. The nausea came swimming up again to make me want to heave. I felt so weakly hot. But God bless America's right-angled thinking. You always know just where you are. Even with your eyes down when you daren't look up. We turned the corner. Flecks of blood, my blood, spangled a flagstone. We kept on. Left again wheel. All I needed now was a stray cop or a mobile blood donor's wagon. Must write a screenplay. The one about the vampires working in the blood bank. 'It's my birthday—let's crack open the O '64.' Why did I hate those far-off, unreal movies so? And love them. All so lovely and unreal. Like this. Far away in a silent movie the major thorough-fare stretched arbitrarily so bereft of traffic a cat could cross its dusty width with all the languid time in this sunny world. Steady the Buffs. Do it by numbers.

'Is it open?'

'Yes.'

'Get inside. Put it in park. Release the hood.'

She did. The bonnet weighed seventeen ton. But counter

balanced ... Otherwise I wouldn't have got it up. As the bishop ... I looked at the car's guts. Mine should be half so good. Concentration cleared my meandering mind. A second chance to get a steal on a car. The coil. The battery. I needed a lead. Well, who needs wipers in California. No tools. I tugged. Oh joy, the wire came free. I tugged again and disconnected the ignition. I ran my wire from the coil to the non-earth battery terminal. I pressed the direct contact button. Contact indeed. She fired first time.

I thought to look round. Outside *The Silver Peso* not a single person stood. Those ear-drum shattering detonations had faded unheeded on the Sunset air. The public would stay home and watch it on TV. Vera had died as unremarked as ... Oops, I felt faint, so I crashed the hood down. Its fall revealed across the street a little fat man in shirtsleeves. He stood outside a grey dry-cleaning store with worry in his bearing and his watching eyes. Who cared? Who cared? I slumped giddily, shiveringly down into the car.

'Where—where to?' I think she said.

Soft black wings embraced me tenderly. I fled in free flight down that labyrinthine shaft of comfort that winds to a velvet, depthless night.

CHAPTER EIGHT

Rippling long-distance from where he'd fled among the red stars, yet massive, occupying all my vision, Che Guevara stared unfocusedly down on me ... Praise Mao from whom all things come; pass the barrel of the gun ... Elect a chairman; halt a revolution ... spinning, at the bottom of the long well, unresisting in the green shade of my own private jungle patch, I went back to sleep. An uncertain Time went surely by. I opened my eyes again and, a little sharper now, Che continued to return my stare. He wasn't the celestial mentor I would have hand-picked myself but at least, still hanging around, he was unblinkingly faithful to his charge. I blinked. Swimmingly superimposing himself in a total eclipse of that son of the revolution came a second dead deity of the underprivileged, Sonny Liston. I blinked again. Liston stayed, a sharper, nearer image. He must have nailed me early in the fight.

'Easy. Easy now. Easy,' he said. A Liverpool supporter.

I wondered why his voice was away using the phone when the rest of him was so near.

Deliberately I shut my eyes, waited, opened them again. He was still there. It was Sonny Liston but death or the needle had made him a lot thinner in the face.

'Easy,' he said again. Mark him low on vocabulary.

'You've been out quite a spell,' he said.

'How long?' I said.

Another strange thing. My own voice was phoning it in too.

'Three, four days,' he said.

The Morpheus Kid.

I shut my eyes. Opened them. The world stopped shimmering. I looked around it. Not a world but a room. Pine panels or some wood, dirtied, aged to a dark brown, horizontal. Ditto the ceiling. A pine box. Unfunctionally large. And with a poster, not an avatar, of the late, late Ernesto. They couldn't have dug a hole that big anyway. There was something ... something ...

'Where's Sam?'

'She's OK,' he said. 'She's here. She's sleeping right now.'

'Oh ...'

That seemed like a good thing. My mouth was like a kangaroo's jock-strap.

'I'm thirsty.'

'I'll get you some water.'

He smiled as he got up. He was small. He wasn't a bit like Sonny Liston. My right arm stung like hell. I pulled on it and it wouldn't move. Panic. I'd never play with myself again. I cocked my head to look at the amputation. Now my head stung like hell. The room went into *The Minute Waltz*. For some hours. When it stopped I could see that my arm was taped to the metal side of the bed. A transparent tube was sticking out of it, into it, rather. There was stuff in it. I traced my eyes painfully along and up the clear run of plastic. It ended in a bottle hanging on a bentwood hat stand. There was stuff in that too.

'Here.' He was back with a beaker.

Gently, so that it was only like being drawn, he half propped me up. The water was like wine. I flicked my eyes up to the hatstand. That was like looping the loop.

'Is that OK for me?' I said. 'I'm B negative.'

'It's just plasma. To help out. It's universal.'

'I lost a lot of blood.'

'Some,' he said. 'But you got a lot in you.'

He lowered me down.

'Have faith,' he said. 'This is my business.'

'I'm your meat ... ?'

'I'm an intern at Los Angeles Children's. Moonlighting, let's say. Now you go back to sleep now.'

I was so blissfully happy to obey.

The sun came dappling down through leaves that were gently

autumnal. I couldn't understand why, beyond, the lake could have such a thick mist thickly rising from its surface. I left the trees and came to the lake shore. I had to get across. I began to panic. There was no way. The lake had no beginning and no end. I knew that. It wasn't a lake. It was a river. I stood on its bank. The river mist began to engulf me. It was cold, clammy. The river had no beginning and no end. I shivered in the mist. I had to get across. The wicket-keeper began jabbing my ribs again. I opened my eyes.

The man who didn't look like Sonny Liston was looking down at me. Behind him I could see Sam. She looked pretty.

'How am I?' I said.

'Pretty good,' he said. 'Temperature got up a little but it's gone down now. It's time you had something to eat.'

Sam had a bowl in her hands. He levered me up. It wasn't so mind-rending this time. All I had was a fierce throb in my thigh. Well that would be because I'd been shot there. The umbilical cord had been severed from my right arm. I took the spoon Sam silently proffered and sipped lukewarm broth from the bowl she held. I was ravenous.

'That's nice,' I said. 'You make it?'

'Yes,' she said.

'It's nice,' I said. 'Where am I?'

'In a house in Laurel Canyon.'

'Whose house?'

'Jimmy's,' she said.

'Mine,' he said.

'Oh. How's my leg?'

'How does it feel?' he said.

'Aches. Quite a lot.'

He nodded.

'You're a lucky man,' he said. 'You got a hole all the way through. Small bullet with a cap.'

'How bad?'

'Took a lot of muscle and some sinew, I'd say, with it. Never touched the bone. Missed the big nerve. You must have had the leg bunched up. Bullet went from inside to out.'

'So how bad?'

'Tissue'll reconstitute in time, if you keep favouring it and don't strain it. I couldn't operate up here in a place like this but I wouldn't have operated anyhow.'

He laughed.

'Even if I was qualified,' he said. 'I did a little stitching and strapped it up real tight.'

'How long have I been here?'

'Four days.'

'And why are you doing this?'

''Cause I anticipate you paying me.'

I relaxed a notch. You can tend to trust people who expect to get paid. I sipped some more soup.

'Besides, Sam's an old customer,' he said.

Ah well.

They waited until I'd finished. Then they went away. The briefcase was in the corner by a ragged pile of *Screw* magazines. I laid back in that cool place and used my pain to sharpen my wits.

I rested my little world of man there six more days. I spent two of them going to the can with Jimmy and Sam pillars of strength on either side. Erect—on my feet—I felt as weak as a kitten. But a kitten has four legs and I only had one. On the third day he said I was stronger and produced some crutches.

'Just barely elevate the foot,' he said.

It hurt and I could feel the strain in the thigh. But he was right. I was stronger and, hanging as heavy as Time-on-your-hands, I could hack it alone.

Time passing was in fact a whole lot less of a problem than you usually find it. I ate like a horse everything that Sam could fix, but, although nominally back to everyday hours, I still felt very tired. I napped the afternoons away. Getting to sleep at nights was the problem.

'Does the leg bug you?' Sam asked.

She was always there, quiet when I needed quiet and ready to talk when I tired of browsing through the little red books.

155

'It's giving me gyp,' I said. 'And that damned group rehearsing to all hours doesn't help.'

'Jimmy says the less dope he gives you the faster your leg'll heal up.'

'I know. He tells me every time he dresses it. He's a great comfort.'

'Nothing much we can do about the group,' she said. 'Laurel Canyon's alive with—'

'Yeah, I know. Just another of life's burdens.'

'You must be feeling better,' she said.

That night the amplified bass throbbed its revenge right into my central nervous system and all the way up to my pain threshold.

'How much got into the papers?' I said to Sam.

There was no help for it. I had to start thinking about the realpolitik of my fantasy situation once again.

'I was wondering when you'd ask,' she said. 'There was just one item the next day. Buried in the news section. I'll go get it.'

A woman, thought to be one Dolores Martinez, had been shot dead in a gunfight between two Negroes who had started a brawl in a bar east of Sunset. The men had both made off unapprehended. The proprietor who had been behind the bar at the time said that they had come in together and then started to quarrel. He'd never seen them before but would recognise them again 'if they get caught'. As for the woman: 'She used to come around once in a while. They weren't aiming to hit her. She just got unlucky, I guess.'

And that was the way it was, Walter. I read it in *The Daily News.*

Requiescat. I put the clipping down.

'Guess we just got lucky,' Sam said.

'I guess. What about the car?'

'I dumped it out at the airport,' she said. 'In the free parking area on the charter side.'

'Good girl. How'd you start it?'

'Jimmy.'

'How'd you get back?'

She blushed a little.

'I hitched.'

'You want to watch out. You can get into a lot of trouble doing that.'

'I'm not complaining. It can have its compensations.'

She smiled. She might boast all she wanted, she would always seem fragile.

'It was the luckiest of breaks for me,' I said. 'How'd you get to know about Jimmy?'

'Like he said. I'm an old customer.'

Ah well.

'What did you tell him?'

'About you? Nothing.'

'Really— He must be— How does he live with the rent up around here? As I recall—'

She smiled again. It wasn't like the first smile.

'He's affiliated, unofficially, to an organisation, you know,' she said. 'They get to need a lot of fixing up. I guess they chip in with the odd donation.'

'I see,' I said. 'I'm being slow.'

'But you don't have to worry. Jimmy's got a considerable ... catholicity of taste.'

'He must have ... Just how much longer do I get to stay here?'

'Oh,' she said. 'I don't know. Not long.'

It didn't take long to find out either. He came back that evening from the hospital and within minutes was conscientiously giving my leg its daily dressing. I didn't like seeing the wound so I was staring straight at him when he looked up.

'Couple more days, three maybe,' he said, 'and you'll be able to stagger on out of here. You're just about mobile, man.'

His point was clear enough.

'Got some place to go?' he said.

I looked at Sam.

'I've got everywhere,' I said.

'How does a commune in New Mexico grab you now?' Sam said. She said it doubtfully.

'I haven't asked any questions,' he said, 'but the way you arrived I reckon there must be people, mean people, looking for you real hard. They find you here and it's bad news for me. And, shit man, you're playing hell with my love life, shacking up here.'

He looked at me.

'You see how it is,' he said.

'Sure,' I said. I looked at Sam.

'Right now New Mexico sounds great,' I said. 'For openers, anyway.'

She smiled in a way full of relief.

'Just how mobile?' I asked.

'Can't totally tell,' he said. 'You'll probably always have trouble with the tendon. Probably got less than a hundred per cent articulation. Leave it a while and then start exercising it till it hurts. That way you can help it.'

'It's OK,' I said. 'I've had a trick knee on that side for years ... Now, what about money? Just how much did your anticipation run to?'

'Oh I don't know,' he said. 'How much you got?'

'I've got a bigger roll on me than an Irish priest at the races.'

'Well ... how's about two and a half.'

'Hey,' said Sam, 'you charged me three, you creep.'

'That was for stopping a life, baby, not saving one. I've got a conscience that's real mean and avaricious.'

'Let's say a grand,' I said.

'That would put me up to AMA scale, sweetheart, and that'd never do. Like I said, I've got a conscience.'

'OK, then, five.'

'OK, Rockefeller. Five.'

We told him goodbye four days later. Two days before I'd had Sam go out and buy us another disposable car.

'Get something used and average that nobody's going to look at twice,' I said.

She overdid it. She came back with a Fishtail Gashog—a stick-shift '62 Chevrolet Corvair. It was true nobody would look at it but neither should she have. Sliding into it with a ramrod-stiff leg was quiet purgatory; getting the seat adjusted comfortably, impossible.

'Shouldn't we wait until dark?' she said.

'We'll go out in broad daylight at thirty-five miles an hour right down Main Street.'

'Jimmy's waving.'

We waved back—for a guy without a shingle he wasn't a bad doctor. She let out the clutch.

We wound ourselves down the precipitous, chalet-hung side turnings of Laurel Canyon, the scent of flower-power heavy in the air. We went out past the Canyon Stores, south on the fast wider stretch and filtered back on to Sunset heading East. Once more the familiar names, the Nathanael West landscapes and then, just beyond, Hollywood Film Enterprises, the turn-off on to the Hollywood Freeway. Like most women she drove well.

'How's the car, now?' I said.

'OK now we've left all those bends behind.'

She gunned the needle up to a freeway seventy and now the smog-capped towers of downtown Yorty land were looming fast to our right. We didn't disturb the delicate monoxidal chemistry of the atmosphere but shot straight on through the awkward interchange for the San Bernardino Freeway. It sped us through East LA a while where somewhere, perhaps, in that Chicano ghetto the man named Olivares who threw a mean knife was getting a second wind. We passed by Commerce and Industry, the greatest of which is Dow Jones. The buildings thinned out. I was back on the road again. I must change my name to Travelling Mat.

The homely pine room where I'd been brought to bed of a plugged leg had had tall, whispering eucalyptus trees outside its window. They had imparted a sea-change, sub-aqueous air to my confinement. Now the madding whirling road in the bright sunshine brought on a strident giddiness. Everyone else was tuned to this streaming world of cars: I was the odd man out. I shut

159

my eyes and, unable to sleep from the pain nagging away below and everywhere, drowsed towards reacclimatisation. We reached San Berdoo first.

'You want to grab some grease?' Sam said.

'I want to drink some drink. Yes.'

We ate at a place from the Donner Party Food Guide and then, four Cokes later, hobbled out into the unclouded, too-hot air to drive a further stage. Sam had only made about a block and a half when on a street that, if it wasn't called Madison, was Adams, a sudden surge of whooping siren assailed us from behind. Ringing a different, distant kind of bell, a red light flashed burningly on and off. Via the rear-view mirror a black-leathered index finger stabbed out it needed us.

'Shit,' said Sam.

She pulled over.

Weak, tired, I wanted to cry. After so much it wasn't fair to be jumped like this from out of a clear blue sky. The Cossack, flared breeches in Gestapo boots, shades, the big iron on his hip, had dismounted, was sauntering up with a masterful casualness. Something in the heart of my resistance begged to be allowed to wilt. It was towel-throwing-in time, surrender day. Why then did I bother at the expense of shooting local pain to cross my good leg over the bad and act as nonchalant as the waves of inside, outside, heat allowed...? He leaned down, peered in, all helmet and shades, tanned whipcord face, through the open window.

'Howdy,' he said.

I'd dismissed all the obvious things—not speeding, not wrong way up a one-way street, the indicators worked. This was a big one and bad.

'See your licence, miss?' he said.

Christ! Had she got one?

She had. She fished it out from her shoulder bag. And current. I could have kissed her.

'There,' she said.

'Where you folks from?' he said. It was his office, not his voice that supplied his question marks.

'Los Angeles,' she said.

'Where you heading?'

'Baltimore,' I said quickly in American. I'd managed some kind of a private Bessemer process.

'Baltimore?'

'See my folks,' Sam said.

He looked hard at us. Handed back the calling-card-sized licence.

'Think you'll make it in this heap?' he said.

'I guess they've got the snow off most all the main routes,' Sam said. 'She's made it before.'

'Well, have a good trip now.'

He started to withdraw. The heat was off. I needed to make it a little more natural.

'What's it all about?' I said. I let a hint of annoyance through.

'Just had word three guys tried to knock over the Crocker Citizens down on First. Driving this model. That's all. Won't get far. One of them stopped a slug in the chest.'

'Hell,' I said, 'who'd ever try a bank stick-up this time of day?'

'Some dumb niggers, I guess ... Take care now.'

Reaching for a notebook he walked away to protect and serve somebody else. We drove on.

'*Che ti dice La Patria*,' I said.

'Whoever wrote the song was never here in his life.'

We worked back to the freeway, accelerated past a bouldered hill from a quattrocento background. The rushing air seemed cool. And as sweet as relief.

Barstow, Klondike, Needles, Powell—our pilgrimage continued. When I get to make a film about the end of the world Barstow's where I'll come. One glance at its dusty edge-of-town shacks and sidings and I shut my eyes, fleeing for long half-asleep miles from further punishment. The Corvair had no air. It got dustily hot inside and then, as we climbed, dustily chill. Then hot. It was uncomfortable plus but maybe, I thought, as we crossed grey, rocky, unromantic desert, Sam hadn't bought a complete lemon after all. Air-cooled, the engine could run on indifferent to the ups and downs of temperature. Besides I heard you can't go down Route 66 unless you're in a Chevvy.

We crossed a black and angry, winter-swollen Colorado—Hi, Arizona—south of Needles and then started a long haul up. By the time we got to Flagstaff I was wilting. Sam broke the tired, protracted silence.

'I take it you don't want to take in the Grand Canyon?'

'Let's just discover a motel.'

'Let's. That snow up yonder's most likely cold.'

We found a place. I laid me down. Sam dressed the wound.

'The stitches are mostly dissolved,' she said. 'It's sort of all glazed over.'

I heard but did not speak. Her hands were cool and comforting and far away. The bliss, the soft seduction of imminent sleep was the voluptuousness I presently craved. I slept as dreamlessly chaste as a post-operative Abelard. When I awoke it was a chill-roomed morning. She was curled about me, granting that ineffable warm comfort and looking like a child.

On the morrow a strange and momentous happening took place. I found myself telling Sam something of my life. It happened thus.

We were many miles beyond Gallup. Earlier we had driven through earth and mesas the colour of dried blood. Beat-up, over-populated pick-up trucks roared up and down in a two-way traffic. We were on the edge of reservation land. Laughing, rolling Navajo kids, unaware of their race's suicide rate, had happily waved us on. Their elders, blood brothers of the useless dispossessed Eskimos, grimly aware of their Federally given lot, stared unseeingly through us with their twenty-twenty vision. Don't ask a Navajo who the Indian givers are. Later, where the New Mexican sixty-six has narrowed down to a single eachway lane, we were breathtakingly buffeted in our grave and lonely eastward passage by a thundering herd of westering freight trucks. Leviathan sons of the pioneer borax wagons, plated by half the Union, the caravan roared by.

It was late afternoon before the last receded, and somewhere about then in the low and orange sunlight when Sam turned to me.

'So what are your plans?' she said.

'I thought you'd never ask ... Just to heal up, I guess.'

She didn't sigh ... She didn't find more words. She just turned back and stared out at the road. I never felt so short of grace. Perhaps it was, again, the subtle intimacy of a long car trip that whetted my sense of obligation, set loose my tongue. Or perhaps in my longer, solo trip across a divide of years, I'd once more reached a time of thaw, the simple need to recognise a loved face, the warmth and wonder of a loving heart.

'I'm sorry, Sam,' I said. 'I just don't know. I'm just so tired. So deep down, inside tired. I've had eight years of the tyranny of non-involvement.'

And then I told her. I told her about London and the films I'd never made. And the films I did—hawking my freelance camera tricks the length of slummocky Wardour Street. I spoke of the sour, dishonest documentaries, the faggotty-smooth commercials, the shoestring, under-financed features, the exploitation from the TV companies. I told her how, just as with everyone, something young in me had died and how I'd woken up one day indifferent, disinterested, convinced by relentless mediocrity that nothing in the game was worth the candle.

'I finally learned,' I said, 'that nothing mattered. What other lesson was there when I'd never done a job I felt had honour in it?'

She was quiet a while.

'Seems like you dropped out before it ever came in,' she said.

'Not exactly. I dreamed myself a foreground interest. Manufactured it. Nursed my wrath and vented my spleen. It helped to pass the time. I set up some jazzy productions and cast myself in the lead. Favourite part was the Self-Destruction Kid. That's a very good one when you want to screw up your marriage.'

I told her a little about Molly. Our marriage. Our divorce.

'Two one-time losers,' Sam said. 'A fellow lodge member ... But I'm sorry that's how it was for you.'

163

I took a deep breath.

'But that was just all warm-up,' I said. 'Because right along then there was a little jumping of the rails. I got involved— quite accidentally, at first—in a very crooked scene. I'll spare you the details because it's very much better for your own good that you don't know them anyway. But you've got to give that "at first" lots of weight. Because once I was in, boy, I could really whip up the foreground action. I was Bogart and Cagney, Marlowe and Spade. The best part of all.

'So,' I said, 'I killed two guys.'

I didn't see her tremble but very slightly, just perceptibly, the car swerved from a straight line.

'Oh, I was the good guy. No question. They were killers and they'd hurt a lot of folks and, ten to one, the law would never have laid its long arm on them. But that's not the point. I chose, I elected, I decided to kill them. Myself. In a kind of dissociated cold blood. It rounded out my fantasy plot.'

Silence fell. The car ran straight and true.

'That's why you came out here?'

'You might say that. Oh, yes. I killed a guy here too. In Anchorage. He was trying to kill me. He killed somebody else. Somebody a little bit like you.'

'How like me?'

'Ask no questions.'

Silence.

'What am I supposed to say?' Sam said.

'Oh—that deep down in your heart you know I'm good and that whatever the world will say you'll always stand by me strong in the knowledge of our love.'

'So I'm an accomplice . . .'

'. . . Thanks.'

'Anything else you might want?'

'Quiet,' I said. 'Sanctuary. An interval. I'm so tired of the surface. Or having nowhere deep to go. And now—now I'm a little better—I'm sick of the smell of killing that's been follow- ing me like a ghost. Like Jimmy would say—I'm bad news. That poor bitch of a hooker that got it—'

'You don't want quiet,' she said, 'you want guilt.'
'Well that's logical. I've got a lot to be guilty about.'
'I know where I can get you a real good deal on penance . . .'
High Sierra. He ran all the way.

CHAPTER NINE

The next, Albuquerque, morning, we breakfasted late. I'd had less trouble getting to sleep, slept longer. Either things were on the mend or I'd grown accustomed to the pain. It was bright, sunny, clear. The old town at the city's centre confronted the present a hint cruelly, with a blank Latin indifference that had seen the parade go by so many times. It's cheap and coarsening, no doubt, to talk about Duke City but at least that gets the sense of history, the awareness of long permanent transience that the Anglo-Saxons assiduously excluded from their West. When, after climbing on fast freeway through the cold blue day, we came to Santa Fé, there was the same air of an old impassive history. The snow-covered, nearing peaks of the Sangre de Cristo had also seen it all before, expected to see and ignore it so many times again. The Indians squatting in the covered walk of the main plaza would sell unchangingly their covetable trinkets of turquoise and cheap silver. Mutability was everything and nothing. That was the legacy the archbishops of Old Spain had left the new frontier before death came to them.

But I am mutable. I can change. On top, anyway. As we approached Taos I could feel my mellower spirits curdling. Maybe it was no more than Sam flipping on the radio and my having to endure the ethnic travesty of Feliciano singing *Muleskinner Blues*. Maybe it was the waves of self-reproach that washed over me when, after thirty raucous seconds, I cut the chords that whined and Sam stared straight ahead in undemurring silence. Or maybe it was the sign in Taos' centre square announcing the diurnal exhibition of paintings by her favourite adopted son. I'd forgotten that we traversed Lawrentine fields. My back went up. When it comes to your liberal fascist it takes one to know one. Kitsch City wasn't big enough for both of us.

Or maybe it was that ever-popular old time favourite, the Trepidation Waltz. Fear springs from the known, anxiety from the unknown. Perhaps the shrill, sour music of inhumanity was being orchestrated in me by the awareness that the next half-hour would conduct me to a world I'd never known. Sam found a barely paved winding rural route climbing through tall pines. I shrank from, was on ageing guard against, the geodesic dome-land I now expected beyond each coming bend. I'd passed my youth a million years ago in the middle of the eighteenth century. What had I to do with Buddha or Lao-tze, Gurdjieff or Kierkegaard, de Chardin or Leary or Marcuse—whichever might be the calf currently in golden vogue among the latterday saints?

'Here 'tis,' Sam said.

She turned the wheel sharply and we jolted off pavement on to rutted corrugated track.

'Hey!' I said.

The cry came less from the momentary stab of pain to my leg than as small release to my overwound anxiety spring. Already I was alienated from the grown-up teenage drop-outs, courtly without but excluding within, gentle but arrogant, promiscuous but narrow, whom I was about to meet. My original meeting invective against Sam had had more of the spontaneous in it than I'd cared to acknowledge.

'Sorry about that,' she said, 'I forgot for a moment you hadn't been this way before.'

'It's OK.'

We were running on smoother, sandy soil now. Two parallel earth-bare lines a Detroit width apart snaked forward through pines that thinly stood on banks to either hand.

'A little earlier and this is snow,' Sam said. 'A little later and it gets real mushy.'

'I imagine. Who, by the way, am I about to meet?'

'Oh ... whole bunch of folks.'

'How come they'll take us in?'

'They'll take me in because I'm what you might call a card-carrying shareholder. My folks left me a little bread and I glommed on to a lump sum once-and-for-all thing out of the divorce. It's quite a big set-up here. You'll see. I was in on the original Louisiana purchase ... We just come and go, you know. Some of us. Some stay all the time. No constitution, written rules. There's a guy called Klaus who's sort of unofficial father figure.'

Klaus. I should have known. Perhaps there'd be barbed wire around the perimeter and packs of German shepherds.

'They'll take me in?'

'Any friend of mine.'

'*Any* friend?'

She turned her eyes off the road in that occasional way she had and smiled at me.

'Any special friend,' she said.

Abruptly the track topped a small rise, ran down sharply and fanned out into a wide clearing. There were buildings and people. I'd sort of expected a clutch of geodesic teepees, their skins beaten out of old car bodies. Or maybe just a crude litter of disembowelled cars, woodies, hearses and such—directly used as domiciles. Instead, to a goodly number, I saw log cabins, creosoted and substantial. They stood at random round a general central grassless area where with a honking, hooting flourish Sam brought us to a halt. Even before she hit the horn or brakes, kids were running from all directions. Behind the kids, more circumspectly, came a handful of tall adults. Arrested, brought up a little short, after the long ongoing motion of the car, I took a deep breath. It was time to become a social animal.

'Hey!'

'Hey, Sam!'

'Hey, it's Sam!'

'Samola, baby!'

I had to take time easing myself out of the car but I purposely dragged it and my legs out for as long as possible. When I raised my head above the car roof, Sam, the centre of a smiling, kissing, clasping, hugging bunch, was the injury-time scorer of the equaliser. A big blond guy had an arm around her waist. A little dark woman was New Yorkedly jabbering away.

'... wondered how it was going for you,' the woman said.

'Like always,' Sam said. 'Cities of the plains. Dust and ashes. Lousy. Zilch. Instant high the moment I see you guys.'

Charming. But accurate in the first particular. Thankful for my à la mode Anchorage parka, I crutched my way round the front of the car and successfully fractured their group dynamic. Faces, Zapata moustache, Negro, pretty chick, big and blond, turned questioningly my way, turned less obviously back to Sam.

'This is a friend of mine—Richard,' she said.

It became 'Hi, there' time, so, making a feature of looking folks straight in the eye, Richard nodded. The big blond guy advanced himself one step forward from the crowd, a sheriff and his deputies. He extended a white-haired, powerful forearm.

'Glad to know you, Richard,' he said, 'I'm Klaus Holt.'

'He's British,' Sam said.

'That right?'

Grave-eyed kids, serious a second, were also trying to sum me up as I took his hand.

He really was big. Taller than me and burlier. And younger. Thirty-eight around the waist, around thirty-two in years. He had yellow, Swedish hair that he wore in receding enbrosse fashion so as, somehow, to emphasise through the resulting high temples the broad, shrewd, thrust-slightly-forward face below. The nose had been interfered with heavily in high-school football days. Faint old scar tissue ringed the wing of one nostril, fading into the cheek. The lips were balancingly thick. But shrewdness came from the grey-blue unblinking eyes. A touch of Beethoven. In Europe it would have been the face of a tough peasant well able to hoe his own row, pull his own plough. In America, three generations later, it had already, indefinably grown far less uncomplicated.

I extracted my hand. Circulation would return in time.

'Here to stay?' he said to Sam.

'Yes ... I guess ... for a while,' she said.

'Two of you?'

Sam nodded. Hesitancy flickered in a brief smile across her face.

'Yeah, well ... Cathy's in where you ... listen, the O'Donnells are on a trip down into Sonora. Their place is empty right now. Easiest thing is you go in there. For a while.'

There was no great emphasis but suddenly everything was for a while.

'That'd be great, just great,' Sam said. 'That's ... ?'

'Fourth cabin over there. Bring any food with you?'

'... No ... I guess we kind of forgot...'

'Come and eat dinner with us tonight. Tomorrow you can get the things you need. Cases?'

'In the car.'

'Drive the car over,' I said to Sam. 'I'll make it easier on foot.'

People said stuff about seeing us later and getting acquainted and, as Sam got in the Corvair, began to go back about their several businesses. The kids were less resoundingly polite. Loosely, not getting yelled at from any source, they hung around. So did one of the men, tall and gangling, a fugitive from a Davy Crockett suit.

'Name's Tom Howard,' he said, 'I'll walk you across. Ground's kind of treacherous, I'd say, for those contraptions.'

Klaus Holt was tagging along as well.

'Thanks,' I said, 'much appreciated.'

I almost had the feeling I could throw them away and walk. Sam was half-way over to the house.

'What you do to your leg anyhow?'

I should have.

'Had a bullet go through it.'

'Gee whiz! Only hurts when you laugh, eh? How'd you manage to get in the—'

'Watch out for that ridge,' Klaus Holt said quickly. 'We put a cable down there a couple of weeks back and the earth needs a mite more tamping down. What do you think? This what you expected?'

'Sam sort of chose to surprise me,' I said. 'And that's what it is. A surprise. I didn't think it'd be anything like so—finished.

170

Did you build all this up from—?'

'Didn't basically build it at all,' Klaus Holt said. 'Speculators put it up. Idea was it should be a sort of hunter's motel. Sort of weekend retreat for citified mountain men. It didn't go. Never was a paying proposition. Not high enough for serious hunters. A little too rugged for your weekend sport. There's no ski slopes round here—too many trees—but there is enough snow to knock three months out of the commercial year. And so on. It's a long story. I'll spare you—but one of us heard about it through a family connection. And finally a bunch of us bought in on it as an association.'

'It must have cost,' I said.

We were nearing the cabin and the Corvair.

'Oh it did, sir, it did. But less than it took to build. And dirt up here's still cheap.'

'Hello again,' Sam said.

We were at the car. Tom Howard darted forward, eagerly beaverly, to help haul at the sparse luggage. I started forward.

'Mind you,' Klaus Holt said sharply and stopped me with his voice. The Confederate eyes stared at me slatily. He not only had peasants but a whole slew of ancient mariners back among his forebears.

'Mind you,' he repeated, 'we've put a deal of work ourselves into this. We've got our own generator and a back-up. We've got a great mother community deep-freeze. We've got officially approved schooling. I tell you this because the physical set-up we've got going for us here will tell you a lot about the sort of people we are.'

He looked at me.

'But we can talk some more tonight at dinner,' he said. The lips went into a smile and then, wavering at last, the eyes had followed crinkling the skin at their corners. I was dismissed.

'Gee whiz. That sure is a sharp case!'

Tom Howard was holding up the little black bag.

'Must be just jampacked full of Classified Information,' he said.

'Nope. Just money,' I said. I don't like being lectured to. I turned to Holt to see he got that message. The crease had vanished away from eyes and lips. I didn't hear him laughing.

'Why don't you mere women go wash the dishes and leave us menfolk here a while to smoke our cigars and have us some mantalk?'

Said Klaus Holt.

'Like shit, fuck, cunt,' his wife said. 'Big deal. I'm seriously considering founding the local SCUM chapter. You just watch it, Svengali. If it weren't for the kids...'

All the same she stood, started to collect the dirtied plates. Short, page-boy auburn, thin, she was called Judy. Sam made a second pile. Careful of their teetering loads they headed for the kitchen.

'Pot-keeling time,' said Judy.

Klaus looked at me across the white Eames table.

'Want one of those?' he said.

He proffered me a smoke. It was shorter, darker, more un-kempt than you'd buy off any shelf.

Ho hum. I was polite enough just to shake my head. His cold flat eyes stared at me. Or were they simply cool.

It was talking time.

And as good a time as any. I'd been wined and dined quite royally. Meatloaf and Californian chianti—but both damned good. And dispensed with an equal, surprisingly courtly mien. Klaus took his role of host with a graciousness that brought largesse to the simple elements of the meal. I found myself ad-miring the slow-paced style as he smalltalked through the courses, unquestioning, with stories of his Madison, Wisconsin, past. Sooner or later the cross-questioning would start but for the moment I let the engendered well-being ease along my veins. It helped efface the mean, bad happenings I'd just been through...

The O'Donnells' place was the refuge right for me. It was fur-nished with books, Indian rugs and, in an inner room, a low wide bed. I hopped in at the door and found myself perusing the line of titles running straight across the longest wall. I felt homesick for the upright spines of my own old friends and only by the weight of concentration—the heart of this collection seemed geology—kept the weltschmerz down.

'It's cold in here,' Sam said.

I realised it was: that I felt very tired.

'I'll light a fire,' she said.

'If you don't mind, I'm very tired. I'm going to go lie down.'

Fully dressed I stretched out on the bed. I didn't close my eyes. I stared, instead, at a Navajo rug hanging on the wall. It was worked in small triangles of black and red, worked in a stark zigzag pattern on a cream background. Suddenly, somewhere inside, I got the shakes. The enormity of isolation hit me. I was in a strange room in a strange house in a strange land. I was estranged from home, from all the people that I'd ever known. Like Cain, my prototype, I was estranged from grace. Alone. I got colder and colder. My thumping heart pumped ice down to the hollow of my stomach. Alone. But then, for the first time in years, not at the point of a gun, abstractedly, I was afraid to die. I only had, what, thirty more years and then the cold, cold ground enclosing, enfolding, extinguishing the uniqueness that was me within that clammy slot. My heart increased in speed. A thought had struck me terrifyingly. Death was not a terminus. Infinitely more terrible it was a terminator and I ... I of all people ... I lay there very still wrapped round with fear for longer than I knew how to calculate.

'Fire's lit!' Sam said.

She came in through the door.

'You OK?' she said. 'You look—'

'I'm cold,' I said, 'sort of got the blues.'

'Well get underneath, silly,' she said. 'Here.'

She lay alongside me and pulled blankets around. I held her uncomplicatedly close. After a while I felt warmer. After a long while it was time to go and eat.

... Klaus struck a match and nursed the joint alight. He shook the match out.

'Thought you'd maybe like to talk,' he said. 'About yourself, for instance.'

I looked around the room. It was surprisingly far less home-spun than the O'Donnells'. Plenty of space had been left around furniture deceptively subtle, simple in its use of chrome and plexiglass, its organisation of strong, basic shapes. On a low white table a brilliantly polished camshaft was displayed for its own sculptural form. The only splash of colour came from a forties Coca Cola autograph dominating on the wall, on a gules field and redolent, somehow, of Patti, LaVerne, Maxine. It was other-wise a case of log cabin to White House. Earlier the furniture had been enhanced by the warm presence of the Holts' two little girls. Both sub-ten, they had that rare quality in kids of a spon-taneous, carefree courtesy. Without angling for cookies. They put me in mind of one chapter that my past had never written. One book that had never been opened. Their niceness was dis-comforting. I was glad when their bedtime came.

'That's a nice lamp,' I said.

'What the machine makes—is good,' said Klaus. 'Functional. Exact. But about yourself?'

The women's voices fluttered in the adjacent, well-stacked kitchen.

'You promised to fill me in some more on the nature of your not-so-little set-up here,' I said.

He smiled regarding me.

'OK. It comes to the same thing in the end, doesn't it?' he said. His eyes were steadier than mine.

'Well, we've got all types of people here. All types,' he said. 'People like Tom Howard who's a simple straightforward country boy who does wonders with our corn but—mostly people a little like me. What for want of a better phrase we will call semi-intellectuals who have opted, for want of a better phrase, to drop out. There are no rules, right? We combine resources when it seems a good idea—go our own ways when the mood takes us. What we aren't is a bunch of acid-head, hard-rock, mainline freakouts. And that's what's important. We try to run a steady ship. Durable. We've got a little money invested in a few well chosen funds, for instance. That may surprise you but we have to if we're to last. What we're about is lasting, solid reality. And part of that is compromise.

'Oh I've been so far down and so way out and up so high and all at once, you wouldn't believe. Man, was I in bad shape. And believe me ... there's no truth there. It's easy, easy, so very easy to flip your lid and trip out all the way. Any way. It doesn't matter which, so long as you get so bad that other people have to come to serve you, save you, minister unto you. Or as long as you go away so far you don't have to do those things to them. But compromise, balanced, open compromise—that's hard.

'So we don't have a personal morality thing. What we have is this. Suppose it was Sam needed an abortion. Now I might not privately think that very nice. But that's OK. That's fine. That's cool. Go right ahead and see she has it. Have it right here. That's fine too. But do it in a way that has the law—the outside law—coming in on us like gangbusters—and that is not so cool at all. They're all out there. There's a whole pack who'd like to see us off. They choose to see us like the freaks we're not.'

He looked at me.

'Dig?' he said.

'I dig a whole heap of old down-home expediency.'

'Well, sir, seeing as I truly do believe you have—or had—a bullet in that leg and seeing's I think that case is full of money, I think a little old down-home expediency might not come amiss.'

There was something in the slow, long-paced delivery, the unhurried pauses while he drew in the sweet, thick smoke, that got to me.

'Well, if you think I'm such a major threat to your Mansfield Park,' I said, 'I might as well—'

'Man, you're hostile. You know that? You're hostile. Is that a national characterist—'

'If I'm hostile it's probably because you've been snotty—inferentially snotty—ever since we met this afternoon. I don't need lectures on the obvious to let me know—'

'It is obvious, then?'

175

'Of course. You've got a perfect right to know what sort of stranger's lodging at your hearth. That isn't in dispute. What I'm sore at is the air of—complacent smugness you wrap the whole thing up in. And it's a two-way street, I might point out. Maybe I don't think the local climate's worth a revelation. Maybe I'd rather just shove off—'

'I don't want to kick a lame man out into the cold, cold world,' he said. 'There's Sam. She likes you and she hasn't had a lot of liking lately. All I want is you should level with me—in the context I explained—about the ... well, the gangsterly vibrations I picked from beneath your prickly skin. I'll tell you, I'm a guy with hi-fi antennae.'

'OK,' I said. 'Sam could tell you anyway.'

'She wouldn't.'

'Well—either way ... actually you're completely justified. I'm not what anyone would call a good risk. In any context—'

'Have you two beaux 'bout finished off your port?'

The aproned Judy didn't shift his eyes off me. He didn't look annoyed.

'Not quite, I'd say,' he said evenly. 'It's kind of personal right now. Why don't you two—'

'Look,' I quickly said, 'three days. To rest. To think. To get my head set right. Then I tell you straight. Or go and leave you, none the wiser, out of my affairs.'

He only thought five milliseconds.

'You got a deal,' he said. He grinned. 'Come on in, Judola,' he said more loudly, looking at the door, 'and pray have pardon on an old curmudgeon who will insist on keeping things to himself.'

The ladies rejoined the men. Judy looked at him with sardonic admiration.

'That's only so I'll pleasure you in worming them all out,' she said.

'Correct!' he yelled and pulled her to his lap.

'It's party time,' he said. 'Let's get some people over.'

He looked at me.

'You can get to know the folks.'

There was a house-to-house telephone set-up throughout the settlement. He picked up the government surplus receiver and, issuing invitations, got on various lines. Over they came. Guy and Carol and Ted and Hanna. Pat and Mike. Jack and Jill. You know the sort. They were all younger, a lot younger than me. They all had moustaches like Elliot Gould. I sat, a tangent to their circle while too little beer and too much talk circulated. I felt withdrawal pains come o'er me fast. This group—further out, en masse, more superficial than the Holts—was precisely the expectation that had put my back anticipatorily up. Their banalities made me feel old and threatened.

I lay low and said nothing. The talk was cheap. Manson should have been gassed, set free, analysed, given life, honoured as the overt Superman and, product of Society's secret logic, was Calley's blood brother. Check one. Repression was the ruin of the middle classes. Patriotism was the first refuge of a President. Christ was a guerrilla freedom fighter, an existential political opportunist. Jackson had had that phony rap beaten a country mile. The best pot came from your own back yard.

Everyone was aware of me, talked a little louder, a little more flashily, on my account. But, for a long time, nobody solicited my views. There were more joints going around than books in a circulating library. My immediate neighbour, a plumpish, dark, Italianate sort of girl turned to me, proffered one with studied, thunderous indifference.

'You use these?' she said.

I shrugged.

'To be sociable,' I said.

Taking in plenty of air as well, holding it, I inhaled. I hung on to the joint and took some more drags. After a while it had an effect on me. I started to get a sore throat. It was about as good stuff as I'd sampled in London and about as boring. I had far too much psychic, puritanical block.

'Pretty good grass, huh?' Lucrezia said.

That broke the spell. I passed on the key to the doors of perception. For a while longer, trying to see for myself, I'd let my flesh be grass enough. I looked at Sam. Across the group she was casually part of the chain gang.

Conversation failed to flag. I began to opt out. My leg ached and it was getting to my head. The sweet smell of excess hung juvenilely in the narcotic air. I became aware, just in time, that someone was addressing me.

'...you do? I mean how do you earn your daily bread?'

General Lull rode in to put down the insurgent talk. With misplaced politeness heads turned. My interrogator was one of the younger girls, intense, fine-drawn, ugly. I was too tired to invent. I tried to pass it off lightly.

'Way back to home I used to screw around in films a little,' I said.

I'd over-underplayed it. It came out as the false modesty of a great man, a glamorous knight. I'd put myself back on the old, old conversational treadmill once again.

'Hey, groovy!' Joan of Arc said.

'What did you do—exactly?' a young man said sharply. He was one left over from Mathew Brady. I knew from his tone of voice that now he felt threatened. Threatened by the imagined kudos of my job. Upstaged. So much was he at one with the Supreme Whole.

'Cameraman,' I said. 'Used to shoot commercials and so on. All very meretricious. Glad to be away from it.'

'Ever work on any real films?' he said, his prejudice showing.

'There are no real films.'

That was too harsh. Blessed are they that suffer fools gladly.

'Well, if there are,' I went on, 'I never found them.'

'Rat race, huh?' said Zappa.

'Pretty much.'

'Too commercial?'

He was making it all seem desirable again. By contrast. I nodded pleasantly. I was thrice blessed. Richard Trebilcock.

'Hey!' said Joan of Arc, 'wouldn't it be just a groove to have a film record of what we've got going up here.'

There were some grunts and murmurs infected with enthusiasm. Something snapped.

'You must be joking,' I said.

It wasn't time yet to possess the patience of a saint.

'No, really,' she said. 'Really! ... Like—completely unstructured ... See, everybody writes down places on a piece of paper —the vegetable gardens, the deep-freeze, the school—and everybody writes down times, dates on another piece of paper. Put all the papers in two hats and draw them out alternately ... Cornfield, Friday, twelve-thirty. So you go film it right there. Doesn't matter if nothing is happening. That's good. That's part of it. Then you put it all together—edit it—in the order it's shot. Maybe you don't even cut out the mistakes. It's random, see. Unstructured. Like it really is. In Art School once we used—'

'Listen, dummy,' someone said. 'You going to have an unstructured f. stop, employ a random focus? Maybe you'd run the film through an unstructured camera. At random speeds. Look, put the damn tripod—if you deign to use one—down in one place as opposed to another and you've made a comment. An editorialising, including this, excluding that comment. Use a given lens, even if it's the only one you've got, and you're imposing a certain framing, certain perspective—'

I liked that, liked it a lot. I liked it so much I realised I'd been the one who said it.

'Look,' said Joan of Arc, finding that burning's not so hot, 'all I wanted to—'

'I don't know why it is,' I said, angry now, wound up. 'Nobody thinks they can write sonnets or cast bronzes but every goddamned sixteen-year-old from Maine to Texas knows all there is to know about film. Everybody is their own favourite film maker ... I mean, I've eaten cheap shit from every cut-price producer who ever tried to pinch a penny. I've run up against every low-key, off-hand poseur of a genius the critics ever myopically acclaimed. But give me one of those two-faced sons of bitches every—'

'All I was trying to—'

'Look—'

'Aren't some people fucking rude ... All I was trying to say was that you could make a damn fine, stand-out documentary right here, right now.'

'You're wrong,' I said. I was sounding more and more American wherever I was speaking from. 'You'd have a mess. An unstructured, unwrought mess. Full—'

'That's just—'

'Full of random, half, quarter, un-truths. And who needs it? You guys don't. Train a camera on a place like this and you kill its spirit stone dead. You bring in self-consciousness, awareness—differences. Just try peeing naturally with a camera focused on your dick. And afterwards everyone breaks his back trying to duplicate what he or she thought they saw hanging there on the screen ... What'll you call it? *Taoists on Parade?* ... You want a documentary—I'll give you a documentary ... How about—how about the one on the Negro poor in Chicago? You ready? Right. Long shot, establishing: Greyhound Bus Terminal. Voice over: "Chicago is their Mecca. Every day, every hour on the hour, the buses wheel them in to what they think will be the Promised Land..." and so on. Or how about a searing indictment of pollution? Shots of garbage dumps and oil-slicks and smoke stacks and phone cables and such while—get this, the Roger Wagner Chorale sings "America the Beautiful" on the track. See, irony. You—'

'Listen, you bastard,' Joan started aiming the stake at my heart.

'Seems to me,' Klaus said quickly, 'they could be two pretty good films. If a man didn't overplay his hand.'

He stopped to light up again.

'You sure you got it right?' he said.

'Sure I'm sure. We'll run them all on NET.'

'Well ... what's the right way, then?'

'The right way's to live with it for x years, then go away and think about it for y. Then set down on paper the residual ... Fiction is truer than fact and ... oh, shit...' I felt the cheap fool I deserved to feel. I stood awkwardly up.

'I'm tired,' I said, 'I'll duck out. Pay no attention. I always got it out of focus anyway.'

Sam was already holding the door ajar.

*   *   *

It struck chill outside. And dazzling. The full moon was whitely brilliant. The country stars prodigal in the cloudless night. My head felt light in the streaming fresh air. Serve me right for looking up. Serve me right again. I all but stumbled. Sam's arm came warm around me. She supported my one-crutch hobble to our little grey home in the west. Reversing tradition, she helped me unlightly cross the threshold. Now it was gently warm. She had learned her fire-lighting lore well. Embers on the hearth still glowed faintly through the dark. She moved away from me and attacked them. Sparks shot their golden shower upwards and then died away with the weight of a fresh log. A silhouette, Sam rose slowly to full height. She stood still, her back to me, looking at the fire. Her hands made indecisive movements. The question hung in the air along with our silence.

Suddenly my sense of shame at my abuse of self, the cheap extravagance of mindless rhetoric I'd just indulged in, vanished away. It ceased reverberating, humiliating, in my consciousness, had happened long ago. I leaned my crutch against the wall and limped across to Sam. I put my arms around her, the left low across her waist, the right high. My hand put gentle pressure to her small breast.

She turned in my arms. Moonlight came into the room from somewhere magically to soften her face. And to show doubt, the shadow of hurt, in her dark eyes.

'I started it this time,' I said. 'You don't have to worry. You don't have to think. I started it because I'm a little old and pretty foolish and I simply want to come here against you and hold you and rest.'

The eyes that looked at me were still hesitant, searching my face. Smoky. Softly, I kissed her.

It was that for a while—the soft, passive kiss of people strayed and lost, finding in each other's tenderness that universal comfort and repose. And then the alchemy that always happens came to pass. Some line of sensibility was crossed. Our mouths were active, probing, fierce, provoking, panting, competing, summoning. We communed with tongues of fire. I surfaced, held her thigh to thigh. My hand at her breast was rougher now, swelling the race of her pulse. Her mouth worried, hot, damp, soft, upon my cheek.

'Do you ... do you feel up to it?' she said.

'In every way.'

She helped me into the bedroom. It was colder there but not, as you might say, so you'd notice. She helped me undress. She'd done so several times in the last few days but always with an almost purely functional, with a mutual almost impersonalness. Now there was a caressing, lingering ulterior motive to lend frisson. She rose erect from taking off my sock. My leg was not alone in stiffness as I lay down on the bed.

More quickly, deftly, as women always do, she stripped her own clothes off. Finishing, she stood a moment, straight and slender, long hair, long body, as I looked up at her through the faint light. There were soft highlights on the upper roundness of her breasts, abruptly divorced by that sweet firm swell from the inky, masking darkness that cupped them below. Black shadow possessed her belly, her hips, the loins that lay between. I sensed rather than saw the long run of leg, sensed rather than saw that inner, darker triangle of primary and final, alpha and omega thought.

Then she was crouched above me, bending, kissing. Her hair hung teasing down, musk-filled, brushing a silky stimulus where it fell with delicious, intermittent unpredictability. I lay passive, letting her work her glorious magic on me; letting her own initiative, own discretion erase the pain from memories of all the times before.

'Like this?' she said.

'Yes,' I said, 'like this.'

Then she was on me, around me, enfolding me. I lay back as she commenced her swaying, gyrating, thrusting ascent towards the summit. I lay back and enjoyed it. And then, as the pace quickened I was no longer still, a trace aloof, but involved and caught, totally joint in reciprocal service. Thrusting myself now, moving with her, ridden, rhythmic, I rose up on one elbow and took her breast pressing hard down at me ripe within my mouth. The film of sweat quickened me with its tang as I bit

182

and tugged. Her driving down was fierce now, hard and instinctive, passed beyond her control. She was panting hard, her breath hissing. And starting to moan.

I fell back heavily and, pain in my leg long since lost in the gathering potential for engulfment in that sweetness from my swollen, unboned, cynosure of flesh, forced from my stomach muscles a last ditch counter stand worthy of the fevered momentum of her own final assault waves.

'Yes. Yes. Yes. Oh yes,' she began. 'Yes. Yes.'

At the base of my spine, something gelid but not cold grew liquid with a seed of tantalising promise. My pulse, an ever faster drum, told me of the same approach.

'Yes. Oh yes. Yes,' she hissed.

It melted, was fire, was ice, was bursting, swooning sublimation. My back arched with the possessed strength.

'Yes! Oh yes! Oh yes!' I ejaculated.

Her walls clasped, slackened, clasped. Damp and velvet warm. Involuntarily they shuddered, clutched, convulsed.

'Yes! Oh God! Yes! Yes! Yes!' she cried out aloud. All sinews at full strength, arc-ed and drawn full bent, we were locked ecstatically for one eternal instant. I felt the milk and honey flow back from the cave. And then, as I lay dying, she was down atop me, across me, still and quiet, all passion spent. That was how, without ever having set foot in Saskatchewan, we came together unto Climax.

I lay there in the dark, royal, kingly, enhanced. I know the how-to-do-it books all say that buy them up and read it up and the tops of your heads'll come off just every time, but it isn't like that, like they say. Not half the time. When it happens for you all the way, humility and gratitude are what you need.

She began to stir. She kissed my neck, my matted hair. She kissed the side of my mouth.

'Thank you,' she said.

I kissed her. She sat up a touch, leaning across me, smiling, looking down. She was older now, fulfilled. Wiser.

'Oh John Wesley ... John Wesley!' she said slowly.

'He never found a canyon half as grand.'

She laughed. Her hair swung as she swayed. The most beautiful curtain that I ever saw. She smiled again, mysteriously. Seriously.

'I'd so like to love you,' she said. 'Perhaps I do.'

I nodded. I almost spoke. But I didn't.

She took my hand and held it to her softly beating heart. I let it lightly rest. For a long time we eased each other so. Who knows how well our two dreams coincided?

Then she shivered, back within the room.

'God, it's cold!' she said. 'And I'm all sticky.'

'So am I,' I said. 'Who cares?'

'Isn't it great,' she said.

She snuggled down within my arms. I drew the clothes around. She slept at once serene and free from stress. I know. Drained as I was, I still found sleep a long time coming. I lay there thinking, listening to her breathe. My bad leg hurt like fuck.

CHAPTER TEN

It was too good to last. I had that feeling. There were a thousand
hardfaced reasons, lining up just offscreen like a firing squad,
that meant I couldn't let it. But I can't take too much rational
credit. It was perhaps my superstitious, Protestant sensibility
more than reality that made me seek Klaus out.

For three more nights, Sam and I made love. We got close but
it was never quite as good. The second coming was not like
the first. But again, we were relaxed. There was no straining
for false effect. We knew what we could rise to, and could
wait for an unforced encore. That took care of the nights. By
day we played house. Sam took the car, went back to Taos and
brought enough provender to stock us through the Third World
Uprising. She swept, she scrubbed, she dusted. She was the
straightest hippy east of Cajon. I found a saw and amputated my
single wooden crutch down to walking stick proportions. Sitting
on a kitchen table I straightened, bent, straightened, bent my
leg. It hurt still, loud and clear, and I soon was glad to stop.
But every time I did it, I could hold on and out that little, vital,
longer. The nightly push-ups helped give it tone as well.

Haltingly, I ventured abroad. Sometimes Sam strolled with me,
her hair held windswept across her tanned face. But it better
suited my mood when, the cold sharp weather an acid com-
mentary, I slowly circled the settlement's central area alone. I
could dwell then on my predicament, its ephemeral status quo,
and inch and edge my way towards decision. As if I had the
luxury of choice.

Passingly, I met adults. Some I recognised from the evening at
the Holts', more I didn't. My cheap and nasty philippic was
never mentioned. I found myself smalltalking with all alike in

an atmosphere of wary pleasantness. And briefly. There were a lot of chores demanding to be done, insistent as the seasons. The men and women, young and old, ex-associate professor, ex-GI, were diligent in seeing they got done. They didn't have a world of time for me.

Their children did. For them I had, pro tem., all the charm of novelty. They clustered round whenever I appeared, all shapes, all sizes and most hues.

'What'd you do to your leg, Mr Powell?'

'I just hurt it a little.'

'Gee. Were you in the war?'

'Oh no. I just hurt it in an automobile accident.'

'Dad was in the war but he wouldn't go.'

It was a long time since I'd been with kids. I had to work hard not to patronise them, every one. There was the fair, wafer-thin, nervously forward nine-year-old, Chuck. There was the dark, plump, never speaking, always watching, Sally. There was Greg, with a beautiful face and an assured self-possession that came from effortless body coordination. There was Nan who got excited and let her words bubble over. There was Leroy who got mean but didn't like it when he did. There were a lot of them.

There were a lot and all, of course, different. But all held in common, inheritance from their elders, endowment of their environment, a type of seriousness, an underlying gravity. They laughed and mocked and pointed fun but never without a saving respect. They had nice, thoughtful manners and, in repose, clear, open eyes in grave, unblemished faces. After they had scampered hollering off, those eyes and faces stayed with me. It was because of them that in my lame circuits my own eyes were going, continually, to the skyline of the fronting hill, were ceaselessly scanning the comings and goings of the adult figures through the slope of pines. I knew as I lay alongside Sam at night that neither with probing prowl cars nor, least of all, with a revenge-driven Tran Chau Chieu, could I violate the worked-at, created harmony of this good place for kids.

All the same, the grenade took me by surprise. I watched from somewhere as, so slowly, so agonisingly slowly, it bounced across the threshold of the Vizetellys' strangely left open door. I ran towards it, willing to smother its detonation with my body. But my leg was still so weak my forward motion was like a child's. I moved through oil on hollow limbs. I tried but never had a chance. The grenade exploded inexorably with a deathly, deafening silence. In violent flash-filled slow motion the wooden cabin was rent asunder from within. Boards, beams, furniture spilled lazily away from the fiery centre of the blast. Furnace flames licked up with yellow greed, balefully, gusting stronger as I watched. Nobody—not the cheerful Vizetellys, not their three kids—could have survived. Horrified, will-less, I glided numbly closer. By empty irony, the door frame stood there still intact. Through the darkening smoke a figure now appeared within its vacuous frame, writhing, clutching, dancing to a noiseless scream of pain beyond all bearing. Mad eyes met mine in final acusation as the face swam large. It was the face of all Vietnam. A face I knew. My tongue cleaved to my mouth's roof and then, set free, ruptured the hideous silence with its shuddering cry of recognition. Elsie!

Elsie! ... Elsie!

'It's all right, darling, it's all right...'

Drenched in sweat, suffused with an oily film of perspiration, I was half up from the bed as Sam clutched a restraining arm to me.

'A bad dream. It was all a bad dream,' she was saying.

In the half-light her eyes were anxious, glad to serve.

'What time is it?' I said.

'Past two,' she said.

'I'm OK now. Sorry. Something bad in my head. Try to go back to sleep.'

I stretched back down while, in comfort, she snuggled to me. My heart still pounded, my stomach was still a sickened hollow, my bones still frozen to their marrow. It was a million miles from the aftermath of sex. Slowly I took in the animal warmth. Slowly, Sam went back to sleep. By that time one thing was incontestable. However convenient a hideout, cosy a love-nest I had stumbled into, I must stumble right on out. Whether

187

or not I could cut it, wanted to cut it in coexistence with the Taoists had nothing to do with the case. It didn't come into it. Didn't appear on the further horizon of outer space. The reality was that Tran Chau Chieu had heard Sam speak of here. I had a duty to assume that, however unlikely, he'd got out of that bar alive and free. I had to make the assumption, however far fetched, that he'd follow me here. Sooner or later. In a manner of ancient, immemorial grace, these people had taken me in, afforded me shelter. I could not subject them, in return, to the chance of murderous reprisal, of random atrocity contrived to coerce my restored cooperation hence. I could not, on my soul, dare not, see visited upon them through my own unholy presence a massacre of them, their grave-eyed innocents. As for Sam ... perhaps much later when I'd come at last...

I sought Klaus out early the next morning. Not that he was far to seek. As I roved out his burly, over-bellied frame was evident on the far side of the settlement. I called and he waited patiently in the raw air as I hobbled over to him.

'Old war wound acting up?' he said.

'It's not too bad now,' I said. 'Getting better.'

'Good. I was just going to check the well over. Want—'

'Well?'

'The pump, actually. Pressure's been down of late ... You didn't think all those faucets were plumbed straight into Boulder Dam?'

'I never stopped to think. Just shows—'

'Want to come along for the ride?'

'If I won't hold you up.'

'I've got all day. It's only just down the trail.'

We started out along the main track out of there. I soon got tired. The uneven changes of ground twisted at my ankle and my stick. There were birches silvered in among the pines.

'Where's Sam?' he said.

He didn't seem to mind my snail's pace.

'Gone into town. I happened to mention I was missing getting my Plymouth rocks off so she's gone to buy a fifth or two.'

I'd planted the thought at breakfast to get her out of the way.

'We've got some gin around the house if you're that desperate,' he said.

I laughed a little.

'Oh I'll hold out till the relief column arrives ... It's the nights that are the worst.'

He laughed. We walked a way. I suddenly found the words stuck in my throat. My pledge to tell him just how I stood was already past due time for being honoured. All I had to do was tell him I was on my way. But, in the cold sunshine, I found it hard to say. It came to me with shock that I didn't want, really, truly, didn't want to go. There was a sanctuary here, a weight of peace, just the sort—

'You know,' he said, looking at me, 'another week and you can have that leg examined. George Ehrnsbarger's due back in then. He makes pretty good medicine.'

I looked back at him. The man was telepathic.

'Thanks,' I said, 'but I won't be around. I've thought things over and ... I've decided to take off.'

'Oh ... when?'

'Later today.'

'You aiming to go before Sam gets—'

'No. I'll see her and say goodbye. But I'm not taking her with me. She could too easily get hurt—badly hurt—tagging along with me.'

'And is that why you're leaving us?'

'Yes. There are people looking for me, people I'm mixed up with who could bring you and yours more unpleasantness up here than you'd ever imagine—'

'Sure that's the right reason?' he said.

'How do you mean?'

In the middle of the track he stopped and turned towards me. The bank behind him rose sharply up into a hill shadowed and striped by the straight, thin pines through which the sun was glinting.

'Well, sir,' he said. 'I've been studying your conversational form as you might say. Since I don't have too much time, it seems, let me put it straight. You're kind of a misfit, aren't you?

189

A misfit here, a misfit generally.'

'Really.' Ire at his impertinence went sourly through me.

'I'd say so. Like listening to you the other night. All that hostility. I'd say you've spent too much of your life getting pushed and pulled two different ways. Part of you has wanted to push forward from needs to be an individual, express yourself, be creative. And part of you has always shrunk from that —thought obscurely that in doing so you'd cut yourself off from others, been inhibited by a sense that expressing yourself was, well, exhibitionistic.

'I'd say,' he said, looking at me, 'movie making was about the worst field you could've gone in for a career.'

'Look, when I need a backwoods analyst to—'

'I'm just telling you this,' he said firmly, 'in the fullness of my presumption, because I thought you might be wanting to light out for pretty much those reasons. Wrong reasons. Because you feel threatened. Feel staying with us might mean being submerged in an alien mass.'

He moved us off again, towards the mid-distant bend in the track.

'Thing is,' he said, casually now, 'I feel a little guilty. I leaned on you too heavily at first. Talking to you, talking to the kids about you, I sort of feel that, underneath, you're the sort of person could help us here a lot. And a person we could help. That's all.'

Limping alongside him, I was lost. I didn't know what level to react on. I sure as hell felt threatened now. But grateful too. And, somehow, spent. An open secret had been voiced abroad and shared, and strain was gone. And then again, he didn't know the half. I felt proud as well.

'There's probably a whole lot in what you say,' I said at last. 'I won't give you a fight or pick a quarrel. Like you also say, there isn't any time. I don't have time for hidden motives and such-like subtleties. The primary reality is this. It really was a bullet that I stopped. The guy that fired it's still around. Probably. There are others like him anyhow. Next time, if I'm here and if they track me down—and that can happen—their aim may be even worse. Then it'll be Sam or Judy or Greg or Leroy who gets hit. And that, if you accept that crutches aren't my style, is all that there is to it. Thanks, but no thanks.'

'OK,' he said, 'too bad. Some other time.'

'Some other time.'

A bird was whistling steadily, a clear, low, soothing note.

'It's beautiful water from the well but, unfortunately, the spring was downhill from the site,' he said. 'We've got a little two-stroke pumping unit that runs on diesel but lately—'

'Hold it right there!'

The voice rang out, loud and clear and very English.

Three guesses.

He came out from behind a tree, slithering sideways down the rise, the gun prominent as ever in his hand.

'Put your hands up,' he said.

'Do as he says,' I said to Klaus.

'Take two,' I said more loudly. 'How's your shoulder?'

He came forward slowly, no expression on his murderously smooth face. He reached out an arm. Stiffly.

'I haven't got a gun,' I said.

He searched me. He searched Klaus.

'The truth, for once,' he said. He moved back out of reach. The gun was pointing steadily at Klaus.

'I've been expecting you to drop in,' I said. 'What took you so long?'

It was the only way to play it.

'In the circumstances,' I said, 'I'll forgo the introductions. Suffice to say this is the gentleman who performed a little blood-letting for me.'

He didn't look quite so good. His clothes, cord sort of shooting jacket over Irish sweater, were as high in quality as ever. But the odd invisible spot or two was somehow staining his overall immaculateness. He was fractionally shrunken, his shoulder plainly impaired by its recent adornment. With so much liable to go so terribly wrong, I still felt oddly calm and unafraid, present and alert.

191

'Well,' I said to Klaus, 'I must be leaving now. I have some unfinished business to attend to.'

Tran Chau Chieu nodded in faint acquiescence. He motioned with the gun.

'Let's not delay it further,' he said.

I started to move forward.

'Powell,' said Klaus, 'you don't have—'

He broke off in mid-protest. Froze. For a second we all three froze. Coming fast round the far bend was a car. A beat-up, mud-bespattered Corvair. For that instant, it was the only thing animate, the only thing with life party to that tableau. It slowed as if puzzled, hesitant and then was surging forward furiously, an outraged, vengeful animal.

In no dream now I tried to move, tried to break the spell. My weak legs let me down. Tran Chau Chieu was on me slashing with his gun. As I went down he grabbed my stick and clubbed with it at Klaus. Postponed pain overtook me. My head swam, my vision blurred from its intensity. On my knees, a fighter who'd been tagged, I shook my head and tried to beat the count. Look up! Look up! I did—and saw the nightmare come to life. Tran Chau Chieu was a few yards off, crouched and taking aim. The car was forty yards away driving down on him. I was immobile, rubber-limbed, powerless to intervene. Watching. Tran Chau Chieu fired. The windshield fractured crazily. At thirty yards he fired again. The car slewed madly, broadside-on from its collision course. Canted over, crashing back down again, the tail coming further around, it lurched on sideways, out of, beyond all control. Its shape seemed to have grown distorted even before the snapping trees, the rise of earth, stunned it to a savagely instant halt. The engine stalled. Something whirred and died. No fire came. There was an all-pervading silence. No bird was singing now.

Tran Chau Chieu was safe. I was about on my quaking feet, sickened by what I knew I already knew, as he ran quite lightly over to the car. He looked inside.

'Let her be! Let her be!' I started to scream.

A gunshot cut me short. A different sort of gunshot coughing harshly from high above. The richochet from off the Corvair's roof whined fierce and humourless within four feet of me. Instinctively I flung myself across the half recovered, slowly rising Klaus. I literally bit dust as, a worse than sitting target, we sprawled ungainly there. No shots came. Again I raised my head.

Tran Chau Chieu was crouched down low beside the ruined car. He held his gun like he had shooting on his mind. Slowly he stretched himself full-length and elbowed forward to the Corvair's tail. He reached it and drew breath. My stick lay in no-man's-land. I was figuring my chance of reaching it, of crawling to him, rising up, of smashing it down with all my strength upon his sleek-haired skull, smashing again, again and again, when, thwarting me, he ventured that same skull, peering out around the corner of the car. Instantly a heavy bullet dug up earth in spurts just inches from his nose. I looked to see its source. On the rim of the small hill, alone among the pines, a silhouette stood dark against the sun. Out of pistol range, he flickered, hard to see with all that light behind. He raised the gun and stiffened. A shell smashed clanging like a gong of doom into the Corvair's front. He was going for the gas tank.

Tran Chau Chieu was hip. Without pause he was away from the potential bomb with low and classic sprinter's form. He came right by us, just too far away to trip, sidestepping just before another bullet came. He flung himself into the trees on the near side of the track. He was running hard away towards the bend. High on the rim above the silhouette ran too, flicking mesmerically through the pines in parallel course. We waited long. A distant engine roared to life and raced away. Another shot. Nothing. Silence. All was quiet again.

I dragged myself up. I helped Klaus up. A mottled bruise flared angry on his forehead. We did not speak. We both looked at the car. I didn't want to—better than he I knew—but we had to look. Shakily we walked across. The air was one reek of gin. He paused, opened the Corvair door.

Like in a film, overly pat and neat, Sam half fell out. A little boy named Jamie would never know again his parents' tug of war. Her head hung down. Miraculously, her face, the soft and dangling hair, were quite unmarked, unflawed. I was glad of that. Of that. Otherwise ... It was pitched past pang of grief. The fabric of her shirt was saturated in a graduated circle of red centred, darkest, most thick, between her breasts. I hadn't known that death could be so bright. Or so ironically apt in its timing. As I looked a trace of blood ran unswerving from her mouth slantwise to her neck. It ran with a liquid, unanswerable finality. Her eyes were open. Upside down, they stared at me with a shrieking, animal reproach. They held my gaze. Upside down. Hypnotic. Transfixing. Malevolently seductive. Unresisting I felt them drawing me across the brink of sanity, luring me down to where in madness I could voluptuously surrender up all knowledge of the too intolerable. Like jumping from a high-rise building. I had almost told her that I'd like to love her too. But not quite. And now I could read so clearly in those all-drawing, upside down eyes that as I, living, watched, something quickened by my seed lay dying within her innocent, lifeless body. I felt my own eyes dazzle. I forced myself to blink. In the lowest depth of bereavement I still groped mechanically for the second-hand.

'Cover her face,' I said.

There was a sort of rescue there. As Klaus reached forward with his jacket, conscious thought was coined, however barely, from the flux of instinct molten in my head. It wasn't over yet.

CHAPTER ELEVEN

I left there later the same day. In yet another car. The one I'd borrowed from Klaus. In that sunny place of death he'd straightened up above her body aghast, an automaton. The saving grace of shock had stunned his quick intelligence. 'Oh my God. Oh my God,' he muttered. On and on and on. I didn't speak. Words were the counters of an age long passed away. This was the new world of aftermath.

'Oh my God,' he said.

His voice died away. We stood in silence as time passed. Tentatively, pausing, starting again, the bird resumed its song. Klaus's head came round to look at me. It moved with effort as if against a great viscous resistance. Still he could not speak.

'Well ... ?' I said.

'I ... have to think,' he said.

The sun cut into me, a laser through the eyes.

'I want to get him,' I said.

We were two disembodied voices now hovering above the death-filled pastoral. Three victims formed the composition.

'That's irrelevant,' one said as I dispassionately observed. 'Wrong ... I have to think ... while I do ... you'd best go.'

The other figure pointed to the car. The mechanics of life began their inward flow again. Of necessity we coalesced.

'I can't go in this,' I said.

'... take mine ... go while I pick up the ... park it in Taos close to the Carson place ... Quick! Before I change my mind!'

His voice came to me underwater while bursting light and bird song pierced my brain.

I offered him much money. He would have none of it. None of my cheapness. So, in a car loaned free, I went down that track past a car that had helped cost me the earth. Its door was shut again now. If you didn't know what was within, you'd take it for tin litter, a just abandoned wreck. It disappeared from the rear-mirrored view. I looked ahead down the undeviating path to what I had to do. And thought on ways.

The mode was mandatory—ice-cold logic, wished upon me naturally by a universe ironically intent at maintaining my chemistry at an acceptable level of function. I would do the trip on the suspension of all feeling. Mechanics were the answer. Logistics. Do it by numbers. I must do no more than regard once-felt emotions through a telescope turned the wrong way round. They could lie there for aloof analysis, suspended in cold blood. All save hope. A compact bullet of hope would be vouchsafed me every day—the hope that Tran Chau Chieu had made a clean escape. Every day I would bite on that bullet until it hurt. He was my meat now. He should keep himself for best.

Mechanics. I parked in Taos by the Kit Carson place, left the keys under the seat. I walked my casual and unhurried steps out to the edge of town. There, banished by the standards of inner pastiche, a car lot lay. Even so, it reflected in its wares the all-conforming eclecticism of the place. There was a Saab, a Mini, a Lancia, two Toyotas. And, in pride of place, magnet to my attention and my need, a '67 Citroën Safari wagon. Life is so cute in dealing out its little ironies. We call it kismet, Hardy. I had just lost the sum of all else. Now in trivial recompense I was proffered a former object of desire. Former ... we are so cute in grief, we burrow back regressively to former states. They were grief-filled too. But never as bad as ... mechanics, damn you! Mechanics.

I bought the car. I went, mechanically, through the motions. I drove it hard around the block (it cornered as on rails). I sent it whooshing up on its own self-elevating hydraulics. I depressed the lever, lowered it all but to the ground. Not a stain beneath. (It was as tight as a drum, sound as a bell. A man would be a fool who didn't buy it.) I haggled, mechanically, for appearance's sake and got the nominal fifty dollars off. The salesman shook my hand. (It was a pleasure to sell to the seventieth Limey in town that week on his Lawrence thesis.) I gassed it up, headed on out. In two miles old familiarity modulated to contempt. It didn't change a fucking thing. It was just a toy and she was dead and I still had a two-day drive stretched out ahead.

I did it in one. Non-stop. On through a dark night. By journey's end just one impression stayed with me. Pain. My leg, a numb ache at first, became embedded with a fine network of white-hot wires. And slowly, icy mechanics melting in the long-houred isolation, so did my soul. The true pain, the pain inside, rose sharper and sharper on the terrible curve up to its peak. Another country ... Dead ... Gone. Gone. Gone. To come no more. *But I am bound upon a wheel of fire, that mine own tears do scald like molten lead....* But with my good biting falchion I'd send him skipping to his grave! The swine! The mother-fucking, mother-raping, two-faced son of a bitch of a whore of a swine of ... Rocked in the cradle of the car my feelings were perversely roused from shock. I got high on grief and physical fatigue, a little crazy. At the top of my lungs, till my throat was raw, it was my version now for endless miles of *Muleskinner Blues.* Only the narcotic of final, total, melting tiredness gave me, as I neared Los Angeles again, a deadening relief.

I collapsed that day into a bad motel somewhere in East LA on Colorado; who cared where, it was a bed. I slept for sixteen hours. The body works medicine of its own. When I awoke I was numb again, insulated for action. I ate. I drove to Echo Park and cruised around. The clapped-out frame houses of the neighbourhood offered plenty of places for rent. Mr Sawaya, a smiling, dusty, elderly Filipino, was happy to let me one on Laguna. Smiles. At a hundred and a quarter a month (first and last month in advance) for that equally old dusty apartment he should have been hysterical with glee. I went out and bought some fresh new clothes. I proceeded on up to Hollywood Boulevard. There was not much risk an ageing face would hail me from film times past. Nothing changes. From Grauman's down it was as gimcrack as ever. I steered my way between the sexual panhandlers, still discreetly rife for those to see, and went into The Supply Sergeant. In that littered five-and-ten writ large of all the vicious surpluses that Governments give rise to, I bought a fresh new gun. Fresh new bullets too. When I found a fresh Swiss Army knife, the boy scout in me was appeased. I took my fresh new purchases back to my stale old pad. There, combining them, I dressed to kill. I did it mechanically. When I looked in the mirror I was shocked. I stared for long hypnotic minutes. It looked so much like me. I knew it wasn't and would never be. My future lay enshrouded in the past. But if I wasn't myself and didn't like the too-close resemblance of the thing I seemed to be, at least that reflected alter ego was standing on his own two feet. He could function for all future needs. One need. He was never going to get involved again. With anything or anyone else. He knew that revenge was a dish best eaten cold. I watched as he put on his unfamiliar fresh new shades. I had a sense that I was growing on him. As he stepped around the corner into the Silver Peso I felt that I knew him as well as I knew myself.

I got the glasses off fast. That way my eyes adjusted faster to the gloom. For a moment I thought it was all duped footage of my previous entrance twelve lightyears ago. The same fat barman. Two identical different guys talking Hollywood shop at the identical approximate table. But as the barman's casual professional scrutiny tightened into remembered wariness and his hands dropped beneath his counter, the dislocation of déjà vu was displaced by a very immediate presence. Stickless, I made it to the bar in two wobbly strides.

'Don't try it,' I said softly. 'Just rest easy.'

He looked at me. A big man with tough, thinking eyes.

'Nobody's behind me this time,' I said.

He looked at me. The men behind had stopped talking.

'I've got to see Olivares,' I said a hint louder.

'Who? I don't—'

'Come on! Come on! Want me to call the cops and say what really happened in here? Tell them how much real truth there was in your—'

'He don't come round here since— Since,' he said.

He said it with conviction. His eyes held steady. I didn't frighten him.

'OK,' I said. 'If you say so. But I've got to reach him. It's important.'

A dark amusement bent his mouth, the line of his moustache.

'Maybe he wouldn't think so,' he said. 'How should I know where he's at right—'

'There must be guys. Numbers you can call.'

Held-down animus gave my voice an edge. He shrugged. Considered. He considered the two twenty-dollar bills I pushed across the bar.

'Just leave word I'm here. He doesn't have to come.'

He shrugged again. Nodded.

'I'll see what I can do,' he said. His voice became public again. 'What'll it be? Gin and tonic, right?'

'Right,' I said, 'easy on—I changed my mind. Make it a beer.'

He drew me a glass and retired down to the bar to his phone. I sipped at the soapy stuff, while he dialled and, his back to me, not looking at me once, spoke low and fast in rapid Spanish. He hung up, dialled again, spoke some more. He came back to me.

'No dice,' he said. 'But I left word. Later—tonight—there's another guy I can call.'

'OK,' I said, 'I'll stick around.'

I stuck around nine days. That's how long it took. I drank a lot of beer. You can do that in nine days. To stay on the right side of unwaterlogged coherence I broke it up a touch. I bought a quality Japanese radio and, late at night, in the slow mid-morning, tuned from the slender band of good jazz to the thin thread of classical music that bordered the mindless acoustic wallpaper in between. There were all the routine crises on the news, but not a word of mine. Well I could keep it in mind by staring at the home-made tote bag, made from an Indian blanket, empty at the foot of the bed. Almost empty. It held a memory or two. Forget that! Mechanics! I went out and ate. I went out and bought a stack of paperbacks big enough to swear on. I came back to my rooms. I read the books, played the radio, caught up on my sleep. Mostly, wondering if it would ever be possible for me to face a gin again, I sat watching in the Silver Peso and drank beer. I got to be quite good at it.

Nothing happened. The barman was as solidly, self-containedly menacing as ever. As traffic waxed and waned in the bar, came and went, we observed a strict neutrality. He replenished my glass betimes with an impersonal efficiency while the phone behind him did not ring and the entering customer to whom I'd turned my eyes looked through me with a total stranger's cold indifference. I occupied always the same barstool—the one that I'd once had those lightyears ago before the shooting had to start. I never ceased to watch the door. If he were as persistent as I gave him credit for, it might as soon be Tran Chau Chieu, that murdering mother-fucker, and not Olivares coming through it. That would be my pleasure and simplify my life. And his. Rather drastically. I felt the gun's weight in my coat. One shot was all I asked. Till that night I held my feelings down. Like the man in the mirror. For the present there was nothing else to do but have another beer, read some more, play some more music, have another beer. Time and I maintained another seeming neutrality. It was a lot like most people's lives. Being a solitary drinker didn't worry me. It never has. It's logical. Only drink with people you'd trust your life with.

On the ninth day the phone rang. I was halfway through the bowl of chile size that every evening, with equal apparent indifference, the barman served me. I had the spoon midway between the bowl and my mouth when, timing its electrifying sound shock to the microsecond, the little black sadist finally gave tongue. Kingdoms crumble these days not to the tramp of legions but to that shrill thing's imperiousness in the night. I started and chile slopped back into the bowl. I had the utter certainty, that way you do, the call would be for me. The barman lifted the receiver, listened briefly, looked at me.

'For you,' he said.

He handed it across. I had to suppress a shiver. It was like handling a loaded gun. The barman didn't move. I looked hard at him. He moved heavily away.

'Hello,' I said.

'Who is this?' a thick voice said. Spanish accent, drawn out vowels.

'My name's Powell. I'm the guy who—'

'Sure. I know you. You want to talk to me?'

'Yes. In person. Face to face.'

'Yeah...? What's so important I should—'

'I want to kill the guy you tried to kill.'

Silence. A sound of breathing. Crackling. Not a local call, now I had time to think. Still silence. I'd scared him off.

'You know Griffith Park?' The voice jumped at me.

'Yes.'

'Know the Observatory?'

'Yes.'

'Park there. Walk back down like you was going out on Vermont. First bend you come to there are trees. On the right going down. Step down into those trees. Eleven o'clock. Morning. Tomorrow.'

'Tomorrow morning. Check,' I said.

There was a dry click. A pebble striking a wall.

I put the receiver down. It had been him all right ... I thought it had been him. I moved back to my stool. Sounded like him. A flutter of excitement ran through my deadened nerves. It was a first release of anticipation. Anticipation of action and initiative. I pushed the congealing chile away from me, turned to the watching deadpan barman.

'Gin and tonic,' I said. 'No lemon.'

It was my portion.

The bullets were coming faster now as I sidestepped through the trees. The last was in both my legs. It was harder and harder to run because of the cotton-wool. My heart was thumping louder and louder. Thud! Thud! Thud!

Thud! I sat upright into a pitch and unfamiliar dark. Terrified. Where was I ... where was I ... what room ...

'Come on, Powell. Open up!'

Thud! Memory found itself as the thudding carried over

from the dream. I fumbled, groped, fumbled for the light switch. Click. Light blinding my sockets shut. No time for decompression. Nude but for a wristwatch, I slid out of bed. I think it was the lack of pyjamas that made me hesitate two seconds before reaching for the pillow covered gun. George Raft would have had pyjamas and ... Too late. The door crashed open and three men crashed into the room. I spun, half-moved, equally unhinged. But my arms were professionally held. I started to plunge and strain. From naked instinct. A fist tore screamingly into my stomach. A hand held back my head. The fist convulsed me again. It was minus the velvet glove. I fought for air, for voice, for an antidote to pain. Thrown with full and well-timed weight the fist smashed hard into my unprotected balls. They let me slump. I fell down foetally between them.

'Richard, you can have a biscuit later—there! I told you you'd get smacked!' 'Please, sir! Please, sir! Powell wasn't wearing a box and Spencer's gone and bowled a full toss right into him, sir!' 'Mummy, mummy, I want a biscuit NOW!' 'Teach you what a protector's there to protect, young Powell. Good lesson for you.' Oh God, oh God, just take this pain away and I promise to be good.

'Stand on your own two feet, son. That's all you can ever do.'

... fade up sound, dissolve, fade down, dissolve, cross fade. Forgotten, always remembered, voices, hovered on the edge of retching, crucifying, branding, all-present, ever-present pain. Coherence came and went. Through the layered, eddying mists of pain my ghostly comforter wraithed blackly, atavistically. He'd long since told me, his grin skeletally said, that it was ever thus.

'Get your clothes and cover up your ass.'

A toe cap bludgeoned home the admonition.

I staggered up. The room resounded with applause that sent it whirling nauseously round. I didn't think I'd ever pee again. I lurched.

'Watch him!'

'He ain't going no place. Look at his leg.'

I breathed in hard, dropped my head, started to get my things.

Half doubled up, I slowly managed it. The pain had subsided now to the mere beat of seven-pound hammers on a taut membrane of exquisitely sensitive nerves. One of them watched me while the other two searched the pitiful room with a coarse tooth comb. They had no more respect for things than people. They took my gun, my money, everything. One of them could manage everything quite comfortably.

'That's it.'

One pushed me hard off-balance.

'Move,' he said.

They pushed and supported me out of the door, down steps and out past neighbours that I'd never seen before.

It was funny. From the first split second they'd been framed in the crudely opened doorway, I'd never had any doubt. You couldn't tell from their plain, anonymous car but I knew well enough. They were a sort of police.

They took me for a little ride. I truly wouldn't have minded if it had been the last. Upstairs and down, I'd shipped too much punishment in the last few weeks. Easeful death would have been so softly sweet had it been forthcoming. But no. From my squeezed back-seat position in the air-conditioned nightmare I could see enough, remember enough, to tell me we were heading downtown. That signified interrogation first. Civic buildings loomed up. Abruptly, with a thrum of tyres, we swept into the underground car park of a building not a million miles from City Hall. You couldn't fight this one either.

An elevator nearly as harshly barren as the three faces with me. Corridors of unending, hellish grey and pervasive inadequate light. Arbitrary windowless boxroom lined with steel, painted steel grey. They flung me in and I was solitary room mate with the bug-eye of the television scanner. Perhaps on its account, perhaps on mine, the light in here was now impossibly bright. I sunk to the floor in a corner of the intentionally chairless, cheerless cell and stared out at defeat. It wasn't so bad. Why all the fuss? Just lie back and be comfortably engulfed. I think at that moment I'd thrown in the towel, had forgotten the fell purpose of revenge keeping me alive. Would have told them whatever they'd asked. I'd gladly have put myself down as Lee Harvey's gunning mate if that's what they'd required. Anything for a quiet death. Yes, quiet. No, worse there was not. I let my mind go blank. Some time I'd sleep out. Incredibly, I did.

That several hours respite, intended to soften me broodingly up, was a mistake. I awoke before they came for me and found that in the face of inevitable defeat I still had one tiny resolution intact. I would make it as hard going for them on their run in to the tape as humanly possible. I bitch, ergo sum ... Along with my pain and soreness I had a sort of equanimity when, the same three, they did come.

'Move,' they said. Perhaps it was the only word they'd mastered.

The sterility of more corridors. Unpopulated. But the distant clack of a machine. Steps down. A sense of basement. I looked at the watch they'd left on me. Five in the morning. Bad timing for my personal darkness at noon. As we came to an end door I found—we never cease to amaze ourselves—I had mustered a detached last dignity. They shoved me on through.

I was in a large, harshly lit, overbright room. It was split in two, ceiling to floor, by a transparent wall of plexiglass. On my side there was a kind of counter against the base of the plexiglass and a few bentwood, chipped brown-painted chairs. A whirring air-conditioner kept the atmosphere aseptic, unnaturally chill. So why should I start to sweat? On the other side of the glass there was also a chair. It was made of steel. It was bolted down. That was all. No other furniture. On the otherwise bare wall was a power box marked '220V 3 phase'. Lying loosely on the floor was a common or garden domestic power drill. I felt my dignity slacken. Fast.

One of my three wise monkeys—the one I was beginning to discern held rank—had not followed us through the door. Through an identical door he now appeared on the other side of the plexiglass. Three men came in after him—two more cops and between them a man with hands handcuffed behind his back. He wore only pyjama type trousers in some coarse, grey institutional material. In spite of that—because of—he looked regal. He looked like an African king. He held his muscled body proudly and straight as if to give fit carriage to his wide-nosed, full-lipped, magnificent head. His hair had been cropped short, his moustache was vestigial. He still looked like an Othello with brains.

My erstwhile turnkey advanced in front of him. His own coarse, thick-pored, glazed features paled by comparison.

'Want to talk?' he said.

I got a start. The voice did not come from where I looked but, metallically, from all around. I looked up. A large un-cabineted loudspeaker was hung in the corner of ceiling and wall. The inner room was wired for sound.

The Negro looked down at his tall interrogator through eyes that were a little closed, slightly dreamy.

'Go fuck yourself,' he said.

Using their fists the three whites beat him up. It was a systematic, professional rotation, unhurried. They did not get in each other's way. It lasted about two minutes. That's a hell of a long time for a man hands tied behind him to be beaten by three who know their business. I watched while they beat the living shit out of him. Literally. For a while he groaned and then he slumped to the floor and lay silent, unconscious. They dragged him out. Still a king.

'Move.'

They marched me out one door, in the other. I seemed to feel again in some shrinking, inner nerve centre, the full force of the blows I'd already had to take. Rough hands, large, seized mine and, pinching skin bitingly, handcuffed me behind my back. I sucked my aching stomach muscles in. The same man stood in front of me smiling slightly, his grey cheeks just faintly flushed from the recent exercise.

'Want to talk?' he said.

I drew a deep breath.

'Whatever you want to know,' I said.

I'm no king.

His smile broadened into an open grin of contempt. It hung on his face. As they unbound me, led me back upstairs, I let

205

him have his cheap moment. After a set-piece like that, only a fool would not have expected a lie.

'In here!'

Another door. Another room. Furnished this time like tourist class on the S.S. *United States*. A matching man, medium to small, middle-aged, well-knit, sat behind a black vinyl and grey steel office desk, furnished only with a phone. His sharp, deep-set eyes looked unblinkingly at me, at them, at me again. He did not rise.

'OK Davis, Schroder,' he said.

He had a dry, thin voice, grey like those ice eyes, grey like his suit. His not quite crew-cut hair had once been sandy but was now half grey as well. The two men left the room. He continued to look at me from behind his desk. I looked at him. I looked sideways at my remaining escort. Silence. Nobody spoke. OK. I waited for the opening ritual to pass. Silence. Only the sound of thinking. I looked at them, trying to see what made them tick. Something had to. Once, and as straight cops, they would have had a day in, day out meanness mixed in with the sense of power. Perhaps there was still a hint of that in the latex Marinesque face of the lieutenant. But none of it in the even, neat, nondescript features of his chief. There the only confederate of power was a kind of unthinking assurance and, yes, a curiously plain not-quite-hidden ambition. I recognised the syndrome. This was not an old style cop, up through ward-heelers and backstairs flophouse raids, liquor store muggings and cathouse kickbacks. This man was product of the military technocracy. He felt himself, literally, elect. He felt hooked in to limitless resources, limitless wealth. And always with the commonweal end justifying the means, overriding the means. Any discrepancy—any that might be made public—was mere matter for some presidential PR statement. I was the last person to dare consider any ends as opposed to means and yet he made me shiver.

'My name's Shepherd,' he said. 'Lester worked for me.'

Thin, precise drawl. Unimaginative precision in the bloodless face.

'Why did you kill him?' he said.

I didn't say anything. For that I got a mule kick in the small of the back somewhere about where the ribs stop and the kidneys start. Think of a bad pain. Multiply it by ten.

'I didn't know he was dead,' I said. 'Who's Lester?'

Another blow wrought havoc on the other kidney. Times a hundred. And pain with a hot line to my scrotes. I made myself stand straight.

'Killed in Anchorage,' Shepherd said evenly. 'Why?'

He looked expressionlessly at me just as a coached man might look on television in an interview.

'Oh, that Lester,' I said. 'He was killed by Tran Chau Chieu.'

I got a reprieve from the devilling on that one. Nothing on Shepherd's plain face got any fancier. I might have just told him Spiro Agnew was a Vice-President of the United States.

'Not him,' he said. 'You.'

'Well,' I said, 'if Lester worked for you and you think I killed him you should be able to think of a reason why I did.'

Again. A thousand. I staggered slightly in regaining balance. If I didn't start coming across, I'd soon be a man of a different...

'Look,' I said, 'the house punctuation to our little chat is becoming monotonous. Can't it be dispensed with?'

'That's OK, Ames,' Shepherd said. 'Mr Powell is quite prepared to talk. We can't ask more, can we? Besides, his leg wound's acting up. Why don't you get him a chair?'

Ames did just that. It was hard and wooden and the best chair I ever met up with.

'A man who'd been shot in the leg might well try pinning a murder rap on the guy who did it,' said Shepherd.

So. That much. I said nothing. Shepherd looked at his watch.

'Now, let's see,' he said, flat, slight drawl, dry, 'a little later today and you have a date with Olivares.'

The wires had been tapped.

'When and where is that?' said Shepherd.

Oh ... Well, I'd only slipped him forty bucks. I couldn't compete with a Federal retainer.

'You've seen we can make you talk,' said Shepherd. The voice was still slow and dry but now, noticeably, there was an accompanying edge to it.

'Lester was a good, loyal operative who—'

'Horseshit!' I said. 'He wasn't good. He made a complete botch of his assignment. Complete and utter. He wasn't loyal. He was trading the store away behind your back as you—'

'So you did kill him.'

'Of course.'

'But you talked to him before?'

I didn't answer. I tried to think what was best to say. For the first time I derived the sense that this might be an open-ended situation. Shepherd leaned forward and touched something, presumably a button, beneath the overhang of his desk top. In another room out of sight and hearing a tape recorder must have ceased its rhythmic murmur. Shepherd looked back at me.

'The best reason I can think of,' he said evenly, 'for one man to kill another is that the other was trying to kill him. If you follow me. Now let us put a hypothetical example.

'Suppose an agency were to receive orders to eliminate a certain alien—let's call him A—about to take up residence on US soil. Sort of lend-lease. And suppose that same agency had an operative who was engaged on a totally different project in another part of the globe, say—'

'Say in a theatre of war in a Far-Eastern country which shall be nameless.'

The lowest form of wit.

'If you like. Now suppose, just suppose, that operative's loyalty had become dubious. Had given rise to doubts. Is it not conceivable that this man might be recalled from his regular duties to take care of this new assignment?'

'So that he wouldn't be automatically suspicious of being suspended.'

Shepherd leaned forward slightly. Now I could see fine lines weaving a mesh under the deep, steady eyes.

'It might be more complex than that,' he said. 'It might be hinted, leaked, to this party that his assignment to eradicate A was a chance to rehabilitate himself and—an audition for his chance of full rehabilitation. The elimination of B.'

'Let's quit pussyfooting around,' I said. 'The names are Lester and Raker and Powell.'

The best half-back line that Chelsea...

'We were hypothesising,' he said.

'Of whom I'm Powell. My government doesn't like me. Neither does yours. Mine was too squeamishly old-fashioned—maybe didn't think it worth their while to knock me off. Yours was less inhibited. Probably has a bigger budget allocation for this sort of operation. Mine, though, was quite happy, in its bland two-faced way—it's old-fashioned in that sense too—to turn a blind eye to any elimination techniques that might be instigated over here. Which explains the insistence on Alaska—a neatly remote place always full of strangers passing through. I knew a little too much for anybody's peace of mind—so my mob served me up to yours.'

'Two faces,' he said. 'That's a lot of blind eyes.'

A joke. A grey, Nixon administration joke. But all the same... a joke. An edge came to me. Did it impassively mask a proffering of contact?

'Yes,' he said, 'I've just told you that.'

'You sent Lester to kill me.'

'Yes.'

'You set it up as a rehearsal, a dummy run, for him killing Raker.'

'Yes. How clever of you to guess Mr B is Mr R.'

'I don't like being taken for a dummy.'

'He was the one got taken... But anyway—we mixed it up for him a little more than that. We fed into him that you were on Raker's team. A key man. A high man. We briefed him that there was little point in getting Raker if he didn't dispose of you first.'

'What a compliment. I do beg your pardon... He sailed for this crap?'

Shepherd shrugged.

'Evidently,' he said. 'Somebody had to be heading things up Merrie Englandwise.'

He would have appeared just as indifferent at that briefing. And with reason. They are expert bridgers of the gap of credibility, these grey men. So are they all. Yes. I saw now why Lester, strangely self-possessed in the death's-head face of my gun, had thought he could buy reprieve with his name-dropping currency. That hadn't been a guess just now. Mr B was not a perfect stranger. Cornered, Lester had been levelling. What he'd had no way of knowing, no reason to suppose, was that those two syllables—Raker—made up, right then, a new one on me. Which was one on him. Shepherd had slipped him notes as negotiable as a dollar on the Tokyo Express.

'I'd like you to keep that appointment with Olivares,' Shepherd said.

Incredible. I'd almost forgotten him and the present. There was more quiet.

'Do you begin to see why?' he said.

'There's only one reason why you'd deal with me. There's only one reason why you don't follow out your original instructions on me and feed me into some boiler in some furnace room somewhere quiet. You want me to replace Lester. You want me to kill Raker.'

'Right,' he said. 'Get to him through Olivares. Get to Olivares through Tran Chau Chieu.'

More silence. I was breathing through my nostrils. I had to change to my mouth to lessen the noise. By rights my brains should have been like buttermilk under a whisk. I found they were crystal sharp and clear.

'What's in it for me?' I said.

'Let me put it this way. You get to go on living.'

Sure, I thought. Like Lester would have.

'What do you want,' he said, 'Mexico? Australia?'

I said nothing. Neutrally he looked at me.

'Probably stake you a little for the trip,' he said.

'My name's Richard Powell. Not Paul. Not Adam Clayton. I've never made much of a hobby of collecting money.'

The creases about his eyes grew a shade more defined. He

was on the point of dismissing me. Without his neo-papal blessing. I sought to get the ball back into play.

'Tell me about Tran Chau Chieu.'

'What do you know already?'

'His version.'

'Autobiographies don't rate much around here. This much is fact. Tran Chau Chieu was on Raker's team in Saigon. And more than that. In bed with him too. He was Raker's boyfriend. They're both that way. He's the obvious, illegitimate by-product, I guess we could say, of World War Two—brought up by the Catholic Mission that found him dying of hunger and cold in some Hué back street. One of the few lucky ones. They gave him an education, a good one: he responded very well. He's clever. No question. But without a scruple in his head. They got him a job as a boy clerk in a Government office. He wasn't interested. He hadn't turned out what you'd call your good Catholic. He'd found out by then that he had looks, charm, intelligence, languages, a foot in both camps, East and West ... he was the perfect middleman, go-between, hustler, you name it, in all the Saigon foul-up of graft and wheeling-dealing. And the world owed him a living. He clawed and cheated and charmed his way into the big leagues. Pretty soon he was a pretty big cog in Raker's wheel.'

He must have at some time, but in all our discussion I hadn't seen Shepherd blink.

'And of course,' he went on, 'he was a favourite son. He got preferential treatment. He was pretty much number two man on the totem pole. Well now ... it's kind of chicken and the egg ... But about two years ago, around the time Raker decided to relocate himself Stateside outside of the military, they had what you might call a lovers' spat.'

For the first time Shepherd allowed himself the sketchy parody of a smile. The compressed lips bared wolfishly over as straight and true teeth as dental surgeon ever furnished.

'King-size,' he said. 'Lover's pique, economics, whatever, Tran Chau Chieu had hived off a lot of Raker's Vietnam operation, personnel. Everyone was playing both ends against the middle.

Lester included. It was the classic set-up and it ended classically. Somebody tipped Raker off his blue-eyed boy had the fix in for him. Raker moved firstest with the mostest. In the shoot-out Tran Chau Chieu's outfit were annihilated. The word we had—from Lester—was he was gunned down along with them. It seemed that way. Wasn't hide or hair of him seen around from that night of the long knives on ... First intimation we had he was still around was a description through channels from the Alaska State Police and a report of a guy walking into a bar on Sunset with a girl, some shots getting fired, another guy coming out wounded with ... but you know about that.

'Who pulled the slug out?' he said.

'It went on through.'

'Who sewed it up?'

I shook my head.

'You don't buy any help like that,' I said.

He nodded, prepared to concede. For the moment.

'The girl?'

I shook my head again. Differently.

'I don't know. We holed up outside Barstow. Slept in the car. She never knew what hit her. I gave her some bills, the car itself. Told her to beat it. She's probably selling it down in Tennessee right now.'

Very thin ice. I had to fling a diversion forward.

'Now you don't know where Raker's gone to,' I said.

He blinked. 'What do you take us for? Of course we know. I know exactly where he is. He's on a big spread south-east of Lordsburg. He's—'

'Handy for the border,' I said. I was blinking too now.

'Among other things.'

'Why—'

He anticipated me.

'You've got two big questions,' he said. 'One: why don't we just go down there and pull him in?'

He eased back in his chair.

'It's like this,' he said. 'He's got a ranch house down there and about thirty hard men working the spread—that's to say mounting a twenty-four hour guard. They're veterans for the most part. They know what they're doing. He's on guard too. Won't hardly step out of there for anything. But for emergencies— he's got a dirt airstrip there, a Lear jet tanked up to go.... Now, OK, we've got the fire power, the horses—we can out-manoeuvre him. Sure. But at a price. Good men would get hurt. He just might escape. OK ... that's one.

'Question two: why you?'

'I'm expendable.'

'Certainly. That helps. And as I've been at some pains to dem-onstrate this morning you've the best inducement in the world to cooperate. But beyond that—it's a hunch, I guess. Or a card I can play and not be any the worse off if it goes down. See, Lester could get to Raker. Raker didn't trust him but he thought he had him pegged. And he needed him. That—'

'He's still in business?'

'Still in business. Bigger than ever. Now you—you just might be able to get to him. They don't know from nothing about you but they're worried right now about Tran Chau Chieu and they know he takes shots at you. Olivares will have passed that on to headquarters.'

'Olivares does Raker's legwork?'

'Exactly. Some of it. Now, if you were to lead them to believe you could deliver Tran Chau Chieu ... OK, you're a maverick, a wild card, but the way you disposed of Lester makes me think it's your style.'

For the second time he grinned.

'One read-out we get from Anchorage is you're better at this kind of thing than our first choice.'

I sat quiet a moment not enjoying his joke.

'That still leaves a third question not answered,' I said slowly. 'The biggest. Kill Raker. Kill Raker. Why do you want him dead? Isn't that just a little bit out of line?'

Very softly, he sighed. I seemed to detect the collapse of some-thing official in him, something ingrained by years of going by the smart young technocrat's book.

'It's an imperfect world,' he said. 'Very imperfect. I'll make you a present. Tell you something. I happen to be one of the guys who sold out to compromise a long way back. I've learned to go for expediency. Like I say I've demonstrated some of the methods I've come to use.'

The clerical precision in his voice had lost out to a bitter world-weariness. I began to feel I'd been premature in judging him.

'But if you line me up against a wall,' he went on, 'I'd still have to say I was on the side of the angels. It's like this. I take Raker alive, there's a trial. Eventually. Years later, maybe. Certainly it's years before the appeals are all through. The guy gets hit with a tenth of what he's got coming. In the meantime his set-up is carefully wound up by the others, the accountants. The traces are dusted over. The small men fade away. The legitimate business fronts go into liquidation ... And so on.'

He sighed again.

'The others. That's really it,' he said. 'Raker's the spider in the middle. Out there on the web there's all kinds of big bright names—names that people have voted for, names that hold commands, lesser and greater, names that have got tradition. And so on. Bring Raker to law—let alone justice—and you've got a scandal. Huge. There'd be another crisis in public confidence in our tattered and torn administration, our establishment, that could rock us all ... Well, you know what I mean.

'Now, if I cut Raker's head off, quietly—and he's earned it, believe me—I cut the head off the whole network. The rest are weak. I can see pressure's brought to bear. There'll be resignations, sudden serious illnesses that require sudden retirement, vacations extended indefinitely overseas. OK, it's a lot less than perfect. But our basic framework—which is all we've got going for us—would survive intact and in the meantime the dope would stop being smuggled and the girls stop being pushed and the Guatemalan rebels or whoever have one less guy left willing and able to sell them their crates of non-permit Mannlicher-Carcanos.'

He paused theatrically.

More pause.

214

'That's why I want him dead,' he said.

'Happens all the time,' I said.

'Who knows?' he said. 'But somewhere along those highly unofficial lines is where I had a hunch this might be your style. I have a hunch you and I aren't so very unalike.'

I found myself recoiling. I didn't know what to say. It puts a nasty taste in your mouth to be taken for an assassin. Especially if you are. It's unpleasant when a man you think you don't like claims kindred with you. Even if it's true. I didn't think I had any wish to take care of anybody else's dirty laundry. Not when it wasn't something personal ... I did have my personal score to settle. There would be no way to that except by doing a deal here ... And even then, thinking about it, did I not detect my revenge becoming duller? Among all my aches and tiredness, did I not feel an immense, sad, further tiredness at the prospect of killing again. For what now, really? ... And yet, I hadn't the slightest, faintest doubt that, if I turned him down outright, Shepherd's regard of me as expendable...

He was looking at me.

'Let's go back to the mechanics,' I said for something to say. 'I'm going to put on a black hat and you're going to give me a bag of marked gold. Then you and your posse are going to put on white hats and chase me along to the Hole in the Wall. And the sentries are going to see my hat and your hats and let me through. And then I shoot Jesse James.'

Shepherd didn't smile one millimetre.

'Sort of,' he said, 'it still works. It worked with Trotsky.'

I thought of the royal spade that they'd knocked into the ground.

'I'm not a killer,' I said.

Deadpan, Shepherd ignored my inaccuracy.

'You don't have to be,' he said. Dry precision had returned to his tones for these matters of fact. 'Raker doesn't come out from behind those guards of his much. But one thought will bring him. The thought of a final revenge rendezvous with his old buddy buddy, Tran Chau Chieu. Set him up for one—I've got one in mind—and leave the driving to us.'

215

'That's something else. I'd have to bluff real well. I'd have to talk an awfully good game.'

'You can do that. Besides, the odds may not be as stacked against you as you think. You can back your hand some.'

He timed it well as he leaned forward again.

'Tran Chau Chieu's holed up in a hotel. The Crescent down on Mission. Room 504.'

CHAPTER TWELVE

Later that same morning I drove north from downtown along Vermont. It was a bright and miraculously clear day. A breeze had sprung up from somewhere to rid the Los Angelic air of all smog traces. On a day like today you could fire an arrow in the air and it wouldn't stick. Between buildings you could glimpse the snow-covered San Gabriel mountains to the far right. You could understand why two generations ago people thought this a nice place to come out and plant oranges in. Even now, up and down this shabby, indeterminate street, it was a day to fall in love on.

But not for me, never again. I had other things on my clouded mind. I cast it over the current balance sheet. On the credit side I had the Citroën back. I had my money back—counted and there behind me on the rear seat. But further behind, probably about half a block, was the tail that Shepherd had warned me I'd never go without now. I'd already made myself stop trying to spot him. That was debit. So was the fact that inside and out I felt as crumpled and soiled as my no longer fresh new clothes. Well, fatigue had become my stock-in-trade. OK, whip, go on for ever so long as my feet hold out. Oh, and one other thing. The little matter that I'd chosen to play ball on Shepherd's Rough Rider team. Therein the biggest debit of all.

I climbed to the top of Vermont, crossed Los Feliz. I ran past houses that had nice lawns and were good to look at and whose owners all looked, I knew, like Barbara Stanwyck and Fred MacMurray. Then I was in the park, on a nice early spring day. All set to keep a date. I drove more slowly, looked in the mirror in spite of myself. No, no visible tail. I passed the Greek Theatre. I didn't stop so I couldn't tell if it were authentic. They were starting off the new season with Johnny Mathis. The road got steep, ascending via tight winding bends. Now I had glimpses of the whole smog-cleared city below. The Observatory lay up ahead. I knew now why Olivares had picked this spot. Forget the music of the spheres. This was jazz from another hotel. The observatory was the perfect place to look down from and observe my solo, unsupported approach.

I gained the plateau on which the telescope, planetarium and so on were set. Once it had been Greenwich, now it was Griffith Park and I ... Forget that! Mechanics! I slid the car into a slot in the two-thirds-empty parking lot and, walking back past the unmanned hot-dog stand, bypassed the Observatory. This might be the one day in the city's history you could see higher than a kite but I had to trail a horse of a different colour. I walked dutifully back down the road towards the prearranged bend. A car came from around it. I tensed. It gathered speed. I got ready to hurl myself into the roadside undergrowth. A sense of the inherently preposterous prevented me. As the family outing accelerated past I was glad that it had. Now I had the road to myself. The city lay laughing in the clear sun in the distance. Still no one. On the bend I stepped off the road, slid a little down steep earth banking and ducked beneath a first line of trees into a small glade. A bird fluttered away in a flap. There was nobody around. I was out in a clearing in a bosky dell. I felt like a dartboard around opening time on a Saturday night.

There was a light crunch. A rustle. Branches parted and, straight in front of me, Olivares stepped into view. He seemed to be alone. That he was pointing a gun at me was merely par for the course.

'You got a gun?' he said.

I nodded and pointed very slowly to the ugly weight in my jacket.

He nodded, not further concerned, it seemed. His own gun stayed out in the open for all to see and think on. His sharp, elemental face looked like an Aztec god's just after losing the world welterweight title.

'Thanks for the assist the other day,' I said.

He stayed silent.

'The guy you were trading shots with,' I said. 'He got away.'

'His gun,' he said, 'had more bullets. I used too many covering you. I had to back out.'

There were Spanish steps in his voice that made Desi Arnez even more of a travesty.

'He got away again north of Taos,' I said.

'Not from me.'

'Raker's tail?'

'Maybe.'

The sharp face stared, implacable.

'What's that to you?' he said.

'He killed my girl.'

Olivares' eyes opened the minutest fraction.

'Later. He caught up with us. I want him. I know where he's at.'

Now the eyes were almost wide.

'Where?' he said.

'Let's talk a while,' I said.

He said nothing. He stood and thought. The sun came filtering through the leaves in a way that made me think of Taos and a dirt road and another bright sun on red blood.

'Who are you?' Olivares said, leaning on the verb.

'Name's Powell,' I said. 'I'm English. I had a job back there for Orbit Arms. You know, selling old surplus guns, planes, tanks to second, third-class powers. It was all nice and legal. Permits. Government approval. I found I could make more if I bent the rules a little. I quit. Did some deals myself. Didn't ask all the questions. You know ... This guy—Tran Chau Chieu he called himself—contacted me, said he could get me new US stuff from Vietnam. I took a chance. I gave him bread to get it set up. You know, bribe guys, grease palms. He double-crossed me.'

'How come you just happened into the Peso?'

'I heard a whisper I could get to Raker that way. I need a job. Contacts.'

'What whisper?'

'From a guy called Lester I was introduced to. Wave money at him and his tongue gets loose.'

'How come Chieu got there?'

'He got it out of my girl.'

'That your proposition?'

'What?' I said.

'You deliver him, you get a job.'

'Pretty much. I want him anyway. Job or no job.'

'Where's he at?'

'Do we have a deal?'

Olivares shrugged narrow shoulders.

'I guess. We get him, Raker won't be sorry.'

'What do you know about the son-of-a-bitch?'

'He's a faggot gook but he's mean. I had a knife into him once but he got one in me. Tell me where he's at and this time it won't be no draw.'

'I mean to be in on the kill,' I said simply. 'If I tell you what's to stop you jumping the gun on me?'

'Best reason in the world,' he said. 'He ain't no pushover. Double-teaming is what he takes.'

I thought about it. Shepherd would have the hotel under constant watch. If he should try, Olivares couldn't really go it alone. If I was going to make friends with and influence him, I'd better be straight. A bird flew above the trees, a darting shadow through the path of the sun. Of course, on receipt of the information Olivares might eradicate the source.

'All right,' I said, milking it. 'Crescent Hotel, Mission Street. I don't know for how long. Room 504.'

Olivares didn't shoot me.

'Tonight,' he said. 'Get him tonight. I saw your car as you came up. They sure know how to make one ugly, huh?'

'Some people like it.'

'Nine-thirty tonight. Cruise the south side of Pershing Square like you're trying to score. I'll be there and—'

Leaves rustled thickly, rasping behind him. He stared hate directly at me for one microsecond, then spun and crouched in a blur I almost couldn't follow. His gun roared out twice like a twenty-one cannon salute.

The hysterical bird went screeching off again, loud alarums

ringing in its beating wake. The branches lashed back and forth as they marked its flight. The sun stopped dancing and stood still again. The cordite smoke thinned on the faint breeze. There was quiet.

I walked, Olivares covering me, to where the foliage began. I parted the bamboo curtain, took a step further. Bark had been ripped untimely from a tree trunk about eighteen inches thick. At about heart height. Olivares was at my shoulder.

'Let's get out of here,' he said thickly. 'Tonight.'

A tree is a tree. We shot it in Griffith Park.

The Crescent down on Mission was a long-standing anachronism. Even by night. A red brick building sicklied o'er with grime, it stood a few twenties storeys high amid a rundown air of perpetual mourning for its lost, marginally better, youth. A service alley, dark, irregularly fanged with the cheap rear ends of air conditioners, ran down its one side. I'd smelled better locations in my time. At the rear there was a Naked City-West Side Story fire escape. And waiting in its shadow, Olivares. As far as was casually possible and to the point, we'd jointly cased the crestfallen outside.

Earlier I'd picked him up with no further trouble than having to fence off with some quick and comic acceleration a couple of night-city, lilac-shirted upstagers of Little Richard—so lurid they just had to be Vice Squad undercover men. He'd slipped aboard without an accompanying train of heavy-gang thugs and, as I picked up speed on the short journey, I told him the right room number. I saw him look across at me without humour and with a lot of malice.

'I take a long time these days getting reassured,' I'd said.

The illwill didn't go but it was a move he understood. As I crossed the street to the hotel's yellow-lit entrance I knew he'd have a working respect for me.

I pushed my way through a heavy old glass door into a small deserted lobby. A rubber mat, then threadbare carpet led to a small curved desk with pigeon-holes behind. Beyond that to the left was a monkey-cage type elevator the size of a phone booth and, spiralling squarely around it, the stairs. Shadows hung pinched in high corners with suggestions of cobweb film. Forgotten dreams had faded on the stagnant air a while then climbed the dingy walls to die. Sadness is an empty hotel lobby.

And opportunity. Decision roughly shoulder-charged my reverie. I moved quickly to the long-since polished desk. With any luck— There was a shuffle. Out from behind the false wall of the pigeon-holes emerged a bald old man. He was white and wizened, wrinkled and stooped. There were liverish blotches on the backs of his hands. Grey ash lent his old-fashioned waistcoat a squalid lace. His teeth were yellowed, nicotined. But his eyes were sharp and lizard-like. Everybody's night clerk. I reached for my wallet.

'Help you?' he wheezed. He rode for the Big C.

'Key to 504,' I said. 'Left mine up there when I went out.'

He squinted up at me.

'You the fellah booked in earlier?' he said. That might have been a grin.

No other way. I pushed the twenty dollar bill across the scratches, the large, faded ink stain.

'Silly thing to do,' I said. 'I'm always forgetting them.'

I never saw an engraving go so fast. Lizard-like. Now he was immobile again. Too immobile.

'Place's got a good name,' he said huskily. 'Never any trouble. Keeps its nose clean.'

I proffered the twin. It joined its brother in nothing flat. The old blotched hand could still deceive the eye. It came back now holding a tagged key.

'Does the trick,' he said. 'You lifted it off the hook.'

'We never met,' I said. 'And the phone is on the blink.'

'Never seed you.'

Already he was shuffling away.

Key in hand, avoiding the certain advertisement of the clanking elevator, I addressed myself to the downtrodden stairs. They ascended shabbily, crepuscularly. Monotonously. I climbed them with a deliberate slowness in a futile attempt to keep my pulse rate down, my breathing easy. Once, a younger man, I would have taken these steps in my stride. But now, I reflected, round-ing a corner, facing a further flight, it was another ... The fifth floor. The same twilight, underlit corridor of dirtied pink, not long but somehow stretching away to a diminishing infinity. Old, old gold lettering on a varnished sign informed me that room 504 was to the right. I went first to the left, limping in thick silence towards the fire escape. It was at the turn of the corner. Waiting there, his hand Napoleonically in his jacket, was Olivares. I held up the key, looked questioningly at him, at the apparently undisturbed window access to the escape. He shook his head.

'He ain't been out this way,' he said softly.

I jerked my head.

'Back here,' I said.

In stealth, breathing through our mouths, we made our un-observed way back along the straight and narrow passage. The world's slowest tracking shot. Tran Chau Chieu had chosen an archetypal hideaway. We halted outside his closed door.

Olivares motioned, took the key from me. Taking for ever but with hands as steady as a Republican majority in Orange County, he slid it fully home into the doorknob-centred lock. He made no sound that I could hear. He straightened up, motioned again as I took out my gun. I could have the dubious honour (and novelty) of venturing first into the dragon's lair. I braced myself, nodded. He gathered himself with hands on the door knob and key. He nodded, turned everything fast, flung wide the door. I crashed on by him and sidestepped fast. Gun out, he was alongside me at once. Together, brought up short, we looked round the light-burning, empty room.

Empty. I jerked open the thin door of the room's one built-in closet. Four wire hangers vibrated with jangling apathy on the dowel rod they were chained to. That was all. Not even a coat. I panned my eyes over the items that minimally furnished the cheerless room. The steel-framed thirties divan was backed into the diagonal corner. No room behind it to hide. No room be-neath, it sat too low. The one easy chair was angled with its rigid back in profile. The dressing table was minuscule. There wasn't a single sign of human habitation within those four close walls. You couldn't have hidden a limp erection there. It had to be the bathroom, then. Either that or I'd been sent on a fool's errand. Olivares tapped my arm. He flicked his eyes across. He'd had the same first thought.

He shut the outside door. The silence in the room grew louder. I looked across at the doorless entrance to the ensuite bathroom. A light burned within there too. I stared at the framed rectangle until it appeared like the mouth of a cave, the entrance to a tunnel. A tunnel of death. Perhaps at this instant Tran Chau Chieu stood within timing his counter-attack to the second. When in doubt have a man come through the door carrying a wisecrack. I almost hoped he would. Else I had some fast explaining to lay upon my trusty, murderous Mexican side-kick. Nothing. Nothing but the musty silence. All right. I'd pursue the dangerous luxury of initiative. At a swift limp I crossed the room.

Amid all that yellowed white tile he was the immediate focal point. And, stretched out face upwards, immediately recognisable. He'd always been dead-pan but never quite to this extent. Not Tran Chau Chieu. Eddie, the late barman from the Silver Peso. His lips were set now in a slight, off-centre curl, showing a glint of white teeth, distorting the line of his moustache. I doubted if it was amusement. The icepick buried to its haft between his sternum and left nipple was no laughing matter. For the record I made myself feel his pulse. He had no pulse. The wrist felt stiff, fell stiffly away on release. It was cold. I looked closer at him. A waxen pallor was already beginning to steal into his face, underlying his darker, living colour. Well. Knock me down and cover me in chile size. I wondered how much of my money he'd had time to spend.

There was a noise behind me and moving shadow. Olivares came curiously in. At the spectacle he grew almost as rigid as his dead compadre. Breath hissed from him. He looked at me very hard. Very mean. He moved forward and went through the same motions I'd performed. In the three's-a-crowd space I stood back and aside, momentarily surrendering to the reality/

224

unreality factor washing over me. Logic said otherwise but it felt like it should be raining outside. Olivares was taking longer than I had. His handkerchiefed hand was cautiously probing the icepick haft. Blood was inconspicuously in short supply around the point it made contact with the oatmeal casual shirt. What there was seemed dry. As I watched, the searching fingers moved, made towards a tiny fleck of white protruding from the right breast pocket. I watched to see what it might be.

Photographs. Olivares took out three or four. Black and white. They seemed a little crumpled but not old. I tried to judge if this meant a fresh development. No chance. The prints were small and, as I craned forward to see more, Olivares' shoulder, not by accident, bent round to block my line of vision. I straightened. He looked long and hard. And then some. When at last he rose, his hand stole into his pocket to slide the prints home inside. He stood quite still, small but very straight. I don't know what he'd seen but his broken hatchet face had set into a pre-Columbian mask. A tragic rage was frozen elementally in those vertical and horizontal lines. I held my gun a little higher, pointed more his way. He turned to me with eyes that lacked all lustre. They slowly gathered fire. His own gun drew a bead, maybe absentmindedly, somewhere around my gut. Maybe.

'What do you know 'bout this?' he said.

I shook my head.

'I don't know. I'm no expert. Been dead some time.'

He looked at me.

'I don't think they know downstairs,' I said. Lamely. He looked at me.

'He got here first,' I said. 'Maybe we got lucky.'

The rigid scrutiny had anger in it now. Had I spent my life in strange hotel rooms with guys with guns?

'We've got to get out of here,' he said suddenly.

I felt slightly drunk. In the States a lot of guys get high on relief.

'Separately,' he said.

'The ways we came in,' I said.

He nodded. Abstractedly. I realised he was trying to think.

'We got to meet again,' he said. 'I've got questions I've gotta get answers to.'

'Where?' I said.

'... Taiwan. 6550 block on Sunset,' he said. 'Tomorrow noon.'

'The what?'

'The Taiwan. Chinese joint.'

'Oh. Got you.'

'Let's go.'

Without a glance down at the corpse, as if it were the firmest assignation in the world, he walked past me and out of the bathroom. I followed him to the corridor door. He didn't turn and cut me down with five shots from his Smith and Wesson. He gave me back the room key.

'Ditch this,' he said. 'I'll go first.'

He edged out through the opened door. I gave him two, hour-long minutes. It was as long as I could bear the thought of him phoning the cops and anonymously sticking me with a rap. Wiping the doorknob clean, I ghosted lopsidedly in his wake.

This time I could detect in the corridor's sound presence a faint, far-off whine. But nothing else. No people. I went along it and then down the stairs. Not even the rustle of spring. The whole place was run on a spirit level. I should leave my personal grinning spectre in suspended residence here. In the deserted lobby, leaning over the desk, I replaced the wiped-off key back on its hook. I could be sure that a beady, lizard-like eye watched from somewhere, but I put my faith in the US Treasury. I went out through the street door.

No blast of gatling guns played havoc with my tripes as I emerged into the brisk chill air. I walked quickly but not too quickly away to the left towards my car. Past the alley. No sign of Olivares. Past squashed beer cans left too long in a civically unswept gutter. Past some store-fronts grilled over for the night. I was hard on the corner to the block when from a doorway a tall, heavy figure was on me. Fingers that should have worked on the vice squad savaged my upper arm, and the small of my back recognised them at once. They belonged to Ames. My arm got sore with henchman's creak.

226

'Keep walking,' he said.

All of two words. I had my motivation. I kept walking. Around the corner, along a short block, over and across, along another intersecting street. We began to near a long black freighter of a car. A Ford LTD brougham. The rear sidewalk side door swung open with abrupt silence, of its own volition, it almost seemed. We drew abreast. Ames strongarmed me in to Shepherd.

'Well?' he said. Dryly. Ames slipped behind the wheel but did nothing else. We weren't going any place. What to say? What part to play?

More talk with another guy in another car. I seemed to have spent my entire life...

'It's got complicated,' I said. 'It didn't work out like you planned.'

'Go on.'

'No sign of Tran Chau Chieu up there. But lots of signs of another guy. A very dead guy.'

I think Shepherd may just have sucked his breath in.

'Olivares,' he said.

'No,' I said.

'Oh?'

'Your messenger boy from the Silver Peso,' I said. 'Eddie, I think his name was.'

'Ed Espina,' Shepherd said. 'Well now.'

A slightly-built man lost in thought, he sat back in the shadow of the overlarge car. I dwelt these days among inscrutables. There was nothing in his attitude that conveyed acknowledgement, let alone regret that in being tricky, not playing it by the book and according to Hoyle, he had brought death violently to a man who could still be alive. The skin on his nose seemed thoroughly intact.

'OK,' he said finally in a voice not addressed to me. 'Go get him.'

Ames slid back out from behind the wheel and, with a soft clunk of the door, disappeared into the night.

'We had the joint staked out, of course,' Shepherd said. 'Saw you go in. What happened next?'

227

'No one on the desk,' I said. 'I slipped behind it and picked up a passkey.'

I broke off. Silhouettes stood shadowily on the sidewalk outside the car.

'Run the window down,' Shepherd said.

I pressed the button. The descending pane of glass whirringly revealed Ames. And, handcuffed to him, Tran Chau Chieu. He smiled slightly. Perhaps at my look of shock.

'*C'est la guerre*,' he shrugged.

His sleek hair was a touch dishevelled; the breast pocket of his sports coat hung at ripped half-mast; there might have been a bruise on his half-in-shadow face. But especially in conjunction with the ape-like Ames he still confidently projected a sense of insouciant, debonair style. I didn't disconcert him in the least. Everything went flat. I found I could discover no connection between the darkened LA sidewalk and that sun-bright, blooded, far-away dirt road. My energy for everything, including execution, seemed eroded. I wondered if I had another killing in me. Such animal facility seemed spent. Sam seemed dead a long, long time ago. Another country ... Doubtless it was as well the Feds had picked him up. He was all theirs now.

'...picked him up outside four minutes after you went in,' Shepherd was saying. 'Must have hidden and slipped out. Had us worried but we thought we'd play it a little longer.'

How touching: they were worried over me.

'How did he do it?'

I described the contents of room 504. Shepherd listened thoughtfully.

'Olivares see it all?' he said.

'Yes.'

'Any idea why the guy should've gone up there?'

'That's your department.'

'Icepick, huh. Anything else unusual?'

I hadn't mentioned the prints. I don't know why.

'I'm no professional,' I said.

Shepherd thought.

'All right,' he said to Ames, 'get him inside. Get a team up there. I'll get this heap back myself.'

He didn't move to look out of the window or bend across me. He just raised his voice slightly.

'Yes, sir.'

Tran Chau Chieu was looking at me, somehow the most human of the three.

'Sorry about the girl,' he said. 'The car came right at me.'

C'est la guerre.

A big lug yanked him away.

'Well?' I said to Shepherd.

'Olivares?'

'He said we should split up. You haven't got him?'

'No.'

'He must be pretty good.'

'That's why he wanted to split up.'

Shepherd fell silent. I began reviewing the situation. I began to feel the prison shades—and worse—closing about me.

'I'm supposed to meet him tomorrow,' I found myself saying.

'You are! Where?'

'A place called the Taiwan.'

Shepherd thought some more. He took out a card and a ballpoint and wrote something in the shadowy light.

'Keep the appointment,' he said. 'Hang loose while you see what he says. Maybe something will break off and roll our way.'

'Your way.'

'Yours too, if you remember.'

'You remember what I've just come from,' I said, 'he's as suspicious as hell of me right now. He may want to see me again to set me up.'

'I don't think so. He'd have finished you off up in the room where he could have framed a nice open-and-shut case. My guess is he's got something on his mind.'

'Like what?'

'I don't know. Maybe he thinks it's time to sell Raker out. Maybe he thinks he's next in line for an icepick. He doesn't know we've got Chau Chieu. Could be he'll try to enlist you full time.'

'To track him down?'

229

'Right. If it's that you might qualify for a ride all the way out to see Raker. That'd be best of all.'

'Oh sure. I'll wear the black hat. It'll save the mortician.'

'You can do some more stringing along. We could bait a trap. I wouldn't be averse to pegging Chau Chieu out some place if I thought it would draw Raker.'

I felt very old and weary. Rudderless. None of this was of my making, had anything to do with me. The heart must pause to breathe and revenge itself have rest. Even if the night were made for killing. Tran Chau Chieu was a dead issue. Only the thought that I could soon be too—a vivid memory of that power drill—kept me from straight out turning Shepherd down. In that hesitating moment he forestalled me.

'Call me on this,' he said.

He handed me the card.

'Where are you parked?' he said.

'About four blocks away.'

Propelled by the full impact of the slightest social gesture nicely timed, I'd assumed a slow momentum. The game was still afoot.

'Better walk.'

I managed it without getting mugged. I slipped into the Citroën. It was like finding an old, comfortable friend. No back seat drivers rose up, howitzers in hand. Save for some confused but silent ghosts it was quite empty.

Olivares had been quite right. The Taiwan was Chinese. I found it on Sunset an egg roll away from where I'd dented the Corvette. It was inconsistently set within the patio precincts of an ersatz two-storey hacienda of strictly Garden of Allah vintage. The hash-house and bar were located on the far inner side of the courtyard beyond a pleasantly plashing fountain. Beach tables of metal with large, gaily coloured parasols allowed you to eat al fresco to the murmured accompaniment of bubbling water and offstage traffic. There was an authentic tree or two to add authentic shade. But for the customers, it wouldn't have been bad.

The babble of people overcrowded around two tables as they all tried over hard to be too beautiful had my hostility index running off the scale. They were all old hands at looking young. Brocaded bell-bottoms, long locks, silk shirts slumming as denim. None of that helped my blood pressure. As I came through into the courtyard the men stopped exercising their larger-than-life larynxes and the girls stopped toying wantonly with their soup. With concerted choreography, eleven necks moving as two, expensive sunglasses turned the trend of a common blank and vacant gaze upon me. In those fairy rings a guy without shades is as rare as a Forbes film without Nanette Newman. They gave it two beats and then the sun flashed darkly as the lenses were averted. I wasn't one to join the circle of the charmed. I didn't look big money from the East. Before I read the brushed steel custom designed shingles respectively to the patio's right and left I knew what they would say. The right wing housed the offices and transmitter of one of Southern California's seventeen thousand, nine hundred and six radio stations: playing on the left was a television commercials house. I was caught in a crossfire of media mediocrity. I wondered why Olivares had chosen such a place.

Then I saw him and saw why. He was sitting in a far corner, his back to two windowless walls, all but camouflaged by shade and smogged beige stucco. Three strides from his chair was an alley-like side exit. The major one through which I'd come was straight within his line of vision and/or fire. Past all the fledgling Stanleys, I went directly to him. I pulled up a chair and sat down.

His eyes were half-lidded, the face more a mask than ever. Despite its sharp lines, projecting planes, it was oddly passive now. A dead dimension of flatness had ironed out the angularity. He didn't speak, didn't nod. In front of him were lined some wooden matches as if the prelude to some party trick. The fountain and the film crowd babbled at my back. Then the waiter, all of fourteen years old, was bowing and scraping, chanting in Formosan. Olivares wasn't eating, only drinking beer.

'Two Coors,' I said. The houseboy hissed, bowed and went.

Olivares wasn't dead. His hand went suddenly into his jacket and came out holding something white. He spaded across to me the photographs he'd body-snatched the night before. I looked at their unlovely views.

The first was puzzling. It showed a large refrigerated truck parked rather incongruously off-pavement in a desert kind of arroyo or dry wash. No name was on the truck's bright silver side. I shuffled the next print up and found it more piquant. In a wide-angle-lens study, seven corpses lay stretched out in a neat and orderly row, face upward. The still was taken from one end and high so that perspective narrowed down the receding line. All the same the farthest body seemed especially small. The terrain seemed that in which the truck had ended up. Olivares kicked my foot. His torso hadn't moved. I masked the stills until the boy had finished, bowed and left. Then I looked at the third.

It was a tighter shot of the first three corpses in the row. They were dead all right. They lay in the farouche, bug-eyed, slack-jawed way that marked, say, the Daltons' rendezvous with violent death. And so many countless thousands more who didn't get their photos taken. I looked at Olivares staring at his matches. He'd already sunk the latest beer. How many before, I wondered? Perhaps that explained the glazed and far-off look.

'What is this?' I said. 'My Lai?'

He shook his head.

'Sonora, south of Nogales,' he said. His accent was thicker, more Spanish than ever. I thought this time he was drunk for real. I looked at the next still. It was the four other men. Now he had keyed me in I could see that they looked like Mexicans. It was hard to be sure. The slack-jawed look was in part derived not only from the ultimate surprise but from the blasted absence of much of the backs of their heads. Nor were they all quite men. The last two of the seven had not lived out their teens. The last, especially, had died young. His features still looked clean and fresh beneath their grotesque recasting. A row of match-sticks, spent, laid out for some cheap trick that held life even cheaper. I passed the photos back. Homespun, or, better, passportly professional, their flat, muddy off-handedness stamped an extra seal to authenticity on the seven times personalised atrocity. Brutal though they were, they were, finally, sad pictures. The ghost who trod with me could not for once conjure a smile.

'Not very nice. What does it mean?' I said.

His head came slowly up from far, unfathomable depths.

'It means,' he said, 'that you want Tran Chau Chieu and I want Raker.'

There was a bray of mindless laughter from behind. And a dark nerve through my dubious sensibility shrilled with a charge of animal excitement. For that second, as I sensed a hunt, I might have been the Mexicans' mass executioner.

'Spell it out.'

He produced the main team photo once again. His index finger, skinned at the knuckle, pointed to the third man from the right.

'My cousin,' he said.

The finger moved on and pointed to the boy at the far end.

'His eldest son,' he said. 'Two of the others I know.'

'Raker?' I said.

He nodded slowly.

'I made sure,' he said.

'Since last night?'

He nodded.

'How? What?—'

'Six years ago I came to Sonora from Guadalajara. To be near the States and try to get in. No way. I bum around. I'm starving. But I stick. I ask questions. Get to know some guys who maybe if the price is right can take me across at night. Price is they need help. I get to do some jobs for Raker. Small but I do good, keep my mouth shut. Raker gets me sponsored to America. Fixes it. I'm not a wetback, I'm a genuine immigrant with a card that says so.'

'Where was Raker?'

'Fort Bragg. In the military. Six months and so was I. They put you at the top of the list if you come from outside. If you want to come to live in this country, you got to be straight off ready to die for it. I think Raker speeded it up. But that was OK. I was getting my three squares and I'd had it a lot rougher in Durango. Anyhow I get assigned under Raker and next thing I know, Saigon.'

He'd been speaking in a fast low monotone, his opaque eyes staring past me. Now they tightened, took on focus, turned to look at me. For the first time in our acquaintance, the working of some faint emotion brought softness to the mask.

'I guess nobody minds screwing the Army. The Army screws you twenty-four hours a day so anything you can get back is all right. But in Saigon, for Raker, I get into stuff that ain't no way Army. Drugs, guns, protection. People there worse than I ever see back home. And worse off. I get to like it less and less. I'm doing fine. I'm fast, I know a lot of tricks. But I feel dirty.'

He stopped, swallowed. I pushed across my scarcely touched beer and he took a long pull. If this wasn't true, he was the best liar of us all.

'And I've got to stick, see,' he said. 'First, I'm in the Army. Second, I need Raker to work a big favour for me. My cousin in Puerto Vallarta wants to come live in the States. But he's done a stretch. They won't give him no entry visa. Raker says he'll take care of it. I keep asking. "Soon," he says. "Later." '

'Mañana.'

'Sí. Yes. Always. I get discharged, he puts me down on his ranch. Pretty soon I get the feeling he's playing me along. He ain't ever going to do it.'

'But the photographs ... that's ...'

'Three weeks ago I get word. Privately. Salvador has disappeared from around home. And his first boy. They're being brought across. But like wetbacks. I ask Raker if this is true. He says yeah but it's tricky. The Narcotics Bureau has a big drive on for good publicity. The border is very tight right now. They may have to wait for a good time. I say that's fine. I'm happy.'

He looked down at his hands.

'Then I see the photographs last night. I know what it is but I can't figure it out. I go down to Tijuana, meet up with a guy who does trips across the border for Raker. We have a little talk. He wasn't on the Nogales run—he makes me believe that. But, after a while, he tells me they got orders. From Raker. Standing orders, you'd say. Don't get caught with any merchandise that talks. Don't leave any behind. I worked with Raker all that time. I should have known. The kid was fifteen,' he said.

I was silent a while. I'd got the picture. The fountain splashed on.

'This guy,' I said, 'in TJ. Did ... did you ... ?'

'Damn near,' Olivares said. 'But no. I didn't. He wasn't worth it.'

I looked at him. If he was born a loser it was because he had a touch of class.

'He'll tell Raker,' I said.

'Pretty soon,' he said. 'I scared the shit out of him but pretty soon he'll remember he's more scared of Raker.'

He shook his head.

'Makes no difference,' he said. 'First time I come near Raker now he finishes me.'

'Whether he knows you know or not.'

'Right. He has to act like I know, figure sooner or later I will.'

'What's your plan?'

He shrugged.

'I ain't had time,' he said. 'I need sleep.'

I sat and thought. A breeze had swirled into the patio to tease at the yellow-green leaves. It was strong enough to roll over the end match.

'It true about Raker and Tran Chau Chieu?' I said.

He nodded.

'Young and pretty. He likes them that way,' he said. 'But that son of a bitch is smart as well.'

'I'm still going to get him,' I said.

He nodded. 'Two could do it better than one.'

'What are you saying?' I pretended.

'You help me first get Raker, I help you next with him.'

235

'Oh ... I'm going to help you first?'

'You know where your guy is now?'

I thought fast.

'No.'

'It'll take time to find him. Raker—we know where he is.'

'So why me?'

'I can't get close to Raker now. Alone. If I come close to him alone, he'll cut loose. It's going to sound like the Fourth of July. After—after what happened down there he can't have me walking around near him. But if I took you in there on the end of a gun, he'd think I was still on his payroll. He'd want to find out about you enough to let me get close.'

A gin and tonic would have been a sovereign aid to thought but I didn't want to snap the mood.

'All I want,' he said, 'is to get close enough for one shot at him.'

'And you and I would get the next two,' I said, shaking my head. 'And my man wouldn't have another thing to worry about. I'd rather do it so I stayed alive. So would you.'

Sam was dead. I seemed to be sitting in a motiveless vacuum. Shepherd was dictating my words. I was passive, flying on automatic pilot.

'You got a way that's better?'

'Maybe. You and I don't know where Tran Chau Chieu skipped to. But Raker doesn't know that we don't know. Suppose now I go see him by myself; tell him I've got his old lover-boy on ice some place. Suppose you're waiting at that place.'

Olivares shook his head.

'He'd never fall for it,' he said.

That was exactly the truth—unless Shepherd would loan me his prize prisoner. But Olivares was a ball I had to keep in play.

'You forget I'm in the arms racket,' I said. 'I've got London connections. I talk a pretty good game.'

'He'd send some of his boys.'

'Maybe. But it'd be me he was holding. You'd be in the clear.'

He looked at me.

'You've nothing to lose,' I said. 'It'd just be me they were burying.'

'How do I know you won't go straight in there to him and put the finger on me? How do I know you ain't already on his payroll?'

'You want me to swear on my mother's grave? That cuts both ways. How do I know you'll come help me get Tran Chau Chieu if we pulled this one?'

Locked in a suspicious trust that needed to believe, we stared at each other a long while across the noontime table.

'There's a place,' he said finally, slowly, thickly.

I felt the old insidious quickening. I looked at him.

'You can see who's coming from miles away,' he said.

I said nothing.

'Old empty store and filling station where there used to be water. Been empty for years. About thirty miles from Raker's when you turn off past Lordsburg.'

It came to me that I hadn't a snowball's chance in hell of getting Raker to do a simple, solitary thing. I'd do better taking my chances with Shepherd.

'I could wait there,' Olivares said.

How else was I to spend my time? I nodded.

'We can talk about it on the way out,' I said.

'OK,' he said. 'First I've gotta grab some sleep.'

I seemed to have heard that before.

'When do you—'

'Tonight. Better for the desert.'

'Where do I see you?'

'Bergin's. Around seven. Know where it's at?'

'I'll find it.'

I got to my feet, started to reach into my pocket.

'On me,' he said.

I nodded, letting him have that, and turned to go. Tomorrow's Oscar winners were still soaking their way through the first of their lunch hours.

'Tell Stanley either right away, like now, or he can go ahead and shoot without me!' I yelled back to Olivares.

237

He didn't react. The eyes all swivelled back to me. It was like being looked on by a pack of lemurs.

I wondered whatever had happened to reality.

CHAPTER THIRTEEN

Far better than any of the previous cars, the Citroën took my latest marathon in its long stride. Olivares had had only his one comment to make as I took him and his large, cheap case over to it.

'Boy, they sure know how to make a car ugly.'

'It works,' was what I'd said.

Earlier, after eating the best meal I'd had since my honeymoon, I waited for him at Bergin's. He studied my plate.

'Carnitas?' he said. The Keaton mask had repossessed his features.

I nodded.

'The best,' he said. 'All set?'

'OK,' I said. 'Let's go.'

Earlier still I'd returned to the no doubt under observation apartment on Laguna. I'd sacked out a while, had a shower, stuffed all the worldly possessions that I didn't have on into a single grip, left the landlord a two-line note. And got on the horn to Shepherd. I dialled the number he'd laid on me and got a result frightening in its instancy. There was a mechanical whirr, the prelude to a ring and then right away the scuffling of a receiver being lifted.

'Shepherd,' he'd said. Dryly, in a manner there was no mistaking.

'Powell,' I said.

'Wait a moment.'

I heard another, different scuffle and a click.

'Go ahead. Whatever you want to say.'

I told him about the photographs; what they meant; what

they meant to Olivares; how they had made him turn his tattered but loyal coat.

'Hmm,' said Shepherd. 'You see him take the photos off the body?'

'No,' I lied.

'How explicit are they?'

'Very.'

I told him about the derelict store; what was supposed to happen there; the miracle of a conducted tour I was supposed to work in my capacity of guide.

'I know the place,' Shepherd said. 'Take one look at the country around and you wonder why it was ever put up. Forty miles of rough road in every direction.'

He was silent. You can hear some people thinking down a telephone wire and know what they are going to say next. But not Shepherd. Listening to that faint, open presence, I could no more guess what was coming than I could when looking him straight in his unblinking eye.

'Think he's levelling?' he said.

'I don't know. I think so. I've kind of given up on believing people. I didn't believe Tran Chau Chieu even when I wanted to. Olivares—I guess so.'

More inscrutable silence.

'He's a better man, a better executioner, for the job than I am,' I said.

'Negative. He's on Raker's hit list. And he's dumb.'

'Not that dumb.'

'Well, he ain't smart. He's not going to sweet talk Raker into as much as batting one eye.'

'But I am. I'm going to have him coming running to the best place in miles for an ambush.'

'If one of his outriders radios in that Chau Chieu is there he'll come licketty split.'

'Let's ignore his sex life.'

'Huh?'

'Forget it . . . He'll just have his boy bring him straight in.'

'No. I'll bait the trap with real cheese.'

From somewhere where I'd once had feelings a silent sigh rose up. Sam was dead. Maybe I didn't want to bother with living. Maybe I just mightn't have to die.

'The words out of my mouth,' I said. 'It's the one way it might work.'

'Play Raker along some, then, when he bears down, let out the location and tell him to run a check. I'll have Ames right in there with Chau Chieu. You can say he's your buddy. His line will be he's not surrendering his prisoner unless you're out there authorising it in person. You can—'

'OK. Don't spell it out.'

'Nice thing about that rendezvous is there's buildings around. It's the one place around there I can hide men away. Not many but enough. I'll get 'em in by night. When are you heading out there?'

'Tonight. In a few hours.'

'Time your arrival for the day after tomorrow. Around noon. That's about what it'll take you, anyhow. I'll have my men hidden away by the time you come through to drop Olivares off.'

'You don't really need him now, why don't—'

'Negative. I want him running down predictable tracks. Take him out there like everything's jake and we'll pick him up on the spot, keep him out of sight.'

'What'll happen to him?'

There was a short pause.

'I can't make a firm commitment on it,' Shepherd said, 'but we'll probably give him a break. Straight deportation.'

'Probably what he most wants anyhow.'

'I think he'll get it. And he'll be a very lucky boy.'

'What,' I said, 'if Raker doesn't buy it?'

'He'll buy it when he gets that radio report.'

'But if he doesn't?'

'Hang in there. Stall. Ask for a job. Twenty-four hours and I'll whistle up help and we'll do it the hard way.'

'Come in like gangbusters, I'll get the first of his bullets.'

'It's better than gas at San Quentin.'

Or a power drill in a basement. I grunted.

'It won't come to that,' he said. 'We'll be out of sight when you drop Olivares. OK?'

'Out of sight.'

'You got it all?'

'Yes.'

'Repeat it.'

I repeated it.

'Good,' he said. 'It's going to work. See you out there when it has.'

Another pause.

'And thanks,' he said. He hung up.

So once again my world was reduced to two men in a car and an outside landscape streaming by. It was fittingly twilight when we quit Sam's shoddy town for probably the last time I'd lay unpennied eyes upon it. Stagnant smog had reassumed the main and as the opposing sun went down it managed delicate effects in pastel—lilac, primrose, mauve—among the thick-eyed layers hanging straight before us in the east. I thought of what I was about and found I didn't like it. It was a good Friday to be riding westward. Not east to betray one man to the law and another to his death. All to save my Judas neck. No, all to indulge my gangrened amour propre. Was Olivares, I wondered, a practising Catholic? How many Hail Marys per pound of smuggled heroin, I wondered. What was the going rate on ten cases of Lee Enfields? Then, at one stride and a half came the sub-tropical dark and the drive reduced itself to the monotony of staring main-beams locked on the darting, everrenewing white lines of a highway.

As seemingly indifferent as the sphinx he looked like, Olivares sat beside me. He might be a mirror travelling down the middle of a roadway but God alone knew what his reflections were. I didn't. Not me, king of the enigma-carriers. We rode long miles in silence, on through the warm night. I must seem as enigmatic ... Lulled by the smooth, swishing progress, I lapsed into a vacant, passive mood. I didn't know much of anything. It was best to let it all slide past without resistance. Olivares, Raker, Tran Chau Chieu, Lester, Powell. Even, in his quasi-official way, Shepherd. A parade of names. Was this all it was? Was this the paradigm? Men circling, spiralling about each other in the stalking pursuit of a revenger's tragedy, a compulsion to get even, come out ahead in the one diversion open to them, the power game? Was it all still a Renaissance dance choreographed by Machiavelli, murderous kids' stuff, or had Klaus Holt proved it could be sat out? Was there life in it only when a skeleton sat at the feast?

The headlights, stabbing across coming bends, were picking out sand dunes now, undulating eerily like waves of a frozen lunar sea. We must be close to Yuma. Hot wind came at us, released by the night desert. The elemental spirit of the old penitentiary seemed abroad: breathing, in the air, homing darkly on its fellow, my cowled doppelganger, riding spectrally at my shoulder to (he could but grinning hope) another banquet of my choice providing.

'What do you figure Espina, the barman, was doing up in that room?' I heard myself suddenly say from out of nowhere.

'I don't know for sure,' Olivares said slowly. 'He was the kinda guy always playing both ends against the middle. You never could tell what that son of a bitch was about. He was maybe trying to work some kind of a shakedown, I guess, or maybe trying to pitch some kind of deal. I don't know.'

'Yeah,' I said, 'there's all kinds of coproductions around Hollywood. How come he had those pictures?'

'Huh?'

'Those pictures you've got. Where'd he get them?'

'Took them himself, I guess. I don't know.'

'Strange,' I said. 'Strange that he should have them.'

We fell back to silence as the car ate up more road.

The vibrations on the rushing wind modulated, changed. We had left behind the friendless souls of shackled prisoners. We ran now through air troubled by the wandering spirits of forgotten long-dead Indians. More reservation territory lay beyond us in the night. There could be no appeasement for the spirits while

243

their descendants rooted and grubbed and got drunk on the arse-end of the world, their patrimony stolen. All that others should enjoy, in this life, a happier hunting ground. It was the same air brushing electrically by us now that had once freezingly whipped at me across the Alaskan runway. Eddying down the Rockies the length of a continent it had come to remind me that the Navajo, Apache and the Yaqui had fared no better than their Eskimo brothers. Born losers. I had only abbreviated the hopelessness of Elsie's cause. And Rafael Olivares sitting there beside me ... His people had been just as brutally deprived. The banality of people, governments, cheating, stealing, killing seemed more and more a pointless norm with every speeding mile. Law was an irrelevance ... I yawned and let the on-rushing night engulf my ability to think.

Rugged rascals, Rafael and I sojourned around Red Rock. We knocked the one-horse motel off balance by our dead of night arrival; there was fine desert grit on sills and shelves within the room. But there was luxury in not having to sleep with open eye; luxury in the separateness of a room apiece; luxury in the truce, however illusory, of our mutual aid society.

Those who are about to betray sleep well. They are lapped in assurance of initiative. Undisturbed, I dreamed a hearty dream. On the morrow I settled the bill to old-fashioned looks from a Ma and Pa Kettle brace of eighteen-carat Goldwaterites. The company I chose to keep stung them to their waspish quick. One must forsake, though, the killjoys of the world. We went back on the road again.

It wasn't a painted desert. It was scrubby, stale, less evocative by day than at night. It was cardboard grey—one more thing covered thick with dust. If you were looking for them, you could search selectively through the motes hanging in the baking, breezeless air and detect a complete rainbow spectrum among the rocks and dirt and desert plants. Assembly, though, produced an en masse effect close to negative. It was with surprise that, after several hours and many miles, I registered that the prevailing grey had modulated to a uniform khaki. That faint increment of red was the one concession to the exotic. To the far north, to the far south, hazy mountains sometimes stalked in parallel course. But where we ran through was as flat as yesterday's tortilla, last spring's love story.

It held like that all the way into Fort Lowell or, as it is known among the tuberculous in these post-imperialist days, sunny Tucson. There was greenery as we approached the old outpost. I started to sweat. The artificial irrigation of a thousand market gardens had introduced humidity into the desert air. As Olivares, breaking a long silence, threaded me through the one-stack litter of some underprivileged quarter, I realised the lungers must move on again in search of arid climes. All we searched for was food. In a beat-up cantina out of late Howard Hawks, Olivares ordered me the best meal absolutely that I ever ate. It gave the city point. It almost gave one cause to want to live.

We made more time. Olivares killed a chunk of it by checking out his gear. Naïvely I thought his big old case held clothes. It did—as padding for an arsenal that would have done for Wool- wich. Driving, I could only look with one eye on his hoard. But there was one thing there, broken in two halves, that must be semi-automatic and on loan from the Green Berets.

'What—'

The wheel juddered in my hand and I knew I'd got a flat. I pulled up to a halt. He looked at me enquiringly. Cushioned on that suspension he hadn't felt a thing.

'Flat,' I said.

Leaving the engine running I slipped out into the oven heat. The pavement was hot through my shoes. Olivares got out too, watching me. It was the offside front. A stiletto cactus had slivered its way right through the tyre. I raised the hood, took out spare wheel, box-spanner and under-bracket. I got the hub cap off, loosened the one central nut. Reaching inside I raised the lever controlling the hydraulic pressure. Hissing gently, the suspension pumped the car up high above its wheels. I placed the bracket underneath and home. I lowered the lever all the way. The hydraulics whooshed the car body down again—lower than its normal road height. The resistance of the bracket raised the whole offside. I slipped the shot wheel off. It all but burned my

245

skin off. Olivares was suddenly alongside holding up the spare. We juggled it on. In due order, I reversed the process. It took perhaps three minutes, start to end. Olivares watched fascinated as the car made its final sighing adjustment to road height.

'Yes,' he said. 'It works.'

And he grinned. It was as expected as Wallace marrying a black. He had teeth like Boot Hill, stained and brown, but the grin was wide and unforced. In that instant I nearly told him. I nearly told him I was driving him to close arrest. But I didn't. I'm not nice but I'm consistent.

'You see,' I said, 'I always tell the truth.'

I slammed the hood back down.

Nightfall found us, the flat meanwhile fixed, in a cheap motel past Bowie. I dreamed that night of long fat knives and Stamford Bridge.

In that flat, sterile oven of a wasteland the clump of shacks stood out like warts upon a baboon's arse, or, if you prefer, like the Miami Beach skyline seen from out at sea. You could see them from as far. And, from as far, be seen. Unbeknowingly, Olivares had picked Shepherd out the best of ambuscades. For minutes we gained yardage in a cloud of dust at eighty miles an hour and seemed to come no nearer. Then, arbitrarily, the buildings took on detail, gained in size, and I was braking to a halt. I looked around. Not a sign of man or beast. Instead, set out at random, as it seemed, seven wind-blown, falling-down drunk, tin-roofed sweatboxes of huts. Free out there from rust, their windows long since blasted in, they stood, two largish and five small, a little less than perpendicular as if some childish giant had left them thoughtlessly behind in tidying up the day before's Monopoly. It was Bad Day at Black Rock, Intruder in the Dust, Tobacco Road. It was subject matter for a time-slipped Saxon poet. It was a good hangout for cops.

'Get in close.'

Olivares was pointing to the penultimately farthest building.

'The shadows are so short, I don't think—'

'That ain't it. Raker has planes up overhead. Get in close in

246

case. We don't want aerial reconnaissance.'

Obediently I bumped the car off the tarmacadam strip and slowly across to the specified shack. The car's was the only noise. I pulled the handbrake on. Silence was the sole sound carried on the swirling breeze. We sat a moment in the glaring light, the furnace heat. The light had a thousand eyes.

Simultaneously, one door's clunk echoing the other, we both got out. There was no drone overhead of piston engine to hurl me back to boyhood on the Weald. No silver fish twisting in the cloudless azure shot down a glint of sun to set me wondering —theirs or ours? The sky was clear, open and endless. And clean. The dirt was all down here. Outside the car the breeze seemed stronger, dryer, dustier. Right by my foot was an age-old soda-pop bottle, stone stopper held by wire. It had been burnished blue by years of desert sun. I saw no rattler, no tarantula, but still I let it lie. The tote bag was enough of souvenirs. Besides, to touch the bottle was to break a spell, unleash amid those silent, stove-in shacks a sudden burst of Sergio Leone violence. I let the bottle lie. I saw no rattler. I saw no men.

Olivares panned slowly to completion his three hundred and sixty degree inspection of the site. He literally sniffed the air. Only now, still holding to the partial cover of the car, did he move towards the shack's half-open door. Then like lightning he was crashing through. No roar of pistols. No weighty blackjack thud. No caught breath, scuffle of shoes on floor. Less like a gangbuster I followed him in. He didn't spin and knife me. I didn't stumble over a new corpse. No cryptic sign from Shepherd hung on the wall in letters of glowing fire. Instead, the barren framework of a room, mottled glass in shards upon such boards as the gnawing desert rats had spared. Charred timbers in one corner darkly testifying to a hobo's passing fire. Holes through to the earth beneath suggesting the scuttlings of dry spiders. On the wall a sere and yellowed calendar, halted on March, had passed into dateless eternity. And dust upon dust upon dust. Stirred up by our entrance it hung thick and dancing in the golden shafts of sunlight pouring through the windows; lay thick and textured on the golden panels they painted underfoot.

A lot of chimney-sweepers had passed this way.

Olivares was looking eagle-faced through the window that gave out on to the shimmering black thread of disappearing road. He moved diagonally across the treacherous floorboards to a second that commanded a ramshackled view of most of the other huts and the distances that spaced them. I saw now why he'd picked this one. He nodded.

'OK,' he said, 'this'll about do it. Just like home.'

I wondered just what loser's history that remark contained. 'Let's get the stuff.'

I helped him get his old and big and, I now found, very heavy case. I carried in the stack of sandwiches, the four gallon Sears Ted Williams water jug he'd made us stop and buy. As, out in the brilliant open, I closed the tailgate I felt the weight of all those watching eyes between my shoulder blades. I felt a jelly-fish in vulnerability, until I stepped inside. Sandwiches—food for a long wait. A sort of banquet. It was academic but I went through the motion. I put bread and water in one corner.

'All right, then?' I said.

'I got the easy part,' he said.

'If I can't get him out here,' I said. 'You won't have a car. How'll you get back?'

'It won't be back,' he said, 'but forward. I'll give you till tomorrow sundown. Then I'll walk on in by night.'

'It'll take all night and more.'

'If it does, it does. Maybe I hijack a truck. One way or another the bastard's going to die.'

I paused aimlessly, with a curious reluctance, in the doorway.

'Good luck,' he said.

'Yeah,' I said, 'thanks. Take care.'

Leaving him for Shepherd, I drove away. I felt cheapened and mean and ashamed.

CHAPTER FOURTEEN

Just turned noon. I was going down the road feeling sad and alone, with only the signal cloud of my own dust for company. I felt like a fly upon the wall of death, the ant tearing along the dotted line. A giant hand was going to come down at any second from out of a clear blue sky and poise above me, and St Francis of Assisi wouldn't be on the other end.

The world was a pancake. Funny farm there or not, I'd be glad to get to the other side. Like an actress trying for an Oscar in a sob part I cast my eyes continually upwards to the heavens. Impatience was rewarded. A fish did glint in its crystal bowl of wild blue yonder. Bandits angels-one-five. Steady chaps, they've spotted us. The road was dead straight. There was nothing to do but not faint. With my head half out the window, I watched the plane making lazy circles in the sky. I think that's how you'd describe them. When I began hearing the drone of its engine I knew that hawkeye was stooping to conquer.

He came suddenly at me very fast and low from almost directly in front. For a second I thought it was a wartime John Wayne movie and he was going to shoot me, tracers zacking down, all the way from here to eternity. But with a violent crescendo of noise snatched instantly away again, with the frantic swirl of a dozen **different** dust storms, he had passed. It was only a reconnaissance beat-up. He climbed again and for a couple of miles stood off from me at about two thousand feet. It was a Piper Comanche. I could tell. Higher cheekbones than the Apache. But lower attention span. Abruptly it got bored and flew away. North by north west. It was just at that point I first saw the other Indians.

They appeared as a column of smoke away, way over to my

right. That would be the old men, the women and the children kicking their heels to throw dust in their enemies' eyes. The fighting braves, General Custer, sir, would be over to the left holding their heathen, un-American breath. It was time for the new Gatling gun. I didn't have a gun to win the West with so, straight as an arrow, I just kept driving along. The Indians closed. When they got to about a hundred yards away I could see that they had cleverly disguised themselves as a Ford V8, four-wheel-drive ranch pick-up truck.

For another five miles, forty yards to the right, one and a half behind, it rode herd on me. I checked off the distance on the clock. Only about five minutes, then. But unnerving as all hell. My eyes kept flicking sideways to look out at it. Involuntarily. In all that open, wide expanse of emptiness, that sun-baked, flat-earthed run to the world's edge, I felt a hint of claustrophobia. This country wasn't big enough for both of us. At four miles my eyes edged sideways once again. Leaping and bucking like a bronco across the unworked ground, the truck kept on apace. If I could have changed into a rhino, I'd have charged. I pushed the needle up. I couldn't get away but, running hydraulically smooth along this even surface, I could certainly play the taws upon the livers of my trackers as they juddered in the cabined confinement of their horseless carriage. Five miles. The truck, at Christ alone knew what cost to spine and teeth, accelerated visibly. On its parallel course it pulled ahead. It looked like the last reel of *Ben-Hur.* I slowed a touch, watched its dust go further on. Eighty yards ahead, perhaps, it jolted savagely from its dead straight course and, left hand down, slewed hard towards the road. Rockingly it braked. Solid and black it straddled the track as I came on. There was time enough and all the room in the wide world to go around it, risking the shot to come. But I was in PR these last, dog days. I came to a gentle halt, twenty-two yards before the token roadblock. I waited to see what the pitch might be. It didn't come. I turned the ignition off and sat on to admire the view.

There was only one man in the truck. At spitting distance I could see that now. In his higher cabin he sat looking down at me through gold-rimmed pilot-style sunglasses. He wore a black and low-crowned cowboy hat. A bad guy, forsooth. Across the ledge of his window-down car door the blue-brown barrel of a carbine poked evil glints my way. We stayed like that, motionless, about a minute. Then he jerked his head. I didn't move. I seem to have spent my life looking down the business ends of guns. I didn't give a damn these days for those held by mere hirelings. It's silly, it makes you sit and sweat, it has you wondering if you haven't made your last, most positive, executive mistake. But it's the only way to demonstrate your class. As if that ever mattered. He jerked his head again. Twice. Still I didn't move. I had too much perspiration invested in time past by now. More time ticked away beyond recall. I held my hands high and in sight upon the steering wheel. It was hotter than Hades out there when you stopped. The heat got down inside your lungs. Raspingly.

He had a problem in decorum. To crook a come-hither finger at me would have seemed unbelievably old-maidenish. A fourth head-jerk would bring to mind the law of diminishing returns. When at length he bestirred himself, and the gun came lightly through the window, I thought it would be to fire a warning shot across or straight into my bows. No such thing. He swung himself down rangily from out his cabin, the carbine always under control. He strolled towards me, hat and cowboy boots and in between a paramilitary, para-cowboy rig of jeans and shirt of many pockets. Brother to the San Bernadino cop. Borgnine, Pickens, Palance, Van Cleef. Pick any one. I wondered if he'd roll a one-handed cigarette.

'Deaf, huh,' he said. He drawled in the manner much approved.

'Yes,' I said.

It gave him pause. He hadn't thought my wit would top his own.

'Where you heading?' he said at last.

'Ranch house.'

'What for?'

'Business.'

251

'Who with?'

'Your boss, sonny.'

Tall, a few feet from my window, he took a pace forward and poked the gun at me.

'Which boss?' he said.

'Raker,' I said.

'There's no one of that name I—'

'Oh yes the fuck there is!' I said. 'And wanting to see me too, whatever you and your idiot pilot buddy might think. Now you get on that squawkbox of yours and call him up and tell him Mr Powell is on his way. And when he says who the hell is that you tell him it's a guy he doesn't know yet bringing him in the head of an old Saigon buddy-buddy on a plate.'

I stared him straight between the eyes. It wasn't hard because I gazed upon my own reflection twinned in the dark, shiny lenses of his shades. On occasions I'm as self-regarding as the last of them. He, though, the hired help, was no Narcissus. He let the scene run on a while and gave me the obligatory if-it-was-just-between-me-and-you-kid heavy villain stuff. I think I may have yawned. When, like a cab driver's, his receiver started a sudden, independent metallic blatting, his loutish face was saved. He unfroze his freeze and, eyes on me, edged back sideways to his cabin. He hoiked a microphone, twisting and resisting on its tight curled lead, up to his ugly mouth. In a voice almost as thin on bottom as the cheap loudspeaker, he filed in his report. Bleat met bleat and faded on the desert air. I couldn't quite make out the individual words. It went on interminably. In the car, in the desert, hot and cross, I felt as snug as a bun in an oven. At last, tiny clouds of powder kicking up from his spurless heels, he was strutting back over to me. He hung it out while, movie-wise, he sought out and set fire to a Camel.

'When I back up,' he said, puffing smoke, 'go on down the road real slow. Thirty miles an hour. I'll be right behind you and, one step out of line, it'll be my personal pleasure to smear you into the dust.'

The resort to cliché apart, he acknowledged in no other way

my inevitable desert victory. I pressed the starter and we left El Alamein.

It only took a few more minutes. They weren't very pleasant because Rommel Road-Runner tailgated me so close I could feel his Jack Daniels breath hot on the back of my neck. But diversion was hard on my heels as well. Almost at once I had a forward view to occupy attention. Spread on the horizon, wide and low, were the palisades of Raker's Rancho Notorious. Wide and long except for two towering, flashing fangs. I tried to read the lay of the land as they grew steadily in size.

From some way out it didn't look like such an Armageddon of a place, not a fortress, not a concentration camp. But, closer in, it was plain it was no Samarkand—any more than the road, running through the arbitrary Ozymandias landmark of an arch, was made of yellow brick. They'd nailed the lonely arch, right between the eyes, with a marble sun-bleached skull. I looked twice, but it was a steer's. Underneath it swung a board and on the board was lettered some brand name. I wondered what a man could grow on that parched bareness of plain. Nothing, it seemed, beyond whiskers, prematurely old and a wire fence.

The fence came first. It wasn't barbed like the sort that divided the West, it wasn't as high as the corn in Oklahoma. It was straight and bright and new, boxing in a seemingly random sprawl of vaguely barrack-like buildings. I had no doubt that if you laid a glove on it you would grasp too that, making up in voltage what it lacked in feet, it was adequately high enough. I halted the Citroën. Where fence and roadway intersected was a gate with railroad-crossing type arms, heavy and metallic. At the gate there was a guard post. By the guard post were two men. They were cowboys too. They had black hats and great big guns. Tomorrow, perhaps, they'd wear their bus-conductor's sets.

Neither advanced, as I anticipated, to recognise me. A telephone, snaking out from its lodging in the sentry box, did the job instead. In my mirror Rommel was talking up a blitzkrieg on his mike. I passed the time counting the men on the two aluminium-painted water-towers, the fangs. Four, it seemed.

Five if that sudden gleam was indication of binoculars. Two, I wondered, why two water-towers? Unless to grant a cross-fire and uninterrupted view. Unless to double up the water instantly on tap. A honk from behind, a phallic lift of barrier in front. Who'd've thought Heathrow would lead to this? The Afrika Korps arcing from behind spattered my car with dirt and dust and shale. More sedately I followed his over-acceleration in. As I passed beneath the elevated arm I shivered. Despite the heat, despite myself, I knew in miniature what Danton felt. My senses knew the crossing of a threshold into evil.

Not that you'd have noticed it. I trundled on in first behind the truck past huts and buildings—bunkhouse, cookhouse, motor pool—utterly unexceptional. Even the droning Piper, touching down now half a mile away, was commonplace in contexts such as this. There was nothing here remarkable beneath the New Mexican sun. It had me jumpy. It was too ordinary to be true. The truck turned left around a long, low hut. Now there was something to react to. Straight ahead was the centre piece of the spread-out complex, a wide porched hacienda, older by far in its directed harmony with the land than the years of all the outer buildings summed together. It probably dated in its founding from times when the presidio was based at Tucson and the territory was New Spain's. Low, rambling, Mediterranean, it certainly had been built before the Federal snatch of forty-eight. There must be water underfoot. No doubt it was in keeping with the present ownership that a pocket-handkerchief sized lawn of ersatz grass should desecrate with virulent green overkill the immediate prospect from the wide, thick-outer-walled verandah. The truck stopped and I stopped too. This time I deigned to descend. All cigarette, shades and hat, Rommel exacted his revenge while I walked up to him and then at casual, oblique gun-point conducted me up the garden path. He should've been in movies. I didn't tell him I couldn't have pulled a thing. The yellow-green bastard sward was like acid in the eyes. But suddenly with the heavy scent of magnolias came coolness and the balm of shade. I had gained the verandah. Another threshold stood before.

Through the thick, open double doors—heavy grey-dark wood and metal studs—I stepped inside. Something flashed. An electric eye was set in the two-foot-thick house wall. I hoped it had grown more accustomed to the gloom than mine. I wondered where they'd hid the camera. I opened the f-stop of my eyes up fast and pondered the point while the desert rat gave me a frisking. I was clean. That seemed to disappoint him. It wasn't like the film.

'In there,' he said. One day he'd jerk his head off. I quit the hallway entrance for a large, open room. Once it had been a fine and gracious place, and the makings were still there. Long column beams ran longways towards a magnificent carved fireplace, a marriage richly worked in stone and wood. Wide windows deeply set in the thick walls to either hand let in a softened and a gentled light. That thickness bestowed the blessing of un-air-conditioned coolness—just as in the desert nights it would lend warmth. Doors in every wall, open and wide, extended the sense of spaciousness. Arches within that acreage of space broke up monotony where they divided and kept proportions down to an informal and domestic scale. Bright, unfading tiles, fetched long ago from Spain or Portugal, set around each window, banished the danger of too sombre tone. Everything else had been fetched from Neiman-Marcus and was wrong.

The fireplace housed a cocktail bar, formica and chrome, brushed steel and plexiglass. A brushed steel fridge hummed quietly alongside. A Coke machine adjacent rounded out the set. It also lent a garish counterpoint to the juke box diagonally over on a second wall. That was the wall hung with the weaponry. Not antique, curio—guns of interest only to collector and psychiatrist—but modern, functional, death-dealing arms stacked up unornamentally in rows as on a catalogued display. The only punctuation to their rigid, prosaic rows was a large, brass, central eagle, wings outspread, perched with gripping talons on a bronze globe of the world. His fierce eyes stared obliquely over to the console of a radio transmitter set on a third wall. He lusted, I knew, to tear at the untidy, tangled clutter of those entrails with his razor claws. That would be fine if en route he would rend the bechromed pool table, centred among the pack of honey yellow leather armchairs and sofas that thirtied up the place. The décor nagged at me. I couldn't place it. Then I could. It was the apotheosis of your sergeant's mess.

The floor was a puzzle too. Once it must have been great flag-stones or, more likely, subtle tiles. Now it was yellow parquet. But of a curious wood. If sprung, it gave just fractionally. Testing, I pressed hard on its interlocking blocks.

'Pigskin, son, pigskin,' someone said. 'Like the footballs, only better.'

I looked up and found myself, at longest last, looking at the man called Raker.

I should have known he'd be just like the room, but it still came as a shock. As usual size had much to do with it. He was a big son of a bitch, his large beer-belly offset by the thick roll of muscle above his shoulder blades. Big blond hands and wrists, heavy upper arms. I knew at a moment's glance he could more than manhandle me.

'Sit down, son, sit down.' The voice was whisky sour, thick with a husky edge.

It wasn't a question of courtesy, but of not seeming ill at ease. I accepted his Southern comfort and sat down. The chair damn near engulfed me, the feather cushion gave so much. The curious yellow texture wasn't vinyl, wasn't plastic and yet its silky smoothness felt unnatural. I rubbed a puzzled palm over its suppleness.

'Unborn calves' skin,' he said. 'Ripped out before they start in growing hairs. Smooth, huh? Hell of a job matching hides.'

I pulled my hand away. Obscenity was now a presence in the room. I was glad. It lent motive to malignancy.

I looked at Raker. He reminded me of someone. Still standing, foreshortened, he bulked even larger, grosser. I could see now a heavy roll of flesh girdling his hips. It was forced down there and held by the wide leather belt buckled tight around his waist. That buckle, a thunderbird in Mexican silver and turquoise, was the only touch of colour to his dress. His tan, bepocketed shirt, his tan whipcord pants wanted only a chevron or so to put him back in uniform. His crew-cut red-grey hair had never been discharged.

Only his head was smaller than life. And disquieting. The faintly bulbous blue eyes, the pinched fat duck's arse of a mouth just faintly hare-lip gave his face a piscine look. I felt that he'd also been ripped untimely from the womb at a slightly less than human stage of evolution. You couldn't hope for fellow feeling there. And yet, for all that, it still contrived to be the most ordinary face I ever saw. It had the mindless ordinariness of every bleacher quarter-back that ever screamed 'Throw the bomb!' with all the downfield receivers covered. It was the face that thought Frazier a great white hope. The face that bought Nixon's used car. It was the face that to keep Troy No. 1 would launch a thousand spaceships.

'What do you want?' it said.

So. A business sense. He hadn't wasted breath huffing and puffing routine opening you've-got-a-nerve threats.

'Well now,' I said, 'I'd have to say it was more a question of my having something you want. Someone.'

A little smile spread over his glazed features, the fish-eyes took on life. It was as if he were just going to tell the boys his favourite dirty joke. He nodded vaguely at the receiver-transmitter.

'I got the message,' he said. 'Someone from sweet Saigon.'

He giggled. His voice sidled huskily up the scale. Andy Devine.

'Only one person I'd want from there,' he said, 'and you ain't got him. What you've got is trouble.'

'Sweet Tran Chau Chieu,' I said. 'And I have.'

I wouldn't say it wiped the smile from off his face. Calculation —the relentlessly pedestrian thinking of a venal man—slowly took control.

'How come?' he said at last.

'He came looking for you,' I said. 'All the way Stateside. I think you must have upset him. Before he found you, I found him.'

'He alive?'

'Yes.'

257

'You got him tied to the back of your car?'

I managed to laugh. Quite well.

'How much?' he said.

I shook my head.

'A job,' I said. 'A job.'

Amusement surprised the mercenary face. The giggle got higher in pitch.

'How come you headed him off?' he said. 'How come you know about him anyhow?'

'We had a deal going,' I said. 'An arms deal. That's what I'm good at.'

Calculation again.

'And?'

I let the question hang there in the cool room.

'I'm a reasonable man,' I said. 'Why don't I make delivery to prove it? We can deal when you've got him under wraps.'

He ambled a few deliberating paces.

'When you've got no more cards?' he said.

'I'll have just done you a very big favour,' I said. 'Shown I'm levelling. You aren't going to kill a gift horse.'

Click, click, click.

'So, where's he at?' he said.

'I've got him stashed away around fifteen, maybe thirty miles from here.'

So he knew almost certainly where it was. He knew for sure he could track it down. That's why he'd settled in that pancake land. The walls of his face grew rigid as he tried not to show his pleasure.

'I've left a friend with him,' I said. 'The friend's got instructions.'

The inner smile left his face. I looked at my watch.

'If I'm not back there in one hour and forty-three minutes from now,' I said, 'my friend's going to cut him loose and they're going to split.'

I was suddenly scared hollow. It was the irrevocable setting of a time limit. The smart money must all say that I'd be dead within its span. Well, amen. He stared down at me and shrugged.

'So I lend you some boys and you go get him,' he said.

'My friend has another instruction,' I said.

'Oh?'

'He doesn't release him alive unless you come out for him too.'

Silence.

'You'd like him alive. First,' I said.

He began to shake as the wheezy, ascending giggle came again. He was furious.

'Now I know you ain't got him,' he said. He stopped laughing. All his ordinariness gathered in a pique of petty, monstrous evil. There was total menace in that sudden silence. I remembered the commonplace buildings on the outskirts of his ranch and realised there must have been just such a prosaic approach to Belsen.

'Clint!' he said.

Beau Geste came towards me holding his gun more pointedly now and wearing a thin grin. It had to have been Clint.

'Oh, I've got your boy,' I said. 'And my friend's name is Olivares. Rafael Olivares.'

Raker's gesture stopped Clint in his tracks.

'He's a little upset too,' I said. 'You got a way of losing friends. Fact is, he thinks I'm bringing you out there so he can get even for that little shindig in Sonora ... Oh, by the way, there's a letter, sealed for the moment, with a mouthpiece in LA. If I don't show up in the next ten days...'

I let my voice tail off and left him room to think. Nothing could be so thin. It was like making ice cubes without a fridge.

'If what you say is true and you've left those two together,' he said, slowly, thickly, 'Olivares will have killed Chau Chieu by now. For laughs.'

I shook my head.

'He's roughed him up some,' I said. 'But family honour comes first with him. He wants you most and first. He wants the bait alive.'

'I can pick up Olivares any time,' he said.

'Sure,' I said, 'but any next time his guns are going to have the slugs back in.'

Mouth a little open, he looked at me. He must have missed insanity by half a gene. I abruptly realised why he'd looked familiar. He was the antithesis, the low-down, no-good reverse incarnation of Klaus Holt.

'I couldn't do anything about the knife,' I said. 'You'll have to watch that. I can show you exactly where he's at.'

He looked at me.

'I told him I thought I could get you to come out,' I said. 'I told him you'd never come out alone. He said he'd take his chances for a shot at you.'

He looked at me.

'Two for one,' I said.

'What are you after?' he said.

'I told you. A job. You're going to be a hand short.'

He looked at me. I continued to look back. He nodded.

'All right,' he said at last, husky almost to the point of whisper.

'But if you're fooling, lying, cheating, you're going to be laughing on the other side of your grave.'

'You can be right behind me all the way.'

Now he giggled.

'Right behind and a little above,' he said.

I stood up. The gun still on me, I left the room of gentle breezes and went out through the verandah and the archway with magnolias around. The sun forearm-smashed me between the eyes. The lawn was acid still. I wondered when man had ever laid his neck so willingly upon the block. The mind is endlessly elastic. With that thought I found, amid everything else, new reason to worry.

CHAPTER FIFTEEN

Out of the guarded gate, out on to the desert road again with the declining rays of the westering sun beginning to be a trouble, that worry continued to vibrate in my mind. It was more of a distraction rocking unsecured, unfocussed to and fro among my thoughts than the fierce stabs of sunlight. It was more of a distraction than Clint Rommel, Camel in mouth, carbine on lap, sitting ramrodly by my side. It was even more of a distraction than the white helicopter, a dark angel for all that, whipping up its own dust storm as, low over the ground, some forty yards behind, it stalked the Citroën. When in a hesitant, iridescent whirl it had risen up from behind some of the buildings I had felt, along with the nudge of carbine in my ribs, the sinking shock of powerlessness. I didn't as an adult recognise the smallish model—it wasn't one I'd ever filmed from—but my childhood did. Here came the chopper to chop off my head. The high ground, the manoeuvrability it bestowed, went some way to explaining why Raker should unnecessarily risk his neck outside his shell. When, as I waited for the gate to elevate, it hovered deafeningly, sand-blastingly near, I could see him, one of three within the perspex dome. He was the one riding sidesaddle behind the world's most awesome airborne cannon. Awesome was the word. Shepherd's men had been so well concealed it was hard to believe that he'd budgeted for a pitched battle with aerial support. The barrier rose up. A rabbit, prey for the steel eagle, I drove out into the enormous, open, landscape.

The temptation was to crouch. It was like a single-threaded sword above your head. And yet it was the problem within my head that, by two miles down the road, had gained the upper hand. Raker was wearing ersatz battle dress ... but I couldn't believe he was humouring me for kicks ... There was something ... the buzzing sense of awryness went, fuzzy, unclear, backwards and forwards, endlessly rocking through my thoughts. If such were thoughts that lacked a centre as much as my latter-day actions lacked everything but suicidal impulse. The miles were being eaten up. I would cop Clint Camel's opener when the shooting all broke out. I didn't fancy that. Me living or dying now was no big deal in general. But it would please him far too much for me to think of allowing him the satisfaction unresisting. I wondered how dumb he was. I wondered if he'd considered that, if his boss saw fit, he'd rake the car from stem to stern and the both of us together.

A lump was up ahead in the middle of the track. It was a motionless tortoise, ten thousand miles from its home. It was waiting for something to nudge it and give it a sense of direction. I swerved slightly and avoided it. Let it try working out its own salvation. No bullets blatted out behind. I'd half expected them, but as the helicopter came on, implacable in my wake, Raker saved his rounds for bigger game. No staccato burst disturbed the constant menace of the chunter of its blades. A lizard ran into the road. Grey-green, it paused mid-way and, turning, watched my fast approach. Then, ancient, ageless, it had vanished in a flash. Lizard-like.

'You the feller booked in earlier ... ?'

It wasn't, Heaven knew, the road to Damascus, but no flash of light could have been brighter. The buzzing dissonances in my head swelled suddenly into one great crashing chord of comprehension. The scales fell from my eyes. The diffuse, shifting half-perceptions that had melted nebulously in and out of each other were suddenly racked sharply home to focus and perspective. Focus sharp as a stiletto. I could see now with perfect, stabbing clarity why Raker should issue so confidently forth' and how I, in the welter of duplicity, had been taken for the longest ride, played for the biggest sucker of all. It was such an *American* way to kill, to use an ice-pick. Tran Chau Chieu would never have worked it that way. *Earlier! Earlier*, the ashen old reptile of a night clerk had said. Not *yesterday*. Not *a couple of nights back.* Not *last week. Earlier.* The same day! Tran Chau Chieu hadn't done an ice-pick job because Tran Chau Chieu hadn't been near room 504 of the Crescent Hotel. I saw now how those officialesque, Olivares-alienating photographs had so conveniently been found upon Eddie the barman's outstretched body. Planted. I saw how uncoincidental it had been that a border clamp-down on narcotics should have been mounted just as seven would-be wetbacks, illiterate and unsuspecting, were started on a last drive north. The same day! The day after Ames had dragged me staggering from my room. Tran Chau Chieu had been no nearer to room 504 than the sidewalk a couple of blocks away. Another plant. The icepicked accessory I'd stumbled on up there was décor of Shepherd's execution. The helicopter was hotfoot pursuing me, not to uncertain rendezvous but, as Raker knew, to prearranged appointment. An appointment he'd been told he ought to keep by the man who'd come to be his boss and who'd proved the most double-featured of us all.

Two things followed. Olivares would be dead by now. Once again, duped up to my eyeballs, I'd unthinkingly delivered a fellow traveller up to his/her (strike out one) uneaseful death. It was a role in which I had become promiscuous. And Olivares had played out the underprivileged hand that Life had dealt to him. That got to me. The vision of his loser's hatchet face came up before me and the speeding road, obliterated the chunter of the helicopter. A deep, animal rage within me grew incendiary, then turned to ice. He'd have thought I'd set him up. For that, for him, before I shortly died, I'd try to take as many out as possible. Although vengeance would, after a posthumous fashion, be his. That was the second thing. After my death, if I were right, the double act of Shepherd and Chau Chieu would, incidental to the pursuit of their own designs, exact for him a full, if wrongheaded, revenge.

Take as many out as possible. Easier said than done with the oomegooly bird above, poised at steel stretch to stoop, and the outline of the abandoned shacks growing taller against the far horizon. The machine-gun was mounted off-centre on the port side. It couldn't have too wide a field. Nor too steep an angle down. I'd never have put a camera there. If I braked suddenly quite possibly the chopper would be past before Raker could traverse and depress enough to keep me in his sights. And—first things first—braking hard might, just might, throw Panzer Pete, the rat riding shotgun, equally hard against the windshield so I could grab his carbine and there possibly etc. etc. It wasn't on. Perhaps therefore ... We were closing fast on the buildings, now able to pick out the broader features. Perhaps better to gamble my co-pilot, derivative of cop-out television, would chicken when the chips were down and, if ignoring the ground fire, I drove foot down hard at a shack ... I caught my breath. Something else was becoming visible as we drove down hard upon it. Something else, dark, lumpish was in the middle of the roadway. It was neither tortoise nor mirror. At fifty yards even with its back hunched and turned away I could tell it for what it was. A body.

I braked. At twenty yards I stopped. The chopper was instantly and deafeningly hovering overhead. Sand whipped in at the open windows like hail, stinging furiously, blindingly. Clint wasn't just for laughs. In the thick of it, just as I tensed to lunge, he got the gun barrel in my throat. That put an end to that. I just sat there eyes closed getting a sandpaper facial while the great power-drill in the sky went round and round. Then noise and driving grit abated in intensity. The chopper was standing further off. I risked opening an eye. A dark veil, shot through from behind with shafts of gold, had been drawn on the world outside. Slowly, filtering down, this dusky pall quite beautifully grew translucent, then transparent. Halfway to settling it softly showed once more what I had almost thought would prove to have been spirited away. A solid lump, as large as life. The body.

The gun muzzle thrust bruisingly into my throat.

'Get out and take a look and do everything real slow.'

Tough guy talk. I moved my eyes to look at him. He was all dusted up.

Slowly, then, I got out of the car. True Grit opened his own door, slid his carbine outside. The chopper noise was instantly more strident, harsh and alive. The ultimate chariot of wrath.

264

It hovered waveringly at short third man. Raker's dark lenses caught the opposing sun as he trained Big Bertha straight on me. Slowly I pointed a Victorian index finger at the corpse and then as slowly turned to limp towards it. Before I'd altogether turned I saw Raker begin traversing his following gun. I neared Olivares. He lay closer than I'd realised to the long deserted shacks. Inside a hundred yards. I wondered as I rounded him which set of guns would get me first.

It wasn't Olivares. It was Ames. And not strictly a corpse. He was breathing his last as I arrived. With some difficulty. A knife was through his throat. It looked familiar. Not Olivares, but his handiwork. I'd seen the counterpart of that knife adorning Tran Chau Chieu's right shoulder. Ames's eyes were open but they didn't look on any of this world. They stared unseeing. I knelt before him. A rich red began by suffusing his white shirt and city suit, then, progressively duller, merged into a darker caking of moist sand. Sand matted his hick face and hair. He must have thrashed about. Now he was all but still. A thin, blood-flocked film stretched at the corner of his open mouth, moved faintly through a quivering millimetre. It might have been the desert wind that blew it. He wasn't very pretty. I had to think hard of that basement room, the steel floor-bolted chair, to ease his passing on. It wasn't the wind. It had been him. A great convulsion shook his doubled frame. A throaty, gasping hollow rattling took on. The film grew greater in a poppy bubble, then slackened as the rattling ceased. The film froze. Between two breaths, one made, the other unachieved, I'd seen, give or take a current medical opinion or two, another death. It was with its understated ebbing out, its dying fall, the most terrible of all. It was almost as terrible as the clear, metallic click that now came to me on the wind from somewhere very near at hand.

I had a moment of pellucid nightmare. I was totally naked, totally exposed on the wide flatness of the world. There was no sheltering comfort ever to be found. I was chained to slow-motion by my leg. I tensed, made myself come back to reality. A man should die in the present. It was the acoustic shock of the rifle's loud report that drove me headlong, like a diver, into Ames. There was the shot, the crumbling crack of shattered glass, a high and brittle scream. I raised my unhurt head. The Citroën's screen had grown a spider's web. Clint Television was jerking blindly out the door. He had suffered a sudden rush of blood to the face. On reflex he was just about up on his feet when the second bullet struck him inches from the first. Written out of the series, he went spatteringly backwards without another sound, a boxer clean knocked out. Murder, kill the bum! Yes sir! there he goes. With all the slowed inevitability of instant replay. Then breakthrough—everything was happening fast. I looked behind. Olivares, the thick dirt and dust of desert camouflage shaking about him like a devil's halo, was rising to a rifle-ready crouch. The helicopter was driving forward fast with Raker's machine gun kicking up a closing trail of vicious spurting sand. Towards Olivares. The noise made me have to act. Just twenty yards. I gave it the college try. Gasping from the inner word go, in despite of my leg, I took off from the ground sprinter style. Some thigh thing tore at once but I tried to pile on the pace. The yielding sand underfoot tried not to let me. It slid away, nightmarishly, too soft for traction. Ten yards. Five yards. One yard from the shelter of the Citroën's hood an incandescent, white-hot hammer smashed stunningly at my wrist. I crashed headlong on to the roadway grit. My head was snapped around. I saw the man who'd shot me running for his own dear life.

Olivares didn't have a chance. He was trying to gain the chopper's gunless side. He moved much faster than I had, zigging and zagging as he went. But the chopper sedately rode back as it trod air, extending beneath it the ground he had to cover. For a moment there was no fire and then the shells started zigging and zagging too. They overtook their man. Olivares danced a broken, one-legged jig. In that instant, with the chopper almost stationary, there was an answering, contrapuntal rhythm of automatic fire. From the shacks behind, an iron flail raked back and forth across the chopper's broadside flank. It staggered in its hovering tracks. Everything in the world seemed shattered by this driving rain of death. And yet the chopper hung. It rose hard up. Gaining something of height, something of speed, it sought refuge in the sky. The pounding rounds pursued it. It wavered drunkenly. The firing stopped. The chopper made noises no chopper ought to make. It bucked and wobbled. But still gained altitude. The firing started up again, working for the rotor. It lacked in accuracy. Losing height a touch, the chopper staggered down the sky. It made sixty yards. No more. From off the desert floor a second machine gun chattered its different note of death obliquely up. A sitting target, lurching and heeling like a drunken albatross, the chopper hung in the balance. Something flew shining from it. I think its engine seized. From about a hundred and fifty feet, gyrating and pitching in wilder and wider areas, it started to fall. Slowly at first. It didn't plummet. It was partly braked by its still turning rotor. But not enough. At forty feet, still under fire, it had gained an alarming speed. I held my breath. At twenty feet, startling me though I'd have done the same, a figure was airborne, sprawling from its side. Even against the sun I still had time to make out Raker by his size. Then, at ten feet, the chopper blew apart. I'm sure it happened before it hit. It was your everyday atomic blast. In miniature, of course. A lurid, orange-yellow ball of fire hung eternally in the all-breath-taken air. Not eternally. A gathering roar of sound was obscuring the flame with an oily shroud of smoke. That's when I ducked my head. I must have been on the periphery. There was a last fading rasp of hot breath and then, all around, the patter of tiny sheet-metal shrapnel. A brief moment passed as a far-flung few spattered randomly down about me. Something clanged on the Citroën but nothing hit me. I heard a last burst from the far, the up-field gun. Then all was deafeningly quiet.

A groaning broke the silence. Mine. I remembered I was racked by action-crippling pain. I bit on some sort of a mental bullet and remembered to remember I was in two lines of fire. I remembered not to look down at my wrist. This wasn't the time or place for passing out. It was time to make up my mind. I took the devil I knew. I had been fleeing Olivares's wrath as

267

manifest in his marksmanship. But bullets work utter changes. By embroidering his own initials on Olivares's shirt, Raker had made that the better way to go. There was silence all around. Without moving at all, I tensed myself. Second down and one. I breathed deeply in and in a dive-semi-lurch-cum-roll moved everything I had. I made it. I was alongside the nice big, lovely, solid Citroën and not drawn a single shot. I'd never seen a better quarter-back sneak. All without Jerry Kramer. If I'd had a sound pair to work with, I'd have given myself a big hand.

I'd landed on it. My bent knees-to-chest posture as I cramped my back into the car was less an attempt at burrowing to safety than an effort to stop myself spewing. Somehow I didn't. I was awash with nausea but somehow I didn't. Not even when, assembling my war weary nerve, I made myself look downward at my bleeding wrist. Smashed to buggery, it was not a pretty sight. I know because I fainted. Only for the space of three heartbeats. But for that time my being tried to blot out what it saw. The bullet had disintegrated the bone on the edge of the wrist. The round, knobbly one. As the wound expanded to comprise the entire universe, it looked like the vilest exploded view of a medical illustration ever made. In a small round area, regular spurting pants of blood were inundating, dripping from, a bright crater of raw flesh and shattered, ragged bone. It was the red on white of it that got me. It made me feel like meat. Steady. I tried to flex a finger. It was like grasping fire. When I stopped the pain, not playing fair, went on ascending its endless, torturing scale until I whimpered like a child. I'd never pan camera again. Or shoot gun. Dead meat was what I was. With that there came the seventh wave of hurt, shaking earth to its foundations, making them reel. I felt myself wanting to faint. But I wouldn't die in the dark. I sought distraction round about to keep my senses alive.

Right arm rigid before me like an ossified priest, I undid my belt. With teeth and left hand I began to twine it tourniquet-tight about my forearm. It hurt. I must think about something else. Think positive. I was at the car. There was just a chance, just, that if I could sneak aboard I might make it out of there.

A slim enough hope, Christ knew. Guns that could down a chopper would blow this trusty steed right out of the water and to Kingdom Come. But if the second gun was a fair way off, and if I could start her unobserved, I might jump the gun in the derelict building. Blood oozed down my sleeve with an extra spurt as I pulled the belt finally tight. Even if I could wrap my one mitt round a gun, I'd never get off a straight shot. Not within half a mile. The blood flow had dwindled now. With a handkerchief I did staunch work. The hand was shot but if I escaped, I'd live. And he who quits and runs ... I heard a groan. This time it did not belong to me.

I looked to Olivares. He was down but not quite out. He was moving now and conscious. And beset by two big problems. One was he'd been hit very bad. The US Cavalry had opened fire too late. They'd prolonged, but not saved, his life. Moreover, in that scrambling, frenzied decapitated chicken dance to the helicopter's tune, his rifle had been flung some dozen paces from where he'd bit the dust. He was making for it now. His residual instincts were a killer's. He squirmed forward full length a yard or so along the sand. Then suddenly was on his knees. The front of his shirt was more saturated than my sleeve. I was too astonished to react when, with a grunt, he was standing on his own two feet. The gun from the shacks opened fire at once. Too much at once. Its staccato aim was off. Dirt spurted up ten feet in front of him. Still he fell. Not in desperate search of cover but in pure, unbalancing shock. Too unsinewed to stand on his own two feet, he was, for a while longer, spared again. The gun held its fire. He had found cover. The strip of desert track had just shoulder enough to keep him down out of sight.

It was the end of my chance of escape. I'd got him into this. Until he died, in case he didn't, it behoved me to try getting him out. A man who couldn't stand. A man who couldn't hold a gun. Put them together ... I lowered my head and looked the other way beneath the car. Clint Carbine was stretched out a little way back on its far side, supinely rehearsing Eyeless in Gaza. The gun was well in view, not an arm's length from the still open passenger door. I reached up and opened the driver's

269

side door. Now it was my turn to squirm. Trying so carefully not to rock the car I pulled myself into it and on to the front seat. It was like a roofed-over sandbox inside, but gritting my teeth I pressed on. I made the sinuous, easy progress of a hog-tied dachshund traversing wet cement. But I made it. I slid to the tunnel-less flat floor and reached out. The open wing of door gave perfect cover. Only my outstretched arm could have been in enemy view as I strained towards the gun. It was out of reach and then, at the cost of agony to my weight-supporting right elbow, was safely within my grasp. Nobody took me for Lew Ayres. Slowly, grunting, dripping with sweat, I drew the carbine up into the car.

Now the door. That was my forte. Slowly, slowly, slowly, so slow the patience of a saint would have been tried, I pulled it to, then tight on the half lock. The sun cast no reflections on me. I got away with it. Head down, I tilted the back of the passenger seat as far forward as it would go. I tilted the driver's seat back and, bent double, scrunched myself down. The shell that got me would have to knock half the stuffing out of the car en route. Or blow it sky high. I slipped the gear lever into first. I turned the key. I pressed the starter button. Without too much judder, she fired. The door my side was still ajar. Thirty fast yards was the aim. I damned the torpedoes and let out the clutch.

They had an if-it-moves-shoot-it-policy. I'd travelled about four feet when they cut loose. Then it was mayhem night in the glass menagerie. The air was lacerated by flying glass as the rivetter outside warmed to his task of destruction. I had my face three-quarters masked by my bad arm. The good one felt the wheel jerk savagely with a sudden wrench. The front end bit. My foot hard down, the engine screamed, a tiny fraction of noise so loud I wanted to mis-steer on its account alone. It didn't die. Keep on, not now but ... now! I pulled the wheel, the car came off the track, the engine missed. So did my heart. The engine fired again and I was home. I hit the key and handbrake all in one and grabbing the carbine took off through the door. The earth rose up and knocked into me a lifetime's sense to replace all the forced-out breath. I rolled and sprawled the ten yards to Olivares. Fresh inner constellations of white pain went radiating from my wrist. What infinite capacity for taking such. I was the Michelangelo Kid.

Olivares had watched. Powerless. He must have thought the Citroën a juggernaut aimed for him. He started now with a face that was all fang. But the firing had stopped. The car wasn't set alight. Save the windshield, there wasn't an intact piece of glass left of it, but, behind it now, Olivares had cover. Through me he had a gun.

If he could use it. I slithered across to him. He had indeed been struck a mortal blow. In that last doubled, dummying run a bullet had hit him around the top of his back and gone on in and down. It must have done for his right lung and God knows what else beside. But not his mind. Dying, he was alive to who I was, what I'd done. The jet eyes transmitting hate from a face drawn even thinner, sharper, left no doubt of that. There was very much Indian in the life-blood spilling from his veins. Now, in a choking, guttural Spanish going back to furthest alley childhood, he cursed me from his other loser's heritage. I shook my head in inadequacy. I had no words. The headsman asks forgiveness before he wields the axe. Now, in English, he was cursing me with steady, unheated hate.

'I didn't know,' I said. 'I swear. They suckered me. I as much as pulled the trigger on you myself.'

Across the sand I pushed the carbine within his reach.

He was incredulous. He stared at me.

'I'm sorry,' I said.

He rolled his weight on to one side and shoulder. He stretched his other arm out. He pulled the gun slowly in. I watched the barrel draw through the sand like an undeviating snake. He shifted weight again, had the gun in both his hands. The muzzle, pointing at me, seemed no wise harder than his eyes. The blood running out of both of us measured an endless time.

'Raker,' he said. Very thickly.

I understood. His basic class had granted my reprieve. I had the grace to take it in my stride. I shook my head.

271

'Not Raker,' I said. 'He's taking orders too.'

'Raker!'

Again I understood. I nodded.

'If I can, I will,' I said.

His eyelids blinked. Just visibly, he nodded too. The hate was changed. For us, it was all right.

I was glad. Glad that, beleaguered though we were; I had taken time to pause and order priorities. The Citroën's last charge had taken no more than five seconds. But the setting it up, my talk with Olivares, might have occupied a hundred years apiece. The time was overdue for having a look around.

I stole looks around and underneath the Citroën, spying out the land. Nothing seemed changed. Santa Ana wasn't charging with all his men. Patton was dead and gone. Emptiness. The cards had been dealt around this desert killing ground for a final, violent hand of bridge. Battlefield or conference, it was all a double-dealing game of bridge. Behind me, Olivares groaned. His breath rasped faster and harsher now. Locally speaking, I had no doubts on who was vulnerable.

It was the gun to the North that worried me. The crashed helicopter to the West was dummy, we might say. It was reasonable that East, the shacked-up gun, should sit pat right where it was. But, the helicopter down, it was North, the second gun to have opened fire, that seemed to have the lead. I squinted hard, shielded my eyes from the low sun. I couldn't see a sign of movement in his quarter. Not a sign at all. With every anxiety that I'd missed it, that he had moved and circled about, I continued to stare. If he was still there, why ... There was a groaning cough and Olivares dug me in the ribs. I turned, looked at him, turned back and followed the line of his gaze. It was amazing. He'd seen it before me. The approach of death had sharpened his earthly vision.

Camouflaged by his battledress, a man was crawling slowly, almost undetectable, around the south side of the charred and gutted chopper wreck. Raker. He'd survived the crash dive. West wasn't dummy after all. It answered two points. It explained why North had not felt free to roam. It suggested that

272

in its dying fall, the chopper had not had time to radio up some help. Raker had else said nothing and lain low, waiting for more of his boys.

Olivares was like a bellows now. His breath heaved in and out. Sweat bathing him, teeth bared, he was trying to hold, to align the gun. He quivered now with the effort to hold life in until his revenge be served. He quivered with the distant nearness of that revenge. Prone like an infantryman, he hadn't the strength. The barrel weaved and bobbed as if sick of the palsy each time he tried raising up his head. I slid alongside him a little to the front. I slid my good arm under the wavering gun. That helped. It was his pool shot, but I was building the bridge. It helped, but not enough. Raker was halted now, low upon the ground. It was a straight shot but over a hundred yards. Try it next time you die. The barrel seesawed on my arm, slithered to and fro. Raker was still. The gun was not. As wickedly simple as that. Olivares's breath was like a lover's coming after half an hour. The wavering grew worse. I willed it to stay still. The gun jerked high and cracked down on my arm. The breathing stopped. I brought my eyes down the barrel's blue-black length and on beyond the stock. The eyes were still open, still looked out, but their eagle sight gazed on nothing now. His revenge was still to seek. On his broken face was the look of a boy told that there's no food. His last vision had been of defeat.

As gently as possible, I untwisted his hands from the gun. I had promised. I could try. Perhaps left-handed I might bring it off. I got it as far as my shoulder, a sinister, awkward weight. I was surely no Billy the Kid. Jesus H. Christ! My right arm would be no support. I fought down the pain. Perhaps steadied on his corpse, the gun could be fired by one hand. I started ... I never found out.

Way across no-man's-land, Raker was on his feet. His arm whipped like an outfielder's. The ball arced fast away. This explosion had little of flash, was dirty, devoid of flame. But not lacking for a mark. Up from the desert floor, akimbo, there started a leaping man. He made no sound as, twisting, he fell back heavily, a flung rag-doll, to be lost back somewhere on the ground. But the cast was small enough now. Revenge had escaped me too. Raker had pre-empted me in despatching Tran Chau Chieu.

Now he was charging on, heading for the shacks. A big man running like a moose.

'Don't shoot! It's me! It's me!' I heard him yell. I don't know where he thought the first shots on his chopper had come from. I don't know what was in his mind. All I knew was, boy, did he have surprises ahead. It came when he was about thirty to forty yards out. The gun stuttered shatteringly. Raker went into the dance of the clowns, stumbling forward, jerking back upright. He was the marionette of a spastic puppeteer. He was the Highland Fling on banana skins. He was—chuckle—falling down dead.

It had come down to me and Old Shep. Or, considering ways and means, me, Old Shep and the Citröen. If it would run after all the punishment it had shipped. I looked at its tyres. By a miraculous stroke of unfortunate luck they were still intact. Unscathed, they afforded no excuse for ducking an all-or-nothing kamikaze run. And I had to go for it. I would be grieved some for all eternity if Shepherd made it a clean sweep without my throwing one last pitch. It wouldn't be all, it would be nothing. That's what kamikaze was about. It would be his pennant, anyway. But I'd have the eternal satisfaction of knowing I'd thrown my heart—that it had happened over my dead body.

In a crouching run, trying hard not to tip my hand, I made for the newly air-conditioned car. Crouched, crunching the sea of glass, I clambered inside. Raker's liquidation had not been without instruction. At the risk of my craning neck I had located from which of the shacks his erstwhile sleeping partner was bestirring himself. Number three. I'd never make the yardage but I was honour bound to try. Let me smash through those bullets and that flimsy wall and I'd drop the two-faced bastard for the biggest loss of all. I'd hold the wheel dead straight through death and dead straight into hell.

Praying she'd fire—I was doing more of that stuff of late—I

reached out to the key. Before I made contact there was the anticipating, distant advance echo of a car starting up. That made sense too. If Olivares and I weren't dead, Shepherd knew there was no chance of us running to fight another day. Bums like us he could snap up *ex officio*. I hit the starter button. She went first time. But even as I offered thanks a Toyota Landcruiser spurted into view from behind the row of shacks. I floored it, started off one-handed. There was still hope of sorts, still scope to kill. If I could stand the draught I still had chances enginewise of staying with him.

I don't know what I had in mind—ramming him, broadsiding him off some road, riding him under a transcontinental freight ... all I knew was that, galled aesthetically that it had not been fought to a finish on this foreign field, I wanted to hang on to him. But the chase was never on. It must have been the desert air that made men die so hard out there. As the Toyota, gaining because it had started first, pulled away from me, Tran Chau Chieu rose, swaying, weaving, but erect on his own two feet. I muffed my change-up in surprise as I cursed my over-simplifying mind. He was flagging the Landcruiser down. He must have crawled some way. He was only about twelve yards from its line of flight as it continued to gain jolting speed.

A hundred yards back, jolting too, the wind savaging my face, I watched. There was a moment—as long as it takes to look in a rear-view mirror—when the Toyota seemed to deviate a fraction, promised to turn from its course. The promise was not fulfilled. The wheels veered back to a hard-line policy. In that instant of correction there was a clear finality. It was like when a running back gets room and a clear way to the line. You get the utter certainty of predestined knowledge that he'll score. So now. That Landcruiser was wanting out. And so, just two beats later, the opening of Chau Chieu's fire. He had an open-frame automatic gun that he fired from against his hip. It was clattering like the chopper as the Toyota came abreast and panning with it in an arc of following lead. Now, palpably, the Toyota veered. I caught a gleam of glass scything through the air. The Toyota straightened, veered again, skidded, leap-frogged

275

and stalled. Forty yards back Tran Chau Chieu began limping after it.

I'd scarcely slackened in my speed, had kept my foot hard down. I was closing on him fast. He started to turn and, not braking, I wrenched the wheel around. It was murder with just the left hand and going the wrong way but I slewed the car off course. In a wide arc I detoured way around him to the far side by fifty yards of the motionless Landcruiser. I pulled my wheel back round. In third, screaming at full revs, I drove head sideways down towards that car and, beyond it, Tran Chau Chieu.

The wheel bucked in my hand like a water diviner's rod, the car like a power-boat gone mad. My head smashed on the roof. But berserk I kept piling it on. I was doing sixty plus as I roared out from that cover with him straight between my sights. Kneeling, waiting, knowing what I was at, knowing it had worked with Sam, he opened fire at once. The world was shattered into galaxies of glass. They knifed into my face, the right arm half covering it. It took steel, my steel, not to drop my head. The wheel kicked at me harder than ever before. The noise was nuclear. Then I hit. There was a sledge-hammer jolt, a sense of him flying wide. I was past, out of the maelstrom and into clear, uneerily quiet waters. I slowed, came to a halt. Sweat, blood, ran into my panting mouth. The animal pounding of victory blood sang within my head. Through! I had come through! I was still—how wonderful—alive!

I looked behind. The victory chant was premature. He too was still alive. Alive and kicking, writhing on the ground. Not writhing now but crawling, dragged on by arms alone. Crawling to his gun five yards away. Him or me, gun or car. I turned the wheel again. It would hardly come. This time the tyres were shot. The car floundered, wallowed, failed to answer the helm. In the mirror I saw him move to the gun. Stay cool! Stay cool! I fought raw panic down. I let the car go forward, didn't try to turn. Now, well under way, I did. My right elbow also on the wheel, I levered for all I was worth. The wheel came round and, in an agonisingly wide arc, I circled back on him. He was halfway to the gun before I was pointed straight, still brokenly moving on as I lurched lopsidedly across the ground between.

The nightmare had invaded reality. Our duel in the sun would conclude in the feverish mode of a straining slow motion. We both crawled to a death. I dared not give the Citroën too much gas in case she stalled. As he neared his goal I once more had to will non-action. I considered leaping out and running, best as I could, to beat him to the gun. But I did not advance alone. My ghost, my revenant to bitter ends and pale mortalities, breathed icily his preference. Tran Chau Chieu's clutching fingers clasped around the gun as I flipped the lever to elevate the car. It whooshed, rose up. He rolled on to his back. I glimpsed the still classically handsome face. It was cool and undistorted, intelligence in control. Let that much be said. Rising I crunched nearer. He struggled to sit up. I didn't think he would but, unbelievably, he managed it. Too late. The final play was Chu Chin Chow on ice. The fender knocked the gun aside as the car straddled over him. I hoped it had knocked it far. As he slid out of sight I felt for an instant as if my open balls were dangling down below. I shuddered. I flipped the lever all the way down. That's when his suaveness broke. As the car hydraulically began to sink a scream came from underneath. A woman's scream. A martyr's scream. The last scream before insanity brings ghastly relief. It was the cry of a peasant napalmed to charred death, a Greek democrat on the Colonel's bench. The ghost's cold fingers stood my hair on end. Ice drilled through my spine. I hit the radio fast. From long ago and far away, a jazz tune came. The car went lower still. I turned the volume high. I knew the tune, recognised the unforced, flowing tenor. Wardell Grey. My ghost's exquisite, appropriate request. Two open fields. A fifties corpse outside Vegas town posthumously playing out an in-the-making corpse far from Vietnam. The car was all the way down at rest. Two inches from the ground. I think I sensed rather than felt the final resisting crunch. Static faded the tune. I sat there a long time. The horns of birdland faintly blew, then blasted high again. *Twisted.*

*   *   *

I sat and sat, powerless to move the car. That would reveal everything to the bright eye of day. I was afraid to look at what I'd done. Finally, arbitrarily it seemed, I opened the door. Not looking back, I limped away. The ghost limped with me, never more present, never more appeased. His hollow, claiming laughter echoed within my skull. He it was who looked behind and, liking what he saw, took off on *Scrapple from the Apple.* No doubt it looked like that. A station break. These few words: what price salvation now?

CHAPTER SIXTEEN

There was a final check to run. Watching the Landcruiser all the while I went over and retrieved the semi-automatic of the late Tran Chau Chieu and worked out how it worked. You squeezed a trigger. I went over to the Landcruiser. Slowly and from behind. Nothing stirred within. I edged around to the driver's door. It only took three hours. That's no time at all to hold your breath these troubled days. It wouldn't be easy, now. One-handed, I juggled the gun into position against my left hip. There still remained the door. With not a fraction of movement, only regularly pulsing, nauseating pain, I'd never get it open fast. Well this thing had helped bring down a chopper, fragmented my car. I stood off fast to about five yards away and opened up at the already punctured, buckled door. It was the loudest, frightening noise of all. Both eardrums nearly went along with my last good wrist. My hip was hammered flat. But the five rounds I got off sliced through the door like backers through net profits.

I waited. The reverberations died. More cordite drifted away on the freshening evening breeze. I slung the gun over my shoulder and limped up to the car. The door, understandably, didn't want to know. I wrenched it extra hard. This time, flying back hard, it came. Shepherd's body fell halfway to the ground, was caught and hung head down. Just like Sam. Only she, thank God, had never known such jagged, such casually impersonal, violation. A slow, muddied dripping commenced. I angled my own head. And looked at Sam. Her features were formed in shimmering superimposition over his. Unrelentingly. Blood was all about, enough to wash in, but I had not bought forgiveness with it. I was unredeemed in her blazing, inverted eyes. Ever condemned. I saw. I understood. The vision temporarily faded and I looked once more on him. He lacked, somewhat, the laconic impression of confidence imparted him by the anonymous eminence of his grey, official authority. It had deserted him, along with the frontal lobe. What was grey about him now was of a different matter. I didn't think I'd done that. I had shot too low. Perhaps a portion of me was obscurely glad. But he'd had it coming. It had taken me too long to see it, but he truly had. I was glad, whatever the last expense to me, that justly, he'd got his. I reached inside, turned the ignition off.

So. The killing had stopped. There was no one left but me to tell the tale. But me. Alive. The killing had stopped because there was no one else left. I was still alive. Just me to tell the tale and garner all the harvest of remorse. If ever again I could, dared pretend recognition of remorse. I was alive but if there were a hell I must be double damned beyond redemption. Not that there was. It was just that I felt faint. The natural aftershock of murder. I leaned against the Landcruiser, and for the first time in fifteen years felt like a cigarette. Perhaps that was the cordite I could still taste in my throat, still see drifting faintly down the wind. I thought of Clint's Camels but no, I mustn't. It was a bad habit. As addictive as revenge. And just as big a depressant. Richard Powell, the Slaughterhouse Kid. Kidding just exactly whom? No, I'd be all right. I wasn't really aghast, and already in the aftermath attempting to suppress the sense of what I'd done. That wasn't why I was shaking like a leaf. It was just that my legs felt hollow and my head felt light and I felt a little faint.

I stayed like that a long, long time. No one disturbed my rest. I had the panorama to myself. No retainers searched for their ring-bestowing liege-lord. At last the mounting pain of my torn wrist burned me back into a kind of present. I bestirred myself and did all the Kirk Douglas things. I went slowly over to the derelict huts and found two pieces of flat wood. I went over and numbly, unfeelingly, stole the broad leather belt from the spilt red sack of Raker's corpse. With all the left-handed awkwardness in the world I contrived some kind of a brace for my shattered, unfixable wrist. Then I went back to the Toyota.

I kicked Shepherd out and shards of glass on top of him. With the thick, short barrel of the gun I smashed away the fragments still remaining in their frames. In back I found a rag and cleaned the front seat and the pedal area. For that I should have had the cigarette. Halfway through, a wave of revulsion hit me and I had added to my work. But it brought a better way. When I resumed I was a half-step from reality, my head detached and distantly observing from the far end of the sky. When, with a minimal steering, changing gear all cacky-handed-like, I drove the quick-to-fire Toyota over to Olivares, my head aloofly nodded in approval.

He was stretched out straight, prone. I rolled him on his back. The set of eight was now complete. The last one laid in line. His features found no joy in it, just as in death they had found no peace. The Aztec harshness of those cruel, hatchet lines had not relaxed into a softer form. Awareness at the end of a mission unfulfilled had left them edged with hate. The loser in death—too narrow in ambition to be tragic. A loser. I looked down for a long time on that mirror of the dark side of myself. My ghost had become incarnate. Perhaps it was that sense, not an age-old propriety, that finally made me raise up his body and, with every difficulty, place it in the Toyota. I drove to the Citroën. With as much difficulty I placed Olivares on the rear bench seat. Panting, I backed the Toyota a long way off. I walked the distance back. I opened up the Citroën's tailgate. I took my money out. Taking careful aim at the wagon's boxed-in vitals, I sent a blaze of hammering rounds into its petrol tank. At about the fifth or sixth it went, louder, more violent than I'd expected. Hot air scorched past me and I all but made a third. I backed off. Olivares, like Elsie, had had a kind of funeral as they both had had a kind of life. As for the other bodies round about, they could take their chances with the dogs.

I climbed into the Toyota and took a last look round. It was quite a view—worth an entry in Poor Richard's almanac. It could have been gorgeous. The low-driving sun made luminous every detail of that ochred stretch-away to the world's rim. The brass had gone from the sky. It was a Cinemascope landscape by Turner. But living, more precise. Battlescape. In the middle distance the corpses took the eye. Not as many as on those other fields of death that had been and would be again, but visited with just as terrible a finality. I closed my eyes. A cooling breeze blew soft with eventide. Fierceness had left the low sun. There was a balm in the air. It was the balm of a Kent cricket green, of summer evening as the players leave the long-shadowed field to a gentle applause. I opened my eyes. I was not in Kent. From the still smouldering chopper, from the Citroën pyre, two black columns of smoke rode ghostly up the sky to drift in silent eloquence across the gilt wasteland. The desert had been painted red. The wind on my cheek had blown on Cain before. I put the Toyota in gear. Even as I did, I heard, high up, the faint drone of a plane. Who cared.

I forsook that place. I went away, that is. There was otherwise no quitting it. It would never forsake me.

I drove back to the main highway and turned east. I drove as far as the Rio Grande at Las Cruces. There I turned north. I drove one-handed and one-eyed, buffeted and smashed at by the night streaming through the glassless window. My head angled round, I kept my left eye closed. The bridge of my nose gave shelter to the squinting vision of my right. I could manage just on that. For a while I noted the freight trucks roaring by, and then the ceaseless rush of wind, the hypnotic coming forward of the ever-renewing road, took me beyond myself. My heart flared with a great ringing emptiness and I had no sense of time and place.

It was the cold that restored me to the present. In the not so small hours I realised I was freezing. Else, it was the instinctive sense that I needed gas. The needle was way down low. I was tempted to pull over and seek sleep. But once off I would sleep all day, and an all-day parked Toyota, much battered, would sooner invoke police attention than one rolling steadily on. I didn't want to end with the whimper of fatigued confession to dumb authority. I didn't ever want another confrontation scene. I kept on keeping on.

I cruised sedately through Albuquerque. Alone this time. Nobody raised a dead of night finger. On the north side of town I found an all-night filling station. I had no choice. To reach the pump I had to pull within the circle of bright light. I stayed inside and held my breath. Nothing. I must have looked more shell shocked than the car. But nothing. The transistor tuned to the tin station, was all. The trainee punk that gassed me up couldn't wait to get back to it. Or pretended he couldn't wait. Maybe he was almost finished the apprenticeship. Maybe a gas war was on. He'd not have done differently by a stray horseman of the Apocalypse.

Now it was easy if I didn't die of sleeplessness or crash nodded off at the wheel. No trance now. I had to finish on will. I made thinking come to keep collapse at bay. There were questions I'd never quite have answered. I'd never know at just what stage Shepherd, acknowledging that absolute officialdom corrupts as absolutely, had bought in, taken over Raker's operation. Quite late in the day, perhaps, before its shift into overdrive and Raker's return to civilianhood. I'd never quite know why Shepherd had wanted Raker removed and dead. Hardly to be sole supremo. His was a totally background role requiring a figurehead. It smacked much of severing the snake's head to bring sure death to the whole long length. Perhaps official enquiry, concerned at the post-My Lai image it cut in the world's press, had been spurred to wrench open its long-sealed eyes. Perhaps Shepherd had been anticipating investigatory embarrassment. Or perhaps he'd had in mind a switch of running-mates. I'd never know exactly when Tran Chau Chieu had acknowledged that he was too far from home to go it alone. I'd never know what kind of deal they'd struck. I'd never know who first had approached ... No, Shepherd, of course ... Perhaps he wanted to revert to a Saigon base. As if that mattered now.

The dawn came up like a long slow yawn eastwards from Santa Fé. I didn't dare stop for food. Not even coffee. I'd never get back—no sane, intervening shadow of a good Samaritan

283

would let me—behind the wheel. It would be instant Sleepy Hollow. For about as long. I put my foot down, fought the wind, tried to keep my brain in gear. My hand. I was finished as a camera-operator now. Finished anyway. Never been any good. All those potboilers had fenced me off from class, put an ultimately final damper on the small spark of inner, worthwhile talent I'd lacked the integrity to nurse. Might lose the hand altogether. Probably would, letting it go unlooked at for so long. As if that mattered now. Getting morose. Self-pitying. What was the German for angst? Reverting to school hymns, layered into my brain by two thousand assemblies, I started, crazily to sing.

I was singing as, long past Taos, I went up the track to Mansfield or whatever Klaus didn't want it called. I was singing as, in the same morning sun, I approached the spot where, brought there by me, Sam had died. I'd avenged all that and that was the most unforgiveable mistake. By now I should have known better. There was just one good thing. I sang so loud I silenced that wiseacre bird. I roared around a bend. Straight in my sights, holding a hoe, was Klaus.

I nearly killed him too. Consistent, at least, that would have been. Such splendid irony. But from somewhere, centuries of miles away, I remembered those things called brakes and how to use them. I employed a heavy foot and not a heavy hand and came to a full stop. I slumped across the wheel. Out for seconds, I suppose. When I looked up again he was still standing stolid with open mouth. The mountain must do the coming. He didn't move in assistance, as, falling, stumbling, stiff as a board, higher than a house, I came back to earth. The Corvair was conspicuously gone. I staggered towards him.

'My Christ,' he said. 'My Christ.'

I found myself lost for words. He looked at me for a long, searching time. Big. A self-contained man at self-ease even in surprise.

'There's death all over you,' he said.

Achingly, I nodded. My mouth was like salami ten years old.

'Is it finished?' he said.

I nodded.

'Sam?' I managed to say.

He shifted weight, shifted his hands on the hoe.

'I didn't dare risk any—authorities—coming in on us,' he said. 'It would have been putting too good a weapon in their hands. They would have seen that it got used ... Some of us buried her ourselves up in the trees. There was more reverence than she would have had in any other place.'

'There was no other place left her apart from this,' I said. 'I helped her...'

I didn't finish.

'Lose that too,' I finally did say.

He looked at me.

'I can show you where,' he said. 'Would you like that?'

'It makes no matter,' I said. 'I...

'Please,' I said, 'I'd like to see it.'

'What else do you want?'

I'd come by instinct. The classic flight to the better, prior, existence. In all that swaying, delirious journey I hadn't once thought of what I would say at its end. Now, asked so simply as that, I knew I had no right to say a word. I didn't speak.

Steadily, recovered from the shock of my appearance, he looked at me. I was a fixed axis. Beneath my feet the globe of the world was, very slowly, spinning. I sensed the very moment that it came to rest.

'There's no way,' he said.

Death sentence. The world spun on again so fast it dizzied me. It came to me that, with abject instinct, I clutched in my good hand the rich black briefcase.

'You're ill,' he said. 'You pack rancour, destruction, killing in your bag. Your sickness feeds on you. You feed on others. You suck destruction to you. You nourish it. It's your sphere.'

The horseman again. For me, too, now, there was no place on the surface of the earth where I could expect to earn shelter or comfort. And, least of all, a place where I could buy them. But I couldn't bear him a grudge, being right. Funny. The hoe was a puny-looking substitute for a flaming sword. Until you thought about it. Then it became so much more solid than the irrelevant weight of paper within the case.

'It's because you're sick,' he said, '...because if I turn you away, this place will cease to be what it could be ... because there has to be somewhere open somewhere for those who have no place to go....'

He broke off and looked at me. He was ten years younger than me and I had met him only that once in brutal passing. But he suddenly seemed an older man who had befriended me long ago and borne me often in his thoughts. The lines on his heavy, broad face were marks of fellow-feeling, wise and peaceful.

'To stay as we are, we have always to take the risk,' he said. 'You can stay here, if it is what you want, and we will try to help you to get well.'

Once more I was unable to speak.

'Is that what you'd like?' he said.

For the second time in that spot, my eyes dazzled. Something within me that had been petrified long since grew soft again. I was very, very tired. It was understandable that for the first time in twenty years I should feel that I wanted to cry.

'Yes,' I said, 'I should like that very much.'